Ringtail Cats are nocturnal members of the raccoon family and are equally adroit in trees as well as on the land. They are non-threatening to humans. This one was only interested in the brownies on the kitchen table.

Also by Charly Heavenrich:

Dancing on the Edge: A Veteran River Guide Shares the Life Changing Power of the Grand Canyon

Spirit of the Canyon: A River Journey Through Time (DVD)

Grand Canyon: A Different View (Coffee Table Book)

UNIMAGINED GIFTS

CHARLY HEAVENRICH

iUniverse, Inc.
Bloomington

Unimagined Gifts

iUniverse books may be ordered through booksellers or by contacting:

iUniverse
1663 Liberty Drive
Bloomington, IN 47403
www.iuniverse.com
1-800-Authors (1-800-288-4677)

ISBN: 978-1-4620-0086-9 (sc)
ISBN: 978-1-4620-0088-3 (ebook)

Library of Congress Control Number: 2011903394

Printed in the United States of America

iUniverse rev. date: 06/17/2011

For all adventure guides who help people go beyond their edges, and my wild, wacky, and wonderful crewmates with whom I've had the pleasure to share the Grand Canyon since 1978

"I had come to the Canyon with expectations. I had wanted to see snowy egrets flying against the black schist at dusk; I saw blue-winged teal against the deep, green waters at dawn. I had wanted to hear the thunder rolling in the thousand-foot depths; I heard Winter's soprano sax resonating in Matkatamiba Canyon, with the guttural caws of four raven which circled above him. I had wanted to watch rattlesnakes; I saw in an abandoned copper mine, in the beam of my flashlight, a wall of copper sulphate that looked like a wall of turquoise. I rose each morning at dawn and washed in the cold river. I went to sleep each night listening to the cicadas, the pencil-ticking sound of some other insect, the soughing of river waves in tamarisk roots, and watching bats plunge and turn, looking like leaves blown against the sky. What any of us had come to see or do fell away. We found ourselves at each turn with what we had not imagined."

Barry Lopez
Crossing Open Ground

TABLE OF CONTENTS

PART ONE UPPER GRAND CANYON MILE 0 TO MILE 90

PART TWO LOWER GRAND CANYON MILE 90 TO MILE 226

PREFACE

After meeting the rest of the crew at the company warehouse, we loaded Blue, the large, painted stake truck, and drove north on Route 89A out of Flagstaff through the Navajo reservation and part of the Painted Desert. I rode in the back of the truck on top of all the gear, straining to keep my eyes open and moist against the desiccating, heated desert air. As we got closer to the Grand Canyon my anticipation and excitement grew, wondering when I would see the Canyon for the first time. I didn't realize we were headed for the very beginning of the Canyon, and there wasn't much to see. In fact, it wasn't until we drove over the Navajo Bridge that I saw the Colorado River and the first four hundred twenty-five feet of Canyon walls. At that point, we were four miles downstream of Lees Ferry, our destination, and the launching pad for our trip.

Lees Ferry wasn't what I expected. There were no buildings, no sandy beaches, and no Grand Canyon. It wouldn't officially begin until we'd traveled a half-mile downstream. Still, I was here, about to begin an adventure that would change my life in ways I could not have imagined just six months before, during a casual conversation with my housemate.

"How would you like to exchange the interest I owe you for a raft trip in the Grand?" The question came from my best friend, Gary, a raft guide in the Grand Canyon. He had borrowed some money from me to buy a truck. "Hell yes" was my instant reply. That was November 1977. In May 1978, I flew to Flagstaff, Arizona to meet Gary and he informed me that as a guest of the crew I was considered part of the crew – also known as "go-fer." My job would be to help out in any way needed.

The day before the trip, I went with Gary to the warehouse to help load the truck with all the river gear, and he introduced me to the trainee baggage boatman. I would be his passenger during the trip. His name was Doug Lord. At the time both of us were in the financial field, Doug as a financial advisor, and I as vice-president of finance for a design-build general construction company. "Lord and Heavenrich," I thought to myself. "Now that would be an interesting partnership."

It took less than two hours of focused activity, inflating the rafts and loading them with frames, coolers, and all the gear and food we would need for our two-week journey. As we jumped in the truck to drive up to the Marble Canyon Lodge for dinner, I looked back to see six fully loaded rafts floating peacefully on a calm river. After dinner, we spent the night back at the Ferry sleeping under a spectacular rotating canopy of stars. About ten o'clock the next morning the passengers arrived. After fitting them with life jackets and giving a safety talk, they then picked their raft for the day, and we embarked.

Since I'd already been on two raft trips on the Colorado River in Utah, I really had no grand expectations. This would be a chance to get away from the stresses of a challenging job in a difficult industry, have an adventure, and collect a few snapshots for my photo album. I shoved Doug's heavy raft away from shore, hopped on, and tried to find a comfortable place to sit in the front of the raft.

As soon as we hit the current moving downstream, tears formed, goose bumps erupted, and I felt a clear sensation of non-physical arms wrapping around me as if to say, "Welcome home, brother, welcome home." I sat there trying to make sense of it all until a wave leapt over the front of the raft and slapped me in the face. It was obvious this would be more than just a vacation.

During that trip, the deeper we floated into the Canyon, the deeper the Canyon merged with me. Before the end I made a commitment to do whatever it would take to keep coming back. At that time, the crew was responsible for scheduling the baggage boatmen. So for the next five seasons I was an unpaid "trainee," rowing a very heavy raft, learning the ropes. And I loved it.

In 1984, I was promoted to a paid guide, with passengers in my raft. After eleven trips with no passengers this was an entirely new experience, one that brought me even greater satisfaction. Over the next few years I learned enough about the natural world to "interpret" the geology, human history, flora, and fauna for my passengers. But something else began happening that engaged my interest even more. I noticed that some people on every trip were particularly open to change, either because they were in the process of that in their personal or professional lives, or because something would happen on the trip that would open them up to new possibilities. Often that involved overcoming some perceived limitation, like the fear of heights or big water.

During this time, I began to gather stories of ordinary people accomplishing extraordinary feats, and as an adventure speaker, I began to share them with my audiences. In 1988, I had what I call my Copernican shift. Just as Copernicus took the Earth out of the center of the solar system and inserted the sun, I took myself out of the center of my "solar system" and inserted the Grand Canyon. I finally realized that my mission was to share the Grand Canyon experience with the world. So I created a partnership with the Canyon, and set out to find ways to share what that experience represented.

Along the way, I have helped people extend themselves beyond the vacation of a lifetime, and embark on a personal journey to places they had never imagined. Some people have left the Canyon and started making different choices: new jobs, healthier lifestyles, improved relationships, greater sense of wellbeing, and more. I'm constantly moved by the depth of courage and ability people have, which they often don't realize, until they come up to some edge and find a way to go beyond it. The reason I keep coming back to the Canyon, well beyond the average working life expectancy of a river guide, is the people I work with and for. And when they take away something of value from our interaction, I am happy for them, and grateful for the opportunity.

Permission for the quote from *Crossing Common Ground* was granted by Barry Lopez.

ACKNOWLEDGEMENT

Many thanks to my editor, David Hicks, PhD, whose enthusiasm and guidance inspired and encouraged me to keep on keeping on when doubts surfaced and procrastination interfered with the completion of this book.

INTRODUCTION

"Show don't tell." This was the first rule I received from David Hicks on the first session of my writers' workshop. When I started this book, my intention was to offer an "ode to the Grand Canyon;" about a sense of place and how spending time in natural places like the Canyon often results in life-changing perceptions and choices. However, as the first draft proceeded, it felt like I was trying to shoehorn that theme into the book. So it morphed into the stories of ordinary people having an extraordinary experience in the Grand Canyon.

When people talk about the Grand Canyon, thoughts inevitably turn to the world-class white water rapids of the Colorado River, and the potential mayhem they offer. In reality, the most significant events that occur on a raft trip in the Canyon happen in the hearts and minds of those who travel through this living geologic wonder. After a week or two living in the natural world, interacting with people from different parts of the world with widely divergent personal and professional perspectives, traveling at 3-4 miles per hour, sleeping under a celestial light show, while experiencing an unparalleled richness and diversity during the side canyon hikes, many experience a renewal of old dreams, and new awareness of what is possible.

The mayhem? Potential - yes. Reality - rare. According to Dr. Tom Myers in his book "Fareful Journeys," rafting on the Colorado River in Grand Canyon turns out to be more dangerous than bowling, and less dangerous than golf - when comparing injury rates. Instead, old and young, male and female, experienced and inexperienced campers and rafters, have their lives touched in subtle and profound ways.

Spending time in the Grand Canyon makes people aware of the difference between what is natural and what has become normal in their everyday lives. This book will take you on a journey with passengers who have rafted the Canyon with me. It is my intention that as you go on this journey with them, you will gain some insight into yourself that will be meaningful to you. This is not an actual trip; but all the people are real, as are their stories. I trust you will enjoy the journey.

Charly Heavenrich
Boulder, Colorado
www.thecanyonguy.com

PART ONE
UPPER GRAND CANYON
MILE 0 TO MILE 90

Lees Ferry is the launching pad for most raft trips in the Grand Canyon. It is also where fishermen launch their boats to seek large rainbow trout upstream. It was named after John Doyle Lee, a Mormon follower of Brigham Young who was asked to establish a ferry for Mormons traveling to St. George in Southern Utah.

DAY ONE –
LEES FERRY TO HOT NA NA WASH

Pastel-colored Vermillion Cliffs dwarfed a white van as it came in to view. Bright yellow waterproof bags containing clothing and personal items were stacked neatly on the roof. Inside the van were ten exhausted and eager passengers, part of a group of nineteen about to embark on a sixteen-day raft adventure down the Colorado River through the Grand Canyon. They had arrived at Lees Ferry, the jumping off point for Canyon raft trips. To get here they had to contend with last-minute details at home and work for a two-and-a-half-week absence, travel hassles, a restless night, an early morning wake-up, and a three-hour van ride from Flagstaff in Northern Arizona.

The van rolled to a stop on the gravel beach near neatly arrayed orange life jackets. Emerging from the air-conditioned van, people from more humid climes received their first taste of the oppressive desert heat. Some smiled as they set eyes on the Colorado River snaking lazily from left to right in front of them. The more observant among them may have noticed the heron rookery atop feathery tamarisk trees three hundred yards across the glassy green river.

A second van pulled up next to the first, the doors slid open, and the remaining passengers emerged one by one. I felt a mixture of curiosity and anticipation. Who were they? Where did they come from? Why did they come on the trip? What must they be feeling and thinking? Would they be eager hikers? What if there was a woman on the trip to whom I was attracted? Would she be single? Would she be interested in me? While I've been single my whole life, it's not because I'm avoiding committed relationships. In fact, I have dreamed of meeting the love of my life while engaged in work that I also love.

This was my twenty-ninth season rafting the Canyon, and I've kept returning into my sixties, far beyond the typical guide's working life expectancy, because I do my best work here. I love helping people go where they've never been, and am very good at transferring to them my confidence that they can do what may seem impossible. I have always been eager to head downstream with fresh faces for an unknown adventure through such a magnificent place.

A bit of chaos ensued as yellow bags, which the passengers had packed the night before at the trip orientation in Flagstaff, were offloaded from the vans. Some of the passengers headed to the bathroom for a last chance to relieve themselves in the privacy of locked doors under a man-made roof. A few walked to the river and dipped their sandaled toes into the forty-five-degree, clear green water. Most removed them just as quickly. Others fussed with their purple mesh bags stuffed with more than they'd need for the day, awaiting word of what to do next, like new students on the first day of school.

They came in all shapes, sizes, and ages ranging from ten to sixty-five. Each one had to be fitted with a personal life jacket. On the back of each jacket was a name. Some identified rapids soon to be run, like Hance, Lava, or Hermit. Others announced historic figures like Bert Loper, Norm Nevills, or Harvey Butchart. The rest introduced a location we might visit or pass during the trip, like Deer Creek, Nankoweap, or Havasu. Michael, a stocky, good-natured, fair-skinned man of Irish descent, and our resident "shade-ologist," Carla, an attractive, very athletic woman in her late twenties, and I – half the crew – helped each person with the right fit. "Remember the name on the back of your jacket," we told them. "It's yours for the duration." While this was going on, Floyd, at 6' 5" the largest member of our crew, and Star, an openly gay woman, and one of the most competitive people I've known, loaded the yellow bags onto their rafts, and sought places for the predictable last-minute additions of beer in burlap sacks and Crazy Creek chairs. Meanwhile, Sue, a forty-something woman of unbounded energy, unflappable demeanor, and tension-reducing smile and laugh, was directing the rest of the passengers, helping them adjust to being here. Sue is my favorite trip leader, and before leading my first trip I asked her what advice she had. She thought about it for a moment, and with her signature smile, replied, "It will work out." It's been my mantra ever since.

With each lifejacket fitting I took time to learn names, which, in spite of my training as a Dale Carnegie instructor (session one was remembering names), seemed to slip my mind all too quickly. When I had a television exercise show in Detroit, people would greet me on the street as if we were bosom buddies. Often I wouldn't recognize them or wouldn't know their name. Being too shy to tell them, I would often fake it.

Among the passengers, Chris and Graham stood out because of their strong English accents. I had known them since 1970 when I had hired Chris as my secretary. I loved her singsong accent, and used to call myself just to hear it. Both were short and stocky and in their fifties. Chris had silky blonde hair and an affable laugh. She hid her nervousness or insecurity behind a bright smile. As I gave Graham a hug he said, "Well it may be hot, but at least it's arid." An engineer by training, he had come to the States as a sales engineer for a major British company.

A passenger named Jane, looking older than her mid-forties, expressed some nervousness about going on the trip, evidently realizing how many questions she had failed to ask in her haste to get away. Another, named Frank, offered me a friendly smile and handshake as I helped him tighten up his jacket. When he observed that it felt like a girdle, I asked him how he knew, and shot him a grin. Time allowed only the briefest of greetings to other passengers, among them a father and son, an attractive, energetic German woman in her early thirties, and a mother and her son who, because of his small size and very young appearance, reminded me of myself when I was his age.

When everyone had been fitted with life jackets, we gathered in a circle for quick introductions. This was for the benefit of the crew, since the passengers had gotten to know one another at the orientation and on the drive up. It was a typically diverse group: eight women ranging from their early twenties to early sixties, and eleven men and boys between ten and sixty-six. Each was asked to say their name and a bit about why they wanted to raft the Canyon. Timmy, a chubby twelve year-old, spoke tentatively. "Um, I came here with my dad to see the Grand Canyon. I just hope I can see it, because I didn't bring my glasses." I was struck by the absence of any emotional expression in his face, and wondered why he would come without his glasses.

Ben, a tall, slender man with a shy smile tinged with a bit of sadness, introduced his "family" - his son Jeff, daughter Ann, and close friends Annie and Tom. Ben said he and his wife had been planning this trip for over ten years to coincide with Ann's college graduation. Sadly, his wife had passed away recently, so while he was happy to be here with his family, he was feeling his wife's absence. I felt my gut tighten.

The rest mentioned fairly typical reasons for being here: get away from work, a longtime dream, share it with her son, the whitewater, chance to hike and sleep under the stars. Everyone seemed pleasant, except for Ralph, Timmy's father, whose slumped shoulders, downcast eyes, and ample belly spoke of a life filled with too many unhappy obligations. In the past I have avoided people who appeared distant and unhappy. But I've learned they can get the most out of time spent in the Canyon, so I made a mental note to get to know him and see what I could do to bring a smile to his face.

As I listened to each person speak, I thought about the trip ahead and how many of them would see a whole new world. Many of our urban adventure travelers had never seen the Milky Way, or satellites, or shooting stars. I have spent a lot of time scanning the star-filled ceiling. In college I took astronomy classes as a way of avoiding natural sciences, which for some reason intimidated me. Now my job requires a fair amount of knowledge of those sciences, because one of our primary responsibilities is to act as interpreters of the geology, flora, fauna, and cultural history of the Canyon. While in the Navy, I spent more time looking for constellations and shooting stars than for enemy subs. Fortunately, we were between wars at that time. Being on a new moon cycle, the darkened sky would be a great backdrop for the Milky Way to stand out like a narrow band of clouds. Satellites from Russia and the West, racing in opposite directions while snapping photos, would vie for our attention while monitoring weather patterns, measuring the ozone hole, and providing intelligence to spy agencies as well as to CBS, CNN and the BBC.

Sue explained that Floyd, Michael, Star and I would be in oar rafts that usually took up to four passengers. Carla, our newest guide, would be rowing the supply boat that carried extra gear. Because of limited space on her raft, she had room for only two passengers. Carla came from an amazing family, and this would be my first trip with her. If she turned out to be anything like her brother, a young man wise beyond his age and very competent on the river, she would be a great addition to the crew.

Finally, Sue introduced my niece, Eliza. She had come down from her home in northwest Oregon and had stayed with me the night before at the home of Sue Bassett, a former crewmate of mine, and one of the first ten women oar guides in the Grand Canyon. In exchange for a free trip, Eliza would help out wherever and whenever needed. This could mean filling in on the paddle boat if there were not enough volunteers, helping to load and unload the rafts, being part of a cook crew, pumping water, putting up and taking down the bathroom, and more. At nineteen, she had been a year older than her other classmates because she had spent a year in

Germany before her senior year in high school. She graduated second in her class, and this was my way of recognizing her for her accomplishments. The time right after high school is one of the most significant periods of transition for a teen and their family, and I wanted to spend some close time with Eliza, since I had lived so far away while she was growing up. Although I saw her every year at Thanksgiving during our annual family reunion, I had wanted to be a more active uncle for her.

Sue announced she would be the paddleboat captain, taking up to six people with her. Back in the early 'eighties we didn't use paddleboats, and when the idea was first suggested I thought no one would want to paddle 226 miles. Boy was I wrong. People love being in the paddleboat, and although there are always some challenging times, like strong upstream winds, the overall experience has always been positive.

She pointed to the fourteen-foot, unloaded paddleboat as she spoke. Some river companies use fully loaded, eighteen-foot paddleboats, which are heavier and more stable, but which demand greater exertion from the paddlers. A loaded paddleboat has a frame running down the center of the raft with a food cooler that can weigh up to three hundred pounds. Waterproof bags and metal ammo cans are usually piled around and on top of the cooler, adding even more weight. Compared to those rafts, our paddleboat, which carries only passengers and their day gear, performs like a sports car – fast, maneuverable, easier to tip, yet surprisingly safe. I have always been impressed with their ability to make it through the major rapids right side up.

Sue was married to another river guide and augmented her time on the river with commercial bike trips in the Southwest and raft trips in Mexico and Central America. She always seemed to have a smile on her face and was not easily rattled, not even when she caught a gastro-intestinal malady that later became known as a Norwalk-type virus a few years earlier.

The sun was getting higher in the sky and it was already around a hundred degrees. Rather than take more time, Sue suggested that everybody select a raft and get off the beach. This was sometimes an uncomfortable time for me. I had always been a bit insecure, being the oldest and usually the smallest guide on the crew, and I never knew who would select my raft, or what criteria they used. On some trips people would choose me right away, while on others, I would end up being the raft of last choice.

When I was in the third grade we moved from our home in Ferndale, Michigan to nearby Birmingham. It was just six miles away, but it might as well been in another state. We had moved from a nondescript, blue-collar town, to a white-collar, relatively affluent village. It was April, and going to my new school for the first time. I was small, shy, and young looking for my age; and very anxious. Would I fit in? Would I make any friends? What if they didn't like me? It didn't make things any easier when I found out it was a combined third-and-fourth-grade class. On my first day I somehow survived until recess, and I went over to the basketball court where the two biggest boys in the fourth grade were choosing up sides for dodge ball. I waited to be picked. And waited. And waited. I watched as they picked all the boys, and then all the girls. Finally I was picked, but without enthusiasm. So I was the last one picked for the first game. When it ended, I was the last one left. I had won the first game. For the second game I was picked first. This had a profound impact on me, and I came to believe that if I wanted to be picked (i.e. loved), I would have to perform better than anyone else.

Fortunately, I didn't have to worry about "rejection" on this trip as Jane, Chris, and Graham quickly chose my raft. They put their mesh bags containing sunscreen, rain gear, long-sleeve shirt and pants (for sun protection), and their river guidebook in two purple waterproof bags. Boots, a book, and a company-issued cup could also be included, even though these would not be used on the first day. It usually took a couple more days before passengers understood what was really needed during the day, and for some, a couple more to be fully organized. The "People" can rested on the floor near my right leg. Since getting into the purple bags can be time-consuming and inconvenient, I suggested that all cameras and sunscreen go into the can, which I could reach in a matter of seconds.

After securing the purple "day" bags to the raft, I coiled up the bowline and strapped it securely to the bow. Then I shoved off, hopped on board, put on my rowing gloves to protect my soft city hands, grabbed the oars and pulled away from shore. One-by-one the other rafts followed with Sue and the paddleboat bringing up the rear. Each guide was engaged in introductory conversations about safety and personal information. Some shared their knowledge of geology and the history of Lees Ferry.

I checked one more time to see if everything had been secured. Three 20 milimeter (mm) ammo cans, 14 ¼" high by 18 ¾" long by 8 ¼" wide, formerly used to house M1A1 Bazooka shells, rested on the floor of my footwell to the right of my legs, each one secured to the floor by short "cam" straps. On the left side was a large "commissary box" containing all the cooking utensils, pots, pans, dish soap, and chlorine bleach. Another strap over the top of the cans would prevent them from floating up in the event the raft flipped over. My personal 30-cal ammo can holding all my toiletries sat on the floor between these cans and served as a prop for my feet. It would come in handy when I needed to pull hard on my oars. To the right of my cooler was the Katadyne water filter in a rectangular container. To the left of my cooler were my two 50-cal camera boxes. One camera came with a wide-angle lens and the other had a telephoto lens. A large yellow tent bag, secured by two long cam straps, rested on the middle of the front deck. Underneath the deck rested the kitchen equipment: stove, propane, blaster, griddle, grill, dish buckets, and windscreens. The two purple day bags were lashed down on either side of the tent bag.

My spare oars ran horizontally along the left and right tubes, with the handles facing the front of the raft. On the deck behind me I had lashed nine yellow bags and my three black bags. On the rear tube sat Wild Thing, her white hair flying in a soft breeze, her arms extended as if reveling at the beginning of another adventure. Wild Thing was a pink-spotted tiger with an Einstein-inspired main of white hair. She had been a gift from a friend. Passengers enjoyed pressing her left palm to hear her sing a chorus of the Trogs song "Wild Thing."

As we floated out toward the current that would carry us through the Canyon, clumps of algae known as chlordophera passed mysteriously under the raft. The suspended clusters of dark green vegetation housed midges, river shrimps, and other microscopic life clinging to their organic home that had been described by one scientist as the 7-11 of the Colorado. He likened the tiny critters to peanut butter and jelly placed conveniently on shelves for ravenous rainbow trout. Rather than pick one ingredient off the fibrous algal shelves, the trout would consume the entire shelf.

Rainbow trout had been introduced to the river in the mid-sixties, after the construction of Glen Canyon dam. The bottom of Lake Powell, the giant reservoir created by the dam, had captured all the sediment carried into the lake from upstream tributaries, leaving the water that spilled out of the dam clear and cold – great for trout, not so great for some endangered native fish. Other algae, clinging to rounded rocks lying on the bottom of the river, swayed sensuously in the current.

The green, clear waters of the Colorado were so smooth as to leave little sensation of movement. Seeing the river cobble passing beneath us made it seem as if we were stationary and the cobble was moving, conveyor-like upstream. Only by looking back at a receding Lees Ferry, or over at the passing shore, did it become obvious we were headed downstream. In no time six canary-yellow rafts had formed a line floating peacefully, each guide introducing their passengers to the marvels of this natural wonder. Without effort, a tribe was forming.

Located fifteen miles downstream from the Glen Canyon dam on the Colorado River in Northern Arizona, Lees Ferry is an historic river crossing. It was named after John Doyle Lee, a Mormon scapegoat whose fifteen minutes of fame had cost him his life. Together with fifty-seven other Mormon men and a band of Paiute Indians, he had been a naïve and reluctant participant in a massacre of settlers heading west in 1857, in what became known as the Mountain Meadows Massacre. At the time of the massacre, the Mormons were close to going to war with the U.S. and distrusted outsiders. Lee claimed that he hadn't shot anyone. The Paiutes called him Yawgetts, a name that meant crybaby, because he had cried as he begged for the lives of the pioneers.

Excommunicated in 1870 from the Mormon Church, he was banished in December 1871 to an isolated, arid, blank spot on the map that would become known as Lees Ferry. It was here that he had been ordered to set up a ferry. His seventeenth wife, Emma Batchelor Lee, called their home Lonely Dell. His banishment was an attempt by the Mormon leadership to deflect attention away from the church during their ongoing struggles with the U.S. government. Fear and suspicion were the prevailing emotions in the Mormon community at that time.

John and Emma subsisted on what they could grow: alfalfa, watermelons, apples, peaches, plums, and pears; what game they could kill; and what they could buy with the meager income Lee derived from the ferry he had established. It was the only river crossing for Mormons heading into Arizona and for young couples traveling along the "Honeymoon Trail" to get married at the Mormon Temple in St. George, Utah. Bandits, outlaws, bank robbers, and Navajos also favored the ferry.

John Lee was executed in 1877, having been the only participant in the massacre convicted of murder. After significant prodding from Lee's surviving relatives, the Mormon Church finally reinstated him with full membership and blessings in 1961. Today Lees Ferry is the jumping off point for commercial and private raft trips heading downstream, and boaters and fishermen heading upstream into the last fifteen miles of Glen Canyon. The rest of Glen Canyon, affectionately called "the Glen," lies under Lake Powell, a two hundred mile long graveyard of water behind Glen Canyon dam.

It felt good to have oars in my hands again. Rowing in the Canyon feels like a dance to me. The oars were an extension of my arms, the blades my hands dipping into the river, moving through the water, and then tickling the silky smooth green water like a lover's caress as the blades returned to repeat the cycle, over and over for 226 miles. At first the raft felt ungainly, heavy, unbalanced. But after just a few strokes it settled into a comfortable rhythm. I was home again.

I looked back one last time at the gravel beach of Lees Ferry where a phalanx of motorized

6

and oar rafts of all shapes and sizes sat obediently at the water's edge. I checked my impulse to start telling my passengers everything I knew about the river, and about the history of the area. Instead I kept silent, affording my passengers time to get settled.

On one of my early trips I had three passengers in my raft – newlyweds, and a woman who had just come from a weekend workshop led by one of my mentors. She was thrilled to learn I knew him and started talking about her weekend experience. To the newlyweds, a banker and lawyer from Chicago, this was all brand new, and they asked me to explain what we were discussing. I was delighted to accommodate them, and instead of offering a quick explanation, launched into a full description of the workshop. I was so enthusiastic about sharing the information that I hadn't noticed that they had tuned me out.

After the trip, one of my crewmates explained that the couple liked me but felt trapped on my raft having to listen to what wasn't of much interest to them. They didn't want to risk getting trapped again, so they never returned to my raft. I realized that I had wandered away from my role and responsibilities as a guide. That's when I fashioned my purpose statement. It has remained the same since then: to do whatever it takes to support my passengers and crew in having a successful experience. Over time I have learned to honor their definition of success, not mine. For some that could mean having the vacation of a lifetime. For others, it would involve helping them go where they'd never been before.

*   *   *

On another trip, a time when I had felt less confidence in my abilities as a guide, I received some helpful feedback from one of my crewmates.

On the truck ride up to the Ferry on that trip I had taken a risk and had invited feedback from anybody who saw areas where I could improve, either as a guide or as part of the team. The next morning, after we had completed rigging our rafts and before the passengers arrived, the trip leader, Peggy, had asked me if I was serious about my request for feedback. I told her I was, and she said she had some for me.

We walked away from the rafts to a spot near the water spigot that we used to fill our six-gallon jugs. In front of us and to our right was a grove of non-native tamarisk trees, their feathery green leaves providing cooling shade while sucking up prodigious amounts of precious water. To our left stretched out the paved parking area and ramp for fishermen to launch their boats before journeying upstream in search of the "big one." Behind us rose the remnants of sandstone formations eroded back from the river by the unyielding forces of water and wind.

Peggy began by saying she wanted me to know that everybody enjoyed working with me. I felt my body tense up, sensing that an opening compliment was setting me up for something I wouldn't like to hear. She then said she had also checked this out with others to make sure it wasn't her "stuff." She told me that she really liked me and enjoyed being on crew with me, but there were times when she didn't know who I was beyond my philosophy. Peggy waited a moment and then finished by saying she wouldn't have taken the time or energy to tell me this if she didn't care.

This was not new information. I had learned to use my knowledge of personal and spiritual growth to stay in control and as a way to avoid feeling vulnerable. Unfortunately, this had, at times, created a barrier to closer relationships.

My raft floated by the gauging station that communicated the river's flow via satellite to the appropriate government agencies. I broke the silence and took a few moments to introduce Jane, Graham, and Chris to our safety procedures. None of them had ever rafted, and I wanted them to get a feel for the way the raft responded in the small waves up ahead, so that when we got to the bigger water they'd be fully prepared. I began by stating the obvious: that this was a heavy raft, and any waves that hit us in the front would have a hard time causing an "endo".

Jane immediately asked what an "endo" was. Her voice sounded subdued and uncertain. I explained that it happened when the raft flipped end over end. When I saw her eyebrows pinching together, I quickly told her it had never happened on any of my commercial trips. She let out a stifled breath.

I explained that waves hitting us from the side had a lot more leverage, making a flip more likely, and that's where they would come in. Wide eyes told me I had their attention. We were just entering a small riffle and I suggested they pay attention to get a feel for how the raft responded in the waves. Then, pointing to some whitewater downstream, I told them it would provide a good opportunity to practice "highsiding" by leaning into the waves. When a wave hits from the side, I explained, it could lift the raft on that side, making it the high side. Their job, I told them, was to get their weight over to that high side. If a wave lifted the boat up, and their weight wasn't on the wave side, especially if they threw their weight towards the opposite, or low side, we would risk a flip. Given the forty-five degree temperature of the water, the tendency would be to shy away from the water. I said I wanted them to kiss those waves before the waves kissed them. This is a whitewater raft trip, I said, and they needn't be afraid to get wet. It is the desert, after all, and we dry out real fast down here. I was the only one smiling.

I finished by saying that by the time we reached the major rapids five days hence, they'd definitely have a good feel for this, and would quickly see how buoyant these rafts were. While there were no guarantees, I assured them I had no interest in flipping. But if we did flip, they'd all come back with a story. Chris let out a nervous laugh, Graham smiled, and Jane tightened her grip on the safety lines.

While we were in a very harsh desert eco-system, I continued, and the Colorado was a high-volume river where many things could go wrong, the reality down here was surprisingly safe. Studies comparing injury rates on the river to other sport activities have shown that rafting on the Colorado in the Canyon is more dangerous than bowling – I paused for a moment – and less dangerous than golf. Graham, an avid golfer, laughed. "I can imagine," he said. "Those golf carts can be real dangerous – especially after the nineteenth hole." I told him about the professional hockey player who had knee surgery after getting his foot stuck between the accelerator and the brake on his golf cart. "Case closed," Graham replied as he raised his bushy eyebrows.

We entered a small but noisy rapid just as a new layer of rock appeared to our left. I watched to see how each person responded to the cold water splashing them. As predicted, their instinct was to shy away. Oh well, we had lots of time to get the hang of it.

Below the rapid, striated light gray rock bracketed the river: the Kaibab Limestone. Just above the forming cliff I pointed to a built-up retaining wall that marked the location of the dugway built by the Mormons so their wagons could reach the ferry. Kaibab is a Paiute Indian word meaning "mountain lying down." It's known as the capstone rock of the Grand Canyon because it is the top layer of Canyon rock and eventually would loom 4600 feet above us at the place where some of our passengers would leave the trip on the seventh day. Here it sat barely ten feet out of the water along the edge of the river.

I told them that as we floated downstream we would become intimately acquainted with each geologic layer as it emerged from its resting place beneath the river. The Grand Canyon is an unparalleled living geologic museum, with the most stable and extensively exposed layers on the planet. The river was constantly cutting through the underlying rock layers, slowly revealing each one as we floated deeper into the geologic history of the planet.

The Canyon, I said in my most knowledgeable tone, was made up of sedimentary, igneous, and metamorphic rock. As Jane released her death grip to lean forward to hear me better, I compared the first nine layers to those of a layer cake, with the river representing the knife. Instead of the knife just cutting down, I explained that much of the forming Canyon we were now looking at downstream had been caused by earth activity pushing the layers up. I held up my right hand, fingers together and parallel to the river, to represent the rock layers, and used my left hand, held vertically, to signify the river. As I raised my right hand to show the uplifting, I lowered my left hand in a carving motion to represent the cutting action of the river. Everybody nodded.

Before dams, rivers were always rich with sediment. This gave the river an abrasive quality, allowing it to cut through hard and soft rock formations. This cutting action had been sharply diminished with the loss of sediment caused by dams.

I then described three basic kinds of sedimentary rock in the Canyon: limestone, sandstone, and shale; and three distinct forms: *cliff-forming* hard rock (limestone and most sandstones; igneous lava or granite; and metamorphic) that are resistant to erosion; *slope-forming* softer rock, notably shale; and one sandstone layer that was *ledge-forming*. Limestone, which we were now looking at, was made up of the microscopic shells of sea animals, phytoplankton, mixed with liquefied calcium carbonate floating in solution in the ocean. When the animals died, their tiny skeletons rained down on the bottom of what geologists called a shallow sea, some five hundred to six hundred feet in depth. Over time the shells dissolved and melted into a primordial mud. This mud then hardened (lithified) from the pressure of hundreds of feet of water into limestone. So limestone could be pure calcium carbonate, depending on the environment in which it had formed.

Contact with water created a chemical reaction that formed carbonic acid and carbon dioxide, resulting in what geologists called "chemical weathering," a dominant form of erosion in the Grand Canyon. Evidence of this erosion could be seen as pockmarks in the rock, in carved out caves and caverns, and in fluting (a feature that conformed to the pattern of water currents and looked as if an infinite number of ice cream scoops had gouged out the polished rock) along the river's edge. In some limestone, the weathering created exquisite, sensuous, primitive sculptures

"I've never heard anyone use rocks and sensuous in the same sentence," Graham said.

Overhead hovered a cloudless, desert blue realm typical for late June in the Canyon. There would be no rain this day, and possibly not during the entire trip. This was typical of my

9

experience rafting down the Colorado in the desert southwest. In fact, I could recall only one trip in thirty-two years that had begun with rain.

It was mid-July and the monsoons had arrived in Arizona. A typical monsoon pattern carried moisture from the Gulf of Mexico on the wings of a low-pressure system anchored around the eastern Colorado-New Mexico line. First a buildup of beautiful, pure white cumulo-nimbus clouds, known commonly as thunderheads, would appear late in the morning to early afternoon. Initially peeking over the rim of the Canyon like a child playing hide and seek, they could soar to 35,000 feet or higher as they built in intensity. Very strong upstream winds were usually the advance warning of these powerful summer storms characterized by lightning, thunder, and pounding rains. Rarely lasting more than fifteen to thirty minutes, they would blow in and blow out, cooling us down while spreading a dark sheen on the Canyon walls. Within minutes they would become a memory. In the desert, that's usually what rain is, a memory.

The sky had been clear as we loaded the rafts and shoved off. We had just begun our journey downstream on a hot, muggy day. Within minutes huge thunderheads appeared over the rim downstream and charged towards us. As we entered the Paria riffle the advancing storm announced itself with unusually strong upstream winds. I was pulling hard on my oars, bracing against my frame, trying to keep my raft moving downstream, trying to avoid being blown to shore. Then the rain, flying parallel to the river, hit like millions of wet bee-bees, instantly drenching us. Because of the short duration of many storms, we tell people it's not officially raining until our shirts are soaked. Within seconds, this was officially designated a rainstorm. Early on, my passengers had seemed terrified. What have we gotten ourselves into? I imagined them thinking. Thirteen days of this?

Everyone on the crew, on the other hand, was thrilled by the unexpected storm. None of us had ever seen one here before. We shouted and pointed to waterfalls rushing over the forming rim of limestone. We marveled at how quickly the river changed color from its unnatural, sediment-free, algae-dyed green, to its traditional sediment-filled reddish-brown. Rio Colorado. River that runs red. Soon the passengers got into the mood and joined us in celebrating this unexpected event. They, too, were getting into the flow of the natural world. Then as quickly as it had arrived, the storm departed, leaving the pungent aroma of fresh organic material flowing in solution on its journey to the sea.

"Why is the river so clear?" Jane asked, perhaps trying to distract herself from her fear of what she had called the Unknown. "I thought it was always filled with sediment. And why is it green?"

I explained that before the Glen Canyon Dam was built, the river was always muddy. "Too thick to drink, too thin to plow," they used to say. The dam had created a reservoir, Lake Powell, almost two hundred miles long, it's shoreline longer than either the East or West coast. With no current to carry it, all the sediment from upstream sources had ended up in the bottom of the lake. The green coloration was from the reflection of light on the microscopic algae growing in the water.

Jane then expressed concerns about the rapids. In her mid-forties, she spoke softly, as if she wanted to avoid something. She was slightly overweight, had gray streaks throughout her dark brown hair, sadness etched around her eyes, and sloping shoulders that reflected the burdens of a caretaker. This was her first vacation after spending much of her adult life caring for her mother, who had passed away earlier in the year. She said she was very anxious about rapids. Even though it would be two hours or more before we would run our first medium-sized rapid, Jane seemed convinced that mayhem lay around every bend in the river. After all, she confessed, she had seen both *Deliverance* and *A River Wild*. I tried to convince her that she had little, if anything, to worry about. But nothing I said seemed to make any difference, so I let it go. I knew that after running the first rapid she would have a better sense of the reality – so long as I didn't screw up by going where I shouldn't.

Four and a half miles from Lees Ferry, we floated under the Navajo Bridge. Built between 1927 and 1929 for $385,000, it was the only vehicle crossing until the Hoover Dam, over three hundred miles downstream. It had become too narrow for modern-day traffic, so in the early 'nineties a second bridge was constructed immediately downstream, and Navajo Bridge had become a footbridge. My main concern about the footbridge was the danger of a pedestrian throwing something over the side and hitting the raft, or someone in the raft. During the construction of the new bridge, engineers had erected a large mesh screen to catch any falling debris loosened by blasting. For some time we could pass under the bridge only between eleven in the morning and one in the afternoon, the time the engineers were at lunch.

Floating into the shadows of the bridges some four hundred and twenty-five feet above us provided temporary relief from the rising desert heat. At river level, the third rock layer was making its appearance. We had already watched the Kaibab and Toroweap limestone layers rise. Now I introduced my passengers to the Coconino sandstone, a layer of sedimentary rock that had formed some two hundred-eighty million years ago. Distinctive diagonal lines, called cross bedding, etched the story of this layer's birth. The lines represented wind erosion as it had traveled down the leeward side of sand dunes that lay near the ocean's margin. Based on the direction of those lines, geologists had determined that the prevailing winds at that time were northeast to southwest, exactly opposite of today's flow.

Just then Graham pointed to a condor soaring overhead. It was by far the largest bird in the Canyon, and had been common until the late 19th century when ranchers and hunters, unaware that condors were carrion feeders, and concerned about losing parts of their herds, had decimated the population, causing its extinction in North American. In the 1990s, the Peregrine Fund began a long-term project to reintroduce these scavengers to the Canyon. Today, there are over a hundred condors in the wilds of California and Arizona, and another hundred in captivity. Their nine-foot wingspan, white patches under their wings, and their unsteady flight pattern made them easy to identify. Unfortunately they are curious about people, and we have to be careful not to allow them to become familiar with us. We have been instructed to keep our distance and actively discourage any contact by yelling to force them away. Birds that have been found eating food, either from tourists at the rim or from river runners, are recaptured and reprogrammed to avoid humans. Repeat offenders are pulled out of the wilds and become breeding birds.

At Six Mile Wash we pulled over for lunch. *In 2002, my friend Dhiana, without my knowledge, had decided at the last minute to come on the trip as a passenger. She adopted an assumed name and arrived at Lees Ferry disguised in a wig and wide-brimmed hat, and she had kept the ruse going by selecting someone else's raft in which to ride. We stopped at Six Mile Wash and ate lunch. While talking with two passengers, one of whom was Dhiana, I meant to ask if we had met yet. Instead I asked, "Do I know you?"*

A coy smile formed on her face and she replied, "I don't know. Would you like to?" As soon as I heard her voice, I knew it was Dhiana. The entire group erupted in laughter. Seems everybody had been in on the ruse.

While the rest of the crew set up lunch in the shade of a tamarisk grove, Sue led the passengers to another shady spot to give the first of two on-river orientations for the day. This one included information about day-to-day activities and safety on and off the river. Eliza came over to help us with lunch prep, but I told her she needed to hear what Sue was saying. Besides, we had plenty of help in putting the lunch together, and would make sure it looked appealing.

We took great pride in how we presented the food for our guests. We arranged the ingredients in a creative way, pleasing to the eye. Star had the lunch boat and was also head cook. She carried all the food required for lunch - meats, veggies, cheese, fruit, and onions - along with the lunch table, cutting boards, knives, the condiments, spices and "utes." She was responsible for managing the food in the coolers and had brought up our lunch menu for the day. We rolled the lunch meats – sliced turkey, beef, ham – individually and placed them in neat rows on one cutting board, stacked the cheese slices like parallel dominoes, cut the tomatoes thin and arrayed them across the top of the veggie board. We surrounded the sprouts with chunks of lettuce in the center of the board. Sliced avocados (still resting in their half shells) and sliced onions filled the rest of the board. We combined sliced apples and oranges, with the oranges lined in rows skin down and arranged the apples skin up between each orange slice. The alternating orange and green colors provided a visual treat. One end of the table had four kinds of bread followed by mayonnaise, mustard, hot sauces, and horseradish. At the other end we put a loaf of bread for pb&j, plus nuts and cookies.

When Sue finished with her orientation everybody went down by the river to wash their hands, then eagerly lined up on both sides of the table beginning with the bread and moving toward the cookies. The need for good hygiene had been one of the most important messages in Sue's orientation. In recent years the Noro-virus, best known from cruise ships, had reared its ugly head on some Canyon trips. Proper hand washing and applying hand sanitizer would help prevent its spread.

During lunch, I asked Jane how she was doing. "OK so far," she replied, looking shyly at her feet. She was still anxious about the first rapid, Badger, which lay in wait two miles ahead. Her shoulder-length hair was pulled back into a ponytail exaggerating the worry lines etched into the corners of her eyes. Most of the other passengers were animated and seemed excited to be on the river. Nathan, the ten-year old with a friendly, upbeat personality, and Timmy, the chubby twelve-year-old without his glasses, were being kids, making designs in the mud near the river. It wasn't long before the mud was flying between the two giggling boys.

As we prepared to head downstream, Chris remarked that the cliffs were already pretty high. After just six miles the Canyon walls, non-existent at Lees Ferry, loomed five hundred feet above us. For a half hour we floated in silence. The world outside the Canyon had receded, soon to occupy a seldom-used part of our memory. A satisfying lunch, calm river, and the energy expended just getting here promoted relaxation. Already I could see the tension of normal life disappearing from people's faces and bodies. Except Jane. Holding tightly to two safety lines in the back of my raft, her brow furrowed, her lips pursed, I could only imagine the turmoil she was experiencing as she anticipated the first rapid.

Soon a new sound floated upstream on the soft afternoon breeze. "What's that?" Jane asked, like a child who has just heard thunder for the first time.

"Badger Rapid," I replied, hoping my smile would ease her concerns. The muscles in her jaw tightened.

Before running this first rapid, I repeated the safety instructions, made sure that everyone's life jackets were tight and they were holding on correctly. This only seemed to compound Jane's anxiety. She was hunkered down in the back, possibly waiting for her demise. Her white knuckles stood out in sharp contrast to her tanned skin. As we entered the rapid I could hear her praying.

Badger is a medium-sized rapid with some decent-sized waves, and is a wonderful introduction to the bigger rapids we would be running in a few days. It is enough to get your attention, but not so big as to put us into any real danger. Unless, that is, we went the wrong way and found a hole or submerged rock.

I was on a kayak support trip in the late 'nineties with nine kayakers and nine passengers riding in oar boats. There was a father and son on the trip and on the first day the son, who had only had twenty hours experience in a hard shell-kayak, floated through Badger and came out the other end right side up but looking like a deer in the headlights. I imagined he was thinking something like, "Oh my god, and this is only a medium-sized rapid!" Meanwhile, the father, in an inflatable kayak we call a ducky, maneuvered his craft right into the hole. Instantly he was sucked down and met the bottom of the river, finally emerging a hundred yards downstream. His eyes matched those of his son, and he had the bruises to back them up. Later in that trip the son earned his nickname - eleven in thirteen seconds – after flipping in his kayak and rolling over and over eleven times in thirteen seconds.

Some rivers demand more technical skill than others, such as the ability to accurately read currents and maneuver around and through rocks and holes often found in steep-gradient mountain rivers. The Colorado River in the Grand Canyon is fairly flat, with a gradient averaging only eight feet per mile. The Salmon River in Idaho, by contrast, drops twenty-seven feet per mile.

To run most of the rapids in the Grand Canyon safely we have to know how to set up correctly at the entry of the rapid, and then be able to keep the raft headed straight into the waves. Most of our runs begin somewhere on a smooth, silky tongue, a wedge in the river formed by lateral currents flowing off the shore or large boulders in the river. The tongue narrows to a point where different forms and sizes of waves await us.

The emerald-green tongue of Badger Rapid shone in the midday sun. It was hypnotic, and I wanted to throw out an anchor and just look at it for a while. On our right, a sizeable hole foamed at the mouth as we gained speed. I gripped my oars tighter and prepared to push hard to add a little momentum as we raced into the first wave. When the cold water engulfed us, Chris let out a loud cry. Graham grimaced as he shook his head like a dog coming out of the river. Jane was silent, her forehead streaked with worry. More waves. Water broke over the front of the raft as we climbed the ten-foot waves.

Thirty seconds later we emerged from the rapid right side up and Jane suddenly broke out into song: "Charly my boy, oh Charly my boy," she sang, a smile of relief on her face. Finally she had a sense of what it was like in bigger water - cold and wet, but invigorating. Maybe death was not so imminent after all. It would be three more miles before running another rapid. Plenty of time to dry out and warm up.

The sun beat down on us from directly overhead. Without the cold Colorado River modifying the desert heat, we would have been too hot. Eventually someone on the crew would tell an overheated passenger "if you're hot, you're stupid" – a phrase reminding him or her that the cooling river was more than willing to offer respite from the sun. What could kill us could also bring relief.

I pulled over into an eddy at the bottom left of the rapid and watched as the paddleboat entered. Eliza, in the left front of the raft, had a grin on her face as she paddled hard. The water drenched her as they broke through the first wave. I gave her a thumbs-up as they floated past us.

Below Badger the river widened and mellowed. As the sound of the rapid receded my three passengers settled back to relax into the day. We passed Ten Mile rock, a large angular chunk from the Coconino formation, the third rock layer. Looking like an unformed sculpture waiting for its image to be revealed, it had planted itself in the river channel after having fallen almost a thousand feet. Long streaks of whitewashed bird droppings tailed off into the river indicating this had been a favorite perch for large birds, probably heron.

The second rock layer, called Toroweap limestone, was referred to by some geologists as dirty limestone. The top of the Toroweap was almost pure limestone, but the lower layers were inter-bedded with sand grains and silts. This meant that the ocean had been shallower in the initial stages when the lower layers of the Toroweap had been forming. Being closer to shore, sand grains and fine silts carried by rivers were being dumped into the ocean, mixing with the limestone mud. In the later stages the ocean had deepened, and no sand or silt had been present.

The low grumbling of Soap Creek Rapid interrupted what had become a peaceful float. Graham slept, while Chris was lost in the fascinating shapes of the Canyon walls. Jane was the first to hear it.

Soap Creek Rapid was named by Jacob Hamblin, the so-called "Buckskin Missionary," a pioneering Mormon scout credited with discovering the area that was to become known as Lees Ferry. He was also the first recorded Anglo to circumnavigate the Canyon. As the story goes, Hamblin killed a badger in what became known as Badger Creek, took it downstream to the next drainage and cooked it in a pot of boiling water. The next morning the pot was full of soap from the combination of the alkaline water and the badger's fat, and when it was dumped into the river, a soapy residue remained in the eddy next to the rapid. Thus, Soap Creek Rapid got its name.

Soap Creek was similar to Badger, only the waves were bigger and the seventeen-foot drop exceeded Badger's by two feet. As it did at Badger, the river formed an "S" as it flowed from right to left and then right at the entry to the rapid. Unlike Badger, where the current pushed to the right towards a pourover near the entry, the current at the head of Soap flowed towards the left shore. I set up to enter on the left side of the tongue so I could hit a big wave head-on. Soap was a bit longer than Badger and the larger, rolling waves made it seem like we were in the ocean running up and down the swells. Again Jane was hunkered down in the back with a death grip on the safety lines. Again her rendition of "Charly my boy" rang out after we came through the rapid safely.

We continued downstream with the Canyon walls now fifteen hundred feet above us. The steep walls looked like impregnable fortresses standing at the ready to repel invaders. Eroded pockets in the limestone cliffs looked like wounds from an ancient battle. The fifth layer was now rising from its watery cocoon. The Supai Formation has four distinct members separated by narrow bands of jumbled rock formed by turbulent ocean waves crashing against the shore. Supai was named after the Havasupai Indian village, containing the only native inhabitants living below the Canyon rim. Their reservation spreads out more than nine miles from the river up the Havasu Creek drainage. The top layer is called the Esplanade, and forms into a sandstone cliff that becomes a significant hiking bench in the Western part of the Canyon. The bottom three layers of the formation have been named Wescogame, Manakacha, and Watahomigi, after Supai family names.

Just below Salt Water Wash at mile twelve we passed a hard-to-spot inscription in the rocks in a large eddy on river left. The inscription, chipped into the black coating of desert varnish about ten feet above the water line, reads *F.M. Brown, Pres. D, CC & PR was drowned July 10, 1889 opposite this point.*

Brown was the president of the Denver, Colorado Canyon, and Pacific Railroad Company, and his objective had been to survey the Grand Canyon at river level to determine the best possible route for his railroad tracks. He had planned to transport coal to Los Angeles, and bring California goods back to Colorado and points east. He had drowned after his boat capsized in the eddy below Soap Creek Rapid, the thick sediment soaking into his wool suit and pulling him down. He wore no life jacket, nor did anyone else on the trip. In his impatience and desire to conserve funds, he had failed to purchase the life jackets that would have saved his life.

Below the inscription the channel narrowed, speeding up the currents, making the river feel more chaotic. It took more concentration and effort to stay in the current and became much too easy to be drawn into one of the eddies. If that happened I could easily lose a quarter mile of distance between my raft and the rest of them. I've always made it a point to stay out of those eddies, which was one of the reasons I usually rowed a non-self-bailing raft. These bucket boats, so named because of the buckets each carries to bail out water, are the most efficient boats on the river. They sat *in* the river, rather than *on top* as the self-bailers with their inflated floors tended to do, "tracked" in the current better, and were not as easily sucked into the eddies.

We floated by the first Supai layer, finely sculpted sandstone offering magnificent examples of art forms created through sedimentation. Thin layers of rock were tilted downward, looking like carefully placed stacks of hardened sand, each a few inches thick. They reminded me of the Pancake Rocks on the South Island of New Zealand. Swirling river currents had rounded off the ends of each stack, foreshadowing even more spectacular natural sculptures to come.

We were now in a quiet section of Marble Canyon. Steep walls enclosed the narrow channel, blocking out the mid-afternoon sun, chilling anyone still wet from Soap Creek Rapid. On mornings when the river was clear, the sun reflected off the surface and danced on the underbelly of overhanging ledges, creating an aquarium effect of light swaying to the rhythm of the river's flow.

Just ahead the soft rumble of Shear Wall Rapid floated upstream. Jane looked at her river map and said "if it's rated only two out of ten, why is it so loud?"

I explained that there were two factors that helped determine in advance the size of a rapid. Chris and Jane were all ears, while Graham remained in his supine position, enjoying the abstract figures in the Canyon walls. The first and most obvious factor was the volume of the sound. Theoretically, the larger the volume, the larger the rapid. However, many things, including upstream winds, close shear walls, and rocks in the current, could influence volume. I pointed downstream and told Jane that the walls hemming in the rapid were steep, hard, and close to the river, the water was flowing against a large boulder in the rapid, and there was a slight upstream breeze. All these conspired to increase the noise level.

The other factor in determining the size of an impending rapid, I explained, was pitch. The lower the pitch, the deeper the growl and the bigger the rapid. I asked Chris what she thought the pitch of Shear Wall was. "A tenor," she volunteered in her singsong English accent. Jane smiled and relaxed her grip on the safety line.

Sheer Wall Rapid, like the vast majority of rapids in the Canyon, had been formed and re-formed by debris bursting out of a side canyon, in this case Tanner Wash, which came in from river left. Any significant rainstorm in that drainage had the potential to create a flash flood. The resulting slurry of rocks, boulders, trees, cacti, vegetation, and sediment narrowed the channel causing the current to accelerate. I had always wanted to stop and hike in this side canyon, but it usually didn't fit our schedule or the hiking ability of our passengers. The only way in was a climb along a narrow Supai shelf. Even though the sandstone acted like sandpaper and gripped footwear very well, there was a lot of exposure, so it was not a hike for neophytes or the timid.

As we approached the head of the rapid, I told everybody to look to their left where the current split. The main channel flowed down the right side into a series of waves big enough to get us wet. The left channel made a sharp bend and flowed close to the wall, then took a sharp right. The sandstone entrance to the side canyon had been eroded into a mini-slot canyon – narrow, sculpted walls on either side of the drainage practically touching in some places. The curves of the naturally carved walls were nothing short of sensuous. Had I been able to pull over there, the eroded and polished rock would have invited our caress.

I set up to enter the silky-smooth tongue just left of center to avoid the bigger waves to the right. As the tongue narrowed to a point, waves breaking over the front of the raft forced Graham to jerk up from his prone position to avoid getting wet. A small squeal of delight erupted from Jane in the back. I turned and smiled. Her face reddened, exaggerated by the iron oxide-painted rock walls shining off the water, and the corners of her mouth curled against gravity. Smaller tail waves rushed against the front of the raft as we rounded a bend and emerged from the shadows.

The sun felt good after that shady stretch. We still had two miles before reaching camp, a place called Hot Na Na Wash, just below river mile sixteen. There we would spend the night listening to a large rapid a half-mile downstream. The drenching we would get in House Rock Rapid first thing in the morning would surely wake us up. Until then, we would hear its voice singing to us all night long.

We had started this morning surrounded by two-hundred-and-thirty-year-old eroded sandstone walls sitting well away from the river. Now steep, narrow walls rose sixteen hundred feet out of the river, hemming us in and erasing images of the world beyond the Canyon. We had traveled sixteen miles downstream and over eighty million years back in time.

We pulled up to a beach in a large eddy on the downstream side of a sand-covered peninsula. Large, river-polished boulders, many peeking out from their sand blankets, dotted the area. All six rafts pulled in side-by-side and were quickly strapped together to make it easier to walk across the rafts, while assuring that none of our rafts would float away at night.

Prior to the building of Glen Canyon Dam the flows of the Colorado fluctuated with the realities of the seasons. Winter and summer rains would create temporary high water flows. Annual spring snowmelt could cause floods as high as 200,000 cubic feet per second (cfs). In between, the river could be as low as a thousand cfs. In the 'seventies and 'eighties, typical fluctuations, now modified by law, would vary between three thousand and thirty thousand cfs.

After the dam became operational in 1963, and before 1992, we had to deal with significant water fluctuations due to releases from Glen Canyon Dam. Depending on our distance downstream from the dam, the water might be rising or falling at night. At some camps we would have to get up late at night and move our rafts to deeper water. If we had failed to do so, we would often wake up in the morning to find our rafts high and dry, sometimes marooned on large boulders. Fortunately, we always had a surplus of people to help us push the rafts back into the water.

An environmental impact statement initiated by James Watt, the Interior Secretary under Ronald Reagan, concluded that the dam's operations had indeed been responsible for downstream damage, including the loss of around fifty percent of the beach areas. The Grand Canyon Protection Act in 1992, the result of thirteen years of science initiated by guides, changed all that. The act mandated lower high flows, and higher low flows, along with smaller hourly changes in volume. The curtailed releases have resulted in significantly reduced fluctuations, and uninterrupted sleep. The two a.m. wake-ups and naked nighttime adventures in bare feet on sharp rocks were now just another memory.

At first glance our camp at Hot Na Na seemed woefully small. In reality there were plenty of campsites just over the rise, offering solitude and privacy for those who wanted it. A flat spot directly in front of the rafts was designated as the kitchen area. As each raft floated into camp, Sue reminded the passengers to form a bag line to help unload all the gear. At lunch she had told them they would help us offload all the rafts before locating their respective campsites. Guy, a short, stocky man with broad shoulders, matted black hair, an ample belly and a booming voice, must not have been listening – or he simply didn't care. As I started to un-strap my bags, I noticed him disappearing over the hill in search of the perfect campsite.

Everybody else cooperated, and within minutes the kitchen was set up. Folks then collected their yellow river bags, matching their blue clothing number and the one containing sleep gear with the same number in red, and headed off to find their bedrooms. As for the kitchen, three aluminum tables, each about seven feet long, were set up in a squared-off "U," with the opening facing away from the river. The stove table was set at the bottom of the "U" to allow for a spectacular, unobstructed downstream view while cooking. The prep table, complete with three large cutting boards, was placed perpendicular to the stove table and to its left. The serving table sat parallel to the prep table to the right of the stove table. At the open end of the "U" rested the large aluminum commissary box full of pots, pans, and utensils. Next to the "com box" rested another surplus WWII twenty mm. ammo can filled with staples like cooking oil, sugar (white and brown), tea (caffeinated and decaffeinated), cocoa, honey, hot sauces, and granola. A similar can contained brightly colored plastic plates, bowls, plus silverware and steak knives in Tupperware containers. We removed a six-burner stove from its black canvas cover and placed it on the cook table, hooked up the hoses leading from a large propane tank under the table to the stove, and to the blaster. We used the blaster to heat water for coffee and dishwashing. It rested on the sand to the left of the cook table.

Finally Michael brought a twenty mm. can with the number "1" on the lid from Sue's raft. Its contents included all the dry goods for Day One dinner, Day Two's breakfast, and lunch if called for. Other cans marked "2" through "15" rested in various rafts, waiting for their day. When empty, the day can would then be converted into a receptacle for garbage. In the morning, it would be the last can to be closed and then loaded on the raft, to remain unopened until its contents could be dumped into a trash bin back at the warehouse.

We finished organizing the kitchen and started preparing baby carrots, celery sticks and a dip for hors d'oeuvres brought up by Star. Meanwhile Michael and Carla set up the "unit." The location of the bathroom, or "unit" was crucial. It needed to be close enough to camp to make it convenient, but far enough for privacy, often behind large boulders or in a grove of trees or bushes. Where possible it should also be close to the river, because that's where we tell the passengers to pee. It sounds gross but is environmentally sound because the river volume is large enough to quickly disperse the urine with no negative impact. Some referred to the toilet as the "groover" in honor of the old days when there had been no toilet seat. Instead, people would sit directly on the top of the ammo can, leaving telltale grooves in their skin.

After using the unit we would wash our hands at a makeshift bathroom sink – two five-gallon buckets situated a couple feet apart. One bucket contained clean river water; the other held the dirty rinse water. A plastic tube led from the clean water to a rubber bulb anchored to a small square plastic board, and then to a hollow copper tube clipped on to the lip of the dirty water bucket. The copper tube rose vertically above the lip of the bucket and was bent forward so that water would flow into the bucket. By stepping on the bulb repeatedly clean water flowed through the tube and up the copper "spigot." Anti-bacterial soap, applied from a small dispenser, would then be rinsed off into the bucket.

Carla set up the sink alongside the path a respectable distance away from the unit. Nearby, she also placed toilet paper, protected in a small Tupperware container. This was the "key." If it was near the buckets, no one was occupying the unit. If it was absent, the unit was in use. Prime bathroom times were always right after arriving at camp and first thing in the morning.

Our arrival at camp coincided with the sun dropping below the rim. On summer trips we often had a couple of hours to relax before starting dinner. Guides might take a bath and then kick back with a beer, a soda, or a mixed drink. Prior to the trip passengers had designated their beverage of choice, which had been bought by the company and placed in individual burlap bags. A name on the tag matched the person to the bag. Some had purchased beer, others wine (often described as "headache in a bag"), others sodas.

We had had a very invigorating day, as was always the case in the Canyon, particularly on day one. After the early morning wake-up, the long ride, the excitement at Lees Ferry, the newness of the Canyon, and a day in the rapids, passengers were now ready to kick back after making camp. But not just yet. There was still a lot of information to pass on. I blew the conch shell and everybody assembled near the hors d'oeuvres, drinks in hand, for the final camp orientation. While they munched, Floyd gave them a tour of the kitchen.

"This is the prep table," he began in his booming, affable voice. "It has nothing to do with college." He paused, raised his eyebrows, and laughed, causing everybody to crack up. "The prep table is for preparing food." Another huge grin erupted on his face as he held two thumbs up. "Anybody who wants to help is most welcome. But noooo graaazing." Walking across the inner kitchen area, he continued. "And this is the serving table. Notice the plates, bowls, and silverware. This is where we all begin our meals. We will have both dinner and breakfast set out buffet-style for your dining pleasure. You can't beat the ambience in this five-star restaurant. Every seat is a window seat." As laughter echoed off the Canyon wall, I wondered where else could you find people who work so hard and have so much fun?

"Here is the cook stove," Floyd offered as he pointed with a flourish to the table holding the six-burner stove. "Be careful of the blaster on the ground. It puts out a mean flame. Now, if you will, follow me to the dish line." He waddled Charlie Chaplin-like to a table near the river with four metal buckets filled with water. On the ground at the upstream end of the table was a white bucket with a screened sieve on top. "This is the 'slop bucket' and you WILL scrape all your juicy garbage into this before washing your dishes, won't you." Laugh-filled replies of "yes, sir" filled the air. "The first water bucket is a cold, soapy rinse bucket. The second is a hot, soapy wash. The third is a hot rinse, and the last is a cold rinse with Clorox to help kill bacteria, and dry your hands to a mass of ugly red splotches." Again he stopped and beamed that "can-do" smile. "Unless you use copious amounts of moisturizer. Clean dishes are then placed in mesh "hammocks" under the serving and prep tables to air-dry.

"Our next stop will be the therapy room." Everybody followed dutifully, some with puzzled looks on their faces. "We take everything out of the Canyon with us. Everything." He winked, and continued. "To accommodate for limited space, all beverage and food cans must be smashed to the thickness of a dime and stored in burlap bags. Notice the metal plate resting on the blue tarp. The tarp protects the beach from any food or liquid in the cans, and the plate is where you rest our empty drink and food cans. Your therapy, sometimes known as anger management, begins when you grab this device." He picked up a two-and-a-half-foot wooden bar around 3-4 inches in diameter attached at the bottom to a round, flat metal plate. Placing an empty beer can on the metal plate, he continued. "For greatest relief and most effective smashing, I recommend two hands, and a quick, violent hit." As he spoke, he demonstrated. "Many times you will notice empty cans not yet smashed. Feel free to practice at your leisure. Our research indicates those who smash more than one can at a time are happier at the end of the trip.

"Next we have the water filter. Stay with me, we're almost done, and you can go back to your drinks. This is a Katadyne filter complete with a ceramic core in a stainless steel housing. The filter eliminates all particulates and bacteria larger than two microns. To take care of any viruses that might be present, we will add a small amount of Clorox to the filtered water." He then demonstrated the proper pumping technique and indicated how to clean the filter and add chlorine. He said it was important to wash hands after cleaning the filter, since we would have come in contact with any bacteria that might be present.

"And now, the *piece de resistance*," Floyd announced with a wave of his arm in the direction of the unit. "What you have all been waiting for. A tour of our fine bathroom facility, commonly known as the "unit" or the "groover," which we guarantee to come complete with a different, unparalleled mural every day." They walked behind Floyd, talking and laughing

19

as he led them on a tour of the unit with instructions about correct use and the need for conscientious hygienic practices.

Finally all the information had been given. Now we could relax and enjoy being in this amazing natural world. Everybody but the cook crew, that is. Two guides would be on cook duty every third day, responsible for dinner and the next morning's breakfast preparation. Everybody on the crew would contribute at lunch. Michael and I were the cooks for tonight's meal.

Fortunately it was a simple meal to prepare: manicotti, green salad, garlic bread, and strawberry pound cake with whipped cream for dessert. We placed the thawed manicotti, layered in spaghetti sauce, crushed tomatoes and mozzarella cheese, in Dutch Ovens (DO), and baked them using charcoal for heat. We placed ten white-hot coals on the bottom of a round aluminum fire pan, twelve to fifteen coals around the lid of the first DO, and another fifteen to twenty coals around the lid of the second DO, which sat on top of the first one.

We chopped up a handful of peeled garlic cloves, sautéed them in butter, spread the mixture over three loaves of French bread split lengthwise, and browned them on the griddle. The tossed salad included romaine lettuce, diced tomatoes, sliced cucumbers, and shredded carrots. A vidalia onion dressing added additional flavor

The sound of the conch shell echoing off the canyon walls brought everybody together. Once plates were filled only the soft sound of the river and the staccato of forks on plates could be heard as the last rays of the sun painted a golden hue on the Kaibab limestone, highlighting the end of a perfect day.

After cleaning up the kitchen area, Eliza and I retired to my raft. I asked her where she planned to sleep, and she said she would like the back deck just behind the cooler. I said that was fine with me, because I actually preferred the front hatch. We sat on the cooler and watched the fading light remove the color from the Canyon's palate. Eliza said she had had a blast on the paddleboat, and Sue had asked her to be available if she wasn't able to find six people on any given day. I told her I looked forward to having her on my raft, and would be happy to teach her to row if she was interested. She didn't reply. I started to say something about her becoming a river guide, but decided to keep it to myself. Eliza said she was tired, and went back to her bedroom. In less than five minutes she was asleep.

Usually guides sleep on their rafts, except in splashy eddies. In the past we would sleep on the top of our coolers which required some creative arranging of throw pillows and lifejackets on either end to provide stretching room. Today we have frames with hatch covers that are around two feet wide and over six feet long. Combined with very comfortable inflatable pads, they afford an uncommon luxury, especially in the summer when night temperatures can exceed a hundred degrees. A virtual swamp cooler of fifty-degree water surrounds us and modifies the heat significantly.

Every guide employed a different arrangement for sleeping. I preferred two pads with a throw pillow at the end so my feet wouldn't hang in the air or have to rest on the metal hatch lid. I wrapped a sheet (cotton in the summer, flannel in spring and fall) around the top pad and the throw pillow and spread the second sheet over the top. I kept a sleeping bag in my waterproof black bag, but usually didn't take it out until early in the morning, about the time the heat captured by the Canyon's walls had dissipated. It was a mummy bag, and since I preferred freedom for my legs, I pulled it on top of me but rarely got in it.

Once the sun set, darkness descended unexpectedly fast and early. I laid out my sleeping kit, brushed and flossed my teeth, applied copious amounts of moisturizing lotions to my legs, feet, arms, and shoulders, and laid down and stretched my legs, forearms, low back, and shoulders. Then I pulled my cotton sheet over me, and explored the stars and constellations emerging above the narrow Canyon walls.

With no campfires allowed due to the lack of driftwood, we were all ready to relax and enjoy the emergence of what for some would be the darkest sky and the brightest stars and Milky Way they had ever seen. Then, hopefully, sleep would come quickly.

My last thoughts wandered to a private trip I had been on with my parents and my brother Sandy. It was 1986 and my dad had recently liquidated his retail men's clothing store, a business that had been well respected since 1925 when his father had purchased it. My parents were not experienced campers, having done only one raft trip, that with my brother Sandy through Cataract Canyon in the late 'seventies. My dad had grown a beard, which looked quite good on him, and was constantly covered from head to toe to ward off any chance of skin cancer. I had never been camping with my parents, and it was a joy to see them so captured by the magic of the Canyon. Like most of my other passengers, my parents had moved almost effortlessly into our daily routines of waking, eating, floating, hiking, and camping. Both were willing hikers, even though they were in their early seventies. My mom's elderly friends back in Michigan couldn't understand how someone her age would willingly spend eighteen days sleeping on the ground. They thought she was just doing it for the sake of her kids. I smiled as I recalled that shared time, and felt gratitude for the opportunity. Within two years of that trip, my father would be dead from a brain tumor.

Charly Heavenrich

Often our first hike of the trip is to this wonderfully sensuous pool. It provides the guides with an opportunity to assess the hiking skills of our passengers. The sounds of my Native American flute deepen our connection to the Earth and the Canyon

22

DAY TWO –
HOT NA NA TO SILVER GROTTO

My travel alarm pulled me out of a deep sleep. I had to get up to put on the coffee and tea before preparing breakfast. First light was just after five, and normally we had coffee around that time. But Sue said she wanted the passengers to sleep in, to give them time to recover from trip preparations and a long first day.

Lying on my back I surveyed the velvet black sky and the outline of the Canyon walls. Listening to the outspoken voice of House Rock Rapid carried on a soft upstream breeze that felt like a cooling touch as it brushed my face, I thought about my first run through that rapid.

It was on a private trip in 1979 with my brother Sandy and six of his friends. We had three rafts. It was my second time in the Grand Canyon, but my first time rowing my own raft, a thirteen and a half foot Miwok. It had been Sandy's first Canyon trip. We didn't stop to scout House Rock. Allowing for his greater experience - he had just completed his third season rowing for a commercial outfit in Utah - I followed him into the rapid without stopping to scout. He took what was known as the highway route, right down the middle. I later learned that few commercial guides chose that route because it could take you directly into a massive hole. Huge waves rebounding off the left shore rushed at me, swallowing my small raft, removing any pretension that I was in control. I tried to put my nose into the waves as they rushed at me, but found it impossible as two currents, one coming off the right shore, the other off the left, merged into a cacophony of liquid sound. Just above the hole, the waves parted as if on cue, and we each got a very close view of the hole. I still like to run close to the hole, but haven't taken that route since.

Before going to sleep we had filled the large pot with river water for coffee, along with a smaller pot for tea. Although river water is first pumped through a filter before drinking, coffee and tea water, when taken directly from the river when it is clear, is boiled, so it doesn't require filtering. Guy's ample, shirtless figure stood motionless by the river at the end of the sand spit. He seemed to be meditating and looked like an East Coast Buddha. I went into the kitchen, found the lighter, and lit the blaster and the stove burner to heat water for coffee and tea. I then

23

opened up the com box and placed the knives, snuggled safely in a folded fabric knife holder, on the inside of the uplifted com box lid. In the box were three other pots arranged in size so that all five pots and four lids could nest inside one another, plus a plastic pitcher holding large serving spoons, a wisk, three spatulas, three ladles, and several aluminum tongs. Also inside were six aluminum bowls -- two large ones for salads, two medium bowls for serving and mixing, and two small ones for serving – plus a container of dish soap, a container of Clorox, aluminum foil, sponges and scrubbies, and a lid for the largest pot.

I also opened the lids of the staples and plates boxes and brought the garbage box up to the prep table. The menu called for blue corn pancakes and bacon, with orange juice. Inside the plates box was a double ziplock bag of pancake mix, two cans of blueberries, and concentrated orange juice. As I was making the OJ, Michael brought up five pounds of vacuum-sealed bacon and dumped it into a Dutch oven resting over two burners. Bacon in this amount takes forever to cook, and we couldn't start making the pancakes until it was almost done.

When steam percolated around the edges of the coffee-water lid, Michael turned off the blaster and poured the ground espresso coffee into the water. He allowed the grounds to settle for about five minutes before pouring the steaming coffee through a sieve into an insulated Gott cooler. Meanwhile I poured the boiling tea water into another Gott, and we placed each cooler on the serving table along with sugar, teas, cocoa, and sliced cantaloupe.

Michael went over to check the bacon and I took a few steps toward the river and then stopped, listening to the silence and feeling the still morning air. It was cool and slightly damp, and smelled clean, like a new day. Beyond the Canyon walls, the world was rising to a new day of rush hour traffic, domestic responsibilities, and the known and unexpected demands of life. I whispered soft words of gratitude for the blessing of beginning my day in this peaceful natural wonder, walked back into the kitchen and blew the conch shell to rouse people for their morning brew. Guy, the shirtless, overweight, no-boundaries passenger, was already pouring his coffee and talking in a voice you could hear over the cacophony of rush hour in Manhattan.

I pulled a large bowl out of the com box and proceeded to mix the pancake batter. After begging a beer from Michael, I emptied the mix, both cans of blueberries. and the beer into the bowl and stirred, adding water as needed. I preferred to use as little water as possible, substituting juices, and in this case beer, to enhance flavors.

Our aluminum griddle had a slight bend to it, and I knew that meant it would have inconsistent heat. I placed it over three burners on the stove, lit them, and poured on a little vegetable oil to prep the surface. Since my first batch always turned out imperfect, I started with one cake, which indicated the griddle needed to be a bit hotter. After waiting for a few minutes, I tested again. Satisfied, I made two rows of four cakes each. Flipping pancakes was always an adventure, not knowing if they would come out the desired golden brown. Sometimes I needed more liquid, and other times the griddle was too hot. But eventually I would get into a rhythm and the second Dutch oven would be filled to overflowing. Michael drained the bacon and placed it in a medium bowl in layers separated by paper towel.

In the past we would save the bacon grease in a glass jar, adding to it until the last night. Then we would make a grease bomb. A guide would be outfitted with a metal bowl for a hardhat, and clothing to protect him or her from the intense heat. We would place the blaster and propane near the river, away from camp and vegetation, boil a big pot of water, and then the fire person would take the grease in a can, suspend it from the end of an eleven-foot oar, *and heat it over the boiling water. When the grease reached a certain heat, it would explode* *into a huge fireball that would light up the night. We don't do that any more. The old days of* *doing pretty much what we wanted were over, and grease bombs were included in the Park* *Service-generated list of no-nos.*

We placed the cakes and bacon on the serving table, brought the maple syrup container out of the heated dishwater, opened up a container of yogurt and a pad of butter, and blew the conch for breakfast. Again Guy was first in line, followed closely by Timmy and little Nathan. Their eyes still preferred to be asleep, but their stomachs spoke louder. Some passengers had already stuffed their sleep gear and clothing into their yellow bags, and had brought them down to the rafts before grabbing their plates. Others would make their beds and clean up their bedroom after breakfast.

I grabbed my food and sat next to Timmy and his dad. The absence of any emotional expression on Timmy's face, even when going through the rapids or playing in the mud with Nathan yesterday at lunch, had intrigued me. I also wanted to get a reading on his dad, who seemed distant. I asked him why Timmy hadn't brought his glasses.

There was an awkward pause. Then he responded in a downcast voice, "I didn't want him to lose them."

That's all he said, but it spoke volumes. This seemed to be a man who saw the glass as more than half empty. How could a father spend three thousand bucks on a river trip and worry about losing a hundred-dollar pair of glasses? And how much would Timmy miss because of this? There must be something more to it, I thought.

Just then, Sue stood up and made an announcement. "Since we're all here," she said, "I thought you might be interested in the plan for the day." Everyone stopped eating and looked at Sue.

She thanked the group for their help in unloading the boats the day before, saying how much difference it made when everybody pitched in. She glanced quickly at Guy, and then said that after being serenaded all night by House Rock Rapid, we'd get to see what all the music was about. Most of the passengers chuckled, but Jane glanced down at her feet. Sue added that we'd be getting wet first thing, and suggested people consider putting on their rain gear, especially since we'd be in the shade. In addition, we'd run a couple more small but feisty rapids before the river mellowed out for a couple of miles. She also said we'd be doing a hike, and suggested that some could wear sandals during the hike, but those with tender feet might want to have their boots available. She lifted up a large blue bag with "Boots" written on duct tape, and said it would be available on shore before the hike.

After the hike we would be entering the Roaring Twenties, nine rapids in eight miles that would definitely get us wet. Before running them, we'd get out the inflatable duckies if anyone expressed an interest. She cautioned there was only one condition, then smiled and paused. Each person would first have to pass a self-rescue test, which required they get in the river. A murmur rose throughout the group. She said one of the guides would demonstrate to show there was nothing to worry about.

From the back of the group, Guy's voice caused everyone to turn around. "We'll be the judge of that," he said. No one said a word, and Sue's gentle voice broke the tension, saying we planned to get to Silver Grotto, about thirteen miles downstream, early enough to go on an adventure hike.

"What's that?" It was Nathan, his eyes now wide awake and his small voice elevated by curiosity.

Star replied that we would be setting up some ropes and swimming through a couple of pools and doing some "chimney moves."

"I know what that is," Nathan replied, a big grin on his face. He had been raised in Northern Montana near the Bob Marshall Wilderness, and even at ten years old, clearly was more wilderness-smart than many of us.

"Well, maybe you can show us," Sue replied. Nathan beamed and looked at his mother next to him. "So, if there aren't any questions, let's finish up breakfast, wash the dishes and load the rafts. I'm sure you can't wait to get wet."

While the passengers finished packing their yellow bags, the crew broke down the kitchen. After cleaning the stove, we stuffed it into its custom-made canvas carrying case. Carla carefully packed the com box and with my help brought it down to my raft. We placed it on the floor to the left of where my legs would be as I sat on the cooler. My front hatch carried all of the kitchen gear, with a very heavy grill on the bottom followed by the stove, griddle, blaster, propane tank, four dish line buckets, and the strainer from the slop bucket. Then I called for eleven yellow bags.

Ben organized a bag line and passed eleven yellow bags down to me, then filled the quotas of the other guides. I took the nine smallest bags for my back hatch and left two longer ones in the front. The shorter bags were usually from passengers who planned to hike out and wanted to minimize the weight they would have to carry. The longer ones were either light sleep kits or personal bags of those going the full length. I carried up to twelve bags on my back hatch, including my three personal black bags, refugees from the past when all river bags were WWII Navy surplus.

I strapped my personal bags on the far right side of the hatch and then three more rows of three yellow bags, all resting behind my cooler which doubled as my seat while I rowed. I then strapped the two longest bags on the right and left side of my front hatch. These would offer convenient backrests for my passengers. Although Sue had encouraged our passengers to vary the rafts they chose, Jane, Chris and Graham again wanted to ride with me. Maybe the sound of the rapid all night had made them nervous. I was happy to have them along, and pleased that they seemed to trust me to ride in the bigger rapids. *On the private trip that I had done with my parents and my brother, my insecurities as a guide had been magnified each time my parents had chosen to ride with Sandy, something they did through most of the bigger water. In fact, it wasn't until day five that my dad actually rode in my raft for the first time.*

Graham coiled up my bowline and stuffed it under the water jug strap on the front tube. He pushed off and jumped aboard with the agility of a former rugby player, albeit with several additional pounds on his frame. I allowed the upstream current in the eddy to carry me into the downstream current. Eliza was again in the paddleboat along with Ben, Jeff, Annie, Stuart, and Jim B, a track coach from a New England college.

"How bad is this rapid?" Jane asked from her hunkered-down position in the back of the raft.

I told her in my world there were no bad rapids, just fun ones. House Rock, I said, was unique because it wasn't like most of the other rapids down here. In the Canyon, we encounter what we call pool-and-drop rapids. Most rapids were formed by debris, either from a side canyon or from a rock fall that narrowed the river channel, forcing the current to speed up. The debris caused the river to pool up and slow down above the rapid – hence the pool – and formed a mini-dam that the water must flow over –the drop.

House Rock and two other rapids – Bedrock and Upset – were unique because of a rock bar at the head. I pointed downstream toward the side canyon on the right, and Jane tentatively nodded her head, her jaw muscles clenched. That was Rider Canyon, I told her, and over the years it had seen many debris flows. As a result, a rock bar had formed, not only pinching down the river, but also forcing the current strongly to the left, towards a rather large hole near the shore. Instead of pushing into the rapid facing downstream, as I had the day before in Badger and Soap Creek, I said I'd be entering backwards, with the raft perpendicular to the flow of the current. That meant Jane would be the leader. I smiled. She didn't.

I explained that I would enter backwards so I could use my stronger stroke, engaging my legs and back, to pull against the current so we could stay away from the hole. If I did it right, which was my intention, we would probably get wet and get a nice close look at the hole. I told Jane I had no interest in going into that hole, and I told everyone they were part of my crew. Their job was to anticipate where the water was coming from, and kiss those waves. They all had their rain gear on, so they didn't have to worry about getting cold. Chris's brow was deeply etched, and Jane tightened her death grip.

I indicated we'd be running third behind Star and Floyd. The paddleboat would come behind us. After we made it through, I planned to pull over into an eddy on the right side to "run safety" and watch the rest of the crew come through. I told them it would be a lot of fun. Silence was the only reply.

We watched as first Star's raft and then Floyd's floated into the rapid. Star's boat disappeared as it dropped over a large wave, reappearing a long ten seconds later as it floated safely to the right of the hole. Floyd entered forward, his oars pushing effortlessly through the current.

On a trip fifteen years ago I had followed a guide named Ray Interpreter into a long, medium-sized rapid with four holes to avoid. Ray, who like Floyd had massive shoulders, had pushed to break through the right current to run down the far right side of the rapid. He made it look easy, and I naively followed. The only problem was I had neither his bulk nor his leverage, and when I hit the right current it hit me back, redirecting me into the middle of the rapid. I barely missed the first hole, and had to find a narrow slot between two boat-flipping pourovers in the middle of the rapid. Since then I've refused to follow others into rapids, and I haven't suffered from any more illusions about my ability to push through bigger water.

After one more glance to make sure Jane was holding on correctly, I turned my raft to face backwards toward river right. Looking for my entry, I reminded everyone to look for waves coming from the side, encouraged primal screams, and pulled hard on my oars. We dropped quickly over a small pourover as I took a couple more strokes, holding tightly to the left (upstream) oar to maintain my angle. If I lost my angle, I could be surfed out into the middle of the current and risk running into that hole. The raft dropped over the pourover with a teeth-jamming thud, and then I let the raft float out a little bit to run closer to the bottom hole. Waves poured in from all directions. As I approached the sharp bend, a large wave rushed at us from the left. I turned to face it and as we broke through that wave, pushed hard with my left oar and turned into a huge wave just above the hole. Chris and Graham lunged forward to meet the wave as I leaned on both oars to add momentum. We broke through and I turned the raft slightly to the right to hit an even larger wave on the right side of the hole. Yep, it was big. Twenty-plus years after my naïve introduction to House Rock in 1979, I still love that run.

As soon as we passed the hole, I pulled hard on my left oar to face the back of the raft toward the right shore. I had to work hard pulling on both oars to make it into the eddy. The current in the tail waves was still very strong, and it took me a good hundred yards to break free and ease into the lower end of the eddy. I then relaxed my grip on the oars and allowed the current to draw us upstream to the top of the eddy. Chris's face reflected her relief at making it through. Graham gave me one of his "well done, old chap" glances, and Jane smiled and pushed Wild Thing's left palm. With her head rocking side to side, the pink tiger, strapped securely on the back tube of my raft, broke out in song.

As we floated up the eddy across from the hole, the paddleboat entered the top of the rapid. We could hear Sue shouting instructions even over the high decibels of the rapid. "Forward, forward, right turn, forward, stop." They cruised to the right of the hole with Ben and Jeff in the front. Suddenly the raft lifted sharply up and Ben went flying out directly over the head of his son. Jane let out a yell and I turned the raft around and headed out into the current to try to catch up with Ben. Jane frantically urged me to catch up to him, and I was pulling as hard as I could, but he was already a hundred feet away. I patted the top of my head to make sure he was okay and he returned it by patting his head and then gave me a thumbs-up and a big grin. The paddleboat, being lighter and faster, reached him first, and pulled him out of the river. He immediately picked up his paddle, slapped the blade on the river, and let out a cheerful shout. We all headed downstream.

A half a mile ahead lay Redneck Rapid, a short but feisty rapid rated a misleading "3" out of 10. *A few years ago I was on a string quartet trip heading for this rapid. One of our passengers was a woman who had been paralyzed from the waist down. A schoolteacher from Denver, she had broken her back when she ran into a tree while competing on her college ski team. It had been six years since the accident and she had clearly recovered some of her physical abilities, but was still struggling with the emotional trauma of losing the use of her legs. Before the trip she had insisted on being in the paddleboat and we had built a custom chair to accommodate her. Everyone admired her spunk and she was doing really well, until Redneck. Entering the rapid, her seat was on the back left just in front of the paddleboat captain. The raft cruised into the third wave that broke as they hit, practically stopping the raft in its tracks, throwing her into the water. Undaunted, she swam the rest of the rapid and the paddleboat turned and paddled upstream to pull her in, no worse for the wear. Her smile was telling as she returned to her seat, to the cheers of everyone.*

The river mellowed as we cruised on a swift current. Graham's King's English broke the silence. "I noticed the water level dropped overnight. I'm assuming it has something to do with the dam, but would like to know how that works."

I told him we were presently running on a current of at least ten thousand cubic feet per second. Our water levels were determined by flows released from the dam. The Colorado River Compact of 1922 had dictated minimum annual levels of 7.5 million acre-feet of water for the lower basin states of Arizona, Nevada, and California. An additional one and a half million acre-feet were designated for Mexico, an afterthought signed into law at the end of Lyndon

Johnson's administration. The remaining 7.5 million acre-feet was held in storage in Lake Powell, reserved for the upper Colorado River basin states of Colorado, Utah, New Mexico, and Wyoming.

I told Graham that an acre-foot of water was the amount of water one foot high that covered an acre. It was 326,000 gallons, enough to sustain a family of four for a year. Each year the Bureau of Reclamation projects monthly flows based on estimates of water entering Lake Powell from snowmelt running out of the Uintas and Rockies. Energy required for heating and air conditioning, as well as other power demands from business, industry, and private use, is generated in part through the southwest power grid. Glen Canyon, which is hooked into the grid, is called an auxiliary dam, providing up to four percent of the energy demands for the southwest. Around six in the morning, when business and industry are gearing up, additional water is released through the dam's penstocks, accelerating the turbines that generate the electricity. Late in the afternoon, when business and industry are shutting or slowing down, the volume is reduced in keeping with the law.

That's why, I told him, we had high flows and low flows – depending on how far below the dam we were at any point in time. The low flows we were floating on now would be coming up around dinner and then falling again by morning. Unfortunately, when the powers-that-be determined the flows back in the 1920s, they had used historic flows from an unusually wet cycle. Since the average inflow of water has been short by over a million acre-feet a year. That deficit comes out of the ground, and has caused the aquifers to be drawn down to levels that have led to sinkholes in Arizona.

Chris wondered how that could happen, so I told her when water levels were lowered in the underground aquifers, pressure was reduced. This pressure kept surface soils from collapsing in. That's all a sinkhole was – falling surface soils due to reduced underground pressure.

"So, how do you determine whether the water will be up, down, or changing?" The engineer in Graham was now fully engaged.

I explained that we assumed average river flows of around four miles an hour. So the water should be starting to increase at our current location around three in the afternoon. Since we were around eighteen miles downstream of Lees Ferry, and the dam was an additional fifteen miles upstream of Lees Ferry, we were actually thirty-three miles below the dam. Dividing thirty-three by four mph, it would take around eight hours for flows released in the morning to reach this location. Since water is let out around six AM, eight hours later would be two PM, give or take. The actual increase would happen over several hours because the dam operators were required to "ramp up" the flows gradually, rather than all at once.

"Look at that," Jane shouted from the back of the raft. "How did that get there?"

She was looking at a massive boulder that from our upstream viewing point seemed to be blocking the river. In reality it had just enough room for rafts to float by on either the left or right.

It was called Boulder Narrows, I told her. The boulder had fallen down from one of the rock layers above. I pointed out some driftwood on top that had been deposited there in 1957 as a spring flood receded. I had spoken recently with someone who had been on the river during that flood, and he told me the water had poured over the huge rock. A block of limestone about sixty feet wide, it loomed at least twenty-five feet above us as we floated down the narrower left side. Behind the boulder, the river rested peacefully in a calm eddy.

29

"Imagine what this place would look like if an earthquake hit," Graham remarked as he surveyed the desiccated driftwood above.

I said it would create a huge lake upstream of any earthquake, depending on the severity of the quake and the amount of debris choking the river. We'd had prehistoric lakes down here that had backed up over two hundred miles into what is now Utah.

"The scale down here is unlike anything I've ever encountered," said Graham. "This is such an unbelievable place."

I smiled. "We've only just begun," I sang, a little off-key. Chris chuckled, and I was pleased to hear it. She had been strangely silent ever since running House Rock.

While floating in silence, I noticed a spectacular reflection on the shaded river just ahead. Like the prow of a narrow ship, the limestone rim on river right soared proudly above and below us in its mirror image. Then we emerged from the shadow into the bright morning sun and the reflection suddenly looked like a picture that had been in the sun too long, faded and indistinct.

As the sound of whitewater pricked my ears, I pointed to the sandy beach on our right and announced we'd be pulling over above the next rapid. We often used North Canyon to gauge the hiking capability of our passengers. It gave us a little bit of everything – flat, sandy trails, scrambling over boulders, a short but steep climb with exposure, and a beautiful pool surrounded by very sensuous rock forms.

"Is it a difficult hike?" Jane asked. "I've never done any climbing and I'm not in very good shape." She looked away as she finished the sentence.

I told her I had no doubt she could do this hike since it was fairly flat by Canyon standards. I also told her if she needed any help, someone on the crew would be there for her. I don't think I was very convincing, but I couldn't worry about that just then. The eddy was just ahead and if I didn't make it I would be forced to run the rapid causing us to miss the hike. Early in my rafting career pulling into eddies made me as nervous as running big rapids. What if I pulled in too soon and had to row against the current while my crewmates watched – and laughed? What if I missed the pull-in entirely? What if it was supposed to be camp, and everybody had to get back in the rafts and row some more just because I had missed it?

As I nosed into shore, Graham grabbed the bowline, leapt off, walked up the angled sand beach and tied the rope to a tamarisk tree that offered the only shade.

I told my passengers we had daypacks for everyone and suggested they bring their water and cameras on the hike. Anyone who wanted to could change into their hiking boots on shore. They'd find them in the big blue bag Floyd was offloading. Since we'd be in the sun quite a bit on this hike, I said they might want to wear a long-sleeve shirt and put on some sunscreen if they already hadn't. Finally I said, if they were really smart, they'd get wet before beginning the hike. This was one of the counterintuitive aspects of hiking in the Canyon. Many of our passengers are from cooler or more humid places. It wouldn't occur to them to get wet in the river before going on a hike. Down here, it's the smartest thing one can do to keep the body cooled down to prevent heat exhaustion.

As Sue pulled into the beach, Mary, a good-natured sixty-something from Washington, jumped from the raft with the bowline. I saw her wince as she landed, and then grab her foot. Sue took the rope from her and tied it to a tammy, then went back and checked with Mary to make sure she was okay.

While everybody got ready for the hike, I walked out on the boulders near the head of the rapid to photograph the beach. On the way I passed a seated Mary with Sue looking at her foot. Mary tossed me a forced smile. As part of the Adopt-a-Beach program sponsored by the Grand Canyon River Guides Association, this was one of two beaches I had chosen to photograph on each trip. At the end of the season I would turn in the disposable camera along with my observations for the sediment scientists to evaluate before presenting their findings. An adaptive management work group would then assess the findings to help determine future operations of the dam. The Grand Canyon Protection Act of 1992 had mandated this.

When I returned, the hike had already begun. Mary was sitting in the shade of a tammy about twenty feet from the river. I asked her if she was all right and she said she was fine. Her foot was a bit sore and she had decided to forego the hike. I made sure she had water, suggested she soak her foot in the river, and offered her a book from the library. She thanked me and said she would enjoy relaxing and doing nothing. I liked her attitude and thought then that this was a woman I would enjoy getting to know. I knew she was married and lived in Washington State, but nothing more.

Hiking in North Canyon was like walking into, and on, a sensuous sculpture. It's a narrow canyon in the Supai formation with steep, exfoliating, iron-oxide-coated walls that curled gently to the Canyon floor. On all our hikes, one guide always brings up the rear for safety purposes, and I volunteered on this one. Walking into the canyon from the back of the line, I noticed Jane walking alone back toward the rafts. Her shoulders were slumped and her eyes averted mine as she passed.

"Not going in, huh?"

She looked up, her face shouting defeat. "It was too high for me. Too hard. I'll just wait in the shade for everyone to return."

I told her this was an incredibly beautiful canyon. And it offered her a great chance to stretch a little bit. There were only a couple places in the least bit challenging, and I said I was confident she could negotiate them. I said I would go in with her, and if she needed any help, I would be there. I wasn't going to force this on her, but I knew she could do it, even if she didn't.

Jane remained silent for several moments. Then she lifted her head, drew her shoulders back, and said, "OK, I'll give it a try." A faint smile slid across her face.

As we walked into the canyon I pointed out features of interest, like the fine dry sediment with current lines that had formed as water had flowed out of the canyon during past flash floods. Many millennia down the road this sediment would be hardened into a soft rock akin to shale. I showed Jane the dark green Mormon tea, a common desert plant with branching stems and dry, scale-like leaves that contained ephedra, a substance that provides energy and, in large amounts, has caused some deaths. In spite of its bitter taste, the Mormons used it for stomach ailments. We passed a large *datura* plant, some of its white trumpet flowers still open. The *datura* is known as a teacher plant by medicine men and women who know how to prepare different parts of it as a medicine, hallucinogen, or poison.

We scrambled up a sandy path strewn with partially buried boulders, and came to a ledge about chest high.

"This is where I turned around the first time," Jane admitted, as she approached the ledge. As she again struggled, I interlaced my fingers and offered her a step up in my hand-made stirrup. With a shy smile and a curtsy she placed her right foot in my hands, placed her hands on top of the ledge, and with a bit of a boost from me, stepped up and over. After following her, I took the lead. Jane grinned broadly as I passed by.

"Amazing how easy it can be with just a little help from a friend," she whispered. I started whistling the Beatles song that contained those words.

We walked up a rock-strewn staircase, paused to let Jane catch her breath, and passed around a huge boulder overlooking a dry, sixty-foot waterfall. Jane requested my hand for comfort. I didn't tell her that two people, a thirteen-year old boy and a middle-aged man, had both fallen to their deaths at this point.

We proceded up a level path through a grove of Mormon tea, datura, and canyon grasses, climbed up the convenient steps of another dry waterfall, and came to a striking, narrow section of the canyon. The sandstone walls, covered with a coating of iron oxide from the Hermit Shale above, curled sensuously to the canyon floor. Shallow pools contained black tadpoles in various stages of evolution. After passing the largest of the pools, I looked back to see the sunlit Canyon walls on the far side of the river reflecting upside down in the pool. Encased on both sides by polished and sculpted sandstone, the reflection brought sunlight into the still, shaded pool. The sedimentary layers of the upper Canyon walls lay reversed in the pool, with the younger Kaibab limestone shining underneath the older Toroweap and Coconino cliffs.

Some of the passengers took a break then, relaxing in the sun or playing in a pool surrounded by more sculpted rock. A few of the guides and passengers went through the pool to explore further. A small trickle of water spilled down the smooth rock bowl into the pool, and when they returned, each person slid down and plunged in, to the delighted shouts of everyone. As I looked around, I was hard pressed to find the tension I had seen on their faces at Lees Ferry. We had been gone for only twenty-four hours, and already the Canyon was casting its spell.

Sue started to lead the group back to the rafts and I decided to remain behind to photograph the pool. Once it settled and recovered from human intrusion, it would offer more reflections. As I looked through my wide-angle lens, I imagined being inside a womb-like space looking out. The polished, curved sandstone seemed very feminine, inviting touch. One reflection reminded me of an eagle's head, half in and half above the pool. I sat by the edge of the pool and closed my eyes, enjoying the silence, broken only by my breathing and the occasional plop of a red-spotted toad jumping into the water.

When I arrived back at the shore, Michael and Star were pumping air into the two inflatable duckies and Sue was talking to the group.

"Remember, if you want to go in one of the duckies sometime during the trip, you have to pass a self-rescue test first." She smiled as several passengers grimaced at the thought of immersing themselves in forty-eight degree water. "We're entering the Roaring Twenties beginning right here" – she pointed to the whitewater a hundred feet away – "so only those who have had experience in a ducky or kayak will go first. Later, the river will mellow out and you'll all have plenty of opportunity to have the experience. So, who's interested?"

Several adults and Nathan and Timmy raised their hands. Sue donned her life jacket, put on a helmet, and demonstrated the self-rescue in the eddy. Grabbing the black safety strap wrapped from side to side under the ducky, she leaned over and dropped headfirst into the water, to the gasps of several passengers. After flipping the ducky back over, she jammed her paddle in the front, raised her feet to the surface, extended her arms with her hands on top of the near tube, kicked and simultaneously pulled the ducky under her. Effortless.

"The key here," Floyd instructed, "is to get your legs up to the surface and pull the ducky under you. It's not a strength move. If you're a sinker, you'll have trouble. You have to get your body as close to parallel to the surface as possible."

One by one, Ben, Jeff, Ken, Diana, and Eliza demonstrated their ability to do a self-rescue. Then Nathan offered to try and he made it seem easy. Timmy attempted next. A chubby twelve-year old with no apparent athletic talent, he was a sinker. In spite of unanimous encouragement, and dogged efforts, he was unable to do the self-rescue. Dejected, he finally gave up, pulling the ducky to shore. His shoulders were hunched and his eyes scanned the wet beach at his feet, as many of us encouraged him to try another time. His father wasn't one.

Only Nathan wanted to go in the ducky right away, so we deflated the other one, stowed it back on Star's raft, and headed into the Roaring Twenties. Between North Canyon at mile 20.4 and Tiger Wash Rapid at mile 27, we would run nine medium rapids. The current would be fast and the rapids fun. When I returned to my raft I was surprised to see a smiling Jane in the front with Graham. Chris had elected to be in the back. Assuming she would remain dry, she had decided not to put on her rain gear. I shoved off and pushed out toward the center of the river. In front of us the silky green tongue fed us into noisy white water. Even as we picked up speed I couldn't help admiring the undulating waves – lush, velvety, emerald-green pillows rushing alongside and in front of us like playful dolphins.

At the bottom of the tongue, the left wall jutted out and large lateral waves rushed in to inundate us. Jane squealed with delight as the first waves broke over the front tube. What a difference a day makes. We all looked back as first the paddleboat, and then Nathan in his ducky, cruised through the rapid. He had no trouble making it through right side up. Everyone shouted "Great run!" and "Way to go, Nathan!" The warming sun made getting wet an easy part of the adventure, and we cruised through 21 Mile Rapid, Indian Dick Rapid at mile 23, and 23 1/2 Mile Rapid before pulling over for lunch. By now the walls of the Canyon had receded slightly, widening the channel and opening up to abundant desert sunshine. Evidence of past earthquakes surrounded us in the broken-down Supai sandstone walls, the first step in the formation of side canyons tracing the path of fault lines. Over many years of geologic time, water running through these cracks eventually widen and deepen them into gulleys, then gulches, and ultimately into canyons.

Star had the lunch boat. Her cooler was loaded with produce, frozen lunchmeats, cheeses, red onions, and other lunch foods. To get to the table, she had to de-rig the front hatch. Unstrapping two waterproof bags containing the passenger tents, she flipped them and the inflated white "paco" pad into the front of the raft and handed the aluminum table covering the open hatch to Floyd who carried it to a shaded area on the beach near the water. She handed the "Lunch" can - containing condiments, pb&j, garbage bags, soap and a sponge - to Michael I took the three cutting boards and the jacketed knives. In a canvas shopping bag Star placed four oranges and five Granny Smith apples, one loaf of bread, six packs of pita bread, two packages of cookies, and seven cans of chicken. She also removed the small fifty-cal. "Utes" and "Spices" cans. Finally, she took out a bag of grapes, a head of celery, a red onion, a head

33

of Romaine lettuce, four pounds of Swiss cheese and four tomatoes and carried them up to the table.

We mixed the chicken for the Waldorf salad with the chopped celery, apples, onion, walnuts, grapes, and lettuce, added a small amount of mayo (leaving the rest for personal taste), threw in some salt, pepper and a little cumin, sliced the cheese, and arranged it on the table next to the salad bowl. After slicing the pitas in half and putting them on the opposite end of the table to the pb&j and cookies, we called lunch. We didn't have to be very loud because everybody was milling nearby. While the passengers made their sandwiches, Carla walked to the end of the beach and bathed. The rest of us would wait until the end of the day, or tomorrow, and bathe at camp either before or after dinner. Carla was very modest, and soaped up with her shorts and sports bra on. Other guides were bolder, and often bathed in the nude, although rarely in an exhibitionist manner. Usually we'd use the rafts as partial screens. Every trip is different in this sense. When we have passengers who bathed in the nude, others are emboldened to do the same. Normal standards of modesty, like other "civilized" habits, tend to dissolve during a Canyon journey.

Chris said she wasn't very hungry and didn't eat anything. She had gotten chilled in the rapids, was feeling slightly nauseous and looked a bit pale, so I suggested she drink water with some Gatorade or Erg (electrolyte replacement) in it. She said she would.

I piled some of the salad into one of the chicken cans, grabbed a fork, and walked upstream to find the juniper tree inscription left in 1890 by Harry McDonald, one of the earliest river runners. I ran my hands over the desiccated grooves, trying to imagine what Harry must have been thinking and feeling. I often try to put myself in the bodies of the early river runners, and of course, it's impossible. I have the advantage of their courage and their experiences when I run the river, not to mention far superior equipment, more than enough food, and a satellite phone. Still, the Canyon walls, rapids, and campsites would be familiar to them. As would this tree. I don't know how old it was, but it probably looks today, as it would have to Harry.

We were now at the beginning of the fifth Cambrian layer, Redwall Limestone, which we had first encountered just above Indian Dick Rapid. Although actually colored various shades of gray, Major Powell, the first explorer to run the Canyon in 1869, named it Redwall for its iron-oxide veneer. Powell also named the section we were now in Marble Canyon in recognition of the marble-like appearance of the Redwall, after it had been eroded and polished by the sediment-rich river.

After breaking down the lunch and returning to the rafts, we had little time to relax before running the biggest rapid of the Roaring Twenties. 24 Mile was one of the newest rapids in the Canyon, formed after some rocks fell into the river in the early 'nineties. It was an exciting rapid with a sharp drop at the entry, and two very large waves requiring good momentum. At lower water the current could push us into a rock on the right side of the wave train. At our higher level today, it wasn't even out of the water. As we slammed into the first wave, Jane yelled in excitement and leaned into the front tube.

Recently, 24 Mile was renamed Georgie Rapid, in honor of the woman who pioneered the use of motorized pontoon trips in the Canyon. Her "G-rigs" – two 28-foot rafts on either side of a 33-foot raft – would take up to thirty "Royal River Rats" down the Canyon. Her trips were inexpensive (she used Los Angeles firefighters who worked for little or no pay) and fun. She was often seen wearing a leopard-skin leotard and a white hard hat. Her passengers loved her devotion to the Canyon, and her feisty personality. And Georgie was notorious for having only one run – right down the middle. I don't think she would have liked having 24 Mile named for her. As far as Georgie was concerned, there were only two rapids in the Canyon worth mentioning – Crystal and Lava. She ran her last trip in 1991, at the age of 80.

24 1/2 Mile Rapid, also known as Bert Loper Rapid, and 25 Mile Rapid, also known as Hansbrough-Richards Rapid, had two things in common. Both formed similar "S" shaped runs, and both had claimed lives. I waited until I had run each rapid and then told the stories.

Bert Loper was known as the grand old man of the Colorado for his boat-building and river-running skills. In 1939, at age seventy, he rafted the Grand Canyon for the first time. Everyone had such a great time that they committed to coming back in ten years. So at the age of seventy-nine, Bert was back on the oars in the Canyon. He hadn't been feeling well, but the prospect of returning to the Canyon had overshadowed any concern. Going into 24 1/2 Mile, Bert's passenger noticed he seemed distracted. "Look to your oars, Bert," he shouted. Instead, Bert did nothing, the raft drifted sideways into the rapid and flipped. His boat was found seventeen miles downstream and was pulled up on shore where it lies today, in a state of disintegration.

"What happened to Bert?" Jane asked, her furrowed brow etched in concern.

I told her his body wasn't found for twenty-six years, about forty-six miles downstream. Most assumed he had had a heart attack.

"Lovely story. Thanks for waiting until after the rapid," Graham chimed in, his fine, thinning blond hair shining in the afternoon light. "And what grisly tale do you have for 25 Mile?"

I told him the second and third river deaths had occurred there, on the Brown-Stanton exploratory trip in 1889, the one that had resulted in Brown's drowning below Soap Creek Rapid. As that trip continued a similar fate befell Peter Hansbrough, the boatman who had etched Brown's epitaph into the desert varnish across from where his boat had been recovered, and Henry Richards, a cook's helper, when their boat tipped over below 25 Mile Rapid. I noticed Jane tightening the straps on her life jacket. Graham had no comment, and Chris was equally quiet.

We ran the remainder of the Roaring Twenties without incident and entered a quieter stretch. The Canyon walls rose straight out of the river on both sides and towered above us, blocking out the sun. Chris was shivering and I suggested she put on something warm.

"It's all in my yellow bag," she replied. It didn't look like she was having any fun.

I unstrapped my black bags and pulled out a fleece jacket that she put on under her life jacket and raincoat. A weak smile replaced her frown. At least she would be more comfortable. I glanced at Graham who had a look of concern etched on his face, but he remained silent.

I announced that we were only a few miles from camp, and suggested that everyone relax and enjoy the scenery. They all found a comfortable place on the tube, with Jane and Graham leaning against the yellow bags on my front hatch, and Chris leaning against the row of black bags on my back hatch. A lazy current contributed to their relaxation. The river was undoubtedly deep here, as there wasn't even the hint of white water, even when we passed peninsulas of fallen boulders that had pinched down the channel. The current flowed in wide arcs, carrying our raft like a tacking sailboat from one side of the river to the other and back

35

again. For a half hour we floated in silence, broken only by my dipping oars and the distinctive, descending trill of the canyon wren. The tiny bird's song sounded like a hearty laugh. It had become the theme song for the Canyon. The wren was also our company's mascot, appearing on the logo. A high-strung bird, it rarely rested for more than a couple seconds before flitting off to some other perch.

We pulled in and camped at Silver Grotto, a long, narrow spit of sand on the left, shaped like the curl of a lower case "j" with the curl lying upstream. The uneven Redwall rising out of the sand at the back of camp provided unlimited hangers for damp clothes and raingear. A small but noisy rapid raced in front of the far wall. Our rafts, strapped together, moved as one unit to the constant crashing of small waves against the shore. A large, shallow eddy created after debris from innumerable flash floods from an upstream side canyon narrowed the river, afforded ample room for bathing. At the downstream end of the camp, a pile of jagged limestone rocks lay in a heap where once a party of private boaters had set up their bathroom. During the night, a large section of the Redwall had given way, crushing the unoccupied "unit." A park service crew, responsible for cleaning up unwanted debris, eventually had the unenviable task of removing the remains.

In short order individual and group campsites were established. Some people set up close to the kitchen. They would be the early risers, whether by habit or by necessity, as the blaster heating coffee water was quite noisy. The family groups located upstream where space afforded a small community. A few wandered off to find more distant spots, either for privacy, or to recharge and enjoy time alone. Guides usually slept on their rafts, except when in a "North Sea-type" eddy like this one. We would find space on the beach.

Day Two and we'd already settled into a routine. As I relaxed on the front tube of Sue's raft, a few hardy passengers bathed in the eddy while the crew enjoyed some down time with a beer or soda before beginning preparations for dinner. Some passengers relaxed at their campsites, reading, writing in their journals, or sitting in their Crazy Creek chairs in small clusters, reliving the events of the day. Hemmed in by steep walls, forced to be present by the excitement of white water and the compelling nature of this living geologic museum, we were a growing community of men, women, and boys with one thing in common – a curiosity about the Grand Canyon and a willingness to let go of normal routines and immerse ourselves in the experiences that nature had to offer.

The crew ranged in age from 23 to me (67). Michael had been raised in cosmopolitan Chicago. I had met him in the early 'nineties when, as a recent graduate of Prescott College, he had been a last-minute addition to our crew. Right away I was drawn to him, and knew he would thrive as a river guide. He loved people, had an engaging personality, and was very competent on the river. He also threatened me. I was doing only one or two trips a year, but I wanted to do more. I was insecure about my place in the company and concerned that Michael would get enough trips to eliminate me. On that first trip together I jokingly warned him not to take my job. There was truth in that jest.

Star looked at her watch and reluctantly got up to do the "shopping" for dinner. Food could easily deteriorate over a sixteen-day trip if we didn't keep the coolers cold. Large blocks of ice rested in the bottom of each cooler. To delay its melting we avoided opening them during the heat of the day, regularly drained the water from melted ice, and minimized air space in each cooler. By the fifth or sixth day, Star would "marry" the produce and dairy coolers, and divide the ice among the remaining active coolers. Her other job was to find the perishable foods for dinner and breakfast and deliver them to the kitchen as needed.

Dinner called for chips and salsa as appetizers, chicken and beef fajitas, black beans and rice, and brownies. Although I was not on cook crew, I volunteered to bake the brownies. I loved baking desserts in Dutch Ovens. It was easy, didn't take that long, and was one less thing the cooks needed to handle.

Sue and Star were delighted to let me bake. While they prepared the appetizers, I got out a medium-sized bowl, two packages of brownie mix, three eggs, vegetable oil, and a can of mango juice to use instead of water. I counted out thirty-three lumps of charcoal into a small aluminum oil pan I had placed on three rocks. This prevented the heat from scorching the sand underneath. I leveled the pan with a small carpenter's level. When my crewmates noticed it, they always ragged on me, but hey, it's all about presentation, and an angled cake just wouldn't do.

After dousing the coals with lighter fluid I returned to the brownies, mixed all the ingredients together, then lit the coals. In less than ten minutes they would be hot enough to use. Meanwhile, I found a jar of raspberry jam, put half in a small pot and heated it, mixing in some mango juice to thin it. At the same time, I placed the Dutch Oven lid on the stove and preheated it. When the coals were ready, I sprinkled the jam over the brownie mix, grabbed the lid with channel locks and put it on the Dutch, and carried it over to the coals. With a pair of tongs I arranged twenty-two coals, which were now white hot, around the outside of the lid, including two in the middle. I then placed five coals in the middle of the fire pan and six around the outside. Finally, I laid the Dutch in the fire pan. I wouldn't touch it until I smelled the brownies. At that time I would remove the lid, make sure they were done, and either return them to the coals, or carry the Dutch to the prep table to cool down.

During the remainder of dinner preparations I gathered my sleep kit and a paddle and headed down the narrowing beach to a spot just upstream of the rock fall. There I made my camp. The beach was slightly sloped, so I used the paddle to scrape out a flat spot the size of my pad, laid my ground cloth down and anchored it with two inflatable sleeping pads. In the morning I would replace the disturbed sand to leave no trace of my camp. I left my black bag closed to prevent any unwanted critters from entering, and went back to the kitchen area. Most of the passengers had come down with their drinks and chairs and were talking in small groups, still invigorated by the day's activities.

Dinner was consumed with gusto and the brownies were devoured amid squeals of delight. The dishes were washed in the waning light, and as the colors of the day turned into the deepening shades of gray of approaching night, everyone wandered off to their campsites.

Soon headlamps illuminated faces as a few read books or wrote in their journals. Laughter from the kitchen bounced off the limestone wall as Floyd, Carla, and Michael swapped river stories. I said goodnight and headed to my raft to brush my teeth and grab some moisturizer, my headlamp, and journal to take to my camp. I spoke with Eliza about her day on the paddleboat and she said it had been a blast. With so few passengers eager to paddle, I knew it was likely she would be there quite often. My hope of teaching her to row, or spending time with her on my raft, was quickly vanishing.

The space between last light and dark was very short. By the time I had laid out my sheets, pillow, and had arranged my black bag within reach so I could remove my sleeping bag if needed, the Canyon wall across the river had morphed into a silhouette against a moonless charcoal sky.

I made a few entries in my journal, applied some moisturizer on my already drying feet, and lay back to watch an emerging ceiling of stars and constellations. Vega, in the constellation Lyre, appeared directly overhead. Part of the Big Dipper appeared just above the Canyon wall across the river, allowing me to follow the pointer stars at the end of its bucket to Polaris, the North Star, hovering upstream near the top of the wall. I followed the arc of the Big Dipper's handle to Arcturus, bracketed in the notch of the North and South Rims. I tried to imagine its size, knowing it radiated millions of times the energy of our sun, and if it were located where our sun was, ninety-three million miles from Earth, it would encompass forty percent of the sky. The size of this universe was unimaginable.

Sometimes referred to as "Shiver Grotto" because we have to swim through three pools of cold water to enjoy this view, Silver Grotto demonstrates the sensuality of the Canyon, best known for its hard rocks and massive white water. The adventure hike to enter the Grotto is often a highlight for passengers.

DAY THREE –
SILVER GROTTO TO EMINENCE BREAK

With the smell of brewing coffee pulling me away from my dream, I rolled over and was greeted by the magic of light dancing on the top layer of the Canyon, the Kaibab limestone ("Kaibab" is a Paiute word meaning mountain lying down.). The brilliant orange-gold line sparkled against a light blue sky. I thought of the opening lines of a Kris Kristoferson song – "I've seen the morning burning golden on the mountain in the sky; aching with the feeling of the freedom of an eagle when she flies." (Cue the flute.)

I stretched my arms overhead and extended my hands and feet in opposite directions alternating left and right sides, like a cat preparing to move from its curled repose. I packed up my sleep kit, filled in the evidence of my bed, and returned to my raft. Michael was shaving with his electric razor, Carla remained snuggled in her bag, and Sue and Star were in the kitchen preparing hash browns, ham, and eggs. Floyd was nowhere to be seen, probably off at the unit. Eliza was still asleep on my back deck, her pajama-clad body half out of her bag. She stirred as I slid onto the raft and gave me a sleepy good morning through half-open eyes. A few passengers had already brought their bags down, while two tents remained up. As I organized things on my raft, Guy came by, shirtless in the cool morning, and informed me he would be in my raft today. I told him that would be great. It wasn't what I was thinking.

During breakfast, Sue announced that we would be doing a three-hour hike that morning, starting with a short climb up a trail, and then following the river for about three miles. We would be in the shade for most of it, but it would still be pretty warm, so she told everyone to bring plenty of water. Afterwards we would head downstream and have lunch in a wonderful shaded cavern right at the river. "It will be a very mellow river day," she said, "and a good opportunity to try out the duckies for anyone who has passed the self-rescue test. Is anyone interested?"

Eliza and Jeff were the first to raise their hands. I saw Timmy talking with his dad. Neither looked happy. When the conversation ended, I thought I could see some tears welling up in Timmy's eyes as he turned away, hands in his pockets, head down.

40

"Great," continued Sue. "When you're finished with your breakfast, go ahead and break your camps down so we can get going on this hike before the sun gets too high."

On my way to the dish line, I overheard Timmy pleading with his dad to allow him to get in the ducky. "You heard Sue," his father replied sternly. "If you can't do a self-rescue, you can't go." Timmy again lowered his head and walked down to the river.

There was no way this kid wasn't going to get in a ducky on this trip, I thought. Somehow we'd make it happen.

Dishes were quickly washed and the kitchen broken down and loaded on my raft. In less than a half hour all the bags were down and strapped in. A few people waited in line for the groover, so I invited the rest to do a few stretches. Guy was surprisingly limber for a big man. Floyd kept us in stitches with his one-liners. Graham revealed he hadn't stretched since he had played rugby in his early twenties. I told him it showed. At the end of our session I asked everyone to stand shoulder-to-shoulder in a circle, turn to their left – Floyd turned to his right – raise their hands overhead, bring them down and exercise their fingers by massaging the shoulders in front of them. This evoked many "oohs" and "aahs." I then had everyone take two side steps towards the center of the circle, and on the count of three instructed them to bend their knees. There we were, sitting on each other's thighs. Except Chris, who had the misfortune of being next to Floyd. She merely leaned against his shins. With lots of laughter he said, "Let's go boating," and everyone dispersed to their chosen raft.

With two passengers, Jeff and Eliza, in duckies, I ended up with only one passenger, Guy. I needed an attitude adjustment before the day had even begun. It was quite unusual to have a passenger who pushed my buttons like Guy, and I wasn't the only one. I had heard both passengers and guides talk about how loud and obnoxious he was. But whenever I have a difficult passenger, which is not very often, I try to tell myself that they are presenting me with an opportunity to learn something about me. After all, if someone is pushing my buttons, well, they're my buttons. So I decided it was perfect that he was my only passenger. I would see if I could determine what this "tyrant" was teaching me.

It didn't take long. I pulled out into the current and a small wave hit the front tube and sprayed Guy. "Not exactly how I wanted to start my day, Charly. See if you can keep me dry at least part of the time, will you?" I tightened my jaw and gnashed my teeth.

We floated less than a mile downstream, ran one small rapid, and pulled over on the left at a break in the growing Redwall limestone. We were in a major fault zone, called Fence Fault, which ran diagonally from northeast to southwest across the river. On both sides of the river, the rising limestone walls had been shattered by prehistoric quakes, leaving a jumble of rocks in a deep gash, through which millions of flash floods were working to carve out a side canyon.

We tied up to a tamarisk tree and scrambled through dense vegetation where we assembled and waited for people to put on their shoes. "Drink some water before the hike," Sue exhorted, "fill up your water bottles, and get your shirts wet." Even so, it was likely someone would not pay attention.

"First wave is leaving. If you're ready, follow Michael. Second wave will be leaving as soon as everyone has their shoes on."

I took off with the first group. Even though I had been on ninety-five trips through the Canyon, every trip had afforded at least one new hike and/or one new camp. I had never done this hike, and I was very curious where it would take us. Michael led us up a short, fairly steep trail through the Redwall. Veteran backcountry hikers are often faced with finding a break like this in the Redwall to find access to routes in and out of the Canyon.

I'm always impressed with how quickly we gain elevation on our hikes. The emerald-green river snaked below us, temporarily narrowing to accommodate a jutting mass of fallen limestone pinching down the channel, and then spreading out into a huge eddy. Soon we stopped our ascent and began following a trail heading downstream. I was delighted to find a trail I hadn't even known existed.

Michael set a quick pace, and we followed the contour of the Canyon. The trail lay on top of the Redwall, about three hundred feet above the river. We were in the shade, but the summer heat still surrounded us, and I could see sweat forming on the back of Antje's shirt. An extraverted, confident, energetic German in her thirties, she was a veteran world traveler who had worked in Taiwan and China. Like many Germans she had strong opinions, but she wasn't confrontational. The Canyon walls formed a set of ascending stair steps that melted into a cloudless azure sky. Our trail was mostly flat, making the hike fairly easy.

The trail moved in and out, following the lay of the land carved over millions of years by earthly intrusions caused by geologic faulting, rain-induced flooding, and freezing and thawing. The trail moved inward and slightly down, and then out again toward the river and up. I stopped for a quick water break next to a weathered limestone boulder and was surprised to see a spectacular display of coral and shell fossils dotting the sharpened features caused by chemical weathering. The coral was quite dark from exposure to the air, and looked like a serpent's body undulating through liquid rock. The shells were a bright red-orange, like pieces of broken clamshells. Both the prehistoric coral and clamshells had probably been swept down into deeper water from more shallow reefs, and had become encased in the primordial ooze of calcium carbonate mud that then had hardened over the millennia. The limestone cliffs had risen above the water line as the ocean had receded, and the fossils I was seeing had been revealed after pieces of the rock had broken off the cliffs above. It was a simple yet spectacular sight.

After a little over an hour, Michael stopped for a water break. We had covered close to two and a half miles. Directly across the river was South Canyon, a predominantly dry side canyon that provided ingress and egress to and from the river. To the right, high up in the Redwall, a shadowed cave peered warily out from the sun-drenched walls surrounding it, like the deep-set eye of a predator laying in wait. On a flat bench of light gray limestone and scattered desert plants about forty feet above the river, a dark brown rock stood out like a blemish on an adolescent face. On some trips we have hiked to that rock, covered with the etched petroglyphs of the Ancient Puebloans who had inhabited and farmed in the Canyon between 750 and 1250 AD. They had existed on what little food the could grow, native plants, and wildlife – notably big horn sheep and mule deer – that could be hunted. Downstream of South Canyon, about one hundred-forty feet above the river, another cave hid behind its shadow. Stanton's Cave was named after the engineer, Robert Brewster Stanton, who, after the three men on the Brown expedition had drowned in 1889, decided to stash his boat and hike out with the remaining four men, to return the next year to complete his survey

A half-mile downstream, we could see our destination shimmering across the river. The red iron oxide veneer covering the Redwall limestone framed a fifty-foot wide by seventy-foot high verdant garden of hanging maidenhair fern, poison ivy, cardinal monkey flower, watercress, and mosses, along with a few trees. This green oasis, adorning bare Canyon walls, was a testament to the power of water to sustain life. Two white cascades flowed into the river directly out of holes in the limestone, created by the erosive power of underground water. The two streams disappeared into a sea of green vegetation, emerged as a small cascade from the mouth of poison ivy, watercress, and monkey flower, and caressed the limestone floor before disappearing into an eddy of the clear Colorado River. Other dry holes in the wall scattered at various elevations indicated that past flows had dried up due to a shifting or damming of underground channels.

Spelunkers who have brazenly explored the dark network of tunnels behind the falls have found two-and-a-half miles of passageways. Powell named this place Vasey's Paradise after George W. Vasey, a physician turned botanist who had accompanied the major on his 1868 Rocky Mountain exploration. While admiring its stunning beauty, one of Powell's crew had remarked, "Vasey could spend the entire day here."

*   *   *

Vasey's also harbored a recently discovered endangered species. Scientist Larry Stevens, a former crewmate of mine, discovered the Kanab amber snail in the 1990s. It's a remarkable creature, known for the parasite that lives in it. To attract birds, the parasite drives the snail to open space at the edge of the habitat, and the acid pink and green sporocysts (parasite cyst capsules) rapidly pulsate in and out of the snail's eyestalks. In 1996, a test flow from Glen Canyon dam resulted in some guides, including Michael, spending several days camped out on hand-made platforms. Their job was to monitor the flow after moving some 10,000 snails from their watercress homes to vegetation above the projected high water line. All that time, effort, and money for a snail. I wondered if it was worth it.

As our second group, led by Sue, approached, Michael continued the hike. I was surprised to find evidence of human habitation, including desiccated two-by-fours, empty food cans, and some bolts in the limestone. These were the remnants of survey crews in the 1950s looking for the ideal location for a dam. Such a dam would have inundated the river we had just floated. I said a silent 'thank you' that it hadn't happened.

We walked up a short rise, rounded a bend, and found ourselves above and directly across from Vasey's Paradise. I set up my tripod and took several photographs. In my thirty years on the river, I had passed this place more than ninety-five times. The flow coming out of the wall was the lowest I could remember, evidence of five years of drought. In the late 'seventies a dye study was conducted in the drainage that fed rain and snowmelt to Vasey's. Before the study, scientists had estimated that it would take two to five years for water to filter through eighteen hundred feet of sandstone, limestone, and shale from the North Rim to the aquifer behind the wall at Vasey's. A dye was placed in sinkholes and natural ponds on the North rim that corresponded to the Vasey drainage, and the scientists went about their business, thinking they had plenty of time to wait for the results. Fifteen days later, guides on a commercial river trip reported the dye emerging in the cascade.

I talked about the area, pointing out the pictograph rock on the first bench, briefly speaking about the Native inhabitants that had lived and farmed here. I also mentioned Stanton's hike out South Canyon, noted the bat cave where he had stashed his boat, and shared information about the split twig figurines and 42,000-year old driftwood discovered there by modern rafters. I had just finished as the second group finally caught up with us. I heard a familiar loud voice bouncing off the walls and noticed Guy, red-faced and sweating profusely, bringing up the rear. We stayed another fifteen minutes, enjoying the spectacular views up and down the river corridor. Eliza sat down next to me and smiled. Like a good uncle, I was pleased that she was enjoying herself. Even though we had only gone half a mile on the river, she said she already loved being in the ducky.

On the way back to the rafts, several passengers, including Guy, ran out of water. The temperature and humidity were rising, and dehydration in this place was an ever-present concern. We shared what water we had, and Star ran ahead to bring up more. When we reached the river, it was suddenly not so cold. In fact, it felt downright refreshing as one-by-one we jumped in and cooled down.

After filling our water bottles we again headed downstream. Guy, still red-faced and sweating profusely, was uncharacteristically quiet. As we passed Vasey's Paradise, I mentioned the derivation of its name and spoke a bit about the Kanab amber snail. His only comment was, "Why would anyone spend millions for a frigging snail?"

I enjoyed the silence for the next fifteen minutes as we floated lazily downstream. The peace was again shattered by Guy's booming voice. "Man, look at that! Bet it's bigger than it looks."

We were looking at Redwall Cavern, a great example of a solution cave. I told him Powell had estimated you could get 75,000 people in there for a concert. Spring floods for millions of years had raced down this stretch of river, and upon reaching this elbow in the channel and banking to the right, had carved a cavern through chemical erosion. This same process also occurred underground, with whole lakes and miles of channels forming behind the limestone walls. The presence of these lakes and channels became apparent only when pressure and gravity finally forced the water to eat through the limestone barrier, to be revealed as waterfalls and cascades – such as Vasey's Paradise. I told Guy we'd most likely be stopping here for lunch.

"About time. I'm starving." Looking at his corpulent body, I bit my tongue.

The river made a sharp bend at Redwall and narrowed. Erosion-resistant limestone cliffs rose directly out of the river like high-rise buildings in a big city. Without a desert blue sky above us, I might have felt claustrophobic. A large, still eddy rested mirror-like in front of the cavern, the reflecting walls plunging deep into the river. Sunlight, reflecting off the river, danced on the wall above the cavern, like light projected from an aquarium. I allowed my raft to float in the current past the beach.

"Where are we going?" Guy blurted out. "I thought we were pulling over here for lunch."

"We are, Guy. Check it out."

I waited until we were well past the beach, and then took a couple strokes to pull into the eddy. We floated upstream, settling in front of the cavern. I explained if I had pulled in any earlier, I would have had to row against the current in the eddy. Instead, I allowed the current to work for me. I described it as maximum efficiency with minimum effort. I asked him if he understood. He cocked his head in a silent "whatever" response.

The roof of the cavern floated above us like a cantilevered awning. As soon as the rest of the rafts arrived, we set up lunch. While everyone ate, I took my Native American flute out of its protective PVC container and climbed a steep slope to the back of the cavern. The shadowed ceiling curled to the sandy floor of the cavern. Looking at the other side of the river with its sunlit red cliff face, the opening looked like a squashed ellipse.

In 1985, I had rested against this same wall, listening to my first string quartet concert: two violinists, a violist, and a cellist sat in front of me silhouetted against the far wall. The sounds of Mozart, Hayden, and Beethoven wrapped me up in their silky notes and carried me to another dimension. It was beyond stereophonic, beyond quadraphonic. It was wrap-around sound that invaded my pores and settled in my cells. Before that trip, I used to say you couldn't improve on a trip in the Grand Canyon. On that trip I didn't just hear the music. I felt it. For several hours after the concert ended, I floated in a different realm.

*   *   *

Music in the Canyon seemed to add another element, perhaps touching an unknown sense. After many years of enjoying other guides playing music and singing, I had purchased my flute. Most guides brought down guitars, although one guide played a saxophone. On my first trip in 1978, one of the guides had brought down a standard flute. Like me, he couldn't play identifiable songs; but the notes he played seemed to float out into the abyss and disappear upstream. Paul Winter, the well-known jazz musician, came to the Grand Canyon and played his tenor sax while at the South Rim. He said he could see the notes disappearing into the chasm. He later rafted the Canyon and has recorded many pieces on the river.

I played for just a few minutes, just enough to avoid being repetitive, returned my flute to its case, and grabbed my lunch. Ben, and Nathan's mom Kathy, both walked over to me as I relaxed on my raft. "Thank you, Charly," Kathy said in a hushed voice. "That was such a lovely sound, and perfect for this place. I only wish you'd played more." I thanked her, somewhat sheepishly. I was still uncomfortable playing in public even though I had been told several times that the music was very moving.

Redwall Cavern was such a comfortable place to hang out, protected as it was from the intense summer sun with sand so soft it felt like a featherbed. It would be easy to take a nap and let the afternoon slip away. But no. We still had eleven slow river miles to row, so Sue signaled time to go. We cleaned up the lunch area, made certain no food scraps remained, loaded up the rafts, and shoved off.

Steep, oxide-painted cliffs rose straight out of the river as it flowed casually beneath a geologic museum of time. The wall on river left cooled in the shade and its rich red tones reflected deeply off the green-tinted river. The pastel, sun-drenched wall on river right waited patiently for its late afternoon reprieve. Above the Redwall, the Supai layer, blanched by the intense midday sun, stair-stepped towards the rim. "Wow, so this is what the real Grand Canyon looks like." It was Guy, reading my thoughts.

"Yep, and it only gets better."

The Redwall layer now rose five hundred feet on both sides of the river, and our newest layer had just revealed itself. The Muav limestone is a defining feature in the Canyon. A Paiute

45

word meaning pass or divide, it is interbedded with clay. Most of the year-round side streams in the Canyon had been born because of this geologic feature. The underground solution pools had been created from rain and snowmelt that had filtered through the overlying rock layers until reaching the impermeable Muav. There the water had backed up in large underground aquifers, waiting to eat its way to daylight, often feeding side streams like Tapeats Creek and Deer Creek that we would encounter later in the trip.

I pulled my raft into a small eddy on river right, grabbed a bail bucket, and stepped onto a flat, polished shelf of Redwall limestone. It took me a minute to find it. "What are you looking for?" Guy asked in a tone that sounded more annoyed than curious. I told him to be patient and he would see. Finally I found what I was seeking.

I dipped the bucket into the river, as other guides, who had been forewarned about this stop, pulled in. I told the passengers they could remain in their rafts as I poured the water over the residue-covered limestone. Instantly a coiled, three hundred million-year-old fossil appeared. "Wow, that's awesome," Nathan said as he jumped from the raft to shore. "What is it?"

I explained that it was a Nautaloid, a member of the aminoid family that around 300 million years ago had been prolific in the oceans throughout the earth. Then some catastrophic event, known as the Permian extinction, had occurred, causing the global extinction of eighty to ninety percent of all living things, including most of the Nautaloids. Just downstream, at Nautaloid Canyon, there were many of these fossils that resided in a six-foot layer of the Redwall. The difference here was this was coiled, whereas the ones in Nautaloid Canyon were straight. They were ancestors of the squid.

I pointed to the inner, smallest segment of the Nautaloid and said the animal initially had occupied the first of these segments. As it grew, it added new, slightly larger segments that it then inhabited.

"What happened with the old segments?" Nathan asked.

I told him that each abandoned segment had become a refuse container, like the bottom of an outhouse. A lot of gas had built up there, and they had used the gas, similar to a belch, to move through the water while ascending or descending. I said that I thought that was pretty cool.

No one had any questions, so I returned to my raft and headed downstream. We passed several mini-springs coming out of the Muav at the river, marked by hanging gardens of maiden-hair fern and cardinal monkey flower clinging to accretions of travertine. The calcium carbonate had ionized out of solution and had attached to other carbonates, eventually building on itself, like coral. I eased my raft next to one to allow Guy to see and hear the spring behind the damp brown travertine formation. He seemed fascinated by the incongruity of vegetation hanging on a rocky outcropping, and took several digital photos as we slowly floated by. I asked him what kind of work he did.

"I've been a consultant in the high tech field for over twenty years," he began. I sensed he was glad to have a chance to talk about himself. "In fact, just before this trip I snagged my biggest contract ever. It's going to keep me very busy for several years. Do you know what a consultant does?"

Like a river guide wouldn't know such things. I told him I had heard consultants are business types who have been downsized, and either couldn't or wouldn't find another job in their field. I said it in a serious tone to see if he would take my bait.

Instead, he amplified on it. He said there were far too many unemployed business executives who hadn't found work and had decided to call themselves consultants. It really pissed him off, he said, because it not only diluted the field, but often gave real consultants a bad name. He belched as if to underscore his disgust.

I thought about asking him to define a real consultant, but decided not to go there. Instead I quoted a friend of mine who says there's always room for a good restaurant, or a good consultant. I tightened the muscles around my mouth into a smile. In so doing, I realized a note of sarcasm had crept into my tone. I don't like sarcasm, either aimed at me or coming from me.

We continued to float through mirror-like waters until a rock bar pushing out from a side canyon on river left interfered with the calm. I warned Guy to be prepared for a quick photo opportunity on river right just past the rock bar, and another close by downstream. As we floated into the riffle, I pointed out Nautaloid Canyon on the left, and told him to look for a couple of small openings in the rock cliff on the right about twelve feet above the river. In the openings he would see large calcite crystals pointed downstream. He finally located them as we floated past. "They're huge. What are they?"

I told him they actually were similar in composition to limestone. They're called hound-tooth crystals and had formed in an ocean environment from calcium carbonate that had precipitated out of solution. The ocean had inundated the already formed limestone cliffs, and the crystals had formed in pockets such as these by the calcium carbonate ionizing out of solution and adhering to other calcium carbonate ions. I added that I had no idea how that happened.

"That was my next question," he replied. "Guess I'll have to ask someone else who knows their geology better."

I clenched my teeth and told Guy we could check at camp if he'd like. Remember your purpose, I reminded myself silently. You're here to serve.

Just downstream of Nautaloid is one of my favorite mini-hikes in the Canyon. Whale's Armpit was a not-so-attractive name for another unexpected jewel in the Canyon. Whale was a much-loved river guide who, unable to ask for help for his depression, had taken his own life. The armpit actually described a maidenhair fern-covered concavity in the Muav. A small beach separated the river from its verdant treasures, grasses surrounding miniature stalagmites in shallow, moss-filled depressions. The depressions had been formed from the incessant assault of water drops escaping from their underground prisons through the limestone wall. Each drop, saturated with calcium carbonate leached from the limestone, helped build clusters of little pointed pinnacles arrayed in receding rows, like rusted lines of shark's teeth. This place had served as a wonderful lunch spot offering respite from the noonday sun, a convenient bathing area at both ends of the beach, and a delightful location for another string quartet concert. *A few years ago Laura Bush's party stopped to listen while the string quartet rehearsed for a concert.*

I pulled my raft up on the beach and invited Guy to follow. There were several places in the Canyon that offered unexpected visual treats, and I liked to make them a surprise for my passengers. Guy was reluctant to leave his reclined position on the front of the raft but grudgingly surrendered. At my suggestion he brought his camera and was quite taken by the mini-formations he saw through his lens. A few of the close-up photos I'd taken in the past had received a wide range of interpretations. Some folks who didn't know that these were small depressions in the sand thought they were gigantic rock formations seen from an airplane.

The other rafts were already more than a quarter-mile downstream as we resumed our float. I could see Eliza and Jeff clinging to the paddleboat like two ducklings hitching a ride on mom.

Another one-of-a-kind place offered Guy his next photo opportunity, so I again gave him a heads-up to have his camera out. Just downstream, a rock bar similar to the one at Nautaloid Canyon jutted out into the river from the left side. I told Guy to look for a natural bridge, the only one in the Canyon at river level, as we floated into the riffle. Five hundred feet above us on the right, a Redwall limestone bridge spanned a narrow side-canyon in the early stages of formation. It's called the Bridge of Sighs, named after a bridge in Venice by the Kolb brothers during their 1911-12 trip

The desert blue sky behind it outlined the bridge and I told Guy when I thought we were at the optimum point for a photograph. "I'm way ahead of you, but thanks anyway Charly."

Don't mention it.

We made a sharp bend to the right, and heard the familiar sounds of a small rapid in the distance. 36 Mile Rapid was short and not particularly challenging, unless you took it for granted, or were paddling one of the duckies. The waves were definitely big enough to flip a raft given the wrong set of circumstances, so a small, lightweight kayak could be a sitting ducky if operated poorly. This would be the first real challenge for Eliza and Jeff. They both seemed to have good paddling control and had managed to deal with some feisty currents upstream. Now they could test their mettle in a real rapid.

I managed to make the rapid seem bigger than it was by seeking out some of the bigger waves at the entry, and then pulled over into an eddy on river right to run safety for the duckies. First came the paddleboat, charging into the same waves I had hit, but with adrenalin-aided shouts of camaraderie and joy. Eliza followed close behind, digging furiously, her paddle a blur of action. She hit each wave head on, at one time rising almost vertically before continuing downstream, upright and triumphant. As she floated by, her broad grin was the only evidence needed to convey how she felt. I flashed her a high-five but she was too focused on the ducky to notice. Just then Jeff entered the rapid, and although his run wasn't as precise, he did very well. Assuming he was safely through, he twirled his paddle overhead and let out a war whoop, interrupted in the middle when an unexpected current twisted his ducky sideways. Over he went. Laughter and then applause rang out from the other rafts as Jeff emerged, paddle in hand, and executed a perfect self-rescue.

"It ain't over till it's over, as Yogi said," shouted Floyd, followed by his infectious laugh. "Nice self rescue, Jeff!" Jeff gave two thumbs up, and accepted a high five from Eliza that almost flipped both of them. More laughter. Suddenly a water fight broke out between Michael's boat and Star's. Nathan, on Michael's boat, seemed to be the instigator, but it didn't take much to get the rest involved. Even Graham and Chris, who seemed to have recovered some of her energy, appeared to be willing participants. Star's boat, with Kathy and Antje, and Timmy and Ralph, were at a decided disadvantage. First, they were downwind, and there was enough of a breeze to limit their throwing effectiveness. Second, they only had one five-gallon bucket, whereas Michael had two three-gallon buckets.

Those new to water fights had several lessons to learn, usually the hard way. First, never fill your buckets all the way up. Five gallons of water weighed over forty pounds, and even a very strong man would be limited in the distance and accuracy of his throws. Second, never start a water fight unless your raft is upwind. And third, to be most effective, you had to spray the water by swinging it from side-to-side. Neophytes usually projected their buckets straight ahead, and rarely hit anyone. Both Michael and Star weighed in with their oars kicking up water with great effectiveness. Recognizing that she was outgunned and outmaneuvered, Star finally pulled away, leaving her passengers cooled down and soaked. Nathan stood on the front tube waving his bucket and declaring victory, until he lost his balance and plunged headfirst into the river. More laughter filled the river channel, while the still laughing Nathan was pulled into the raft by Michael.

What else was there to do after a good water fight than to kick back and relax? We would have seven miles before having to run the next rapid.

Ahead, a gray-green slag heap about twenty feet high stood out against the red-tinted cliffs above. We closed ranks and tied our rafts together. Carla took a few minutes to tell everyone that the opening we saw in the Muav represented one of several test borings made by engineers in the 1950s to determine the capability of these limestone walls to host a dam site. This was one of two proposed by the Bureau of Reclamation that would have directly impacted the Grand Canyon. If a dam had been built here it would have raised the river over four hundred feet and would have created a reservoir beyond Lees Ferry. That would mean every bit of the river we had just run would have been under a reservoir. Glen Canyon dam had drowned all but fifteen miles of one of the most pristine canyons in the world. "If it hadn't been for the Sierra Club and other environmental groups," Carla said, "a dam would be sitting here too, and we wouldn't be rafting in the Grand Canyon today." She pointed out the slagheap above us. "The test bore you see above us," she said, "runs a quarter mile into the limestone, and then T's off at the end. An air vent had to be drilled from the top of the Redwall, over five hundred feet above, into the shaft to provide air for the engineers. At the end of this stretch, where you can see a dip in the Redwall, a tram had spanned the river and was anchored to very large bolts at the base of the wall on river right. Workers would camp above the Redwall and descend every morning. Fred Harvey, who had the concession for food for the engineers, had a hell of a time finding cooks. One ride down the steep, fifty-degree tram cable would often be one too many.

"The era of major dam building in the United States is over, Carla continued. "There is currently a drive to remove many dams because some have been found to be inefficient, expensive to maintain for the value derived, and wasteful of precious water. Lake Powell, created by the building of the Glen Canyon dam, loses over 800,000 acre-feet of water each year through evaporation and leakage. The Glen Canyon Institute, established by David Brower, past Director of the Sierra Club, is dedicated to removing the dam, or at the very least, decommissioning it and diverting the water to restore the historic natural flows of the Colorado."

Michael then interjected. "Glen Canyon dam was supposed to pay for itself through the generation of electricity. That's why they called it a "cash register dam." However, it hasn't even paid off the cost of constructing the dam, let alone generated any revenue. This is because both electricity and water are subsidized by your tax dollars."

Sue jumped in to ask whether anyone had any questions. The only responder was Nathan. "I'm glad they didn't put a dam in here." Others nodded in agreement.

We untied and continued downstream, fortunate to have no winds. This section of the river, with its steep walls and narrow corridor, could act just like a wind tunnel, channeling upstream winds that test any guide's ability to move downstream. Marble Canyon, being the farthest north and highest elevation in the Canyon, could also be quite cold, especially on cloudy, damp days. None of those conditions existed on this day, however, and we enjoyed a peaceful float with only four miles to camp.

I pointed out the location of the tram anchors to Guy, as well as the location of a "punt," a boat that had been used by engineers to carry equipment from one test site to another. Just below the tram site the remnants of two of these vessels sat partially buried in the ground. Filled with soil and vegetation, they had become historic planters. Hiding behind a grove of tamarisk trees, they were not apparent from the river, and I had only become aware of them a couple years ago.

We floated casually down a long stretch, passed Buck Farm canyon on the right where mule deer were often spotted, rowed through a wide section with large eddies on either side of a snaking current, and passed the remnants of Bert Loper's boat deteriorating on the side of a slope where it had been dragged in 1949. Just downstream, at the head of another long, languid stretch of river canyon, loomed the Royal Arches, three developing caverns high up in the Redwall 250 feet above the river. Over the millennia these depressions in the limestone had eroded from water flowing in underground channels. Eventually, the thinning limestone ceilings would collapse, and new side canyons would begin to form in their own geologic time. Colonel Claude Birdseye, the leader of a USGS expedition in 1923, gave the caverns their name.

Black streaks running vertically down the inside walls of the arches silently spoke of water flowing out of the porous rock. These dark streaks, called desert varnish, had come from the evaporated residue of rivulets that had drained down the cliff face. Floyd, who was well versed in the geology of the Canyon, had told me that desert varnish was comprised of manganese and iron oxide residues carried in water and drawn to rock surfaces by capillary action.

Both sides of the river were in shade as the descending sun pushed light up the slope to the base of the Muav/Redwall cliff. We rounded a sharp bend to the right and heard the sound of a rapid downstream. Directly in front of our raft, on river right, I pointed out the Anasazi Bridge, a blackened wooden bridge left by the Anasazi or Ancient Puebloans close to a thousand years ago. The bridge spanned a fifteen-foot gap along an unlikely trail used by the Puebloans to get from the East Rim to the West Rim. They would climb down an arduous route from the east, dropping some eighteen hundred feet, cross the river, apparently without the aid of any watercraft, and climb up the west side, cross the bridge, finally emerging at the top of the Redwall through a series of caves and tunnels.

The bridge was hard to see, the gap sitting in the shade under an overhang. The wood had become blackened and brittle with age and was off limits to any visitation. The indians must have seen this route as normal and part of what was required to survive in this harsh desert environment. It seemed like an impossible route to me.

President Harding rapid, at river mile 43 3/4, was the shortest, rated rapid in the Canyon. Some described it as hardly a rapid, and he hardly a president. One large boulder rested in the right center of the river with a frothy-white pillow of water channeling the current to the right and the left. In the past we usually ran to the right of the rock; but in 2000, part of the Muav had peeled off the right wall and had blocked the right side. It had always been an easy run, except in two instances.

In 1955, before the dam, Bill Beer and John Daggett swam the Canyon from Lees Ferry to Lake Mead. They kept their clothing and food in waterproof, rectangular, WWII-era generator boxes. Each man floated with two boxes attached by a line. When Daggett attempted to swim Harding, he found himself in dire straights, headed straight for the rock. One box floated left of the rock, the other right, the line connecting them pinning Daggett against the rock. He was lucky to free himself, and came away only with facial contusions as a reminder of his close encounter with death.

*   *   *

In the early 'nineties I was on a commercial trip as the "mother ducky," responsible for the safety of passengers in the duckies. I told Darrell, a well-meaning but unfocused man on the trip with his precocious sixteen-year old son ,Darrell, Jr, to follow me. I instructed him to be sure to start as far right as he could, and break through the lateral coming off the shore surging towards the rock. Once past the rock, I told him he could relax. I entered ahead of him, following the same line, and once through looked upstream to check on Darrell. To my horror and consternation, he was in the middle of the river headed straight for the rock. A huge "pillow" of white water rebounded off the rock, and Darrell's ducky bounced off the pillow and turned over instantly. Fortunately he was right of the center of the rock, and was caught in the current that flowed down the right side. I watched, my breath stuck in my chest, as duckier and ducky emerged beyond the rock. At that moment a strong upstream wind arrived and blew off my visor. It had several pins I had collected while at the 1980 Winter Olympics in Lake Placid. I was so upset with Darrell for not paying attention to my directions that for just a moment I was tempted to rescue the visor rather than him. But I pulled him into my raft, and soon afterwards a thunderstorm roared in, dumping a copious amount of rain in a short time. Within minutes the river turned a rich iron oxide red from the sediment-filled flash floods coming over the rim. It was a spectacular sight, one that totally distracted me from the loss of my visor, or any frustration I had felt about Darrell.

I ran my raft down the left side of the rock, soaking a complaining Guy through two big standing waves, then floated down a very wide eddy the last mile to camp, a narrow beach on river left. We set the kitchen up at the point and the groover behind some "tammies" (tamarisk trees) about two hundred yards downstream. Passenger campsites soon dotted sandy alcoves upstream and downstream of the kitchen, most behind a row of tammies. With three hours before dinner, Sue announced that a hike would begin in about twenty minutes. Michael, Star, Sue, and I would take any volunteers up to the top of the Redwall, in a relatively short but steep hike up Eminence Trail.

Half the passengers decided to go and Michael led the way. Carla and Floyd would stay behind and prepare dinner.

My brother Sandy had taken this trail in 1983 while on a science trip sponsored by National Geographic. They were seeking evidence of ancient condor in the Redwall caves. He had to leave the National Geographic trip early to go on a private rafting trip with me, so he had hiked up the Eminence Trail with only a map written on the back of an envelope. Unable to decifer the map correctly, he made a wrong turn and wound up in a blind canyon. It took him an extra two hours to get to the top. He also lost about twelve pounds in the July heat. The trail near the top was so steep we had to throw him a rope to help him climb out. After drinking the beer we had given him, he threw up. Those who had continued on that research trip found a full skeleton of an ancient condor with a twelve-foot wingspan.

We picked up the trail at the back of the camp, walked through a dry drainage that had run red in that thunderstorm years earlier, and began our ascent. The trail grew steeper as we went. In some spots we actually had to grab waist-to-shoulder high boulders on the side of the trail, being careful not to allow gravity to pull us down. The trail had lots of loose rocks and fell off precipitously to the left. We weren't in a hurry, so we stopped regularly to drink water and catch our breath. With each rest stop I looked down on a receding river, our yellow rafts becoming toy-like, floating peacefully in front of camp.

We arrived at the top in small groups. Behind us spread out the upper layers of the Canyon surrounding us in a wrap-around bowl of geologic history. Looking upstream, we could see, and vaguely hear, President Harding, streams of white water wrapping around Darrell's boulder. Downriver lay a spectacular three-mile vista of Canyon walls framing an undulating river channel that we would float in the morning. Directly across the river rested Point Hansbrough, named after Peter Hansbrough, who had drowned in 25 Mile Rapid in 1889 on the Brown-Stanton trip. His body was found by Stanton the next year and buried across from this point, a rounded Muav and Redwall limestone cliff rising from the river, topped by the jumbled, receding members of the Supai formation. Created by a major fault, the river wrapped 270 degrees around the point, flowing from northeast to west-southwest.

After exhausting our photo opportunities we headed back to camp, and dinner. If I thought the trail was steep going up, I realized just how steep it was going down. One misstep could lead to serious injury. Antje was less than fifteen feet away from me on the trail and I was looking down on the top of her head. The detritus that littered the trail made it very easy to slip, and heightened the danger.

Halfway down we heard the conch shell announcing the serving of appetizers. When we reached camp, most of us headed straight for the serving table to snap up the remaining Gouda cheese and crackers. The aroma of cooking salmon, wild rice, and broccoli only increased my appetite. I couldn't wait for dinner. Carla let us know it would still be a half hour, so after grabbing drinks from the drag bags, several passengers and guides headed off to take a bath and relax.

The last golden rays of the sun finally crawled over the rim as the dinner conch sounded. Now the entire Canyon that was visible to us rested in early evening shadows, and a slight chill descended on us. We were all assembled in a loose circle just upstream of the kitchen, and while we enjoyed our dinner Sue outlined our plans for the next day. It would be another leisurely day in the beautiful canyon, with a hike in Saddle Canyon and only one rapid. Again she encouraged the less experienced passengers to try out the ducky.

I noticed Timmy again speaking with Ralph, making his case for the ducky. Just like his response on day two, Ralph told him he knew the rules, and if he couldn't do a self-rescue, he couldn't go in the ducky. He said he should just forget about it. There were plenty of other things to do down here. Besides, he could get into trouble in that thing.

Ralph wasn't a bad guy; he was just protective. In fact, I was surprised he had chosen this kind of trip. The awareness helped me understand the absence of expression on Timmy's face. He wasn't used to being acknowledged and didn't know how to react. While straightening up in the kitchen, I told Michael about my observation to see if I was on track.

"Makes sense to me," he replied. "I'm going to help Timmy get in the ducky. Maybe at the Little 'C'."

After closing up the kitchen, I checked the beach to make sure nothing was left below the high water line. The water would be coming up at night, and the river would claim anything left in the wet sand.

I gave Eliza a goodnight hug as she prepared her bed and headed to my campsite about a hundred yards downstream. After laying out my bag, I set up my camera on the tripod, attached my remote shutter release cable, and looked for Polaris. It stood proudly above the rim upstream and would be in the same location all night. The Little Dipper, the Big Dipper, Leo, Bootes, Corona Borealis, Draco the dragon, and all other stars and planets in the Northern Hemisphere rotated counterclockwise around Polaris at the center. A long time exposure would create an impressive display of concentric rings of various colors and thickness, depending on the age and magnitude of each star. If a shooting star or two happened to come into view, all the better. I opened up the aperture by locking the shutter release cable down. Then I lathered up my drying feet, stretched, and lay back to enjoy the brightening canopy of stars.

*One of the most diverse as well as spectacular hikes in the Upper Grand
Canyon, we begin by hiking through a riparian zone of tamarisk trees,
pick our way through a grove of prickly pear cacti and mesquite trees, past
bushy shrubs of four-wing salt bush and brittle bush. We then have an
aerobic experience climbing up man made steps cut into a limestone slope,
follow a winding trail up and down past resurrection moss and a wide
variety of desert plants, before dropping down into a lush, narrow canyon
of hackberry, redbud and box elder. As we follow a shallow, meandering
river we step around a lush garden of cardinal monkey flower with some
beautiful columbine scattered about. After scrambling up a wet, narrow
limestone path, we climb eight feet up a small cascade to our destination, a
sixty-foot waterfall plunging into a shallow pool where summer hikers can
cool off and enjoy a soapless hairwash.*

DAY FOUR –
EMINENCE TO NANKOWEAP

I slept so heavily that I failed to hear the blaster or the coffee conch. I woke up when Floyd walked by, a steaming cup of coffee in his oversized hand, on the way to the groover. He never walked quietly. I rolled over on my back and pulled my flannel sheet and sleeping bag up to my chin, reveling in the warmth my body had generated. I could hear the water lapping up on the shore just twenty feet away, and the impatient calls of the camp ravens, exhorting us to eat our breakfast and leave so they could swoop in for their meal. A subtle downstream breeze carried the smell of sausages cooking. The breeze shifted from off the water to off the shore, changing the temperature dramatically from cool to warm.

After some quick stretching, I packed away my bed and walked up to the kitchen to see if I could help. Carla stood over a griddle packed with golden brown French toast. The sausage had been cooked and snuggled in one of the small aluminum bowls, covered by a paper towel. The serving table held the big orange cooler with coffee, a small pot of tea water, cereal and granola, yogurt, evaporated milk for coffee and tea, packaged milk (UHT fridge-free – scary), warmed maple syrup, butter in a bowl, OJ, and a bowl of sliced honeydew melons and grapefruit. As soon as the current batch of French toast – sourdough and raisin bread – was done, breakfast would be called.

I filled my cup with water, poured in one of my packets of green powder, and stirred. I have a glass every morning as part of my program for healthy aging. The powder is a mixture of deep greens like spirulina, alfalfa, and kamut, sea vegetables like kelp and dulse, and a blend of cruciferous vegetables. It helps with energy, cellular repair, a healthy acid/alkaline balance, and blood sugar balance. And I like the flavor, although it left a dark green residue on the inside of the cup that aroused the curiosity of some passengers.

"That looks like something I'd give to my rabbit, if I had one," volunteered Graham as he walked by with his morning tea.

"I must have been a rabbit in a past life," I replied. "You probably wouldn't want this, though. It makes you younger."

"Now why would I want to do that? Aren't you the one who says don't mess with Mother Nature?"

"I'm just working with Mother Nature on this one, Graham. Personally I'm not focused on how long I live; but I do care how well I live."

"Touché, mate," Graham replied, as he pulled out one of his mini-cigars and lit it with a sly grin.

Most of our passengers were nearby when the conch blew for breakfast. Guy was the first in line, with Nathan and Timmy right behind him. I was tempted to go for the French toast, but I had been trying to control my sweet tooth. So I grabbed a bowl, filled it with granola and yogurt, and sat on one of the ammo cans to eat. Timmy came up, still with that flat look on his face, and asked if he and his dad could ride with me. I said I would be glad to have him in my boat, and asked if he had any interest in learning how to row.

He looked down at his sandaled feet. "Um, I don't know. Maybe." As he walked back to sit next to Ralph, he looked around, and the corners of his mouth lifted a bit.

It wasn't even eight in the morning and the July heat was already rising. The soaring cliffs behind and upstream of our camp guaranteed shade until mid-morning, so there would be no real hurry to load the rafts. Sue allowed us to clean up at a leisurely pace. This was a good group of passengers. Many had packed up before breakfast so it was easy to throw the yellow bags on the rafts and start rigging. Carla, who carried all the burlap drink bags in her front hatch, called for a line to bring them down to her raft. Floyd had his raft loaded first and called for everyone to come over for story time.

In his hand he held what looked like a children's book. "Snowball," it said on the front, a picture of a small white pony eating grass in front of a bleached white barn. The entire group assembled like a classroom waiting for the teacher to read to them. Floyd began.

"Before we head downstream for another day in paradise, I have a story for you all," he began, his laughing eyes dancing below lifted eyebrows. He opened the book and began. "Snowball was a pony." He paused and chuckled. "He lived on a farm." Another pause. "They have VERY GOOD grass." He smiled broadly and showed the picture of Snowball eating. Everyone got the double entendre and cracked up.

We laughed through the entire book. Floyd had studied improvisational comedy in college, had hosted his own show on public radio, and had made a run at improv in New York City. Having Floyd on crew guaranteed a laughter-filled trip. He was also a strong leader, and had encouraged me to lead trips for two years before I had agreed to do it.

After Floyd finished, Sue piped in. "Let's go boating you guys. After all, this is a river trip."

Animated by the humor of the moment, people were still laughing as they selected their rafts. In addition to Timmy and Ralph, Chris and Graham asked to ride with me again. I thought about encouraging them to ride with other guides, but decided to wait another day before doing so. As Mary attempted to hop on Floyd's raft, her foot slipped and a soft whimper escaped from her mouth. Floyd grabbed her and helped her into the raft, and asked if she was all right. It was a minor slip, and she said she was fine.

Graham volunteered to wrap up my bowline and pushed off. Looking down the river corridor, we had an uninterrupted view for almost two miles. The walls on river right were partially in sunshine, washing out the iron oxide colors, while the walls on river left were still totally in shade, marking the typical contrast of dark and light common in the recesses of the Canyon.

After we floated through a small riffle I offered the oars to Timmy. He looked at his dad who offered no response, and reluctantly climbed over the bags to sit on the cooler. I sat behind him on those same bags.

I began by saying that the first thing he should know was this would be like any new skill. It would take time to get it into his body. So I suggested he just start by getting a feel for the oars. The eleven-foot ash poles were pretty heavy, but I had put counter-weights near the handles to minimize the strain on my wrists, elbows, and shoulders, so I didn't think he would have a problem. I urged him to grab the oars and see how they felt.

He picked up the oars and immediately tried to row. His confusion was obvious. "I can't do this," he whispered, letting go of the oars and starting to climb off the seat. Ralph looked away and I could see the muscles around his jaw flex.

I put my hand on Timmy's shoulder and assured him he could do this. I urged him to give it some time to get used to a new way of rowing. I asked if he had ever rowed a boat on a lake.

"Yes, but it was smaller than this, and I rowed backwards. You row forward. It's so different."

I agreed that it was different than he was used to, encouraged him to grab the oars one more time, and promised I would help him get the hang of it. I also assured him we weren't in a hurry.

He sat back down and reached for the oars. I put my hands over his and helped him get started. I explained that instead of starting off by pushing with his arms, he should hold the oars in front of his chest and lean forward using the stomach muscles to start the stroke, then finish off by pushing with his arms. I demonstrated with him holding the oars and pushed his upper body forward. Then I showed him how to press down on the oars to lift them just out of the water, lean back and pull the oars back at the same time. I said he should do this a few times with me helping, and after he picked up on the motion, he could take over on his own.

After three more rotations I let go of the oars and sat back on the bags, offering words of encouragement. I said he should keep his feet on the floor so he could use his stomach muscles more effectively because they were a lot stronger than his arms. He started to appear more comfortable with the motion, so I told him sometimes I push one heel against the cooler to get more leverage. After five minutes he looked very comfortable, so I sat back and watched, making subtle adjustments from time-to-time. After awhile, he wasn't thinking about it any more. This was a perfect stretch to do this. No squirrelly currents, no snaking eddies, no upstream winds, no rapids, just a gentle current to give Timmy a chance to gain some confidence. Chris and Graham told him what a good job he was doing, and then the paddleboat floated by, everyone shouting words of praise and encouragement.

Turns out he was a natural. All he needed was a nudge. Here was a twelve-year-old kid rowing an eighteen-foot, fully loaded raft on the Colorado River in the Grand Canyon. How great was that? I couldn't wait to let him run a small rapid. Maybe I'd have him row through Nankoweap after lunch.

After a long straight stretch of river, we floated around a slight bend to the left. Downstream on river right I pointed to a slash high up on the downstream slope of the side canyon. I announced Saddle Canyon, and said the hike we were about to do was one of my favorites.

"Is there a hike you don't like down here, Charly?" Graham asked with a wink.

One hike up Saddle in 1982 had left a lasting impression on me. I had rowed one of the rafts for several well-known scientists whose job was to study the succession fight between the native coyote willow and the non-native tamarisk, also known as salt cedar. Although the willow was native to the Canyon, the building of the dam at Glen Canyon had created a stable high water line where the tamarisk could get established. Tammies put down very deep roots and require a lot of water. They are not useful plants in an arid ecosystem. The scientists wanted to find out which tree had more staying power.

On trips I had worked before this one, I had noticed a pattern among some passengers on our hikes. We would stop at a place like Saddle Canyon and they would ask where we were going and what we would see. At Saddle we would point to a slope behind camp and indicate the first part of the hike would be a very aerobic workout up a fairly steep, dry trail hacked out of the limestone. We would then drop down into a narrow, lush canyon with running water, and less than a half-mile in, would come to a waterfall. At that point, some passengers would program their mental computers – "Waterfall, look for the waterfall" – put their blinders on, rush headlong into the side canyon, look at the waterfall for a short time, and then, as if checking this destination off their list, turn and go back to the boats.

I wasn't surprised when the scientists asked the same question – where were we going and what would we see? – and we provided the same answer: aerobic hike, lush side canyon, waterfall. But that's where the similarities ended. No sooner had the hike begun than the botanist was off checking the trees and declaring that they were in a weakened and diseased state requiring water for survival.

Further on, as we entered the lush part of the side canyon, the biologist stopped to look into a small pool. He pointed to something moving on the pool bottom and said it was a Dobsonfly larva. Not far away he scooped up an empty, translucent shell, and announced it to be the discarded shell of the Dobsonfly larva. A few yards from there he pointed to a dark spot on the canyon wall, and in a matter-of-fact manner said it was the mature adult Dobsonfly. Within fifty yards this scientist had discovered the life cycle of one of the many inhabitants of the Grand Canyon, one that I had not previously known.

Once we arrived at the waterfall, I again observed very different behavior than I had expected. Instead of checking it off their list and returning to the rafts, they approached the waterfall and explored all around it. And on the way back, they looked for, and discovered, more life. To these scientists this was a living place with an infinitely rich landscape filled with more than we would ever know. They were opening my eyes to a much larger, richer world.

Later on that same trip, we camped at a side canyon and in the morning hiked into it. I brought up the rear and found the biologist sitting by a stagnant pool of water. Lots of yellow-green algae on top of still, seemingly lifeless, water. He motioned me to come over, and as I approached he asked me what I saw. Feeling a bit flip, I told him it looked like scum on dead water.

'Well, did you know," he asked with the knowing smile of a teacher, "that in this supposedly dead body of water, there are five layers of life? Five: one layer on the surface, two intermediate layers of life, one on the soil at the bottom, and one in the soil. Why don't you take a seat for a few minutes and check it out?"

So I did. At first, I didn't see anything but scum on dead water. But then I noticed some movement from one of the intermediate layers, and before long I was seeing all five layers, teeming with water beetles, water striders, tadpoles, and strange-looking larvae of varying shapes, sizes, and colors. It was a wake-up call. How much had I missed because I hadn't stopped to look? How many rich experiences had I avoided by judging the scum on the surface rather than looking for the richness underneath?

I helped Timmy guide the boat to the beach at the point where we would embark on our hike. The view downstream was spectacular, with walls alternating between slope and cliff. At the end, the river bent sharply to the right, giving the appearance of a dead end.

After all the rafts were tied together and secured to the shore, we made sure everyone had filled their water bottles, and headed out. Sue and Michael took the lead and Floyd brought up the rear. I positioned myself in the middle behind Jane, because I knew there would be some places on the trail that had serious exposure. We walked through a thick grove of mesquite trees, their long straight needles warning visitors to keep their distance. Several stands of prickly pear cactus drooped in the stifling desert sun, waiting patiently for a drenching rain. We came to another small forest of mesquite trees and had to duck under branches leaning over the trail.

Turning a corner, we took our first look at the aerobic part of the hike, a steep trail hacked into the Muav by Park Service personnel and volunteers. The dusty gray limestone, polished by thousands of human feet, was bordered by enclosing banks with a variety of cacti, desiccated agave, and yucca. In some places, the ends of agave leaves had been worn down from intimate contact with passing hikers. I wondered how much pain they had inflicted along the way. On one hike, one of my crewmates had been speared in the shin and had trouble walking for two days. The leaves of agave and yucca are similar, especially from a distance. What differentiated them were the teeth along the margins of the agave leaves. Yucca leaf edges were smooth.

After an elevation change of around a hundred feet, the trail alternated between dusty and rocky. The elevation was still a constant up, just not as steep. Coming around a corner, we started to move into the side canyon. Looking back at the river, a wide green liquid ribbon flowed quietly near the far wall. If you looked closely at a section of that wall, about forty feet up, you could see a lighter segment in the middle of the Muav cliff approximately thirty feet square. On one of my hikes into Saddle I heard the rock fall that had created that square. Returning from that hike, I saw the jumble of rocks lying at the base.

We stopped in a shaded section of the trail to allow people to catch up and drink some water. Jane, Ralph and Timmy, Chris and Graham, and Ken and Diana, a middle-aged couple from Western North Carolina, seemed pleased to have a chance to rest. Guy was the last to arrive, and in spite of his substantial girth, seemed no more the worse for wear. While we rested, I called Timmy over, saying I wanted him to see something that was way cool.

Although a bit reluctant, he got up off his rock seat and came over. His face was red and damp, and his breathing was slightly labored. I asked him what he saw, pointing to the slope just off the trail.

"Looks like dried-up dirt to me," he replied, squinting his eyes.

"Watch this," I said, opening up my water bottle and pouring a small amount of the life-giving liquid on the slope. Suddenly, the dried-up, black mass turned green.

"Oh my god," he declared. "How does it do that?" By now everyone else had come over, issuing similar declarations.

I identified this as my favorite little plant in the Canyon. It's called Resurrection Moss, and they had just seen a perfect demonstration of desert adaptation. Vegetation turns green by a process called photosynthesis, a process by which plants and other organisms produce simple carbohydrates from carbon dioxide and hydrogen, using energy that chlorophyll or other organic cellular pigments absorb from sunshine. Plants require a prodigious amount of water to support this process. In some places in the desert, creek beds that are dry in the daytime become small streams at night when the vegetation releases water sucked up to aid in photosynthesis. To survive in such a dry environment, this moss adapts by closing its tiny petals to hold in what little moisture it has. Then, when it rains (or some guide pours water on it) the petals open to take in the moisture, revealing its true color.

The trail meandered up and down, with very little room for error on the right. A slip here would mean a fall of several hundred feet. Jane seemed a bit uncomfortable so I asked her what was going on.

"I'm not sure I can do this hike, Charly. This trail is so narrow, and I'm afraid of what might happen if I should slip." I told her that I understood, and would walk with her to help out if she needed. Then I told her about a trip in the 'eighties with a friend who had told me she had been an avid hiker back in Michigan.

Betsy had also been afraid of heights. I had told her that if she started feeling fearful she should stop and take some deep breaths, and if she needed help I would be right behind her. We made progress even though most of the people had passed us. When we got to a particularly sharp bend in the trail, Betsy suddenly stopped. I asked her if she was all right. She didn't move. Her breath seemed trapped in her chest, so I told her to stay where she was and just breathe. I then offered my hand. She shook her head in a frenzied, herky-jerky fashion, like a silent scream. It was as if she was more willing to hug the cactus on the inside of the trail than reach out for my hand.

I told her we didn't have to go any farther. I would walk back to camp with her. Again she shook her head no. Finally she took a small breath, and then a little bigger one. After one more, she took a step. Then a breath. A step. A breath. Then two steps. Then three. Finally we were past the exposure and her body relaxed.

We ended up spending a half hour in, around, and under the waterfall. The water was cool and very refreshing. On the way back, Betsy barely noticed the spot where she had been so terrified. I wondered how this experience would play out as she made some decisions about her future. She was in transition in her life, and had to decide whether to go back to her old job.

"What did she decide to do?" Jane asked.

I told her she had quit her job as a top manager of a Fortune 100 company, had gone back to school for a degree in counseling, had become a therapist, and was now married and living in Arizona. Jane smiled and set off down the trail.

After one last aerobic climb we descended into a very different world. A small, barely flowing creek moistened the desert soils as it disappeared underground just beyond our crossing. We followed a trail through a grove of hackberry trees. Along the trail, desert grasses caressed our bare legs. Barberry bushes, resembling holly, rose among the grasses, their blue-green leaves ringed with sharp needles to discourage foraging animals. The creek was bare of much vegetation, a stark contrast to its tangled mass of trees, nettle, cardinal monkey flower, and lush datura bushes just three years ago. A flash flood had scoured the creek bed, removing everything in its path. Now, instead of crossing the creek multiple times, we hiked straight up the drainage.

The canyon narrowed as we came to a six-foot, polished limestone boulder blocking our path. A narrow creek flowed to its right, next to a fern-covered limestone wall. This was where I loved to challenge people to keep their feet dry. Beyond the rock was a narrow Muav gorge with small pools. Maidenhair fern clung stubbornly to the damp walls. When I first rowed on trips down here, my crewmates used to play a game with our passengers. They would pretend that the gorge was a thousand feet deep, and any slip would mean death. The challenge was to stay dry. It was designed to encourage people to develop a new skill of maneuvering on rocks, while protecting life in the algae-covered stream. Now, practically everyone slogs through the creek, and most of the eco-system has been destroyed. I still like the challenge and usually find people willing to take it. Timmy was up for it, but quickly abandonned the challenge when he slipped into the water right at the beginning. If Nathan hadn't been up ahead, he would have been up for it. On this trip, I was the only one to take the challenge all the way.

At the end of the narrow challenge course a large, square boulder had become wedged between the walls, and a small flow of water danced down the right side of the boulder. The narrow space and hard walls magnified the sounds of falling water, making the flow seem bigger than it was. There were few obvious handholds. To get above the chock stone, everyone had to climb over the cascade. I stayed down below showing everyone their handholds and foot placements, and Michael gave people a helping hand at the top. Chris and Graham, both of whom had short legs, needed a hand at the top. Jane, at first tentative, giggled when I pushed on her butt to help her up, and let out a triumphant yell after Michael pulled her up. "You sure have come a long way, baby," I said. She turned around and smiled, and then continued on.

The walls ended in a moss-covered notch highlighted on the right side by a thin, thirty-five foot waterfall feeding a pool three feet deep and ten feet long. At the top of the falls, another chock stone rested in its own notch waiting for a powerful enough flood to carry it away. Nathan stood under the falls, one foot wedged on either wall. He had a big grin on his face as his mom photographed him under the clear, cool water. Clear liquid splashed off the top of his head and dribbled down his shirtless body.

We shared bags of "salty" and "sweet" gorp – "good old raisins and peanuts" that sometimes included M&Ms – that Sue and Floyd had carried up, and enjoyed the beauty of the waterfall. Then Sue and Floyd headed back to the rafts to help prepare lunch, while Michael, Star, and I helped people down and back on the trail. This time I challenged Nathan to the dry hike and he was only too happy to comply. He was so agile on his feet and free of fear that he made the challenge look effortless. Eliza, who had reached the top with Nathan's group, also took up the challenge. I watched as Nathan lowered himself down the cascade, hopped from one side of the gorge to the other, then scrambled down another short water slide with one foot on the right side and one on the left, and maneuvered around the remaining section with ease. Eliza did the same, and was doing well until her foot slipped and she stepped into the pool. She laughed and walked the rest of the way through the water. By the time I had emerged over the top of the limestone rock, Nathan was long gone.

As we emerged from the narrow canyon, I invited Eliza to follow me up a short drainage. I ducked under the bare branch of an acacia tree being careful to stay off the vegetation. We came to a blackened slab of Redwall limestone about eight feet high that had been split by the impact of its fall. In the crack I showed Eliza some large calcite crystals that had formed in the limestone. She pointed to crystals that weren't pointed, and I said that someone had chipped part of the crystal off, probably as a souvenir. She let out a breath accompanied by a scowl on her face.

When we arrived back at the rafts lunch was already being prepared. After washing our hands, I joined the rest of the crew gathered around the shaded table to help finish preparing my favorite lunch: taco salad. Cans of kidney beans, salsa, black beans, green chilies, and black olives had been opened and drained. Two pounds of cheddar cheese needed grating, tomatoes and avocados diced, limes sliced, and lettuce shredded, then mixed and seasoned with cumin and chili powder. The last addition, broken corn chips, signaled the lunch call.

Floyd volunteered to demonstrate the proper way to fill the oversized flour tortillas. With a flourish he pulled a tortilla out of its plastic home, carefully folded one side diagonally toward the middle, then the other side, forming a wedge. With a flourish, he then bent the bottom up to form a cup. Picking up the large serving spoon out of the bowl, he placed a measured amount of the salad in the tortilla cup, added some sour cream and a liberal dash of chipotle sauce, and bowed to the attentive crowd. Since this was a particularly messy meal, we reminded everyone to eat below the high water line. As we ate down by the river, scraps of food escaped from inattentive hands and were pushed or thrown into the river, settling on the shallow bottom. Out of the depths, a dozen rainbow trout, attracted by the smell of food, gathered for their own lunch. Better to feed the fish than the red ants, which were also attracted by the food. Red ants have been here as long as I have, but their numbers have increased over the years. More people creating more micro-trash, sustaining more ant colonies. It's a good thing they were so small, because their venom was the most toxic of any critter in North America. Fortunately they're diurnal; when the sun goes down, they do as well. We don't have to worry about them at night.

We ate quickly and jumped into the rafts for another five gentle miles before camp and an opportunity for another great hike. We would be free of any rapids until just before camp, and this stretch was filled with the grandeur that personified the Grand Canyon. The rim, when we could see it, was now more than two thousand feet above us, still less than half its daunting height where we would say goodbye to our upper Canyon passengers. After a long, straight stretch, we floated around a corner and passed from warm sunlight to cool, moist shade. The early afternoon reflections of Canyon walls and shore greenery suddenly turned from washed-out pastels to deep, vibrant shades of red, green, and blue, as if a faded masterpiece had been restored by master artists. We were floating in and on unparalleled murals, in a museum of rock and water.

Graham volunteered to row, and was comfortable on the oars. No one spoke, and in the silence *I recalled an incident in this part of the Canyon when one of my crewmates, a beautiful, fearless woman, began to sing. It was a song written during a singing workshop, and simply spoke of places in the Canyon.*

Shinamo Hakatai Chuar Nankoweap

Her voice was clear, strong, and evocative, and her words expanded to fill the Canyon. I was transfixed, and felt my eyes moisten.

Coconino
Cheyava
Unkar
Awatubi

Paria
Watahomigi
Kwagunt
Moki

Havasu
Shinarump
Toroweap
Shivwits

Kaibab
Hot Na Na
Tatahotso
Moho

Moenkopi
Sinyala
Tapeats
Matkatamiba
Matkatamiba
Matkatamiba

That simple piece evoked a journey through the Canyon, through time, into cultures, into the heart of floating through this natural wonder. I couldn't do it justice with my flute, but on this trip I was moved to take it out and play. The notes seemed to dance out of my flute, being everywhere at once. People on the paddleboat stopped paddling and listened. Sue smiled and nodded.

We passed Fifty Mile canyon and saw a beautiful view of the North Rim in the hazy distance. Just upstream of Fifty Mile we had passed the emergence of the Bright Angel Shale, a slope-forming soft rock of alternating bands of purple, sand, and green. Besides the distinctive banding, the Bright Angel was noted for an abundance of worm burrows, raised sections created in the mud of the Cambrian Sea, much like those we see today with the telltale dirt trails created by moles and voles, only smaller.

We were about to run Nankoweap Rapid, one of the longest in the Canyon. It is rated only three out of ten, and is a very playful rapid for the duckies. Nathan and Ben were in the duckies this afternoon, and as long as they avoided the hole at the top, they should have no problem.

In the high water year of 1983, when river levels were ten times higher than they were on our trip, a guide on a thirty-seven foot motor rig, who apparently wasn't paying enough attention, went straight into the hole and immediately flipped, sending his eighteen passengers and one helper on a long, cold, fast swim. A helicopter had to fly in to help turn the massive rig back over so they could resume their journey.

Graham spotted the hole and maneuvered the raft to the right to avoid it. He sported a wry grin and his eyes sparkled in the afternoon sun. He sat ramrod straight with one foot propped against the cooler, and one foot pressing on my ammo can on the floor. When we were about two-thirds through the rapid I told him to pull over into a huge eddy on the right, where Michael and Floyd awaited the rest of us. The camp we planned to take was already occupied by a private trip. While we waited for Sue to show up, I told my passengers about the granaries established almost a thousand years ago by the ancestors of the Hopi. Their common name is Anasazi, but that is a derogatory Navajo name meaning "ancient enemy." The Hopi had asked us to call their ancestors Hisatsinom, which means "those who came before." However, both the Zuni and the Puebloan people had also claimed ancestry to the Anasazi, so the politically correct term has become Ancient Puebloan People. I pointed to a cliff face at the contact point of a steep talus slope. There were five shaded windows recessed into the cliff, around seven hundred vertical feet above us. The windows were actually the openings to the granaries, where the Puebolans had stored seed after the fall harvest. They would then migrate to the North Rim where game was plentiful, returning in time for spring planting.

Sue came through the rapid and indicated that we would camp on the point, another camp just downstream. I loved the point camp because it provided a spectacular river-level view of the downstream corridor. The steep cliffs across the river hemmed us in, and late in the day would project an orange cast onto the water, like the glow of a fire on the horizon.

We set the kitchen up in front of the rafts in a small clearing surrounded by willow saplings. The groover was hidden just downstream in a grove of riparian vegetation. Behind the kitchen, hidden from view by a row of willow saplings and arrowweed, boulders bordered sand enclaves that became temporary home sites for the passengers. Chris and Graham found a site near the river nestled in the two foot tall horsetail, a silica-based, segmented refugee from the age of the dinosaurs, when they were as much as thirty meters tall. We were now in a more open section of the Canyon that would allow the summer heat to dissipate quickly after sunset. A spot close to the river would provide relief even sooner.

Floyd announced a hike in fifteen minutes, and everybody scurried around finding their boots, filling their water bottles, and making sure everything at camp was tied down or put away.

Our hike would take us upstream through the "main" camp to the top of the delta that pushed out to the head of the rapid. It had been created by debris flows coming out of the side canyon that reached fourteen miles back to the North Rim. On top of the delta were the remnants of an Ancient Puebloan habitation site from a thousand years ago. They had lived and farmed there until forced by drought to abandon the Canyon.

Also on top of the delta were large, weathered blocks of Kaibab limestone resting on the hard packed soil. Geologists and sediment scientists today are still uncertain about the origins of these boulders. What they did know was they could have originated only from one of two locations: the North Rim, fourteen miles away, in a massive debris flow; or from the top layer of the South Rim directly across the river, some twenty-five hundred feet above us. From a purely visual perspective, the latter seemed more plausible. It was hard to imagine those boulders traveling fourteen miles only to conveniently come to rest on top of the delta. But in fact, that has become the most accepted scenario. In debris flows that contain as little as ten percent water, the heavier debris tends to "float" to the surface.

Everyone would come on this hike except Mary. When describing it earlier, Sue had painted such a spectacular picture of the views from the granaries that all were looking forward to it. As he was lacing up his boots, Guy said it had better be good.

Sue and Michael started the hike off. Star and I followed in the middle and Carla brought up the rear. Floyd stayed back at camp to write some letters to his wife. Every crewmember carried extra water, snacks, and first aid kits. While injuries on these trips were rare and usually minor, we had been trained to expect the unexpected, and all of us had a minimum of wilderness-first-responder and CPR training. Many guides were emergency medical technicians, and a few were paramedics.

On a past trip, I had led a group of passengers up to the granaries. The trail began behind the main camp through a grove of mesquite trees and willow saplings. Initially the elevation change was gradual, and hikers could get a glimpse of the spectacular view downstream without too much effort. A third of the way up, the trail turned sharply to the left and became very steep. This was a trail created at least a thousand years ago by Ancient Puebloans who had used it to carry part of their annual harvest up for storage.

As we sat in front of the granaries, I watched a man on another commercial trip jump off a large motor rig and land awkwardly in the shallow water. Even from my elevated place I could hear his scream and figured he had probably broken an ankle or a leg. For the next hour we watched as the guides carried him to the sand, assessed him and prepared him for evacuation. As the sound of the helicopter shouted from downstream, a bucket line was formed to dampen down the sand. The helicopter landed in an open area we often used for the kitchen and two men in orange flight suits emerged. After ten minutes of assessing the injury, the man was placed on a gurney and carried to the chopper. As the rotors gained full speed, trees swayed and sand kicked up, creating a mini-sandstorm. The helicopter lifted up, swung around, headed out towards the center of the river and floated downstream, rising to the top of the Redwall cliffs before disappearing.

At the top of the delta, Michael talked about the habitation site for a few minutes before continuing on. While he spoke I surveyed the cliff face and slope directly across the river. One segment of the slope was covered in red sediment, in stark contrast to the remainder of the gray-green slopes leading to the river's edge from the base of the sheer cliff. The source of that red rock looked down on us from twelve hundred feet above, in the middle of the mottled Supai formation. If you knew where to look, you could see a section about seventy-five feet high by twenty feet wide. This was the origin of all the red rock covering the slope below, a rock fall in 1996. I knew where to look because I was looking at that place when the rock had peeled off.

I was leading a "loop hike" up Nankoweap, into the Chuar Valley, and back to the river through Kwagunt Canyon, two and a half miles downstream. I had stopped on top of the delta to allow stragglers to arrive and catch their breaths. I was casually surveying the immense cliff across the river when I heard a loud crack and then a shout from one of my crewmates. I watched as a big slab in the middle of the Supai formation peeled away. Loosened by eons of erosion from water lodged in cracks, freezing and thawing innumerable times, the last straw had been a thunderous storm the previous night that had shaken the earth beneath us and had loosened rock that had been stable for well over three-hundred million years. I watched in amazement as tons of rock careened off the cliff and plunged a thousand feet to the slope below. My first rockfall. After a period of silence where the falling rock seemed suspended in air, the staccato reports of large and small rock striking the earth sounded like mortar rounds being shot off. Dust appeared, and with each new thump more arose and co-mingled to build into a giant mushroom cloud. The expanding and rising dust eventually filled the river corridor and was carried on a soft breeze downstream.

Some of the rock would make it into the river and be carried downstream. Were it not for all the dams on the Colorado River, this sediment could eventually be carried to the ocean where it would settle on the bottom and eventually take on another form. Larger, heavier sand grains would fall out near the ocean's margin. If its location were on-shore, it would eventually lithify (solidify) and form Aeolian sandstone. If it reached the ocean, it would mix with liquefied calcium carbonate that would glue the sand grains together, forming sub-aqueous sandstone. Smaller, lighter sediment would build up in a delta or be carried farther from the shore, settle to the ocean bottom, and turn into shale, or mudstone, or siltstone. All this was now inhibited by the dams.

The higher we climbed, the steeper the trail became. How the Indians managed to carry their weighty baskets of grain up this trail was a mystery. The river looked like a long undulating pewter snake moving in a winding channel bracketed by green vegetation along both shores. Two and a half miles downstream the snake stopped, halted in its progress by what appeared to be the end of the channel – in reality a sharp bend in the river hiding another rapid lurking just around the corner.

As we approached the granaries I looked back down the trail to see a human serpent edging its way toward us. At the far end, like the rattles on a rattlesnake, Guy, his ample, sweat-soaked, hairy upper body glistening in the sun, struggled to take one more step, intent on making it up.

We sat in front of the granaries, lost in our own thoughts. Finally, Chris wondered out loud if the Indians had chosen sites like this just for protection from the elements, animals, and other humans; or if they, too, were in awe of the views and beauty of the Canyon. No one had an answer, but I silently had no doubt that they held a deep appreciation for the beauty of what they called Mother Earth.

On the way down, I told Graham a story of a prior trip that had planned a loop hike up the Nankoweap drainage. Only one of the guides had been on the hike before, and it had been some time, so she was uncertain if she could remember where they had to turn to link up with the entrance to the canyon downstream. What should have been an eight- to nine-hour hike turned into an eighteen-hour marathon. They had missed the turn and headed far up the valley. Eventually they ran out of water, and at one point early in the morning, a dehydrated guide had chased what he thought was a big horn ram. It was actually one of the other guides.

When we arrived back at camp, laid out on the serving table were cream cheese-and-pesto appetizers with pita bread. The smell of Greek chicken being grilled over charcoal further whetted our appetites. Rice pilaf was cooking on the blaster, and Floyd was tending to the tarragon bread on the stove. A tossed green salad waited in one of the large aluminum bowls.

During dinner, I noticed Mary limping as she carried her plate to the dish line. I asked her how her foot was, and she said it hurt, but tried to minimize the severity of it. Star spoke to no one in particular as she pointed out the light on the river. The last rays of the late-day sun reflected the brilliant orange off the cliffs onto the slowly moving river. Downstream, the blue sky was slowly turning lighter until dissolving into a faint gray. In less than fifteen minutes shadows removed the day's color from the Canyon walls. We were two days from the full moon, and a large, orange orb peaked over the rim downstream as we finished up the dishes and closed up the kitchen. As the earth rotated, the moon lifted off the rim, turned from orange to yellow to white, and cast its reflection on the river downstream, a white streak on liquid pewter.

I gave Star a hug and went in search of Mary. I found her at her campsite, located directly behind the kitchen in an open, sandy area with willow saplings on the riverside. She couldn't see the river, but had a great view of the silhouetted west rim across a boulder-encrusted field behind camp. I removed her sandal and gently touched the area of her foot near her ankle. She winced when I pressed on the inside top bones, and felt some pain just under her anklebone. There I found some minor swelling. I went to my raft, got some moisturizing lotion and my first aid kit, and gently massaged the areas where she felt the pain. To take her mind off any discomfort I asker her about her work. She told me she was a human resource consultant for a large paper company in the Northwest. I asked her if she happened to know a good friend and mentor of mine, and was surprised to learn that she not only knew her but had also worked with her. I was delighted, and we spent a few minutes talking about our mutual friend. When I finished, I wrapped her ankle with an ace bandage to minimize the swelling, and said I would check her again in the morning. She smiled slyly, and said she would probably need another massage. I told her not to get greedy. Saying goodnight, I returned to my raft.

Eliza was over on Sue's raft, and I could hear her laughter mingling with Sue's and Carla's. I felt a warm glow knowing she couldn't have found better role models of strong, competent, loving women.

I decided to sleep on my raft, and laid out my sleeping bag. After lathering up my dried-up skin, brushing my teeth, and stretching, I laid back and scanned the sky for my celestial friends. Soon I was asleep.

*One of the most spectacular and best known images in the Grand Canyon,
this shot was taken near Ancient Puebloan graneries where grains were
stored for the winter, to be used for planting and food in the spring. The
snaking river corridor is about 2 ½ miles long.*

DAY FIVE –
NANKOWEAP TO CARBON CREEK

My least favorite breakfast: roast beef hash from a can, eggs, and orange juice. I felt as if I were in a Denny's, until I noticed the downstream view. The long rays of the spectrum from the rising sun had just started to paint the upper Canyon on the west side of the Nankoweap corridor a brilliant golden-orange. The shaded pewter river was framed on both sides with riparian vegetation, primarily willow, tamarisk, arrowweed, and farther off the river, at the 125,000 cfs-highwater line, catclaw acacia. The last time water had reached those heights was during spring floods in 1957.

A clear sky had begun its transformation from gray to ever deepening shades of blue. Goosebumps appeared on my bare arms as the warming Canyon walls drew a tender upstream breeze into camp off the fifty-degree water. The aroma of brewing coffee mixed with the organic flavors of the river.

Once the hash was done breakfast was called and devoured quickly. My unspoken complaint seemed to be a minority opinion. Sue described the day as a play-day, assuming the Little Colorado was clear. If not, we would go to plan "B".

"And what would that be?" Guy asked, in an "I-have-to-know" tone.

"I'll let you know when I have one," Sue replied, grinning and letting out a quick giggle.

"So glad I asked," Guy said.

Everyone was so in sync with the morning routine that the kitchen was taken down and the rafts loaded with remarkable ease. While waiting for Star and Carla to take down the groover, I offered to lead another stretch session. Having been an aerobics instructor for six years, I had come to appreciate the value of stretching to create more comfort in the body. Most of these passengers were urban residents, not used to sleeping outside on the ground. We had taken two hikes the day before, and everyone, guides included, could feel some tightness in their bodies.

I began by declaring that stretching was not a competition sport, and offered some guidelines. I told them to avoid ballistic stretching, meaning no bouncing while holding a position. I demonstrated this as I explained it. I also warned them to extend only to the limit of their range of motion, and back off if they felt any pain.

I had everyone warm up with some deep breaths while raising their arms in a sweeping motion overhead, loosened up the neck by slowly lowering their chin to their chest, and then bringing the right ear to the right shoulder, then chin back to the chest, and left ear to left shoulder This was followed by a side-side rotation of the head, and finally by taking the right ear directly to the right shoulder and lowering the left shoulder to increase the stretch, and then to the left. After shoulder rolls forward and backward, we did some side stretches, worked the inner thighs (much to the discomfort of some of the more sedentary in the group), had everyone sit on the sand, and worked their hamstrings, hips, thighs, and calves. We finished in a circle where I again had people stand shoulder-to-shoulder, turn right, inhale and raise their arms overhead, then exhale and bring the fingers onto the shoulders of the person in front and give them a massage. Then I had them turn around and do the same to the person behind them. Finally, I yelled out, "Let's go boating," and a group of smiling, slightly more flexible people grabbed their life jackets and headed for the rafts.

Before I finished rigging my raft, I checked on Mary. The night before we had given her the option to fly out and have her foot x-rayed to see if it was broken. She decided to stay, and we gave her a removable plastic cast to help stabilize it. She said she was feeling fine, and I told her I would work on her foot again at the Little Colorado. She said she looked forward to it.

Jane, Ben and his son Jeff, and Frank, a nice man in his early 70s, requested permission to ride with me today. I was looking forward to having Jane back in my boat. Ben and Jeff clearly had a very close relationship, closer to a friendship than that of father and son. Ben was lean and quiet, with a sweetness uncommon to the male species. Jeff was six inches shorter, in his twenties with thinning hair and a stout body that spoke of lots of physical work. He had shown an eagerness to pitch in around camp, whether it was pumping water, smashing cans, carrying bags, or helping around mealtime. I hadn't had much opportunity to speak to either of them. The day would be calm, except for one medium-sized rapid.

We jumped into the rafts and headed downstream to run Kwagunt rapid. The two-and-a-half mile corridor between Nankoweap and Kwagunt was one of the most spectacular in the Canyon, whether from a high-viewing place like the granaries, or from the river. On both sides, steep slopes rose six to seven hundred feet to the base of the Muav/Redwall cliff. Small riffles announced a temporary narrowing of the channel, often accompanied by a slight change in the course of the river. On either side of the current were wide, calm eddies with recirculating currents that answered Nature's drive for homeostasis, or equilibrium.

Soon after shoving off from camp the current split, wrapping around a large rock island with stringy tamarisk saplings straining in the downstream current. Sue and Star floated ahead of me and took the line to the right of the island close to shore. I floated to the left of the island, a shorter stretch with a slightly slower current. At the bottom of the island the currents merged into a small, splashy rapid. We drifted past the remnants of a former camp on the left, now stripped of most of its sand beach.

In 1986, my brother Sandy and I had celebrated my mom's 71st birthday at this camp. Everyone donned party hats, my mom put on a pair of crazy glasses, and we made her favorite meal – hamburger (very rare) and French fries. I baked a carrot cake with "Annie" written in the white frosting, and we all celebrated with some fireworks. The festivities were abruptly halted when a rocket went off-course and sailed just a few inches over Sandy's head. "That's it!" the protective lioness roared after watching her cub being threatened. "No more fireworks."

After four days hemmed in by sheer cliffs rising out of the river, the widening Canyon brought an unanticipated feeling of freedom. The walls receded. Small rock-and-vegetation-strewn islands provided a haven for ducks, heron, and the occasional egret. Jeff spotted a beaver swimming towards its home in the mud bank at the river's edge. As we approached Kwagunt, a medium-sized rapid hidden by a ninety-degree bend in the river, the banks displayed a splash of green, including grasses, shrubs, and small trees, home to a variety of birds. In the stillness of the river, ash-throated flycatchers, violet-green swallows, and blue-gray gnatcatchers, warblers, juncos, lesser goldfinch, and buntings could be seen in paroxysms of aerial aerobatics. The air was filled with the calls of the shy bell's vireo and the extroverted yellow-breasted chat. A mated pair of ravens waited on a small beach hoping for visits from crumb-spilling humans. Overhead we saw small flocks of common mergansers, blue-winged teal, and mallards flying in formation. We could tell the mergansers by their stable flying pattern and fast wing strokes, while the smaller teal flew in a more frenetic, rapid pattern. Sandy could tell these birds without even seeing them, just by their calls.

Most rapids announced their position on upstream winds, and provided plenty of time to don rain suits and prepare mentally for the ride to come. Kwagunt remained hidden and silent until we turned the final bend at the end of the Nankoweap corridor. The sudden raising of the river's voice, exaggerated by a hard rock cliff on river left, jarred my sleeping passengers into adrenalin-induced action. The channel drew a giant "S" taking us towards the left bank at the head of the rapid. The silky green tongue slid past a hole on the right at the entry through drenching waves that carried us around a big bend to the right. At higher water levels that hole was a big wave we loved to hit on sunny days. Below the rapid, a long beach on the right rested in front of Kwagunt Canyon. Several miles up the canyon loomed Cape Royale on the North Rim, over five thousand feet above the river.

Kwagunt had a great campsite, and perfect lunch spot with a shaded grove of Tamarisk trees behind the beach, a sun-drenched river nearby for bathing, and great views. *On one trip I watched for a half hour as an osprey swooped low over the river, fishing at the head of a small rapid just downstream.*

The Colorado River in the Grand Canyon used to serve up trophy trout as large as twenty-nine pounds. But after unusually high water in 1983, the larger fish had been swept downstream, and the Park Service began introducing a new, smaller species of trout. The era of "the big one got away" was over. Today, the Park Service is trying to hold the trout population in check to protect the native species, like the humpback chub and razorback sucker. Both had been forced to retreat to warmer side streams like the Little Colorado and were threatened by non-native predators like the introduced trout and striped bass that had migrated up the Colorado from Lake Mead. Between 2005 and 2007 the Fish and Wildlife Service conducted experimental flows from January through March, letting out 20,000 cfs in the morning and dropping down to 5,000 cfs at night, to take advantage of the time between the hatching of non-native species (trout) in late winter and that of the native species (chub) in early spring. The higher flows, they hoped, would flush out the non-native fingerlings to prevent predation of the native species. Results have been positive, at least for the humpback chub. The impact of the high flow/low flow pattern, however, has not been so good for the beaches. Higher water inundates the beach area, and when the river level drops quickly, gravity pulls the water back into the channel, along with the sand, thus reducing, and in some cases eliminating, camping areas.

We ran the small rapid where I had watched the osprey fishing, and settled in for a five-mile float to the Little Colorado. Aside from a few riffles and one small rapid at 60 Mile Canyon, it would be a smooth float, barring any strong upstream winds. *On one trip such winds had been so fierce, and our progress so insignificant, that we had decided to pull over and camp on the point just upstream of the Little Colorado-Colorado River confluence. It was the only time I had camped there and it provided me with a chance to explore the area for any remnants of a June 30, 1956 mid-air collision between a United DC-7 and TWA Super Constellation. With 128 fatalities, it was, at the time, the largest commercial airline tragedy in history. While hiking the steep slopes beneath Chuar Butte, I managed to find a large rusted CO2 canister. It was still full.*

As we approached the confluence, I alerted my passengers to be ready for a visual treat. If the Little "C" was clear, and it should be since we had not seen any evidence of rain during the trip, the beauty of the azure blue Little Colorado in contrast to the algae-dyed green Colorado was one of the great pieces of eye candy in the Canyon.

A long, slow eddy traced an upstream path in front of a narrow beach just upstream of the Little Colorado. Behind the beach a jungle of Coyote willow saplings hid the freshly emerged Tapeats sandstone, the last of the Cambrian sedimentary rock layers in the upper Canyon. At the end of the eddy, a muddy point marked the mouth of the Little C. A long, boulder-strewn island stretched from left to right just below the mouth. Flowing out of the mouth, both in front of and behind the island, I saw the blue color of a clear side stream. I anticipated exclamations of awe and surprise when we turned the corner to discover paradise. Jane said the color was so vibrant it didn't seem real. Frank smiled, while Ben told Jeff to grab his camera.

I pulled over to the shore, warning my passengers about the very slippery mud next to the river. A slightly pungent aroma pervaded the area from the exposed mud. Evidently the volume of the Little Colorado had dropped recently. Tapeats sandstone ledges sloped down to the river's edge, their large-grain, gray-brown pebbles a stark contrast to the blue water flowing lazily toward its disappearance into the green Colorado. A white bathtub ring encrusted boulders dotting the river channel, evidence of recent higher flows. On the far side of the Little C, deep green cattails and luminescent green reeds danced in the breeze. The view upstream was impossible to capture in words. Cliffs broken up by soft rock slopes stair-stepped into the summer blue sky. A quarter-mile upstream a shallow cascade turned blue water a frothy white as gravity exerted its pull.

We walked along the Tapeats shelf towards another cascade farther up the drainage, where adults could remember when they were children. After slipping their legs into lifejackets turned upside down and backwards, Sue led a line of adults into the water and linked them one-by-one by wrapping their legs around the person's waist in front of them. The human train floated in the gentle current, accompanied by cries of joy and playful laughter, headed for a slot between two boulders near the right shore. The back of the line began drifting to the left. Amidst feigned panic calls of "get right," people paddled frantically and narrowly averted mock disaster as the river quickened and a sharp drop pulled each laughing adult below the surface, emerging fifteen feet downstream. The line broke up and people swam to shore, many to do it all over again. And again.

I left the group to hike a bit further upstream to one of my favorite spots in the Canyon. Walking through a grove of catclaw acacia trees, curved thorns snagged my shirtsleeves and skin, raising small welts and liberating a few droplets of healthy red blood. *I had recently heard a story of a man in his early thirties who was scratched by a catclaw acacia at the Little "C". Thinking it was just a scratch, he ignored it. But by the next morning his leg had become inflamed, and within twenty-four hours it had worsened. Rather than call in a helicopter, the group decided to wait another day for them to get to Phantom Ranch. He was immediately evacuated, and by the next morning his leg had been amputated. From a scratch! It wasn't from the acacia, but the scratch had allowed a particularly virulent staph into his bloodstream, and his compromised immune system had been unable to fight it.*

In front of me waited my refuge, a small pool of liquid turquoise overlooked by a house-sized conglomerate boulder. Conglomerates were formed from debris flows consisting of mud, boulders, organic debris, and as little as ten percent water, saturated in lime. Over time the organic material had degraded, and the jumble of rocks had become encased in concrete-like mud. Imagine an unfinished concrete block with a wide variety of pebbles, stones, rocks, and boulders – most angular and unpolished – scattered throughout. Conglomerate rocks must surely have been the inspiration for concrete, which is composed of cement (a fine limestone sand), pebbles, and water.

It was easy to determine whether rocks were from a riverine or a dry environment. Rounded rocks, stones, and pebbles resulted from angular rocks colliding together as they were tumbled over and over in moving water – like steep mountain streams and rivers with the energy to move rocks long distances. Angular rocks, common in conglomerate formations, have not been carried far enough to round their edges before coming to rest once the debris flow loses its momentum.

My conglomerate boulder doubled as a jumping platform. Scrambling up one side, I walked to the edge and looked down into a deep blue pool, the current rushing from left to right. In the middle of the river, a series of travertine dams created sitting pools bordered on each side by current rushing to meet the main flow. The yellow-brown walls of the travertine pools combined with the sky-reflected blue waters into a landscape architect's masterpiece.

Stepping off my platform, I plunged into the cool waters of the Little Colorado and swam underwater towards the right shore. Once out of the current, I rolled over on my back, took a deep breath and lay spread-eagled on the surface, feeling the cooling waters on my backside and the warming sun on my front. Exhaling, I felt my body sink below the surface. Inhaling, I bobbed back to the top. I repeated the cycle several times before rolling over and swimming to shore. I then found a flat rock and lay down to dry off.

When I finally arrived back at the rafts, everybody was preparing to head four miles downstream to Carbon Creek, where we would camp and hike in the morning. Jane had pulled her mesh bag out of the purple day bag to get her sunscreen, and I told her to give it to me when she was finished so I could put it in my people can for quicker access. I grabbed my life jacket and zipped it up. It was tighter, having dried out in the harsh desert sun. After untying my bowline and wrapping it up, I pushed off and jumped on, resuming my position on the cooler. As I pulled out into the current, a strong upstream wind forced me to turn the raft around and row backwards. We wound our way down the channel upstream of the long island and turned sharply west, watching as the blue Little Colorado disappeared into the green Colorado. Within a quarter mile, any evidence of the Little Colorado had been swallowed into the larger flow. The Colorado now had a slightly translucent appearance, reducing the ability of the sun to promote photosynthesis in the colony of algae, the primary food source for the rainbow population.

A strong headwind was never a good sign here. We were about to enter the "land of a thousand eddies" where the narrow, snaking current undulated between huge eddies on both sides. With strong upstream winds obscuring the current, I had to rely more on the feel of the oars than my eyes to stay in the current and move downstream. Slipping into an eddy could cause me to lose a quarter mile or more in progress. Factor that in over sixteen days, two hundred twenty-six miles, and thousands of eddies, and you can imagine how much harder rowing could be.

While I rowed I told Ben I was sorry to hear about his wife's passing, and I was honored to share the Canyon with him. I found out that Jeff was currently working for Habitat for Humanity, and was considering his next career move, something he hoped to realize during the trip. I offered to help him in that exploration, since I enjoyed coaching people in finding work that didn't feel like work. He said that sounded real good. I asked Frank what his story was. He chuckled and told me he was happily retired, living in California, and enjoyed spending time at his cabin on the northwest coast of Vancouver. He also told me how much he enjoyed hearing my flute and hoped I would play it some more. He asked me where I had purchased it, and I told him it was made by Cristi Coom, a friend and master craftsman who had made flutes for some of the best-known professional Native flutists. He said he might like his name, since the flute would be a great instrument to have at his cabin.

On river left a frozen cascade of sodium chloride oozed out of the Tapeats sandstone, a sub-aqueous sandstone formed in the Tapeats Sea some five hundred-thirty million years ago. The salt had been trapped in the form of ocean water, just as water remains in a sponge. Over time, as the weight of overlying sedimentary layers squeezed the Tapeats, trapped saline water had leaked out and evaporated in the arid desert heat, leaving a residue of salt.

The land on river left below the confluence of the Little Colorado and Colorado Rivers was considered sacred Hopi land, and was off limits without the permission of Hopi tribal elders. Just upstream of mile sixty-four were several horizontal windows that had been carved out of the salt-encrusted base of the Tapeats. These were the sacred Hopi Salt Mines where, according to tribal tradition, warriors would journey to gather salt for ceremony and consumption. The braves would come down the Salt Trail into the Little Colorado drainage, travel downstream along the Tapeats shelves to the mines, gather what they could carry, and return to the tribe. *On a guide's training trip in 1989, some unsuspecting or sneaky hikers were found on the beach in front of the mines. Unfortunately for them, a park ranger was riding along with us, and we became an audience to their arrest.*

Just below the mines, on the right side of the river, awaited our camp. Commonly known as Carbon Creek, *I call it Condom Camp after an incident in the early 90s on a private trip. A friend and his wife had selected their campsite in the soft sand amidst privacy-affording boulders. After laying out their ground cloth and pad and changing into dry clothes, they headed to the river to wash off the salts from the Little Colorado. Behind their backs a raven dipped down, then soared overhead with something in its mouth: a ditty bag from one of their river bags. Soon the air was filled with multi-colored condoms. And laughter.*

The camp looked out on a large eddy with a swift, noisy downstream current traveling near the far wall. The wall displayed a hard-to-comprehend example of an unconformity. These were geologic anomalies identified when two distinct rock formations were not contiguous in time. In this case, the Cambrian Tapeats Sandstone, 530 million years old, sat atop the Pre-Cambrian Nankoweap Formation, 850 million years old. At this contact point, 320 million years of earth history were missing. Missing. Many things had occurred during that time – deposition, erosion, layers lifted through earth movement two to three miles, then faulted, dropped, tilted, and eroded. It was hard for me to wrap my mind around this, and the best I could do was assume that each year of earth history had been written on one page of the earth history book, with page one being the present, page two the prior year, all the way to the last page representing the oldest rock in the Canyon. So the Tapeats story was written beginning on page 530 million, and the Nankoweap on page 850 million. All pages between these two had been written, and then ripped out of the book, leaving 320 million pages, or years, missing. This was a testament to the erosional power of water and wind over a long period of time.

We parked our rafts in the middle of the eddy on a hard-packed beach. We set the kitchen up a short path to a flat area surrounded on the downstream side by a grove of tamarisk trees that provided shade and shelter from upstream winds. The groover rested between large sandstone blocks about thirty yards downstream from the rafts. It was reachable along the beach at lower water levels and along a dry path behind the kitchen at higher water levels. The dish line stood below the high water line, and would have to be moved away from the river before going to bed, as the river would rise during the night. The water that had been released from the Glen Canyon Dam that morning would reach our camp, seventy-nine miles downstream around twenty hours later. Sometime around three in the morning the water would come up and anything below the highwater line would be swept into the river.

On an earlier trip we had camped at mile 216 and celebrated a passenger's birthday, which I had photographed. After dinner, everyone had gone to sleep, tired and happy; but around one in the morning we were awakened by the sound of kitchen tables falling over. The water had come up and was in the process of claiming a bit of our kitchen. We rushed around to save all we could, moved the kitchen higher, and then returned to our beds. I made one last sweep of the camp and discovered my camera sitting in some grass less than a foot from the water.

On this trip the flows were much easier to anticipate, because the dam operators couldn't increase the river volume as much as they had prior to 1992. The normal operation of many power-generating dams, also known as "cash register dams," has been to open the floodgates in the morning and shut them down at night. It's called peak power, and it's the most financially efficient way to operate hydroelectric turbines. However, during the 'seventies and 'eighties, river guides in the Canyon had noticed a significant loss of beach area that they had attributed to the high flow/low flow regime of the dam.

A group of science-savvy river guides began making scientific observations that led to the decision by James Watt, Ronald Reagan's none-too-environmentally sensitive Secretary of the Interior, to commission an environmental impact study. It would be the first ever EIS on a standing dam, and the first to study the downstream impact of a dam's operations. The results of the study verified our "anecdotal" information and led to the passage of the Grand

Canyon Protection Act in 1992. For the first time Congress mandated that a dam be operated in a way that attempted to repair what its prior operation had damaged. This meant lower high flows and higher low flows in terms of volumes released from the dam, and smaller daily and hourly changes. In the past it was not unusual for fluctuations to vary as much as twenty-five thousand cubic feet per second. After 1992 they were limited to no more than eight thousand cfs in any one day. This minimized the saturation of beaches, which reduced erosion from gravity pulling the wet sand into the river along with the draining water.

Dinner tonight was chicken cacciatore, tossed salad, garlic bread, and cheesecake. Eliza and I were on cook crew and I was a bit disappointed that we didn't have a baked dessert, since I enjoyed doing that so much. On the other hand, it would mean less work and fewer dishes to wash. During the day, in a moment of unbridled enthusiasm, I had offered to lead a moonlight hike up Carbon. The moon would be full the next day, and I had always wanted to be up in the Chuar Valley at that time. Eliza had already said she wanted to go, as did Ben, Jeff, and Nathan. I told them we would leave right after the dishes were washed, although I secretly hoped they would change their minds. I tend to get lazy at times, and with the heat of the day, my energy was a bit low.

We sautéed the chicken, onions, mushrooms, and garlic in a Dutch oven (DO), added a little "headache in a bag" (wine), let it boil, and then lowered the heat and added green peppers, black olives, tomatoes, tomato paste, and seasonings. Ben, Jeff, Mary, and Chris offered to help with dinner, and we were happy to let them chop up the ingredients for the tossed salad.

While the chicken simmered, Eliza sautéed the garlic and butter, spread it on the French bread and browned it on the grill. After preparing the serving table, I blew the conch, and a hungry group descended on us. During dinner, Sue again described the plan for the next day. We'd be getting up earlier than usual to go on an adventure hike up Carbon into the Chuar Valley, and then down Lava Chuar, a side canyon less than a mile downstream. The hike would take around three hours. We'd walk up a dry river bed with lots of gravel and small boulders, do some scrambling over some big boulders, hike up a fairly steep rock fall, walk through a dry, narrow sandstone gorge, follow an easy trail through the Chuar Valley, and come down a flat canyon with a trickle of water, finishing up at the beach where the rafts would be tied up.

"What if we come to a place that we can't do?" Diana, the North Carolina tree farmer, clenched her fists as she waited for Sue's answer.

"I don't think that will happen, but if it does, someone will help you get back to the rafts if it's early on. Once we get to a certain place, however, the rafts will be gone. At that point you'll have no choice but to go with us. I'm sure you can do this, Diana. In fact, there isn't anyone on this trip who can't. We'll have three guides on the hike, and they're very good at these things." Diana smiled weakly as if embarrassed by her question.

"Oh," Sue continued, "and Charly has agreed to lead a night hike up Carbon. If any of you are interested, let him know. You'll be leaving right after the dishes are washed. Enjoy the rest of dinner." She smiled softly and walked back to her raft to finish her dinner. I flashed a weak smile.

After cleaning up, all I wanted to do was relax on my raft. I half-heartedly announced the hike in ten minutes, hoping everyone else felt the same way. Instead, Eliza, Ben, Jeff, Timmy and Nathan showed up eager to go. I checked with Nathan's mom and Timmy's dad, who was less than enthusiastic, then filled up my water bottle, checked my headlamp, put on my shoes and socks, and set out. The moon was already up and its reflected light provided plenty of visibility – at the beginning.

We walked across the cobble-studded sandbar toward the drainage coming out of the side canyon. The hike would start off in the drainage, and I was pretty sure I could find my way. My first hope was that after going just a short distance, everybody would be satisfied and we'd be back at the river in a half hour. Steep canyon walls blocked out all light, so I switched on my headlamp. I've always liked walking in the dark in the Canyon and didn't like the light, so I turned it off. I liked the challenge. Soon everyone was walking without his or her light. The air was still, and the temperature high without feeling oppressive. I inhaled the dryness of the desert and with it felt a surge of energy.

We scrambled under some big boulders resting against each other. I ran my hands over each one, like caressing a good friend. We hiked up the dry creek bed stepping on and over various-sized cobbles and boulders, and came to our first climb. A stack of flat, slate-like stones, piled against a short cliff, formed a stair step to make our climb easier. The canyon was still and hot, and sweat had already formed on the back of my hand. Brushing the back of my hand over my mouth, I tasted the salt leaching out of my body. I stopped for a moment to remember the way, moved over to my right, found the creek bed again, and continued up the drainage. Looking up, I could see the bright moonlight at the top of the canyon wall. This was so cool! I decided to go a bit farther, maybe to the bottom of the rock fall. When we arrived there, I suggested we take a water break. As I drank, I noticed moonlight hitting the top of the slope and thought it would be very cool to be bathed in that light.

I pointed to the moonlit rocks at the top and said we had come all this way, why not at least go up there?

"Hell yes," said Eliza.

"Fine with us," said Ben.

"Let's go," said Nathan.

Now I was excited. I started up. The trail led up a huge rockslide that had appeared just a few years ago. I could see the trail without my light, but missed it a couple times and had to retrace my steps. My heart rate increased with my legs demanding more oxygen to negotiate the steep trail. Loose debris made walking an adventure. It would be easy to slip and fall, or kick a stone down on someone behind me. I called down reminding everyone to yell "rock" if they happened to kick one loose. That way the people below would have a chance to cover their heads.

I wondered how we would do on the way down, when gravity would pull harder. One by one we arrived at the top, and stopped to catch our breath and drink more water. We were now in the spotlight of the moon, reflected light devoid of color.

It was just too moving a moment to remain silent, so I asked if everyone would give me one word that described how he or she was feeling at this moment. I said "blessed." Eliza added "fortunate." Ben chimed in with "grateful." Jeff offered "wonder." Nathan said "excited." And Timmy, after an awkward moment of silence, made us all laugh when he said "tired".

We were too close to the Chuar Valley to turn back now. I told them I'd always wanted to camp up there on the full moon and asked if they were up for going the whole way? I added it was through a dry gorge with very little elevation change. Everybody agreed.

I led the way down a short slope to a cut in the sandstone wall, entered the gorge, and headed up toward the valley. It was darker in the gorge and Ben and Timmy turned on their lamps. In fifteen minutes we came to the opening to the Chuar Valley. On both sides of the drainage we could see that the Tapeats Sandstone had folded – not broken – *folded*, ninety degrees. A major faulting that had occurred over a very long time had caused this. We stepped out into a literal moonscape. The North Rim, several miles to the West, seemed like a backdrop on a movie set, since there was very little depth perception in the moonlight. I walked a hundred feet up the drainage into the valley feeling and hearing the crackling of salt residue under my feet.

I said that this scene reminded me of a line from a Moody Blues song, and without waiting, recited it.

"Cold hearted orb, rules the night, removes the color from our sight; red is gray and yellow white; but we decide which is right, and which is an illusion."

I suggested we take a few minutes of silence and just enjoy this amazing scene. I told them

they could see what it looked like in the daylight, if they decided to go on the loop hike the next day. I knew that relatively few people had seen this place at night.

I walked up a short way, stopped, and listened. The loudest noise was my heartbeat.

Finally I said it was time to go. Just before we re-entered the gorge, I took a moment to talk about the brain rock, fossilized algae that was over a billion years old. It had sat in this one spot since before I had started working here, and now it was gone. After all these years a flash flood had taken it away.

When we reached the river, we shared sweaty hugs and everybody thanked me for taking them up. I thanked them for giving me no choice. It was one of the most amazing hikes I'd ever done.

The very distinctive patterns of the Collared Lizard along with bright orange or yellow markings on the body and feet stand in stark contrast to the earth tones so common in the arid lands of the Canyon

DAY SIX –
CARBON CREEK TO RATTLESNAKE

After five days of floating through rising walls and a relatively narrow channel, the Canyon was about to open - wide. In two days, we would welcome in eight new passengers, and ten of my new friends would be hiking out, their trip over. From camp, people like Ben, Jeff, and Jane, could see the enormity of their task. In the distance the top layers stood tall, burning golden in the early morning sky, as if to say "If you want to get home, you have to find me first. It won't be easy." A small structure on the rim pointed to the heavens, the only evidence of the outside world that we had seen since the trip had launched. It was known as Desert View Watchtower, designed by Mary Jane Colter in 1932. People from all over the world have flocked to this place, the only tourist spot on the south rim from which to see a long stretch of the river. Large telescopes have afforded visitors a chance to view unsuspecting rafters as they float downstream.

I lingered for a few minutes after hearing the coffee conch. Upstream, the stair-stepped Canyon walls receded to a point near the horizon. The rims on both sides created the illusion that they had intersected at a point, like railroad tracks on a long straightaway. The early morning sun on the cliffs and slopes upstream shouted hallelujah, with brilliant colors celebrating the start of another day. I could almost hear trumpets blaring over the soft sound of the river moving downstream. This was one of the "shoulder times" of the day, when the early morning brilliance of colors returned from their round-the-world nocturnal journey.

Time to get to work. It was already five-thirty. At home, with a roof over my head, I would still be asleep. Here it was so easy to wake up early. Even when I woke up at night I had a rotating canopy of stars overhead to entertain and hypnotize me; or moving shadows painting a mysterious canvas on the cliff across the river as the moon traveled from east to west; or foreboding dark clouds suggesting the possibility of a storm.

Breakfast had been called early today so we could enjoy the loop hike that would take us back up dry, vegetation-sparse, boulder-strewn Carbon Creek, into the surreal moonscape known as Chuar Valley that we had visited in the moonlight the night before. The 180-degree view of the North Rim in the distance would become our backdrop as we then followed a trail to the vegetation-rich creek bed of Lava-Chuar Canyon. The creek was more of a trickle of brackish water contained by steep, contrasting slopes of rust-colored Dox sandstone and Cardenas Basalt, ancient black lava that had flowed more than a billion years ago.

The first time I had hiked Lava-Chuar Canyon I was the "go-fer" and had been "volunteered" with another guide to row our six rafts three quarters of a mile downstream from Carbon. We would each row a raft with a second one tied behind, hike up Lava-Chuar through the valley, down Carbon, and bring the remaining two rafts down. My companion was Jimmy Hendrick, who liked to go by Hendrix, after the rock star. With flaming red hair to go with his live-free-or-die approach to life, Jimmy was irrepressibly energetic. He smoked a lot of dope, and I used to joke that he had to do that to keep from exploding. He was brilliant, in his own twisted way, and would regale us with a nonstop menu of hilarious jokes. After tying the first four rafts up at the beach at Lava Chuar, we hustled to get into the valley before the hikers arrived there. Jimmy wanted to launch a mock surprise attack. We moved quickly up a fairly flat grade until Jimmy found an appropriate ambush site behind a small ridge. As the unsuspecting passengers strolled on the trail beneath us, we erupted with screams while charging over the ridge. Then Jimmy took off, and to my surprise he wouldn't stop, not even when we had to scramble over house-sized boulders, or down a steep talus slope; nor when we jumped fifteen feet off a large boulder; nor when we navigated the dry riverbed strewn with loose debris; nor when Jimmy twisted his ankles, twice. We only stopped after reaching and plunging into the river. I can't remember when I had concentrated so hard. I don't even remember what Carbon looked like. I missed the stromatolite rocks, fossilized remnants of the Earth's first life. I missed the undulating beauty of the narrow, purple-and-white-swirled walls in the Tapeats gorge. I was so focused on where my next foot had to land that I hadn't noticed geologic formations that were revealed only in this and other side canyons. It was intense. It was exhilarating. It was nuts.

This time I would be part of the crew going up the right way. Before getting ready, I went over to Mary, who was sitting on a boulder near the kitchen. As I removed the plastic splint Floyd had given her, I asked her what she thought had actually happened. She said she had no idea, because all she had done was step out of the raft. She had only felt a slight twinge in the top of her foot. The pain had diminished somewhat, but she said it was still hard to walk on. We discussed the possibility of it being broken, and I again asked her if she wanted to be flown out for x-rays. She said Floyd had offered the same thing and she had decided to stay on the trip. I told her the option was open if she wanted it. After lightly massaging the areas of discomfort I rewrapped the ace bandage, replaced the splint, and helped her back to her campsite. Ben had offered to carry her yellow bags down to the rafts, so I gave her a hug and returned to my raft.

I dug my backpack out of its hiding place at the bottom of one of the waterproof day bags, found clean socks and my hiking shoes, filled my water bottles, put my first aid kit, some salty snacks, and my camera into my pack, applied sunscreen, and waited for the passengers to get ready. That's when Connor came to mind.

His full name is Connor Epstein Kraus, a mouthful for anyone, let alone a skinny eleven-year old. His parents called him bagel boy. We were in the Chuar Valley having completed half of our "loop hike," which had begun two hours earlier. Our path meandered through soft rock revealing signs of cataclysmic earth activity more than nine hundred million years earlier.

Connor wore an off-white cotton shirt – it had begun the trip pure white – and swung his arms and shoulders freely as he strolled down the trail. This was the walk of a strong adult, I thought, as I followed behind him. He and his mother were carrying on a conversation as any two extroverted adults might, talking on top of each other, speaking with exaggerated animation, and finding no end of things to say.

During a water break I approached his mother and told her that I had been struck by the maturity of Connor's gait. "He looked like a twenty-something on a stroll with a slightly older woman," I said.

She smiled, watching him as he stalked an unsuspecting adolescent frog. "It's pretty amazing," she said, "when you consider that twenty-one months ago his left foot was dangling at a grotesque angle, attached only by the grace of a resilient and resistant Achilles tendon."

The image made me gag. I asked her what had happened.

"He was hit by a car," she told me. "He was on his way to the store to buy some chocolate chips so his sister could make pancakes." She stopped for a moment to take a deep breath and smooth out the wrinkles on her forehead. "He was in a crosswalk when an impatient driver pulled out from behind the first car waiting for Connor, and ran him down. I was teaching an exercise class at the time, and had to ride my bike to the hospital. It wasn't easy seeing my carefree son all drugged up with his foot covered in a bloody bandage. The doctors told me he might not walk again, but I knew better. I worked with him for a year after he had recovered to make sure he would walk as naturally as possible." A tear appeared in the corner of her eye.

Connor and his parents had left our trip on the sixth day, hiking out the Bright Angel Trail. While they were still on the trip, I paid special attention to him. One day a dragonfly decided to ride along with us on the raft. Connor seemed engrossed in the details of the creature's gossamer wings and intricate yellow and green patterns on its body. It remained on his finger for an hour, and if I didn't know better, I'd swear by the way he was concentrating that he was having a telepathic conversation with his new friend.

The night before they were to hike out, we were all sitting as a group on the beach. It was dark and we found ourselves reminiscing about the past five days. Connor sat on the front of a raft facing us. When someone would recall a special time on the river or during a hike, Connor would reply with his own reflection. His words, like his walk, were not that of a "normal" eleven-year old, but of someone wise beyond his years.

Once everybody was assembled, we began the hike. Eliza remarked at how interesting it was to see the canyon after hiking in it at night. When we arrived at the rock fall, Timmy told his dad we had climbed that the night before. His dad threw a glance my way that was both accusing and impressed. The Tapeats narrows remained cool and shaded, and then we arrived at the Chuar Valley with the North Rim looming off in the distance. The rest of the hike proved enjoyable and uneventful.

Arriving back at the river after the hike, we all jumped in to cool off, took some time to refill our water bottles, stowed away boots in the boot bags and day items in the day bags, and then shoved off for a whole new visual experience of the Canyon. Up till now we had become accustomed to progressively higher, narrowing walls giving a feeling of being enclosed in a geologic museum of time. A major fault, the Butte Fault, which crossed the river at our location, changed all that. For the next ten miles, we would be floating through the Palisades of the

Desert, a section of the Canyon with wide vistas of tall cliffs, buttes, points, and terraces still climbing to the rim. It had always felt to me like the very bottom of the Canyon, even though we would not reach that point for another twenty miles. This was a place where you could take deep breaths, a place where you could shout to the heavens only to have your voice disappear. It was a place where freedom floated all around us.

On river right, the deep rust color of the Dox suggested formation in the presence of shallow water, like a delta, a floodplain, or near-shore ocean environment. It stood close to the river and while we floated on a near-shore current, we got a close look at the sedimentary bedding planes. Thanks to the soft Dox, the Canyon for the next few miles would be very wide, the widest by far in the upper Canyon. The gently undulating slopes wandered up to the cliff-and-slope-forming Cambrian layers. Directly across the beach at Lava Chuar, the Tapeats Sandstone, the last of the Cambrian layers, had rested just above river level. Now, because of the lifting power of the Butte Fault, it soared 1500 feet above the river. And we had traveled only a quarter-mile downstream.

On both sides of the river, the rim had receded several miles. The current was swift, and it took only a half hour to reach Upper Tanner, a camp on a point that offered spectacular star gazing, especially during a new moon cycle. We pulled over for lunch and I took advantage of some free time to hike up and behind our lunch spot. The panoramic view from this elevated platform was a photographer's dream. Upstream the river flowed out of the narrow confines of its Cambrian-encased channel. Directly across the river loomed Comanche point, resembling a large hand with straight, closed fingers reaching skyward. All around me were wonderful shapes of eroding earth highlighted against a desert blue sky with classic names like Lipan Point, Apollo Temple, Venus Temple, Jupiter Temple, Juno Temple, Cape Final, and Ochoa Point.

Before shoving off, Sue reminded us about the bigger water just ahead. We had lunched on a large peninsula that forced the river to make a sweeping "S" revealing Tanner Rapid and an unobstructed view for several miles. It was a section of the river known as Furnace Flats for its super-heated summer winds. As we floated around the corner, Tanner announced itself with a deeper growl than we had previously heard. It was a long rapid with big waves, and at lower water, a hole on the right edge of the current near the middle of the rapid. It was not a big rapid in comparison to those coming up, but it felt different than the ones we had been running for the last two days. It foreshadowed a shift to the bigger water beginning in four miles with Unkar. I could sense a change in my passengers, Nathan, Kathy, and Ben's daughter Ann. They had joined me after lunch and their carefree attitude had shifted to one that seemed to anticipate the possibility of danger.

After running Tanner safely, we enjoyed a swift current and the panoramic views all around us. Taking another sharp bend to the left, I looked upstream at Comanche point, which now appeared as a mitten with a small, thin thumb. Another sharp bend to the right took us by one of my favorite rocks, one I called the "manta ray" rock for its resemblance to the ocean flyer. It was embedded in an old river channel with clearly differentiated rocks nestled together indicating the direction of the river's historic flow – from left to right. Something had caused the channel to relocate to the right, perhaps a lava flow that had filled the old channel. Since water resisted nothing, it merely did what it had to do to continue on its journey. Over the succeeding millennia, the new sediment-laden channel had incised through part of the old channel, leaving a forty-foot wall of cobble that had lain on the bottom of the old riverbed.

Here the current pushed left, directly into a sizeable hole that lurked a hundred yards away, waiting to catch any unsuspecting rafter. Those who didn't know of the hole's existence stood a good chance of being drawn into it. From upstream it wasn't easy to spot. In 2005, the 17-year old son of a congressman who had brought his family on the trip decided to take the hole head-on. Later he admitted the hole had "kicked his ass!" Below the hole the current rolled through five-foot waves as it bent sharply to the right. On the left was a strong eddy that could easily suck in a raft. Straight ahead, on shore about fifty feet off the water, stretched a broken, ragged line of dehydrated cottonwood trees that had been deposited by the last flood to exceed a hundred thousand cubic feet per second. To the right of the current flowed a huge eddy framing a long, narrow beach and camp called Basalt, for the side canyon in the background.

The current slowed as the river channel widened. I pulled over into a small eddy on river right and pointed out a pictograph on the smooth vertical wall fifteen feet off the river. It was shaped like a spiral, and was said to be a Hopi migration symbol, interpreted as the journey of Hopi ancestors, the Hisatsinom, out of the Canyon. Modern day Hopi elders have said they had never abandoned the Canyon. Rather, they had just moved out from it. The center of the spiral represented the Canyon, and the spirals the extension of their movements away from this center.

According to the Hopi, places that have been inhabited in the past, or story walls of petroglyphs and pictographs still retain the energy and spirits of their ancestors. As a result, it is deemed necessary to request permission before entering any of those places. This is usually done with an offering of corn meal or tobacco, their way of asking for permission to come in. According to my Hopi friend William, it is like visiting friends and family.

Just downstream on river left was Cardenas, a camp that we had stopped at often in my early rafting days. I saw my first rattlesnake there as I had walked into the ample undergrowth to pee (we don't do that any more, but back in the 'seventies, we were just beginning to become sensitive to the impact of urinating off the river). The snake was coiled and relaxing against the base of a small willow sapling. While I was relieving myself, a Desert Spiney lizard ran under the flow and took a shower.

The camp was located just upstream of a wetlands area with large tamarisk and willow trees which had become home to at least one nesting pair of endangered willow flycatchers. The camp was declared off-limits during nesting season between May and July. Behind the camp was a trail leading to Hilltop Ruins, a rectangular-shaped rock structure about two-and-a-half-feet high. Archaeologists suspect it had been used as a blind for hunters, or maybe the location for ceremonies revolving around astronomical events, like the solstice and equinox. A hundred feet away rested a barely visible circle of stones that lined up perfectly with the notch in the thumb of Commanche Point to the north, and an indiscernible arch on the rim to the south. Archaeo-astronomers had determined that the sun rose in the thumb notch on the Autumnal Equinox, and in the arch on the Winter Solstice. So this could very well have been a ceremonial spot. The case for the structure being a hunter's blind was reinforced by animal trails that crisscrossed along the top of the slope. On the far side of the ruins a sheer cliff plunged a hundred feet to the river and Unkar Rapid. Across the river we could see a large delta with the excavated ruins of one of the Canyon's largest habitation sites.

We floated past Cardenas and came around the bend where the sound of Unkar Rapid raced upstream to greet us. Sue signaled for us to pull over on river right for a hike to the top of the delta where we would share some information about its former inhabitants.

We pulled into the eddy and hiked up a series of stairs, logs buried in the slope of the delta to provide a pathway to the ten habitation sites while also preventing erosion from summer and winter rains. Unkar is a Paiute word meaning red creek or red stone. The delta had been created from debris coming down the Unkar Creek drainage from the North Rim. The normally dry creek flowed into the Colorado near the head of the rapid. Across the Colorado, the shear cliff below Hilltop Ruin curved gently from left to right, providing a sounding board that magnified the volume of the rapid. From the top of the delta we could see the white water at the head of the rapid, diminished by the scale of the cliff. While it didn't look very big from where we stood, I knew from experience it could be quite harrowing. On a prior trip, I had casually followed one of my crewmates' rafts into Unkar, and watched as his raft headed straight for the hole, where it lifted up on its side and flipped. I too should have flipped, but was thankfully spared the embarrassment, reminded once again never to follow another raft or take a rapid for granted.

We walked along a loop trail on the delta and stopped to view various sites. Dwellings had been constructed from local rock for the walls and organic material for the roof. The only evidence of habitation that remained were outlines of small common rooms, bedrooms and ceremonial kivas, along with a diminishing number of pot shards that have too often found their way into people's pockets. It is illegal to remove anything from a national park, but the volume of potshards today is miniscule compared to my first visit here in 1978. The Ancient Puebloan People had occupied the delta seasonally (spring and summer) from 800 AD to 1250 AD, scratching out a living by farming, harvesting native edibles, and hunting.

We returned to the rafts and pulled out to run Unkar. The current carried us from the right side toward the left shore. Anyone taking the big run had to enter on the left side of the tongue, break through a large entry wave coming off the hole-you-don't-want-to-visit, and then run the wave train of large rollers rebounding off the shore. At the far bend in the rapid, it was necessary to pull away from the wall to avoid rocks and holes along the left and left-center of the rapid. The safer run entailed entering on the right side of the tongue and skirting the large rollers. Since my near flip, I have usually taken that option.

We were now two miles from camp and I didn't even bother to row, just allowing the current to carry us along. I asked Ann how she was enjoying the trip. She said it had already exceeded her expectations, and she didn't want to leave. She also said her mom would have loved being here. I asked Nathan how he liked the duckies, and he said they were way cool. He asked me if he could run some of the bigger rapids, and I told him he would have to check with Sue and his mom. Kathy said she would leave that decision up to Sue.

The Canyon was already narrowing down, a foreshadowing of more narrowing the next day as we would be entering the inner gorge and much bigger water. Nathan asked me how big the rapids were going to be, and I told him much bigger than anything we had seen thus far. He said he couldn't wait. The only other responses were tentative smiles.

I pulled into the small eddy at camp, sliding next to Star's raft and attaching the strap from my frame to hers. The camp stretched for several hundred yards up and downstream, with small saplings near the river, and a wall of dark, Precambrian sandstone, a hundred feet behind camp bracketing the open sandy area.

It didn't take long to set up the kitchen, conveniently located twenty feet from the rafts. We still had a couple hours before Star and Carla had to cook dinner, so we hung out on Floyd's raft and Sue talked about the early morning hike, before sunrise, and plans for the next day. I offered to lead the hike up to the Tabernacle, an eroded butte at least 2500 vertical feet above us. I had already done one hike up there in the dark, and it was spectacular. The objective was to get there to watch the sunrise, and then head down in time for breakfast. Sue, Eliza, Michael, and Carla all said they would go, and Floyd volunteered to help Star with breakfast.

We talked briefly about the trip and agreed that the passengers were great. Even Guy had toned down. Everyone said it would be sad to see Ben and his group leave, but that was the nature of "split" trips in the Canyon. People leave, and new people come in. We had all become good at saying goodbye to great folks, and almost always enjoyed the passengers who hiked in.

Some of us took advantage of the free time to write letters and post cards to friends and family. I send cards out from Phantom Ranch with a stamp declaring "Mailed by Mule from the Bottom of the Grand Canyon." I also enjoy receiving mail, including cookies from my mom. Michael already mentioned that he hoped she would be sending some.

In the early years we didn't even stop at Phantom, and getting mail was unheard of. When we started doing split trips in the 'eighties, I used to be envious of others who were receiving mail, in part because I didn't have a girlfriend or wife, and in part because I felt left out. Then, in a blinding flash of the obvious, I thought I would ask people to send me mail and provided the address. Now I often receive more mail than anyone else.

During dinner of black bean posole, cornbread, and rice, Sue described the early morning hike, saying it was a serious hike but well worth the effort. She asked for a show of hands of those who definitely wanted to go and eleven hands were raised. She said we would be waking up at three and starting the hike at 3:30. We would need plenty of water, would have snacks and fruit available, and everyone should use the groover before going up. She then talked briefly about the plan for the next day, saying it would be a really fun, big water day, and our last full day together. A few frowns and words of protest arose, and Sue asked everyone to not get ahead of themselves. We still had a lot of Canyon to experience.

After dinner I found Mary and we went through what was becoming a daily ritual. Jane was camped nearby and she joined us. Mary talked about her experiences being unable to hike. Initially she said she had been disappointed; but had found that she was seeing things she probably wouldn't have seen since she was forced to be stationary. She found that critters were coming to her, including several lizards that got very close. While she was used to being active, she was happy to be in the Canyon. She thought her foot was getting better, and hoped she would be able to join us on future hikes. Besides, she said, she was enjoying the attention. Jane just said that I was good at that, smiled, and said good night as she returned to her camp.

I said good night to Mary and returned to my raft. I was hoping to spend some time with Eliza, but she was nowhere to be seen. So I gathered my stuff, including my clock and flute, and found a nice flat sandy bed for the night. After playing my flute for a few minutes, I put it away and lay down. Three o'clock would come early.

*Close to five million people visit the Grand Canyon at the North and
South Rims, while only 25,000 venture on the river. What the latter see is
unimagined by those at the rim. These rafters are floating on the Colorado
River surrounded by unparalleled reflections while being enfolded by
geologic formations as old as 1.84 billion years.*

DAY SEVEN –
RATTLESNAKE TO CREMATION

The full moon shone brightly, highlighting ominous-looking clouds just downstream. I lingered, enjoying the warmth under my down bag. Polaris, the closest star to true north, shone just above the west rim from the end of the handle of the Little Dipper. The song of a small rapid penetrated the darkness, reminding me that big water waited just around the next bend. I took a deep breath, inhaling the dry desert air mixed with the moistness of the Colorado River. I threw off the comfort of my bag and slipped on a t-shirt and shorts. Time to get to work.

If I were to calculate my hourly wage, it would be ridiculously insufficient. In summer I can wake up at 3:00 AM, as I did on this day, and work until 9:00 PM. I've done this for thirty years, rowing an eighteen-foot, fully loaded raft with four passengers two hundred and twenty-six miles, carrying the weight of responsibility for their safety. And I still feel the privilege in that.

Because a big part of my job is interpretation, I must know about numerous subjects I had shunned in school– archaeology, history, botany, biology, geology - because they had intimidated me. Some of my crewmates are experts in one or more of these fields. I am a generalist, knowing just enough to be dangerous. Because safety is "job one" in this big-water, harsh desert environment, I am also trained in emergency wilderness medicine, CPR, and swift water rescue. I cook, clean, load, unload, lead hikes, tell stories, play instruments, sing badly, tell jokes even worse, and organize games. All for relatively low pay and little or no benefits. When I first started working in the Canyon, in 1978, guides were paid sixty dollars a day. Today, I receive a hundred fifty dollars a day. We're definitely not keeping up with inflation.

I put my sleep kit away and gathered what I needed for the hike: two water bottles, camera, tripod, daypack, first aid kit, shoes and socks, rain jacket, Polypro. Even though it was summer, the temperature could turn dangerously cold if a drenching rain and wind blew in. The clouds seemed poised to remove our moonlight but didn't appear threatening. The extra weight would be worth it if there were a storm lurking beyond the rim.

On my first night hike to the Tabernacle, in 2000, we had arrived at the top an hour before sunrise and the early morning chill, compounded by a strong breeze and no shelter, had left us at risk because everyone had dressed for heat. To adapt, we clustered in small groups, and then lay down side-by-side. Finally we formed a tight circle so we could share body heat, like the Emporer Penguins do. No one seemed concerned. In fact, there was quite a bit of bantering and humor. One of the women cracked everybody up when she blurted out, "whose hand is that?" After a spectacular sunrise, during which no one felt cold, the air warmed up rather quickly, especially on the hike down.

Sue and Star were up, waking the eleven passengers who had said they wanted to go on the hike. I made sure a jug of water was available to fill water bottles, and fruit and energy bars were on hand. I poured myself a cup of water, mixed in my rejuvenating green powder, and headed for the bathroom located in a grove of willow saplings two hundred yards upstream. A few years ago Sue was the paddleboat captain and we were camped here. Suddenly the raft came loose from its tie and started floating up the eddy. Sue sprinted up the path toward the groover, which was occupied. She yelled to the occupant that she was coming in, because that was the only way for her to head off the raft before it reached the downstream current. The occupant merely replied, "Why?"

Since I was the only person on the crew to have done this hike at night, Sue asked me to lead it. At 3:30 we were ready, and I headed off, using my headlamp to light the way for those who would follow – Ben, Jeff, Annie, Tom, Nathan, Ann, Ken, Diana, Antje, Eliza, and Jane. Michael, Star, and Sue found spots between the hikers.

I walked away from the river behind camp, climbed some fallen Shinumo quartzite slabs, found the trail, and headed upstream towards the far ridge. It was actually harder to see the trail with my light, but I kept it on until everybody was up on the ridge. Clouds now completely covered the moon that I had hoped would light the way for us. The trail had probably begun as an animal path, and then human footsteps had defined it more clearly. This trail was less apparent than most of the others we'd hiked because human footsteps had been less frequent, so finding and staying on the trail required a fair degree of concentration. I likened it to following a ghost trail, like trackers who claimed to be able to follow the energy lines of an animal that had wandered by.

Once off the ridge I followed a narrow and at times barely discernable trail. The unbroken rise in elevation challenged my lungs and heart. As we moved away from the river, the air grew still and hot. All I could hear was my breath, the sound of my shoes on the trail, and my niece Eliza walking behind me. The rest of the group had been swallowed up by the night, but I knew the other guides were spread out, with Carla bringing up the rear.

My first marker was an outcrop of Tapeats sandstone quite a ways up. It stood out as a dark mass against the gray, cloudy sky. We trudged up a steep incline and I stopped to take a water break so people could catch up. I had no watch, but felt we were making pretty good time. Eliza was breathing hard and said she appreciated the rest. Michael joined us, followed by several passengers. I gave them all a smile in the dark and headed off.

We reached the top of the incline and the trail led off to the left towards my outcrop. The trail steepened sharply, and my quads burned with a demand for more oxygen-rich blood that my racing heart and straining lungs were supplying. I reached the base and headed towards the darkness inside the outcrop, picking my way over and around huge slabs of peeled-away sandstone. I slowed my pace and looked back to make sure the others had followed. Once past this section, the trail led across an open stretch of soft soil. Clumps of prickly pear and hedgehog cacti stood by the edge of the trail like spectators watching a parade. Some guides have said there were snakes along this trail, but I doubted it because water was so scarce up here. First light made it easier to see the trail and the cacti.

The Tabernacle loomed directly in front of us, appearing in the early dawn darkness like a fortress atop a steep slope. It was hard to make out any distinguishing features, but from past visits I knew it was from the Bright Angel shale formation. The soft shale eroded easily, and an infinite number of green and purple shards were scattered everywhere around the landscape. To the left of the Tabernacle stood another prominent feature, eroded into the shape of a pyramid with its top rounded off. In the saddle between, the descending full moon peeked in and out of the silver and gray clouds. I reached the base of the Tabernacle and followed the trail along the upstream edge. In places it was difficult to stay on the narrow trail that often lay hidden in the shadows. A steep slope to my right made any misstep a potential disaster.

Coming around the backside of the Tabernacle, I looked up at our final destination. The trail was steepest here. I placed one foot in front of the other and kept moving. My lungs were screaming, and my legs felt like rubber, but the end was in sight and I wasn't going to quit.

I climbed up the last obstacle, a small ledge, and was there. The top of the Tabernacle, which from the river looked like the profile of a nipple on a prone woman's breast, was a rough rectangle about fifteen feet wide and twenty-five feet long.

One by one everybody joined me on the top. Far to the east, the upstream rim was receiving its early morning paint job. The edges of the gray clouds had begun to turn a soft magenta as an ever-brightening gold replaced the darkened edges of the Canyon. Ben erected a small cairn next to a bush as a testament to his wife. Although saddened by her absence, he was heartened at having his son and daughter with him. He motioned to his kids, Jeff and Ann, and to their friends, Tim and Annie, and together, with arms around each other, they took some time in silence to honor her presence and her passing. Streaks of tears shone on their faces as the sun broke the horizon. We spent the next fifteen minutes in awe as the light crawled down the Canyon walls, shining on the cliffs and slopes around us as brilliant golds and oranges celebrated the beginning of another day. Exclamations of delight erupted from some; others remained respectfully silent.

We were just about as far above the river as one could reasonably reach on this kind of a trip and still be inside the Canyon. We could see far upstream, beyond the narrowing curve of the river flowing around Unkar Delta, and into the Palisades of the Desert, the wide-open stretch most visible to tourists gaining a telescopic view of the river from the Cooks' tour safety of the South Rim. Below Unkar, the river, still awaiting the morning sun, stretched towards us like an iridescent slate ribbon.

After enjoying the sunrise and taking a group picture, we started down. The steep trail and gravity that had stressed our hearts, lungs, and quads on the way up now pulled us towards camp and a well-earned breakfast. My body practically floated down the trail, as if I had just removed twenty-pound ankle weights. In some places I had to slow down to prevent an out-of-control tumble.

On one of my trips, a very athletic young woman fell on the way down this trail and hit her head. When she was unclear about the incident, we monitored her for a possible concussion. Head injuries can lead to increasing pressure from swelling in the brain, and can be fatal. Not remembering the incident is an indicator of concussion. The next morning we stopped at Phantom Ranch, where she and her father planned to hike out. As a precaution, the trip leader discussed the incident with the ranger, who promptly placed the woman on a gurney, where, because of safety protocols at the park, she was forced to remain against her will until a helicopter arrived to fly her out, two hours later. Turns out she didn't have a concussion, but the rangers decided it was better to err on the side of safety.

It had taken our lead group less than an hour and a half to reach the top, but it took us half that time to get down. I felt sorry for anyone with bad knees. The silver ribbon of river far below grew in size as we descended. By the time we reached camp, the sun was bathing the kitchen area and encroaching on the river. The early morning clouds were dissolving in the heat of strong thermals shooting out of the Canyon, and breakfast was ready. The aroma of cooked bacon, scrambled eggs, and potatoes fed our already ravenous appetites. Soon the food would become another memory, and our attention would be focused on the whitewater downstream.

Our long, narrow camp was bordered on its front by the river and groves of willow saplings along the shore. Behind camp stood a fifteen-foot wall of newly emerged shinumo quartzite, a purplish-brown mix of erosion-resistant quartzite and sandstone. Quartzite is sandstone altered by intense heat and pressure. Often this occurred deep in the earth, the heat emanating from the mantle, combined with the pressure of overlying layers of sediment. Downstream, the Shinumo layer rose dramatically out of the river, like a steep-gradient roadbed. It formed nearly vertical walls resistant to erosion, pinching down the river channel. Sheared off slabs of Shinumo, partially buried in soft sand, were scattered around camp. Several flat chunks behind the kitchen provided convenient seating for fine dining. Two domed tents were nestled in a thick grove of willows just off the path to the groover, a few yellow bags rested in front of our rafts waiting to be loaded, and several campsites were marked by blue tarps under thermarest pads and empty sleeping bags. During breakfast, hikers talked about the glorious sunrise on the Tabernacle. Many said it was a highlight of the trip thus far. As for the crew, we were a bit more subdued, aware of big water lurking ahead.

After cleaning up from breakfast, I turned my attention to our day on the river and began rigging in a more focused way than usual, as did the rest of the crew. Undoubtedly some of our passengers noticed the difference. Even though we had already run many rapids – some fairly large – today would be our introduction to the first major rapid, and to the Inner Gorge, a stretch of river unlike any we had yet encountered.

On big-water days most guides "rigged for flipping," not because we expected to flip, but because the bigger water made flipping more possible. I was carrying nine yellow passenger bags in three rows of three, plus my three black bags on the deck behind my cooler/seat. By now Eliza had learned the routine and had loaded those bags. I checked them before shoving off, just to make sure. I strapped the six-gallon water jug to the nose of my front tube to provide an extra fifty pounds of stabilizing weight, and added a heavy tent bag and two purple day bags onto my front hatch for my passengers to lean against. I also made sure there were adequate handholds for people to grasp fore and aft, so they felt adequately prepared to throw their weight around should the need arise. In the back, I fashioned loops on the straps holding down the yellow bags, again for secure handholds. Then we all checked to make sure there were no loose straps to prevent foot traps. I've never had that happen to a passenger on any my trips, but an old river guide, Shorty Burton, had drowned in 1967 when his motor rig flipped and his lifejacket snagged on the motor mount, trapping him underwater. I have also seen video from a private trip when one boatman flipped in the ledge hole at Lava Falls. He was seriously bruised and battered after his raft rolled over and over, his loose bowline wrapped around his ankle.

Finally, I checked my oarlocks, which are shaped like an upturned "U." The oars slid into the oarlock and floated freely to provide more flexibility when running the river. We can "feather" the oars by rotating them slightly as we lift them out of the water. This was particularly useful in strong upstream winds because it cut down on wind resistance. We can also pull the oars in to avoid hitting rocks, or when the current runs close to a wall or other obstruction in the river. I wanted to make sure the opening of the oarlock was narrow enough to prevent an oar from leaping out at an untimely moment.

That had happened to me in 1983, on a private trip with my brother Ned and some of his friends. Ned had worked for one summer with Sandy in Cataract Canyon. Sandy had become a guide the year after he and I had taken our first river trip in Cataract with my lifelong friend, Gary, who also had invited me on my first Grand Canyon "homecoming" trip. After that trip, I had called Sandy and told him he needed to be down here, and that's when he applied for, and won, a private permit for a trip in 1979.

River levels in 1983 were the highest they'd been for over twenty years, and everything on the river was different. It was like running it for the first time. I felt like a rookie, even though I had been on four trips through the Canyon. My confidence in reading water was not high, and I had naively chosen to row my thirteen-and-a-half foot raft. It was very small and light, and the increased volume and power of the river could make it seem like a toy in a bathtub. We had launched on seventy thousand cfs and the eleven-to-thirteen mile per hour current made every moment on the river an adventure. Swirling currents, boils, and near-whirlpools required constant attention. Normally we could relax on the ninety percent of the river that was devoid of whitewater. Now we had to be more alert in these stretches because an unexpected boil could erupt and threaten a flip, or a whirlpool could suck down a tube and pull a relaxing passenger into its void.

Sandy told me about an experience on one of his '83 trips. He and another raft were floating side-by-side when suddenly the other raft was sucked ten feet down by a whirlpool. After a few revolutions, the raft was spit out and they continued downstream.

Then there were the "eddy fences," where the combination of the racing downstream current and the equally fast opposite current in the eddy created a standing wave that made entering and leaving every eddy a moment of anxiety. Not only could that eddy fence flip any raft, just making it into the eddy was problematic. We had to anticipate our entry far sooner than we had in the past. Missing a pull-in could mean missing camp.

In the middle of our private trip, we had been surprised to find an old friend on the beach at Phantom Ranch, waiting to hitch a ride with us. Gary, the man who had introduced me to the Grand Canyon, had retired as a river guide the prior year, but evidently he hadn't gotten the Canyon out of his system. He later told me that lying in bed one night, he couldn't stop thinking about us being on the river at such high water levels. He had to be there. So in the middle of the night he had packed up his truck and driven nonstop in order to hike down the Bright Angel trail in time to meet us. His wife said she had wanted to kill him.

Most of the rapids at this higher water level were either washed out or had been turned into enjoyable standing waves – but not all. Two rapids, Crystal and Lava, had become enormous.

When we arrived at Crystal and saw how massive and scary it was, my brother Ned, nervous about running it, asked Gary if he would like to row. An experienced and very competent river guide, he was happy to take over the oars. He would go first, and I would run second. I had two passengers, a good friend, Bill, who had been my brother Sandy's schoolmate in junior high, and Lulu, my sister-in-law. This was Bill's first raft trip, and his first experience with camping.

We shoved off and were carried quickly to the head of the rapid. I watched in horror as Gary entered too far left, got swept directly towards a monstrous hole, and flipped faster than I could say "Oh my god." Crystal had always been a "white knuckle" rapid for me, having flipped there on my second trip. A strong lateral coming off the right shore required a precision entry and good momentum. I hadn't learned to use momentum, preferring to position my raft as close to my desired entry as possible before beginning my strokes.

With the volume so high and the current so fast, I needed to be even more accurate with my entry. After watching Gary flip, I must have been even more juiced up, and I entered farther right than I had wanted. My oar blade struck a rock and popped out, leaving me with one oar and no hope. In a matter of seconds I found myself approaching a massive hole that spanned half the river. Next to the hole was a huge standing wave. With no way to maneuver my small raft, I became a witness as my small raft climbed the wave and flipped end over end, leaving me, Lulu, and Bill to swim in the fast, cold current.

I was immediately swept downstream, over the rock island, which fortunately was under water. I looked for my raft, Lulu and Bill, and couldn't find either one. All I could do was save myself, because there were no rafts downstream to rescue me. So I looked for an eddy I could enter to get to shore. I had heard about people swept downstream and dying of hypothermia, so I swam towards the left shore, knowing there was another rapid less than a half mile away. Finally I spotted a small eddy just upstream of that rapid and managed to swim into it. As I reached slow water, I was swept over some submerged rocks and banged both knees, but hardly felt anything. I crawled up on a small beach and checked my body for broken bones and found nothing. Then I looked for Bill and Lulu, and spotted them on the right shore. The powerful current had stripped Bill of his shoes and he was forced to walk a half-mile over heated, sharp rock before being rescued by one of our other rafts. Later, after we were all reunited with our own rafts, I learned that Gary had injured his hip on a rock while swimming to shore. He would be inconvenienced for a few days, but had received no permanent injuries. Bill was fine, although his feet had been abused while hiking downstream. Lulu was shaken, but okay. We had been lucky.

My final task before running big water was to check each passenger's life jacket to make sure it was snug enough. Wet life jackets expand, and in turbulent water could be sucked off a body. That had happened to a private boater on a late fall trip, when his raft flipped in Hance rapid. His body was recovered days later without a life jacket. Others on the trip said he had it on when he had entered the rapids, but may have not had it buckled up.

After completing my rigging, I again invited people to stretch. This would primarily be a river day, and having a flexible body, especially after the long hike we had just completed, would allow people to react more quickly should they need to move to the "high side." We finished with shoulder massages. Ben was in front of me and I had to stretch to reach his shoulders. Because his muscles were so tight, I asked him if he ever received massages. He said he hadn't, but knew he should. Chris stood behind me and her knowledgeable fingers found several knots in my shoulders. To the words "Let's go boating," we headed for the rafts.

Ken and Diana, the tree farmers who were going to hike out the next day, joined me. Mary came too, and in spite of her injured foot, decided to ride in front with Ken.

We shoved off, and I let the eddy pull me out to the current. Until recently, this had been a mild stretch of river that at times had become frustrating to navigate in low water amid strong upstream winds. Recently, after a flash flood had roared down the drainage from the north side, this placid stretch had been altered. The additional debris that had flowed into the channel had created a small rapid where none had existed before, at least not in my time here.

Change is happening all the time in the Canyon, and it's our job to adapt. Sometime, and I hope it's in my lifetime, I expect there will be an event, perhaps an earthquake, that will cause a landslide that will completely block the river, creating a temporary lake stretching miles upstream. Will the dam operators release enough water to break up the natural dam? Will the Park Service bring in dynamite? Or will they resist the pressure from the public and the concessionaires, and allow nature to take its course? I want to be around to find out.

We entered a wider stretch of calm river with verdant grasses and horsetail lining the banks. Up ahead, another new rapid, formed in the same flood event as the one at Rattlesnake, spit its venom and exercised its lungs. At the head of the rapid, the river bent slightly to the right, flowed against an uplifted cliff of Shinumo Quartzite, and snaked left. A deeper growl floated on an upstream breeze to greet us, heralding a larger rapid, Nevills.

Norm Nevills had been the first man to run boats commercially through the Grand Canyon. His hard-shell wooden boats had a center seat for the oarsman, and his passengers rode on the deck fore and aft, lying spread-eagled while running in the bigger water. In 1937, Lois Jotter and Dr Elzada Clover, a botany professor and her student from the University of Michigan, became the first women to run the entire Grand Canyon on a Nevills trip.

Nevills is a long rapid with several pourovers, depressions in the river caused by water flowing over some obstacle that could easily flip a raft – or eject a guide. *On a trip in the mid-1980s, Dave, a good friend of mine, had been drafted at the last minute to row our baggage boat. A lawyer by education, he had a great sense of humor, played guitar, and was a wonderful addition to the crew. He had run many trips as a motor guide, but had not rowed before. Dave followed me into the rapid, but I focused on my run and didn't see his entry. In the lower end of the rapid I looked back to see how he was doing and found him in the river climbing back onto his raft. A wave had sneaked over the rear tube and had slapped him right off his seat.*

Nevills Rapid had formed from debris pouring out of 75-mile Canyon, creating a long rock bar at the head of the rapid and pinching down the river. Upstream of the rapid, on river left, a narrow beach fringed by saplings had often provided a convenient shade spot for lunch. Behind the saplings an ancient cottonwood tree and sandstone overhang provided shade and shelter from desert sun or rain. Over the years industrious beavers had applied their teeth to the four-foot diameter base of the tree. It had withstood this onslaught until 2001. Arriving that year with the expectations of shade, we were amazed to find the carcass of the fallen tree with freshly carved teeth marks on the large stump and tree bottom.

75-Mile Canyon had also been the site of a number of string quartet concerts. A quarter mile up the boulder-and-gravel-strewn creek bed, a ninety-degree bend provided both shade and shelter from the sound of the rapid. It offered an ideal location for a concert, with narrow walls to keep the sun out, and a hard gravel and stone floor for better acoustics. On the trip I guided in 1985, classical musicians had offered formal concerts in this and other natural amphitheaters in the Canyon. They performed during dinner preparations, and occasionally woke us up to Mozart. The quartet was made up of two violinists, a violist, and a cellist, all from California. We carried the violins and viola in a cooler, put the cello in a body bag and strapped it to the back of one of the rafts. It was such a treat to be around musicians who were passionate about their music. And there turned out to be something unexpectedly powerful about the combination of the music and the setting of the Grand.

In 2002 I was on the crew of my fifth string quartet trip. We had camped just downstream of 75-Mile near the bottom of Nevill's rapid. It was early afternoon and I was relaxing on my raft in spite of the high-decibel noise from the rapid. One of my passengers, Russ, walked up with a casual hello. His body language was anything but casual. A slim, bearded man, he looked like someone out of a "Jeremiah Johnson" novel. As it turns out, he lived in a small mountain town in western Colorado. In a very quiet voice he told me that something had just happened and he was feeling overwhelmed. His brow was creased, and he seemed on the verge of tears as he nervously scratched his beard. I invited him up on my raft and offered him a soda, which he softly delined. Then he began his story.

He had been hanging out at his campsite just downstream from the rafts when something he didn't understand drew him upstream. He said he felt he had no choice but to go along. He ended up sitting on some rocks away from the river feeling very confused. By way of explanation he told me he had been in the Navy during the Vietnam War, on a ship in the Gulf of Tonkin. He hadn't seen any action, but the ship had housed Marines who would go off on missions. Some didn't return. On one mission, 175 didn't return. And he'd felt a survivor's guilt ever since. That was in '72. His eyes moistened and his voice died in his throat. He closed his eyes and rubbed them. When I asked him about the guilt, he only said he hadn't shown the Marines enough respect.

So there he was, sitting on that rock, knowing something was about to happen, but having no idea what it might be. His voice choked and he started to cry. Then he told me that suddenly it was as if all 175 Marines were there, like they had just materialized out of the earth. He stopped to wipe the tears and compose himself.

I wanted to ask him how these Marines had shown up. Were they ghosts? How did he know they were the same men? But I remained silent.

He asked me what I thought it all meant. I hesitated to answer, saying it was really something only he could answer. In a pleading voice he said he had no idea, and again asked me what I thought it meant. Finally I said I thought they were telling him it was time to move on. I then told him that in many cultures, when a person passed on, they would hold a ceremony to honor them and let them go. The Lakota performed a hoop dance to close the hoop, believing that if they didn't, their spirit would be trapped on the earth plane. I then shared with him a ceremony I did after my dad passed on, called "a washing away of tears."

My dad was a sweet man who had the genes and lifestyle to live to be a hundred. Yet at seventy-three, soon after liquidating his retail men's clothing business, he began to show symptoms of what turned out to be a brain tumor. It was hard to see such a vibrant man reduced to an expressionless human. The tumor was in the part of the brain that influenced the expression of feelings and emotions; so after the surgeon had performed a craniotomy to reduce the pressure on his brain, the procedure also removed any evidence of feelings on his face. My dad survived ten months. While he was still alive, I told him I was hesitant to leave to go to a raft trip in the Canyon because I was afraid I wouldn't see him again. He replied that at some point I wouldn't see him anyhow, and encouraged me to go do what I loved. He passed on while I was in Arizona.

Just under a year after his passing, I participated in a "washing away of tears" ceremony with a group of people who were studying from the same medicine man. First we passed around and smoked from a ceremonial pipe, and then one-by-one, each of us was asked to bring the person who had passed away back to mind, and to recall all of them, not just their glorified aspects. We were then told to recall and anchor a memory that we had had with them that we wanted to carry with us into the future, say what we hadn't said to them while they were alive, and then say goodbye. As my anchor I chose a time when my dad and I had played a game on our private trip in 1986 in the Canyon. It involved two small paddles and a rubber ball, and we had managed to hit the ball back and forth 235 times before it hit the ground. Several times my seventy-one year old father had to dive to keep the ball off the ground.

Tears are the Great Spirit's gift for cleansing and healing. I had never really shed tears for my father, and the release and relief I felt during this ceremony were palpable, deep, and humbling. I received a clear picture in my mind of my father, beaming, as if to say, "I'm in a good place."

I suggested to Russ that he consider creating his own ending ceremony where he could let go of his guilt, do something to honor those Marines, and bring closure to that period of his life.

He said that made sense to him, and would have to think about it. He walked away, head down, looked back, smiled weakly, and then disappeared into the saplings. After that trip I asked him if he would write to me about his experience, if he created a ceremony. I'm still waiting for that letter.

As we approached Nevills, Sue let out a war cry. Floyd was in the lead, followed by me, then Star, the paddleboat, Carla, and Michael. I felt a strong connection with my crewmates, especially when we were running bigger water. While our safety record has been remarkably good for such a hostile place, the potential for danger was ever present, and having a group of competent men and women who were dedicated to looking out for one another added an element of respect and intimacy that proved unusual in most work environments.

The entry to the rapid was either on the left or right side of the tongue. This time I entered on the left side, missed the hole at the top, and purposefully pushed back out into the middle to run between the two pourovers halfway down. I miscalculated the current and narrowly missed dropping over the right pourover. Frank and Mary applauded, thinking I had run it that way on purpose. I wasn't about to correct them, but silently engaged in some self abuse as I wondered when I would make the leap to full competency in reading water and maneuvering perfectly.

Below Nevills the river bent sharply right, entered a small riffle near the right wall, and emerged into a calm stretch. Diana asked if she had time to remove her rain jacket and I said yes, since we would be pulling over to scout the next rapid. Ken and Mary, who hadn't put on rain gear for Nevills, leaned against the bags on the front hatch and relaxed. The current slowed to a crawl. To our left, Papago Creek cut a swath through the newly revealed Hakatai shale, a dark bed of soft, easily eroded rock lying under the harder Shinumo quartzite. Softer rock erodes easily, and when lying underneath harder rock, removes the support for the upper layer, causing it to peel away. This was one of the mechanisms Nature had used to contribute to the widening of the Canyon.

Three quarters of a mile downstream awaited Hance Rapid, the first of six major rapids in the Canyon. Water that had pooled upstream of the rapid resembled a narrow lake due to its slower current – Hance Lake – providing us with more time to feel the anxiety build as we drew nearer to the rapid and the gut-churning sounds and images of impending doom.

We were about to experience one of the most abrupt changes in the Canyon and the river. Just below Hance, the Canyon formed a gorge of hard, steep walls, fast water, and powerful rapids. Hance was the gateway to the Inner Gorge, so named because of 1.8 billion-year-old metamorphic rock which appeared just below the rapid. This steep, dark, iridescent, erosion-resistant rock rose directly out of the river, narrowing the Canyon. Major John Wesley Powell, in the journal of his 1879 exploration of the Canyon said, "hard rocks make hard rapids." Many of the biggest rapids of the trip awaited us in the next thirty miles.

We pulled over above Hance to scout. At low water our entry into the rapid was right of center, and the run was a downstream ferry pulling away from waves and holes towards the left shore. In order to have the best view of that run we pulled over on the right above the rapid and hiked up a short trail. At medium to high water, our entry was on the left side and we would pull over above the rapid on the left, walk downstream and up a rock-covered dune to have the best view.

My first run through Hance had been in 1979 on the private trip I shared with my brother Sandy. Hance can be very intimidating, especially to a neophyte. It has a vertical drop of thirty feet in a quarter mile, one of the steepest in the Canyon. When Sandy and I arrived at Hance, we surveyed the rapid from high on the sand dune on river left. The river was very low and I was horrified. My eyes seemed to be seeing for the first time, and I wanted to shut out the roar in my ears. There were boulders the size of pickups, and angry holes spitting undisguised anger. The water frothed from one side of the river to the other. It was pure chaos. Its deep, guttural sound reminded me of an out-of-control freight train bent on destruction. My mouth dried up, my heart raced, and I began to sweat. A novice at reading the river, I could not see a safe way through this minefield. Soon, the slope across the river appeared to be moving, an optical illusion that added to my anxiety.

Finally, with Sandy's help, I had been able to visualize a possible run, sort of. We would enter to the right of a large pourover and pull hard to the left to miss some monster waves while avoiding fabric-ripping rocks and boat-flipping holes.

Sandy had run first. He was six inches taller than me, with sixty pounds of extra muscle, and two years experience running rapids in Utah. This was my first trip rowing my own, small raft. As planned, Sandy entered to the right of the pourover and even with his powerful legs and strong upper body I could see him straining against the overpowering flow of the Colorado. He barely made it to the left of all the danger.

I knew I couldn't do the same run, so along with my passenger, I decided to enter to the left of the pourover. Floating on the calm water above the rapid with my passenger Frank white knuckling the safety lines in front, all my attention was focused on the spot where I had wanted to enter. But I failed to notice the direction of the current that was moving to the right towards the pourover. My raft hit the side of the pourover, ripping my untethered oar out of my hand. Like a powerless bystander, I watched as it slithered into the river. Reaching for the oar, I slipped off my cooler seat, and in horrifying slow motion, slid headfirst into the river – right at the top of a major rapid.

The oar slipped under my raft. The water temperature was fifty degrees, but I was so focused on getting my oar back that I failed to notice the cold. Even the roar of the rapid didn't speak to me. Taking a deep breath, I submerged, grabbed the oar, pulled it out and yelled to Frank, who was staring at the danger ahead and hadn't realized his guide had jumped ship. Blood drained from his face and he screamed,

"What are you doing? We're in the middle of this rapid and there's a huge hole right in front of us. Get back in this boat!"

I handed him the oar, pulled myself back into the raft, and shoved the oar back into its oarlock. As I did, I noticed a crack in the shaft of the oar. I looked for a place to change oars, and somehow managed to pull to the right shore. Looking back upstream I was stunned at the minefield of boulders my raft and body had miraculously navigated. I should have been eaten alive in the massive waves we call the Land of the Giants. To this day I don't see how I made it through all that to the right side. The thought of going back out there was frightening – and unavoidable.

I replaced my injured oar with a healthy one that had been strapped to the right side of the frame, took a deep breath, said a silent prayer, and pulled back out into the drenching fury. The river now had my full attention, and with a death grip on my oars I pulled as hard as I could, turning my raft to hit each massive wave straight on. Frank was plastered to the front tube holding on for his life, his weight helping to avoid an "endo." We dove into a deep trough and a wall of water engulfed us. Somehow we re-emerged, and I yelled to Frank to bail because we had another short but intense rapid, "Son of Hance," to run. The river bent to the left and then sharply to the right. After facing my bow towards the left shore to hit strong lateral waves, I then pushed hard on my left oar to square up for one more cruncher.

Sitting on my cooler in a calm eddy below the rapid while Frank bailed water out of the raft, my whole body began to shake. For the first time on that trip I felt trapped in a primordial, unforgiving wilderness. Was I going to lose it now that I was safe? Or was my body just releasing pent-up energy? Finally I let go with a raucous roar of relief and joy. The shaking subsided and I felt the corners of my mouth lift in a smile all the way to my ears. I had made it through Hance Rapid. It wasn't pretty, but it sure was memorable.

On this day, more than two decades later, the early morning clouds had given way to a deep blue sky, the sun was high, and any drenching would feel refreshing knowing we would dry off quickly. We were a half-mile from the head of Hance, and that's all I could see – the head of the rapid. A large boulder peaked out of the river not far from the left shore, like a sentry guarding the entry. Fifty feet downstream the river wrapped around a car-sized piece of sandstone. As we got closer, the sound deepened. I could see the spray of spitting whitewater everywhere. A low, gutteral roar spoke volumes about what I couldn't see. The words from a Bob Seger song popped into my head: "Wish I didn't know now what I didn't know then."

A side canyon opened up to the left at the head of the rapid. Brilliant red-brown slopes offered insight into its name, Red Canyon. On the right slope, a dark line ran through the Hakatai shale, dissecting the iron-oxide rich slope as it traveled diagonally to river's edge. It was an igneous dike, molten rock that had been injected from a pressure-filled pool of magma beneath the surface. After untold millennia, it had been revealed through erosion. The head of the rapid was less than a hundred feet away and we now heard the full basso-profundo roar of Hance. I felt pressure in my groin. Suddenly I had to pee.

Since we were going to run this rapid from the left side of the river, we all pulled over in an eddy and hiked up a trail to the top of a large boulder-encrusted sand dune. After running Hance over ninety times, I now had a pretty good feel for it. While Sue was pointing out the path to the paddleboat crew, my mind wandered to another trip early in my career, in 1982.

This was the research trip studying the succession fight between the coyote willow and the tamarisk. One of the scientists on that trip was a geology grad student named John who had never traveled west of the Allegheny Mountains. Now here he was, in this living geologic museum called the Grand Canyon.

One look at John's face would tell you that he was in heaven. After all, the Canyon had some of the most stable and extensively exposed geologic formations on the planet. Formations he had only seen in photographs and read about in geology texts had come alive before his very eyes. John had clearly loved his experience, until we arrived at Hance.

We had pulled over above the rapid on river left to scout and determine the safest run. John had remained below sitting on a rock overlooking the rapid. When I approached him on the way back to the boat some fifteen minutes later, he didn't look well. His face had gone pale, which was not exactly normal in the desert; and the sparkle in his eyes had disappeared. John had just spent the last fifteen minutes staring at this mighty rapid, listening to the sounds of a freight train, and seeing nothing but white water and rocks. He later told me he was convinced he was going to die.

Wanting to distract him from his fears and get him more involved, I told him I needed his help in navigating Hance. Because of its technical nature in low water, I told him, there were many "markers" - exposed rocks, submerged rocks, current lines, slack water, standing waves, and holes - that had to be memorized to safely maneuver the raft through the rapid.

He said he didn't see how he could help, but he would try. I then showed him the route we were going to take. We had to enter to the left of a pourover with the rear of the raft pointing downstream to the left, break through a lateral wave coming off a group of rocks, pull left into slack water, a place we called the duck pond, to take advantage of slower current, pass to the left of some exposed rocks, continue to pull left in a current intent on pushing us right to miss some holes, find a slot between two holes, and hit some huge waves straight. And then we had to negotiate "son of Hance.'

He looked very intently at the points in the rapid as I had described them, asked me to repeat the run once more, studied it carefully like he was preparing for his PhD orals, and then indicated he was ready. We walked back to the raft and I noticed the color returning to his face. John took his place in the front while I coiled up the bowline and shoved off. As we floated toward the head of the rapid, John looked intently downstream, searching for the pourover that marked our entry.

The current above major rapids moves agonizingly slowly, until you get right to the head of the rapid. Then it can speed up to 35 miles per hour and all hell can break loose. Just as we were entering the rapid, John stood up and took charge, shouting directions and offering encouragement. "Looks good, Charly! There's the hole, hit that lateral, move left and grab that slack water! There's some rocks ahead, get a little left! Watch that hole! Straighten the boat up! I don't see the slot! Oh, there it is, off to the right! I think we're good! Yes!!! Now hit those big ones straight! Great run, Charly!"

That night, after dinner, I asked John what he remembered most about the day. Without hesitating, he said, "Going from the brink of death . . . to sheer exhilaration in thirty seconds at Hance!"

Once the guides finished their scout, we returned to the rafts and shoved off. This time I would lead. The trip leader normally ran first, but because Sue was on the paddleboat, she couldn't do that. We positioned them in the middle of the pack to make sure to have rafts in front and behind them for rescue in case the paddleboat flipped, or one or more of the passengers ended up in the river.

As the first raft to run the rapid, I had to take on the safety role for the rest. That meant finding a safe, conservative line, to avoid a flip. But in Hance, there was no conservative line. As I pulled out into the current, I felt a heightened responsibility, not only for my passengers, but also for the rest of the trip. If I flipped, there would be no one downstream to help out, and that could put my passengers and me at greater risk, and leave the rest unprotected.

I instructed Mary and Ken, who were in the front, what to look for. We had to enter backwards just to the left of a large rock. We floated to the right of the sentry rock upstream of the entry and the rapid's roar increased. I looked behind to see Diana hunkered down in the back, plastered against the yellow bags, looking intently at the entry rock. She looked at me, a glance that said "I hope we make it." I nodded my head and sent her a reassuring smile.

I maneuvered the raft to hit a small wave that set me up on the current line I wanted, checked my angle, and held my oars firmly as we rode up on the pillow of water coming off the rock. I could feel a small crack running down the oar handle, smooth from many years of use. I didn't want to pull hard because we could end up in the eddy behind the rock and it would be difficult to get back in the current. Too little momentum and the wave could push us down the left side of the rapid, where numerous exposed rocks and holes would make it a very bumpy ride.

We entered and floated past the rock on swift current. From upstream it would appear we were being carried swiftly to the right, instead of downstream. In fact, the diagonal current was doing both. We picked up speed and I looked for "the goalposts," two rocks hiding just beneath the surface. I wanted to run to the left of them, and prepared to turn my raft around to pull hard towards the left shore to avoid the land of the giants.

Waves rushed against the left side of the raft as I continued to pull away from the mass of water in the middle of the river. Ken and Mary, now seasoned high-siders, were doing a great job of responding to the assault against us. I looked for "Whale's Rock," named for the same man for whom Whale's Armpit was named, to commemorate the time he had wrapped his motor rig on the rock at low water. If I could get to the left of it I'd be in great shape. If I went to its right, I'd still have some big waves to run.

I finally spotted it and knew I wasn't going to get left. So I straightened up to face downstream, let everyone know we were about to go into some big waves, and pushed hard. The raft dropped into a deep trough as Ken and Mary threw their weight onto the front tube. The raft shuddered, practically stopping as a mountain of cold water engulfed us. For a moment, all light was extinguished.

We broke through, our raft now heavy with water. I yelled over the roar for them to bail as I pulled hard on my right oar to again face my back towards the left shore. I wanted to get into a small eddy to run safety for the rest of the boats now entering the rapid.

Diana in the back, and Ken in the front, bailed feverishly. I needed the raft to be as light as possible in the event I had to go out for a rescue. With a couple hundred gallons of water, and two-and-a-half-gallon buckets – great for water fights, but less efficient for bailing – it would take some time to empty the raft. Meanwhile, Floyd came by pulling towards the right shore to run safety on that side. True to his character, I could hear him laughing as he passed by.

Star flashed a smile as she broke through the big waves and headed for "Son of Hance," two hundred yards below. The paddleboat came next, six paddles in sync, with Sue making calls – "left turn,' "stop,' "ahead two," "all forward" – while acting as the rudder and seventh engine. After Carla and Michael came through, I pulled back into the middle to run "Son of Hance."

At the head of the rapid the river made a sharp bend to the right. Strong waves rebounding from the shore raced out to meet us. I faced my raft forward and pushed into them, then pushed hard on my left oar to run one more wave, and we were through. We floated into an eddy where the paddle crew were exchanging high fives and talking animatedly about their run. I had no doubt exhilaration was mixed with a bit of relief for making it through the first major rapid. That would include me.

We headed downstream towards more big water. Not far below the rapid I pointed out a small square hole at the base of a short cliff about five hundred feet above the river. It had been an asbestos mine, now abandoned and off limits to visitation, established by "Captain" John Hance, the first permanent settler on the South Rim. Extracting asbestos from hard rock required grueling physical labor. The value of asbestos is proportional to the length of its fibers, so it could only be hand-mined out of very hard rock.

Floating beneath the mine entrance, I marveled at the early twentieth century ingenuity, drive, and persistence of men who had mined down here. First they had to get to the river, which was challenging enough. Then they had to make their way safely across, climb with their heavy equipment to the mine, extract the asbestos fibers, return to the river, re-cross it, and climb out on a primitive trail, with no guarantee of finding a buyer for the hard-won insulation material. I told my passengers that some of the asbestos had wound up as fire retardant in theater curtains in Europe. We used to hike up there, but when asbestos fibers were found to be carcinogenic, the Park Service declared the mine off limits.

On our left we passed a small beach we had used once for a lunch stop because it offered a shady spot for the table. During one trip, the last raft had entered the small eddy with too much speed and had slammed into the side of one of the parked rafts. A loud, disconcerting rush of air immediately got our attention. Looking down, we saw the right front tube deflating. A sharp screw head on a clamp that held a clip on the spare oar had punctured the tube. We were stunned. This raft had a very tough plastic skin that we had thought was practically impossible to puncture. No worries, mate. While we prepared lunch, the guide and another on the crew patched the hole.

The raft had to be pulled up on shore, an easy task with plenty of strong backs around.

After drying off the tube and roughing it up with sandpaper in the area of the patch, special two-part glue had been applied to both the tube and the bottom side of the patch, which was then placed over the six-inch tear. After lunch, the tube was filled with air, and the trip had continued as if nothing had happened. Back at the warehouse after the trip, a new patch would replace the temporary one.

I could hear the now familiar sound of a large rapid downstream. I might as well get used to hearing that sound, I thought. For the next three days we would be expending a lot of nervous energy running rapids with names like Sockdolager ("knock-out punch"), Grapevine, Horn Creek, Granite, Hermit, and Crystal.

Sockdolager was a long rapid shoehorned between narrow, iridescent metamorphic and igneous walls. It had a standing wave left of center near the top, which turned into a hole at low water. Just downstream and to the right was another large wave, positioned diagonally towards the middle of the river. I could run the left wave, the right wave, or thread the needle between the two. I usually liked to run the left wave because it was straight on and would give us a big hit. To be set up for it I positioned my raft facing downstream and pushed through the left side of the tongue at the head of the rapid. I then found the big wave and made sure I was near its center. If I hit that wave on its right side, I had to be ready to pivot to my right in order to hit the large diagonal wave just below. Turning a raft quickly can be very difficult when it's sitting flat in the water. The best time to turn is when a raft is on top of a wave, where there is less resistance.

This time we slammed into the left wave as it was building and soared up and over. I let out a whoop of excitement, echoed by Mary. She was smiling broadly, really enjoying the adventure. The rest of the rapid felt like a small roller coaster ride. Six to ten foot waves greeted us as we raced down the narrow channel. Ken and Mary leaned into each wave with no concern for getting wet. At the bottom, I pulled into another eddy as Diana and Mary unclipped the bail buckets for more exercise. I enjoyed the sense of comaraderie and teamwork we had developed. Big water will do that.

We were now below the biggest rapids of the day, but still had several that could create problems if we started to relax and take things for granted. Whenever I've heard a guide say, "this rapid's a piece of cake," I've known something was about to happen. And it usually wasn't pretty.

My first lesson in this reality happened on the Tuolomne River in California. We were at Clavey Falls, considered one of the ten biggest "drops" or rapids in the country. A guide had hesitated to take his raft through, so another rafter who had already rowed his boat through volunteered.

"Shit, this rapid ain't nothing," I heard him say. "I'll show you how to do it." We all watched as he walked back upstream, untied and entered the raft, and shoved off. Clavey has a steep drop and then an immediate right-angle turn. The challenge was to find the steep chute between two holes at the entry, and then immediately pull back on the oars to avoid a huge hole next to the left wall, with much of the current pushing hard towards the hole. The guide managed the first part well, but couldn't pull the raft back enough to avoid the hole. I have a picture of him and his boat in the middle of that hole. The raft is folding in half, and the guide is in the process of being ejected. You may call it a boatman's superstition, but I've

seen something like this happen too many times when a guide "disses" the river. I have great respect for the power of the river, and don't care to test it when I'm rowing.

The current slowed down, even though we were still in a narrow section of the gorge. One common interest of many passengers is the depth of the Colorado. In the Canyon it can range from three feet to 122 feet. Our slower current probably meant the river was quite deep here.

We had two miles of calm water ahead of us before running the next rapid. With a warming sun and subsiding adrenalin, it provided a perfect opportunity to kick back and relax. As Diana, Ken, and Mary found comfortable positions, I spoke about the ancient rock rising above us. I told them that at one time, some 1.8 billion years ago (give or take a couple hundred million), this layer had rested on the bottom of the Pacific Ocean. Then the Pacific Rim tectonic plate, moving eastward, collided with the North American plate, moving west. The collision had caused the sandstone, limestone and shale deposits to fold, like a piece of aluminum foil being pushed from opposite edges, and be driven deep into the Earth's mantle. What had followed was one, perhaps two, orogenies, mountain-building episodes that had created alpine-like mountains fourteen to eighteen thousand feet high. The combination of extreme pressure from the overlying mountains, and the intense heat generated from beneath the mantle, caused the metamorphosis of the crystalline structure of the rocks. Thus was born the metamorphic Vishnu Schist. Lying deep within the earth, the viscous rock took many hundreds of millions of years to cool and harden. Like diamonds that cooled slowly, the crystals formed parallel to one another. This meant that the schist could be cleaved, or split. It took many more hundreds of millions of years for the overlying sedimentary layers to erode, plus the cutting action of the Colorado River, before the schist would see the sun.

I mentioned how much I still marveled at the dynamic reality of nature's cycles, which led to an interesting conversation on the raft about how different cycles appeared down here. Rocks became other rocks over long periods of time. Water that fell in the Canyon returned to the ocean by river, was pulled up into the atmosphere through evaporation, and again rained down in or near the Canyon. Mary indicated this was the first time she had heard about the hydrologic cycle and wondered about other atmospheric effects. I told her that the prevailing winds from west to east carried lots of particles, including toxins from coal fired plants, and sediment from sand storms. Some years, I said, dust from the Gobi desert in China have found its way to the Canyon on the wings of the jet stream. The sunsets, exaggerated by all the particulates in the air, had been spectacular. That beauty all too often had masked the negative impact on many people's health from the toxins in the dust.

I told them a story of a presentation I had made to the Michigan Recycling Coalition. Because of a deadline for getting out their newsletter announcing my presentation, they had been forced to come up with a title, since I was on a river trip and unavailable. During a board meeting my client had announced she had hired me as the speaker for their annual conference. One of the board members then asked, "What the hell does the Grand Canyon have to do with recycling in Michigan?" The title they had chosen was "What does the Grand Canyon have to do with recycling in Michigan?"

I wasn't happy when I was informed of this, but immediately went to work to make the connection. During my research I discovered many things about recycling, including the term "secondary feed stock." A 7-Up bottle, after being reduced to plastic chips, could be turned into carpet. The chips are the secondary feed stock. After thinking about it, I realized that the Grand Canyon is made up entirely of secondary feed stock – eroding sandstone, limestone, shale, schist, granite, and lava – that ultimately will become other rock. During my presentation, I was able to make the connection.

Mary, who had been to many corporate meetings, said she would have enjoyed hearing me make that connection.

Even though it was only 11:00 AM, Sue decided to pull in at the Grapevine camp for lunch. We had eaten an early breakfast and had burned off all those calories by now, and then some.

A long, wide, sand-covered beach spread out in front of a granite wall a hundred feet from the river's edge. We carried the table and food up a steep sand slope and set the table in the shade. We enjoyed a deli-lunch of cold cuts, turkey and roast beef, and then Sue declared siesta time. After an adrenaline-filled morning and a full lunch, no one argued. The sand was soft, the shade cool, and we weren't in a hurry to reach our camp, appropriately called Cremation. I found a comfortable spot near the wall, wiggled my body to fit the sand beneath me to the contours of my body, and closed my eyes.

When Sue's pleasant voice too soon announced the end of our siesta, I struggled for a moment to wake up. Midday naps are wonderful, but never long enough, and it takes me a while to come back fully to my senses. Once on the river, however, I had no choice.

The sound of Grapevine Rapid greeted us as we shoved off. It was similar to Sockdolager, without the two huge waves at the top – a long run down a narrow channel with playful rolling waves. I entered on the right side of the current, slipped by a hole on my left, pushed left to get to the center of the river, and enjoyed dousing my passengers in the front. By now Ken was a premiere high-sider, throwing his weight around like a seasoned pro. Mary was subtler, but her ocean sailing experiences came in handy a few times when she needed to move quickly. I encouraged them to "kiss the waves before they kiss you," and Mary never shrank away.

Even though we still had a few rapids to run before camp, the biggest water of the day lay behind us, and it proved easy to relax. We ran a surprisingly feisty rapid at 83 Mile, a short, noisy one that didn't seem like much until we entered and saw what could have happened had we missed the entry. Sharp rocks peeked out of a cascade hidden from upstream view. The entry was on the right side of the river, and the current above carved an "S" from river left along consecutive ninety-degree bends before entering the tongue. It seemed to take forever to reach the entry.

The current was still strong in this narrow section. Up ahead I could see some of the current pushing up against a prominence on the left wall. I should have been on the right side of the current, but wasn't paying enough attention. Pulling hard on my left oar, I faced the rear of the raft to the right and pulled hard. Too little, too late. We got sucked up against the polished schist and the right side of the raft began climbing the wall.

"High side!" I yelled, as I threw my weight to the top of the right tube. Mary and Ken were already there. At first Diana went the wrong way, and water began to pour over the lower, upstream tube. "Get high, Diana!" I ordered in my best autocratic voice. If more water poured over the lower tube, we could flip, and I would never hear the end of flipping in an eddy from my crewmates. She responded quickly and reversed her direction, and between surges the raft settled back down. I didn't say a word, but I'm sure my look broadcast both the embarrassment and relief I felt. It took me two attempts to break through the strong eddy line. Fortunately all the other rafts were downstream, so I didn't have to hear their ribbing – just my own.

"Thought you might want to get a closer look at that beautiful, polished schist. Pretty amazing, eh?" I said as I winked, smiled, and pulled on my oars to catch up.

We were approaching Clear Creek, where on a sunny day we would normally stop and hike. It was a very narrow side canyon with dark gray metamorphic walls rising into sheer cliffs directly from the creek. Hiking through the warm, clear water, always provided a refreshing alternative to the cold, often muddy, Colorado. Rock walls almost two billion years old would enfold us. Before it had disappeared due to erosions caused by the operation of the dam, I had photographed the beach at Clear Creek for the Adopt-a-Beach program.

On two trips, I had learned how quickly danger could arise here. The first was a private trip in 1993. We had been pulling in to camp to hike up Clear Creek. Two hikers, teenagers who had come down from the North Rim, were relaxing on the beach. One last raft was just entering the eddy, rowed by my friend Kathy, who was a wilderness veteran, but new to rowing. She had underestimated the swiftness of the current, and was having difficulty getting into the eddy. One of her passengers scrambled to the back of the raft to grab the stern line. It was thin and long, and she suddenly became entangled in the rope, lost her balance, and slipped precariously towards the edge of the raft, holding on to some of the gear without her life jacket on. At the same time, a spare oar fell off the raft into the eddy.

Seeing this, both hikers plunged into the river, without life jackets. This all happened so quickly we had no time to react. I was amazed at how quickly things had turned potentially deadly. In less than a minute, three people had put themselves at risk, and one raft had almost floated downstream and would have missed camp. One of the hikers managed to grab the oar in the shallows, while the other plunged out into chest-deep water, grabbed the raft, and somehow managed to pull the raft into the eddy. Kathy had been spared the embarrassment of missing camp, and her passenger had been able to pull herself back into the raft with just her ego bruised.

*　　*　　*

The second incident occurred in 1999, after I had pulled into the Clear Creek eddy to photograph the beach. Normally, I would pull to shore at the downstream end of the beach, tie up, climb over beautifully polished schist, photograph the beach, and return to the raft. This time I decided to float into a small eddy directly below my photo spot. It turned out to be smaller than it had appeared from upstream. I jumped out of the raft, bowline in hand, and tied up to a small sapling. The black schist had soaked up the desert sun and I could feel the heat through my sandals as I looked down at my raft, only half of which floated in the micro-eddy. The current was still tugging the rest. To be safe, I tied my stern line to a rocky outcrop, and quickly took my photo. I didn't bother to write down any notes of perceived changes and their causes. I had to untie my raft, now straining impatiently in the current.

I asked Michelle, my only passenger, to come up and untie the stern line while I held the bowline. As she did, the raft swung farther out into the current and was threatening to journey downstream without a guide or a passenger. Michelle scrambled up to help me hold the bowline. Even with both of us holding on, the current was winning. The line was digging into my hands, and we had to act quickly, or lose the raft. I told Michelle to let go and jump into the raft that was directly below us. Without hesitation, she did so, almost tripping on the straining bowline.

The raft was now pulling me towards the water and I had visions of being dragged behind my raft into the next rapid. Finally I leaped into the back of the raft, scrambled over the bags and resumed control of the oars. It was embarrassing, and served as another wakeup call. It can take just a split second of indecision, or a moment of carelessness or miscalculation, to create a potentially life-threatening experience.

Because of the time we had spent at lunch, Sue decided to forego a hike into Clear Creek. Too bad, because not only was the water clear and warm, there was also a wonderful pool fed by a dual cascade that dropped over a car-sized boulder wedged in the narrow channel. One stream dropped down a center chute into a shallow pool, the other traveled along an eroded groove in the right side creating a horizontal flow that merged with the center cascade. I understood Sue's reasoning, but I was still disappointed; and if our passengers had known what they were missing, they would have been disappointed as well.

We were now less than four miles from our camp. We could see the clear water from the creek merging with the Colorado as we floated by the mouth of Clear Creek and ran a small rapid at a camp called Zoroaster, named for the ancient Persian religious leader. We got drenched in the medium waves of Zoroaster rapid and the no-name rapid just below it, and floated under my favorite wall, a massive sloped wall of exfoliated schist and granite.

Finally we ran 85 Mile, the last rapid of the day. In no time we were through and on calm water. The roar of the rapid faded as we floated calmly to camp at Cremation, a double camp a half mile upstream of Phantom Ranch. Here we would enjoy a last dinner with those hiking out, help them prepare lunches and their packs for the hike, reflect on our time together, and spend a satisfying and restful night before introducing new passengers to even more intense whitewater the next day.

Dinner the night before an interchange, is always an experience in organized chaos. While Floyd and Eliza prepared dinner, Baja tacos, tortilla roll-ups, garlic bread, and cherry cobbler baked in a Dutch Oven, the rest of the crew set up a separate table to provide lunch options for those hiking out in the morning. Cold cuts, cheese, lettuce, tomatoes, onions, pb&j, apples and oranges, gorp, nuts, Cheez-its, and granola bars, would provide everyone with plenty of choices to add more weight to their backpacks. The hikers would be instructed to make their lunches before dinner and place them in a paper bag with their name on the outside of the bag. These would be placed in my cooler and distributed at the beach just before the beginning of their hike. While we did this, Sue talked to the passengers, instructing those hiking out – Jane, Guy, Ben, Jeff, Ken, Diana, Frank, Annie, Tom, and Ann – to empty their personal dry bag and fill up their backpacks, which we had taken out of their hiding place in somewhat waterproof bags. In the morning, we would load their backpacks on two or three rafts and take them downstream a mile-and-a-half below Phantom Ranch to begin their seven-and-a-half mile hike up forty-six hundred vertical feet to the South Rim. Sometime during their hike, they would pass those hiking in to join us for the second half of the trip.

I have always grown fond of my passengers. In fact, the longer we're in the Canyon, the more beautiful people become. As the days pass we all become more attuned to the natural world and rhythms. Working together in such intimate circumstances strips away our pretences, and we become more relaxed and more comfortable with each other. This was a particularly wonderful group, and I would miss all of them, except maybe Guy. I was particularly drawn to Jane because of her courage in allowing me to support her, Frank because of his feisty personality, and Ben because of his vulnerability and authenticity. Tom was a real character, and Annie, well Annie was one of the most outrageous woman I'd ever met. She was always ready for a quip, and never lacked for a retort. Her interactions with Carla and Star had been flat-out hilarious, like the night they stayed up late engaging in nonstop verbal jousting and laughter.

Having some people leave and others join us in the middle of a trip presented several challenges. We had just spent seven days in intimate connection with people we would probably never see again. More often than not, they had chosen a shorter trip out of concerns that they may not like the experience, and wanted to avoid feeling trapped for two weeks. Or maybe they could only afford a week. Many often regretted having to hike out. Clearly, the Canyon had captivated them. That was certainly true for many of these folks. The remaining passengers, who had also been part of this same intimacy, would soon find themselves feeling different from those hiking in. After all, they were now Canyon veterans and were comfortable with the day-to-day routine. I knew from past experience that if we failed to do something to acknowledge the loss of our departing friends, and then consciously invite the new folks in, they would subtly remain outsiders.

To prevent this from happening, Sue, who has many years experience in working with groups in wilderness settings, invited everybody to spend a few minutes after dinner reminiscing about the trip and what those leaving would take with them into the rest of their lives. We assembled in front of the rafts in a close circle, and waited for someone to break the silence. The dark schist radiated its sun-soaked heat, while the coolness of the river pushed back.

Jane was the first to speak up. She talked about her terror on the first day, how she had felt like a fish out of water – that brought a laugh from the group – and how important our support was in helping her realize how much more she was capable of accomplishing. She said she would take this experience and apply what she had learned to other areas of her life, particularly her work, where she hoped to find more meaningful employment, and in a relationship that had begun just before the trip. After spending much of her adult life caring for her mother, she said she was a bit inexperienced in personal relationships. However, she assured us she now knew she could go where she had previously never imagined possible.

Ben spoke of his challenge of coming without his late wife. He praised the crew as an amazing group of talented, caring, fun people, and said he had gained so much more than he had expected. He said he was also very grateful to have experienced the Canyon with his kids. He announced that he planned to take them all to the south rim for one final celebration for his wife. Frank said he was speaking for the "old farts," wishing that more people in their senior years would be willing to come on trips like this. Annie said she was sad to be leaving her sisters, Star, Carla, and Sue, who she described as the most amazing women she'd ever met.

Others spoke of enjoying quiet time with a loved one, away from the stresses of everyday life, how much fun the guides and the rapids were, and how much they didn't want to be leaving in the morning. Finally Guy, who had been uncharacteristically quiet, cleared his throat. He said he had come for a vacation and hadn't wanted to think about work. He'd accomplished that, and much more. He also said he wasn't looking forward to the hike out. We all laughed, knowing exactly what he meant. He finished by saying that as a consultant, part of his job was to help build effective teams. What he had seen on this trip, he told us, was a model of teamwork he'd never imagined possible.

The imposing silhouette of ancient rock drew its undulating outline against the approaching night sky. Upstream, the earth's rotation created a tapestry of moving light as the brilliance of the sun climbed slowly toward the rim, removing brilliant golds, oranges, and reds, the long rays of the spectrum, to be replaced with dull, shadowed cliffs and slopes marching toward darkness.

The river was smooth and quiet. An organic smell of soft earth mingled with the delicious aroma of leftover cobbler. Headlamps danced up and down and side-to-side as passengers laid out their sleeping bags, and guides sat on their coolers writing last-minute odes to missing friends and loved ones. The morning would come soon, with a quick breakfast and an early goodbye to get hikers on the trail. This would maximize their time in the shade before a desiccating sun, enervating trail, and complaining shoulders from too-heavy packs took their toll. After a long, exciting day, sleep was easy.

*After running thirty miles of some of the biggest white water in the country,
we often enjoy a respite in Shinumo, with a cascade of relatively warm
water and a pool in which to play. On this trip, the creek was in flood,
and I was the only person who was foolish enough to go in, not knowing
whether this was the front or backside of the flood.*

DAY EIGHT –
CREMATION TO MONUMENT

It was hard to crawl out of my cocoon after hearing Floyd turn on the blaster to make coffee. It was still dark. The only other sound was Floyd setting up the kitchen. We needed to wake up earlier than usual to make sure the people hiking out would get on the Bright Angel Trail as early as possible. The seven-and-a-half mile trail rises forty-six hundred vertical feet, with the most significant elevation changes occurring in the last three miles. The park service has been kept busy rescuing dehydrated and heat-exhausted tourists who had failed to appreciate how arid the trail was.

Ten years ago one of my passengers was a Philadelphia lawyer who had had major spinal surgery in January. A very bright and pleasant woman, she had been told by her doctor, who had no idea about the harsh conditions in the Canyon, that she shouldn't hike much during the trip to preserve her energy for her hike out. She had been faithful to those orders and hadn't done any hiking. The morning she was to hike out, we emphasized the need for her to drink copious amounts of water, eat plenty of food, take her time on the way up, and rest frequently. She told us she had her cell phone with her just in case she needed help, and was surprised to hear there would be no reception on the trail.

One of the other guides who worked for our company had hiked down the Bright Angel Trail to see his girlfriend, who was on our crew. While hiking back out, he found the lawyer almost unconscious about three miles up the trail. Her respiration was five – very low – and he knew that she needed immediate attention. Someone had run up the trail for help. When a ranger arrived, he assessed her and declared that she was suffering from hypothermia. It is impossible to get hypothermic hiking out the Bright Angel Trail in the summer. In actuality, she was probably suffering from severe heat exhaustion, and her body was in the early stages of shutting down. Bill told the ranger that he taught wilderness medicine and that she couldn't be hypothermic. He is a big man with a deep voice and long hair. For some reason the ranger felt threatened, although Bill said he was only concerned about the woman's well being. When the ranger placed his hand on his gun, Bill just walked away.

After I finished the trip, I heard the story. The ranger had called for a gurney on wheels, and they transported her to Indian Gardens a short distance away, where a helicopter picked her up and flew her to the clinic on the south rim. There she was treated for heat exhaustion and later released. I called the woman in Philadelphia and asked her how she was doing. She told me she was fine, and the ordeal was "really no big deal." Bill told me she could have died.

*   *   *

In 1993, a good friend of mine became a story in the Canyon when he hiked out the BA trail after six days on a private trip. At our trip orientation prior to launching at Lees Ferry, the ranger had warned people to drink plenty of water, saying you just couldn't drink too much water on a river trip. That was the prevailing wisdom at the time. During the trip, I had reinforced that message. Allen took that advice seriously, during the trip and on his hike out. On his way up the trail he noticed an increasing sense of weakness, dizziness, and nausea, possible symptoms of dehydration. He told me he had stumbled into Indian Gardens, just over halfway up the trail. He was disoriented. After being assessed by a ranger, he was flown in a helicopter to the clinic on the south rim. The doctor diagnosed Allen with early stage hyponatremia – water intoxication. This occurs when someone drinks a lot of water and doesn't eat enough protein and salts, diluting the body's sodium, causing cells to swell. When brain cells swell, they put pressure on areas of the brain that can cause organs to fail.

The doctor at the clinic later told me this was one of the earliest diagnoses of what had often been mistaken for dehydration. Allen was told he could remain at the clinic and receive an intravenous saline drip, or he could go to a restaurant down the road and have a steak. He chose the steak. As a result of his and other cases, the park service has altered their orientation to discuss the symptoms of hyponatremia, and how to avoid it. We tell our passengers to make sure they're eating enough protein and getting sufficient electrolytes through salty snacks, especially during long hikes on hot days.

Breakfast was oatmeal, cold cereals, and bagels to load the hikers up on carbs. Most of the hikers had already filled their backpacks, which had been distributed the night before. Last-minute preparations, like a final visit to the groover, filling water bottles, applying sunscreen, and saying goodbye to those who were continuing on the trip, always took more time than planned. Then there were the group photographs. In this case, Eliza offered to be the photographer, and she looked like the quintessential tourist with six cameras hanging around her neck while she photographed all of us standing and sitting on Sue's raft.

After the photographs, Ben asked me whether I had a moment, and walked down by the water upstream of the rafts. As I approached him, I could see his moist eyes shining. He told me it would take a while before he could grasp all the gifts from this trip. What he did know, he said, was even though his wife wasn't here to share the trip with him, it was deeply meaningful to him, and he knew he and his kids would cherish it for a long time. He also told me that he would write me a letter when he had some clarity. He thanked me for the conversations we had had, especially regarding my support of him doing what he loved. And he said his experience swimming House Rock rapid had been a great gift. He said it was the river telling him "take this, old man." It was a wakeup call on his birthday, and he remembered having a huge smile on his face as he was pulled into the raft.

Time to go. Ben had asked if his "family" could take the paddleboat down, and Sue had agreed. Since she would be stopping at Phantom to call the office and deliver and pick up guide's mail, Star agreed to take the paddleboat. All the backpacks were loaded on two other rafts – Michael's and mine. Floyd, Carla, and Sue would take the rest of the passengers with them to Phantom. Floyd wanted to call his wife whom he hadn't seen in over a month because either he had been on the river, or she had been, conducting science trips in the Canyon. Carla had recently hooked up with another one of our crewmates. He hadn't come on this trip, but worked for our company, and she was eager to call him as well.

All the guides had given Sue letters and postcards to mail from the ranch. I had given Sue some money to pick up a package I knew would be there, containing my mom's ginger-molasses cookies. They were always a bit of a mixed blessing for me, because I can go the entire first part of the trip without eating any sugar; but as soon as Mom's Cookies arrive, I'm a goner. They feed my sugar addiction, and for the rest of the trip I wind up succumbing to my sweet tooth. By distributing the cookies to the rest of the crew, I get to share them while minimizing my intake.

Jane and Frank slid into my raft and found comfortable places in the front; Jane was wearing her rain jacket and rain pants to remain dry. She seemed very relaxed and much more comfortable in her body. The tentative way she carried herself at the beginning of the trip had disappeared. Her smile seemed to come straight from her heart. Frank wore a sparkling white tshirt and tan shorts. An old sea dog, he hadn't worn a rain jacket during the entire trip. Guy, Ken, and Diana went with Michael, while Ben, Jeff, Ann, Tom, and Annie settled into the paddleboat for the three-mile float to Pipe Creek beach. Everyone else stood by the river shouting his or her goodbyes. They would be going to Phantom Ranch, about a half-mile from the beach, to relax in the clear, warmer waters of Bright Angel creek, or hike up to the Ranch and write postcards and enjoy ice-cold lemonade. Otherwise they would have to sit around Pipe Creek waiting for the new passengers to arrive. They could also use the phone at the Ranch, but I had discouraged them from that lest they take themselves out of the Canyon. I liked it better when, in the old days, we didn't even stop at Phantom.

It was six thirty, and we would get the hikers on the trail before eight. That would give them a couple hours of hiking in the shade before the sun would find them. The sky was clear – a good sign for us because we would have heat to dry off from the major rapids we would be running with the new passengers. But it was not good for the hikers. The farther up the trail they hiked, the more exposed to the sun they would be, with no relief until they reached Indian Gardens, more than three miles away. There they could relax, use the bathrooms, eat their lunch and prepare for the final assault up the trail.

We floated on a snaking current under a cable strung above us across the river. On the right side, an empty hand-cranked cable car rested, waiting for a ranger or a scientist to come along to measure the river bottom for sediment build-up, or to check the turbidity of the river (how much sediment was being carried in solution by the current, and how far the light penetrated). In the past, rangers used a housing at the other end of the cable to measure river levels. A satellite panel on top has replaced the humans, and the information is beamed to a satellite, which then relays the data to the proper sources. On my first private trip in 1979, a male peregrine falcon with its distinctive slate gray topcoat, heavy dark mustache, white throat, and fine leg feathers like dainty pantaloons, sat on the cable, unperturbed by my presence.

A quarter mile downstream and about eighty feet above the water, the Kaibab suspension bridge spanned the river. An unstable swinging bridge built by the park service had been replaced in 1921 by a stronger bridge after six months of backbreaking work. The current model, completed in 1928, was made of ten 548-foot steel cables, each cable weighing just over a ton. One cable at a time was carried on the shoulders of fifty men, mostly Hualapai Indians, down the seven-and-a-half mile Bright Angel trail, and then another mile-and-three-quarters to the bridge's location. Mule trains – some with people, some with duffels, some with garbage and trash from the ranch and campground – crossed the bridge and headed through a tunnel cut into the schist, either to trudge up the Kaibab trail, or down to the Bright Angel trail and up to the south rim. The riders looked bored, and many peered at us with that "I wish I were down there" look.

We cruised around the corner and the beach disappeared from sight as another bridge loomed up ahead. The Bright Angel suspension bridge not only offered a shorter route to Phantom Ranch from the south rim, it was also instrumental in transporting water. Built in 1970, a water pipeline attached to the underside of the bridge carried water by gravity from Roaring Springs on the north side to Phantom Ranch and Indian Gardens, and from there by pump to the South Rim. The man who had maintained the pumping station since it had first opened in 1969 was a New York City artist who had come out to the Canyon that year for the first time. As the story goes, after spending some time there, he decided he wanted to live in the Canyon. Everyone told him that was impossible, but just by coincidence, an announcement appeared seeking a maintenance man for the about-to-be-opened pumping station at Roaring Springs. Even though he had no experience or skills as a maintenance man, he applied and got the job. He's raised three kids there. Shopping was an inconvenience, to say the least; but that was nothing compared to the effort it took to get to a Little League baseball game. That required a four to six hour hike and road trip, one way. As of this writing he has retired and is living in Flagstaff.

As we floated under the bridge, I pointed out the black pipeline about eight inches in diameter. The river took a sharp bend to the right, and then back to the left, and the current created a minor rapid that required some concentration. After that, we enjoyed a long stretch of swift water before making another sharp turn, this time to the left, and then another back to the right. Up ahead I saw Pipe Creek beach on the left.

Ever since I almost missed the pull-in on my first trip carrying passengers to the beach, I've been a bit more attentive in my approach. The water level back then was high, the current swift. I was the only raft, and wasn't paying enough attention to my location. I found myself out in the middle of the river when I realized where the beach was. It was too late to get over, so my only other option was to try to make it to the lower beach, which was far more difficult to arrange. I quickly faced the back of my raft towards the left shore and began pulling frantically. Over my shoulder I saw three women waving at me: A beautiful blonde named Kelly, her mother, and her aunt. They were from Michigan, and I had booked them on this trip. Wanting to impress Kelly, or at least look like I knew what I was doing, I removed the frantic from my face, and continued pulling. Just as I was about to reach the impossible beach, my friend Dave, the one who had been washed out of the baggage boat in Nevills years earlier, motored by and yelled, "Nice trash run, Charly!" So much for impressing anyone.

I had no trouble pulling over this time. We were in a small eddy parked behind a large rock in the water. At lower water levels the rock is closer to shore and we have to tie our rafts farther upstream. Frank grabbed my bowline and wrapped it around a small sapling behind a narrow beach. Jane remained in her seat for several minutes as I unstrapped the backpacks from my rear hatch. She had been silent during the entire float, and as I handed her backpack to her, I noticed streaks on her cheeks. Still, she had a smile on her face, and seemed ready to tackle the trail out of the Canyon. The paddleboat drifted next to my raft followed by Michael's raft, and everybody climbed out. After offloading all the backpacks, I pulled the lunches out of my cooler and distributed them to each hiker as they were putting on their boots and tidying up their packs. I told them to get wet, ideally by dunking in the river, but in lieu of that, by soaking their shirts and hats. Michael and Star made sure all their water bottles were full, and I added suggestions for stretching after every stop. I also predicted that their lunches would be gone before ten. Since there was only one trail, and one direction – up – we didn't need to send a guide up with the hikers. That has since changed, and now the Park Service requires that a guide accompany the passengers up the trail until he or she meets the hiking guide who is accompanying the new passengers hiking down the trail.

Frank came up to me and gave me a heartfelt hug. He was looking forward to getting his flute, he said, for when he spent time at his cabin on the northwest shore of Vancouver Island. As Ken and Diana passed by me, Ken invited me to visit them in Western North Carolina. I told him I would be in Asheville in the fall and would stop in. Guy lifted his pack, and as he was heading towards the trail said thanks, it was more than he'd expected. I told him to take his time and drink plenty of water. I figured I'd get a report from the new passengers about his condition. I didn't doubt he would make it up the trail, but I was certain it would be a challenge.

Ben and his gang were ready, and I knew I would miss them the most. Ben was such a gentle man, and had been profoundly touched by his experience. In his communications with us he left no doubt how much he respected the crew, and how grateful he was for the time with his family. Tom was still as carefree a spirit as he was at the beginning, only now he could brag about being the first to beat Star in leg wrestling. As he did, making sure Star heard him, she feigned anger and grabbed him in a headlock. They both wrestled a bit and almost ended up in the river. Ben came over and gave me a big hug and looked me in the eyes. I've become used to saying goodbye to my passengers, and I rarely choke up. But seeing Ben's moist eyes and hearing his soft voice saying thank you, touched me deeply.

Finally, Jane and Frank were ready. I told them I would walk a ways up the trail with them. We scrambled over well-worn black schist stepping-stones for fifty yards until we came to the Pipe Creek drainage. It's all up from here, I told them, a big grin on my face that they didn't match. I was glad they had each other as support on the hike. We started up the trail with the clear creek speaking to us from our right, and a stone wall along the side of the trail. We came to a "Y" with one trail heading to the left and upstream a mile-and-a-half to Phantom Ranch, and the other trail to the right going to the South rim. A sign announced the Colorado River, elevation 2400 feet, and warned about strong currents and no swimming.

The trail now had a cliff on the left with pink Zoroaster granite slicing through the Vishnu

Schist, and a built-up stone wall less than two feet high on our right. Across the creek was a stone building used as a shelter from the heat or rain, with an emergency phone that actually worked, from time-to-time.

Fifty feet up the trail we crossed the creek and I told Jane and Frank they would be making two more crossings before they started the real climb. I suggested they get wet at the second crossing, and again reiterated the importance of taking their time, eating, and drinking plenty of water. I then told them I would be saying goodbye. Frank wrapped his arms around me in a bear hug and said I was always welcome at his place. He then headed up the trail. Jane also gave me a big hug, and, choking back tears, told me I would never know how important this trip and our support had been for her. She then gave me a lingering hug. She smelled refreshing and natural, even after seven days in the Canyon. I heard the call of a raven up the trail, along with rushing water and wind rustling through a nearby mesquite tree. With some hesitation, Jane pulled away, and without looking back, walked away. I followed her for a while, listening to her footsteps. I waved and smiled when she turned towards me one last time, feeling a lump in my throat, and then watched as she disappeared around a bend.

PART TWO
LOWER GRAND CANYON
MILE 90 TO MILE 226

When I got back to the beach, Michael had found a spot in the shade and was sleeping, and Star was on her raft straightening it up. The lifejackets had been laid out by size: small-medium, large, and universal. In the shade were cans of fruit juice and V-8 juice cooling down in a bucket of river water for thirsty and possibly dehydrated passengers. The blue backpack bags had been laid out next to the yellow, waterproof clothing bags waiting to become the dresser drawers for a new set of strangers.

I grabbed my shampoo, soap, and a small bucket, and headed over to the creek. It was tempting to bathe in it, but park regulations had banned bathing in any side stream to protect any endangered species. So I filled up my bucket with the warmer creek water, and walked over to the lower beach to bath. After taking off my clothes, I walked into the river until I could dunk my entire body. It had warmed up a bit since Lees Ferry, and felt very refreshing. Deciding that I didn't need the warmer creek water I soaped my body, applied biodegradable shampoo and washed my hair, and then dunked myself one more time. Emerging from the river, I stood with my eyes closed, my skin tingling and feeling the heat of the sun. The sound of Pipe Creek Rapid drowned out the relative trickle of the creek.

It was only 8:30, and we probably had a good hour-and-a-half before any of the new passengers would show up. I thought about the hikers going up the trail and sent them some good thoughts. I figured they'd all make it out, with some, like Ben's family, getting to the rim first, followed by Ken and Diana, then Frank and Jane, and finally, a beet-red, soaked-to-the-skin, heavy-breathing Guy.

Hikers have died on the Bright Angel trail, but to my knowledge no one from a commercial river trip. I'm sure there have been some close calls, like the Philadelphia lawyer. But I'm not up on the rim when they emerge, so I've never seen how they look. I have, however, seen many passengers who have hiked in, and some of them have looked seriously challenged. *One year we had several passengers who were late, so a couple of us hiked up the trail to see if they needed any help. About a mile-and-a-half off the river, just below the Corkscrew – a series of switchbacks with log checks that served as both a stairway and erosion control – I came across*

119

a passenger, who I later found out was the head of a large Chicago financial institution. He looked terrible: sweating profusely, red-faced, and breathing hard. I gave him my brightest smile as I introduced myself as a CanX guide and asked him if he'd like me to carry his pack. "No!" he replied, determined that he was going to carry his load all the way. Twenty yards back was Gordon's wife. When I offered to carry her backpack, her only response was, "Oh thank God."

When we got to the beach, the lunch table had been set up and Gordon slumped against one of the legs and closed his eyes. He seemed to have immediately fallen asleep. A moment later, one of the guides looked at him and asked, "Should we be concerned about this man?" He was being facetious, but he had a point. It turned out that Gordon suffered from sleep apnea, a fact discovered by another passenger, a cardiologist, on the same trip. Gordon had been on another Canyon trip five years before, and on our trip felt discouraged by how much stamina he had lost in the interim. One day, as he and his wife were riding in my raft, he told me I was only person on the crew that he didn't like. Stunned, I asked him why that was, and after a moment he told me because, even though I was older than he was, I could do more than he could. He also said he did like and respect me.

*   *   *

On another trip, my first as a trip leader, we had a complete exchange at Pipe Creek: twenty people hiked out, and twenty hiked in. Several of those hiking in had experienced difficulties; so four crew members had hiked up the trail to see how folks were doing. One man had slightly dislocated his fibula and was hiking in some real pain. A former army Ranger, he at first refused the guide's offer to take a load off his shoulders. However, this guide was Floyd, who can be very persuasive. The man finally agreed to let Floyd carry his pack as long as Floyd would let him carry it the last couple hundred yards to the beach. He didn't want anyone seeing another man carrying his pack.

Another man, in his early seventies, had missed our pre-trip conversations about keeping the weight of his gear down. He brought an oversized backpack so crammed and heavy that he had some difficulties right at the beginning of the hike down. Early on, a slim woman had traded her backpack for his, and she hadn't taken too many steps when the size and weight of the man's pack caused her to fall face first onto the trail. When she arrived at the beach, her eye was purple, but she was smiling.

I erected my umbrella so I could sit on my cooler in the shade. This would help keep the temperature in the cooler, as well as my own, down. Star had done the same thing on her raft. Now it was a waiting game. For the most part these times have been relatively droll: not much happening, except a few hikers, on their way to or from the South rim, to greet as they walked the trail a hundred feet above us. Once, we found a rattlesnake coiled up in the shady corner that Michael currently occupied. It wasn't bothering us, so we didn't bother it. Then a German hiker came by, stopped to ask about the trail to Phantom, and instead of going back to the trail, decided to climb up the steep slope behind our rafts. He had failed to see the snake, but was fortunate that as he began his climb, he had stepped right on the snake's head. He never knew it. The snake, on the other hand, was very aware that something had just happened, and slithered away, perturbed at having his rest period so rudely interrupted.

We were all given a roster of our passengers at the warehouse, and I retrieved mine from my ammo can to see who was coming in. I saw that Jim and Diane were from the Denver area, a half-hour away from my home in Boulder. I always enjoyed meeting my neighbors. A mother and son, Miriam and Tyler, were from South Carolina. I thought there was a typo when I read that Tyler, although only twelve years old, weighed two hundred-and-twenty pounds. I weighed around sixty pounds at that age. Finally there were four Israelis: Liz and her daughter Doron, and Elli and her daughter Roni. I figured Roni and Doron were friends, since they were both fourteen, and concluded that Liz and Elli must also be friends. I'd only had one other Israeli on a past trip, and I was very eager to speak with them to find out what it was like living in Israel with all the fear, uncertainty, and constant tension they must, I thought, have felt.

Around 9:30, the two girls, Doron and Roni, showed up. Roni, an enthusiastic girl with dark hair and dancing eyes, talked nonstop about the hike down, how excited she was to be going on a raft trip, and just couldn't wait to get started. She was a bit chubby, but carried the weight well. As verbal as Roni was, Doron was just the opposite. Her dark hair framed a very pretty but guarded face. She didn't show any feeling, and was more business-like, setting immediately to work unpacking her backpack and transferring her personal stuff into a yellow bag. Ten minutes later, Liz and Elli arrived. Like her daughter, Elli was friendly and extroverted, with a similar body type. Liz, her face flushed by the exertion of the hike down, was more like her daughter – quiet and smoldering. She was a beautiful woman with very curly black hair, a sweet smile emanating from pouty lips, high cheekbones, and mysterious, deep-set, clear black eyes. I introduced myself self-consciously, aware that I was immediately attracted to her. It was not only her looks that drew my attention, but also a certain mystery that she seemed to carry.

I have always enjoyed my passengers, but have rarely been attracted to them. In fact, the last passenger I was really attracted to happened to be on a trip with a large group of women who happened to be lesbians. When this woman arrived at Pipe Creek, the crew assumed she and her friend were also gay. She was perfect for me: very attractive, slim, and warm. Two days into the trip, she found out that we had assumed she was gay, and was quite amused. It was from that trip that I had received my T-shirt that says "Lesbians Love Charlie." The seed had been planted while we were camped around mile 193, with one more full day remaining on the trip. One of the women was sitting in a raft and I was up on shore talking with her. Out of nowhere she said, "Charly, even lesbians love you." I immediately replied "That would make a great T-shirt." Five weeks later, I received one in the mail.

Liz was married, and I knew there was no chance to connect with her, as I would have liked had she been single. About the only thing I could do was to enjoy having a beautiful, mysterious woman on my trip.

Elli told us that Miriam was having some difficulty carrying her pack, so her son was doing double duty. Star and I decided to head up the trail to see if we could help. On the way up, we talked about the folks who had hiked out. Star and Carla had both loved Ben's group, particularly Annie, whose non-stop repartee proved hilarious. Both Star and Carla had great senses of humor, and to find another woman who could match their energy was exciting for them. They had spent a lot of time together, and wherever they went, laughter followed. Sue added to the frivolity with one of the greatest laughs around.

Up ahead we saw a tall woman and a taller boy. He was carrying two backpacks and a huge grin. He walked in a Charlie Chaplin-like waddle, and carried a lot of baby fat. He couldn't be twelve, I thought, and be that big. We introduced ourselves, and I offered to take one of the packs off Tyler's back. He was incredibly polite, saying "Thank you, sir," and I told him to call me Charly. Miriam seemed to be very protective of her son, checking with him regularly to make sure he was all right and drinking enough water.

By the time we reached the beach, the rest of the crew had arrived. Sue handed me a box of Mom's cookies and three letters from friends. The beach was alive with activity. The familiar voices of our veteran rafters mingled with unfamiliar voices and accents. Nathan and Timmy stood together near the rafts, checking out the Israeli girls. Periodically they would whisper something with a quick glance. Floyd's booming voice and laughter, mixed with Sue's laugh and supportive encouragement, set a light note for the new folks, who were efficiently packing their yellow bags. Miriam, a cancer survivor, had bounced back from the hike, and was having an animated conversation with Chris, who had gone over to help her figure out the best way to pack. Mary was settled in the shade of a small bush near the rafts. Graham came up to me and said he had rather enjoyed Phantom Ranch, although the odor of the mules was disconcerting. It seemed that was the price we had to pay to accommodate the mules that carried most of the gear, food, garbage, riders, and mail in and out of the Canyon. No pooper-scoopers allowed.

Finally Sue called all the new passengers together in what little shade remained as the sun approached its zenith. She introduced the passengers who had rafted with us on the upper, introduced the crew, and gave the same safety talk she had at Lees Ferry. She then talked about the paddleboat and said she had room for two more people. Jim and Diane, my neighbors from Denver, quickly volunteered. Jim was a scientist and Diane an artist. Eliza, Jim B, Antje, and Nathan were the other paddlers. Sue said we would be running one major rapid today before lunch. She also said we would find an early camp and may not run any more major rapids until tomorrow. Those plans were contingent on finding no other campers at her intended site.

Miriam and Tyler, who were from South Carolina and sounded like it, asked if they could ride with me, and I welcomed them aboard. I showed them how to fit their mesh bags into the purple day bag and offered to put any camera or sunscreen in the dry box rather than the day bags. I told them it would be easier to get to them in the box. I also asked them if they got cold easily, and if so, they should put on their rain jacket. Both said they were looking forward to being soaked, and I told them I would be happy to comply. The night before, Mary had asked to ride with me, so I helped her into the raft. She moved gingerly to the back and reminded me that she missed her physical therapy session this morning. I told her I'd make up for that at camp.

One by one we pulled out into the current. Floyd carried Chris and Graham, followed by Star with the Israelis, Carla with Timmy and Ralph, Michael with Kathy, and the paddleboat. Liz's life jacket made her look small, almost childlike. I thought I noticed her taking a quick glance in my direction, but maybe she was just looking back at the beach. A small but feisty rapid waited just around the bend. It would be a good introduction for Tyler and Miriam: I told them to notice how the raft moved through the water, and instructed them on how to hold on with one handhold in front and one handhold in back so they had good body control. I told them to use the "chicken line" along the top of the front tube or the loop on one of the "D" rings at the level of their outside knee as the forward handholds, and one of the loops I had tied on the purple day bags as the back handhold. As the first wave hit the front of the raft, I talked to them about leaning into the wave. Tyler understood quickly and enthusiastically. After a few more waves, Miriam was also on board. Seeing how quickly Miriam and Tyler had picked up the lean, I relaxed a little. In ten minutes we would be running Horn Creek, a short but intense major rapid.

We have a saying on the river. "In the Canyon there are only two kinds of guides: those that have, and those that are gonna." At some point almost every guide will flip. *In the early 'nineties, my friend Peggy was running the paddleboat and also leading the trip. We had just said goodbye to a group of returning passengers from Texas, six very strong men who had spent much of the trip in Peggy's paddleboat. Now she had to select from a group of tired, dehydrated, and – from the look of them – far less physically fit men and women who had hiked in. With a brand new crew, we could hear Peggy shouting instructions all the way to Horn Creek: "forward, right turn, stop, left turn, all back, hard forward." Knowing there was a major rapid just downstream was always a great teambuilding motivator. Before entering the rapid, Peggy gave me a look that meant she was not feeling good about her crew. At least it would be a straightforward run that wouldn't involve any maneuvering or bursts of strong paddling. The idea was to enter between the "horns" – humps in the center and right center of the river caused by water flowing over submerged rocks – and hit some very big waves head-on. As the paddleboat was preparing for the entry, a strong sheer wind blowing from left to right seemed to pick up the paddleboat and deposit it to the right of the right horn. A dramatic corkscrew wave then turned the raft over in an instant, ejecting all the paddlers. Welcome to the Grand Canyon. It was Peggy's first flip after forty-five trips, and she was upset, mostly for the trauma that any of her new passengers might be feeling. But it turned out they all had a story, and the trip was only twenty minutes old.*

The river began a sharp left turn, and I focused on staying out of a very swift eddy on the right. On one of my trips, the trip leader had been sucked into that eddy and had made four revolutions before he could escape. The current was so strong that at one point it ripped the oar out of his hand, out of the oarlock, and severed the half-inch tether he had attached to the oar to keep it from floating away should just such an incident occur.

After another sharp bend to the right we entered a calm stretch with metamorphic walls rising straight out of the river, hemming us in. Sue's voice rebounded off the walls as she whipped the paddlers into shape.

While I was resting on my raft at Pipe Creek, I had looked for the marker rock out in the current and just upstream. We knew from past experience that when water flowed over the top of that rock, we could run between the horns. But if the rock was showing, we had to make a tricky right-to-left entry to avoid three huge depressions with big waves. On this day the rock was submerged, so I knew we would have an exciting run between the horns. Of course, I still had to set up my raft to make a good entry. The time I didn't do that proved far too exciting – for me and for my passengers.

We had pulled over on the right to scout the rapid because we had an inexperienced guide rowing the baggage boat. I had three passengers, including a woman who had sprained her knee on the hike down the BA trail. Our rafts were parked just upstream of the rapid, and we would have very little time to set up for our entry. I pushed into the current and pulled out to the middle of the river just as a big wind blew upstream, obscuring the current lines I had intended to follow. Too late I realized that I was too far left. We were going where no one should ever go. I quickly straightened out my raft, told my passengers to hold on tight, and slammed into a hole at the top, then bumped through a series of pourovers, one of which was so violent my passenger in the back, the woman with the bad leg, would have been ejected had she not been holding on tightly. She did grab some pretty good air, I later heard. I felt embarrassed at having missed my entry, and avoided eye contact with my crewmates, who were not at a loss for words. "Nice run, Charly. I didn't know you could do that one." "Congratulations for pioneering a new run, Charly." I heard about it for the rest of that trip.

We watched as first Floyd, then Star entered between the horns and dropped out of sight. Tyler was at first aghast when he saw Floyd's raft disappear after his entry, until I told him to keep watching. When Floyd's head popped back up downstream, Tyler let out a held breath and smiled sheepishly. I looked over my shoulder and Mary flashed me a smile of confidence. The roar of the rapid was increasing as it bounced off the closed-in schist cliffs, and the smell of excitement permeated the air. I told everyone things were about to speed up and get very big, and reiterated the need to "kiss those waves," whether they came from the front (ideally), or the side (not preferred). The raft dipped as we slid down the smooth, sensuous tongue into the throat of Horn Creek. We raced past boat-flipping holes on both sides, and straight ahead loomed three huge waves, each preceded by a deep trough. We slammed into the first wave, and both Tyler and Miriam kissed it. I yelled as loudly as I could, telling them they were awesome as we slammed into the second, and then immediately the third. We were soaked, and exhilarated. Tyler let out a loud whoop, releasing the pent-up energy of months of waiting for this trip, the stresses of travel and hiking down the BA trail, and the anxiety of not knowing what the big water would be like.

I yelled for them to bail as my raft slid off a wave toward the left wall that seemed to be moving out to meet us. I pulled hard on my right oar, turned the raft toward the left shore, and cranked on both oars to get into the eddy just upstream of the jutting wall. Here I could run safety for the paddleboat that was just entering the rapid. Eliza and Antje were in the front, digging frantically to gain enough momentum to break through the huge waves. They disappeared into the trough and rose up the wave, cresting at the top, almost stalling out before sliding down the backside into the next trough. I could see the bottom of the raft as it seemed to hesitate at the top of the next wave, and hear Sue's voice exhorting her crew to "Dig!" They came out of the second wave a little sideways and all had to high side into the third wave. They all yelled and looked exhilarated as they touched their paddles high over their heads before slapping them on the water.

By now all the newcomers had been initiated, and we were headed for the first shady spot for lunch. I asked Miriam to tell me about herself and Tyler. She told me she had raised him as a single parent from the age of four. She was a cancer survivor, and Tyler had become her best friend through the ordeal. That explained why, in spite of his age and childlike demeanor, he seemed more mature than most twelve-year-olds: Tyler had been forced to grow up early. Miriam also told me that both of them were outdoor enthusiasts, and they had spent a lot of time in the marshes around their home in Sumpter, South Carolina. I asked Tyler what he had thought about his Grand Canyon trip, and he said he was really looking forward to seeing lizards. A shy, boyish grin enveloped his chubby, child-like face as sunshine set his blond hair on fire.

The basement rock of the Canyon, the Vishnu Schist, rose out of the water on both sides of the river. This was "normal" for the newcomers. It was all they knew. Those who had been with us from the beginning had met each of the nine Cambrian layers, and parts of the Grand Canyon Supergroup and schist below, one layer at a time. They had floated through the sheer confines of Marble Canyon, watched the Canyon widen dramatically in the Palisades of the Desert, and experienced the closing in of the Canyon as we entered the inner gorge. Our eight new passengers had hiked down through each of those upper layers, but with no one to interpret and explain the different formations, they had no understanding of the geology. Now they were at the bottom looking up, and for many passengers it was just too overwhelming to learn the layers and grasp the scale, both in terms of its sheer size and its extreme age.

The sun beat down on us from directly overhead and shade was at a premium. Sue had not indicated where she planned to pull over for lunch, but I figured it could be at "Wanna-Be Trinity" (actually 91-Mile Creek), a beach with lots of sand and a few tammies for partial shade. Or we could go downstream another half mile to Trinity itself. If we went there, we would probably carry the table up the side canyon to find enough shade to put out the lunch, which today would be a deli menu.

We passed "wanna-be" so I maneuvered my raft towards the right shore in anticipation of the pull-in at Trinity. There was a strong current coming off the right shore that pushed hard to the left just upstream of the side canyon. On one trip I hadn't realized how strong it was, and I barely made the pull-in. Fortunately there was a long eddy, and I was finally able to pull in and float back upstream. The power of the Colorado, even in the calm stretches, is so great that it is practically impossible for all but the strongest guides to row against the current. Since I had been the lunch boat on that trip, we would have been forced to find another shade spot downstream. No one said anything at the time, but there were "those" looks.

Sure enough, Floyd started to pull in to the narrow beach at Trinity. After making sure I was inside that strong current line, I relaxed and cruised in next to Star. Carla came in next, and we helped her de-rig the front of her raft so we could get to the table, three cutting boards, the sheath of knives, the "lunch" can, and the fruit that had remained cool under the hatch. Carla's front hatch lacked a permanent cover. Instead, the table had been manufactured to nestle smoothly on top, providing the lid.

Floyd carried the table across a small sandy area often used for campsites, down into a draw and up a cobble-strewn, dry creekbed to a place next to the left wall that provided shade. I carried the lunch can and the knives, Michael came up with a bucket full of fruit and produce, and Star arrived with the rest of the food and the "utes" can. A six-gallon water jug was pulled off the front of my raft and set on the beach along with the "drinks" can that contained Gatorade, lemonade, and Erg. A pump container of hand soap remained near the water for people to wash before lunch. We had a container of hand sanitizer at the table for the final bacterial elimination process.

Sue had assembled the eight new passengers in a small shaded area down by the river, and was giving them information about sanitation, river etiquette, peeing below the high water line, micro-trash, and other pre-camp essentials. After that, everyone devoured their lunch while

Mary remained down by the river soaking her foot. Eliza, who had grown up in a very loving community surrounded by adults at every turn, made a sandwich and carried it down to her. She was not only comfortable around older people; she loved them.

While we were cleaning up after lunch, Sue said she wanted to make it a short river day, and planned to camp at Monument, just upstream of the next major rapid. Since there was plenty of shade there, she said we should head down and snag the camp before anyone else. There was a very real possibility that hikers or a private trip would already be there, and if that were the case, Schist camp would be the fallback. It was downstream of Hermit, the third of four major rapids in the first eight miles of the lower Canyon. While Hermit was my favorite rapid, I agreed with Sue that an early camp would be best for the folks who had hiked in. In the morning, they would be more refreshed, be able to enjoy the big water, and be more active on the rafts, something that could be crucial in those major rapids.

The one-and-a-half mile float to Monument was very mellow, interrupted only by one small rapid at Salt Creek. I managed to get both Miriam and Tyler wet, and offered no apologies. After all, I told them, there was a reason that this was known as the wet boat. They took it in a good-natured way. As we floated, I thought about the folks hiking out. By now some may have reached the rim – maybe Jeff, Tom, and Annie. The rest would probably be past Indian Gardens and trudging up the many switchbacks in the top three cliff-forming layers. I then looked at Miriam and Tyler, checked out the Israelis in Star's raft, and Jim and Diane in the paddleboat, and felt good about the new passengers. Liz and Doron were in the back and seemed to be napping. The guides were regaling the others with stories and jokes. No doubt we would continue to have fun on the lower end.

Large eddies on either side of the snaking current below Salt Creek slowed us down to a crawl. The river had opened up a bit, but just ahead the ancient walls were again closing in, and then opening back up. Downstream of the narrowed section lay our camp at Monument Creek. I couldn't see any rafts there, so if there were no hikers, the camp would be ours. Even if there were hikers, we could probably work something out with them. A freshly prepared dinner with dessert and beer would offer a great incentive to be flexible and neighborly.

In fact there were hikers camped at the lower end of the beach. Sue went down to talk with them and came back with a thumbs-up. She told us it was a man from Flagstaff and his two daughters, and they had no problem with us camping there. The roar of Granite Rapid filled our ears as we unloaded our rafts. A long, narrow, hard-packed beach perhaps a hundred-fifty yards long, covered the length of the camp. A thick grove of tamarisk trees forty feet deep stretched out behind the beach, backed up by granite-encased schist walls. The groover was placed in a stand of willow saplings upstream of the kitchen, which was located in a grove of tammies right in front of the rafts. The roar of the rapid would drown out the early morning sounds of breakfast being prepared. This would allow us to sleep a little longer. Except for Carla and me, the cook crew *du jour*.

It was only three o'clock, and Sue suggested that people set up their campsites and relax for a couple hours. She announced that when they heard the conch blow to signal that the hors d'hoeuvres were ready, everybody should assemble around the serving table for one last orientation talk. I told Carla I would be happy to bake the cherry cobbler that was on the menu, and since we had at least two hours before beginning, I would probably bake the dessert early. All I would need was three eggs. The rest was already up in the kitchen.

I walked up to the kitchen and looked at the rest of the menu: Greek chicken, tabouli, green salad, and tarragon bread, with crackers and cheese for hors d'hoeuvres. Easy enough. I walked through the camp and checked in on the new passengers to make sure they were set up and didn't have any questions. Miriam and Tyler had found a spot at the far end of the beach, and Tyler was busy checking out the tadpoles in the small pools in the Monument creek drainage. Jim and Diane were napping behind the kitchen, and the Israelis had found home in an open area surrounded by tammies. I asked if everything was okay and Roni took time away from reorganizing her yellow bag to say all was just great. She had a wonderful smile, and an air of confidence that impressed me. Liz had put up a tent, and I advised her not to lay out her sleeping bag until she was ready to get in it, to avoid any unexpected company at night. I didn't mean it to have a double meaning, but I was relieved when she flashed a shy smile and thanked me for my concern.

As I walked back to my raft, Sue called for a crew meeting. After everybody had selected his or her beverage of choice, we gathered on Floyd's raft. Sue began by thanking us for making the exchange go so smoothly. She then said she planned to run the rest of the inner gorge the next day and camp either upstream or downstream of Elves. We were currently at mile 93, and Elves Chasm was located at mile 116. So that meant the next day we would cover up to twenty-five river miles, the most of any day thus far. It would actually be pretty easy, assuming no mishaps to slow us down. The current was fast in this section, and we would be running three major rapids, stopping at one to photograph the runs, and at another to scout. Otherwise, it would be a wild and wonderful whitewater day.

We talked about the folks who had hiked out, particularly Ben and his family, who were clearly our favorites. Michael mentioned he'd had some really interesting conversations with Ken. I spoke about Jane and what a breakthrough experience it had been for her, and Star surprised us by saying that Guy had confided in her just before he hiked out, saying how moved he had been being in the Canyon, and how impressed he was with the crew. No one seemed to miss him, but we had to admit he had come a long way.

We talked briefly about the new passengers, sharing information we had gleaned on our rafts. The early consensus was we had a good group, and Tyler seemed to stand out as someone to watch. We weren't concerned about him, just curious how such a childlike kid could also seem so . . . adult-like.

I went back to my raft and checked my mail. Mom's cookies were well packed, and I decided to distribute them early. I went up to the kitchen and found six ziplock baggies and divided the cookies in equal amounts. When I had the chance, I would deliver the cookies, dropping them on each cooler top for the guides to discover. I decided to check out my three letters after dinner. Then I went over to the dairy cooler, took out three eggs, and set about making dessert.

The camp was now quiet, except for the roar of the rapid, which had by now become white noise and had lulled some folks to sleep. The song of the yellow-breasted chat was the only other sound. All the rafts had been strapped together and were floating calmly in an unruffled eddy. Star, Michael, Floyd, Eliza and Sue had hiked up Monument Creek to check out any changes since their last visits. Carla was lying on her cooler underneath a large red umbrella, reading one of Dan Brown's books. Life was good in our office.

At 4:30, Carla began shopping. From the meat cooler she removed thirty, eight-ounce chicken breasts; three pounds of havarti cheese, peeled garlic, a half-pound of butter, and a pound of feta cheese from the dairy cooler; and four cukes, three head of iceberg lettuce, and ten tomatoes from the produce cooler. Finally, from her rear hatch she located three loaves of French bread and six lemons. We carried this up to the kitchen, washed our hands, and first prepared the hors d'hoeuvres by slicing up the cheese and laying it out on plates with crackers in the center. By now the rest of the crew had returned, and after putting the hors d'hoeuvres on the serving table, Carla blew the conch. Immediately, hungry campers surrounded us, and Sue began the same camp orientation she had given on night one.

While we prepared dinner, the crew handled the orientation with Floyd finishing up with his rousing groover talk. I could hear Roni's high-pitched laugh even over the roar of the rapid. Carla prepared the chicken, and after removing the cobbler from the coals, I fixed the salads and the tarragon bread. I added one item to the bread menu by grating up some cheddar cheese. After melting butter, and sautéing it with some garlic, I added the tarragon, pasted the French bread halves, and put them face down on the heated grill. After the bread toasted for a minute, I turned it over, sprinkled the grated cheddar, and again placed the wet side face down to melt the cheese. Each loaf was cut up into small cross sections and put in a pot.

After placing the chicken, bread, and salad on the serving table, we announced dinner, which didn't last very long. Again we received kudos for another great meal, and some of the new passengers, Tyler and Roni in particular, couldn't believe they were eating a baked dessert, with whipped cream no less.

While we enjoyed dessert, Sue announced her plans for the next day. She told everyone who was interested in the paddleboat that she would have the same crew for the first few big rapids in the morning, and then others could switch out if they wanted. She also said we would be doing a picture run in Hermit in the morning, and people who were particularly interested in taking photos should check with me because I would be taking photos as well. As I was closing up the kitchen, making sure no food was left out for any marauding ringtails, Liz came up to me and said she had a pretty new Nikon camera, and was very interested in learning more about photography.

We sat on the com box and talked for awhile. I found out she was happily married and had a son as well as Doron. Her husband and son had been to the Canyon two years before and had encouraged her to go. Elli was her best friend, and she had invited her and Roni along. They planned to meet their husbands after the trip and tour around more of the western United States. I was even more taken by her after talking to her, and reminded myself that she was married and I was a professional.

I told her a bit about my experiences with photography, beginning with my first photograph when I was in the fourth grade being published in my local newspaper. It was of an automobile accident at the end of my block. I was on my way to school, raced home to get my mom's Brownie Hawkeye camera, raced back and took the shot. One showed a car "T'-boning" another car against a light pole, the ambulance and paramedic tending to an injured man, the police car, and a cop writing a ticket. I told her I had no idea how the photo wound up in the paper, but it hadn't occurred to me that I might have a future in either photography or the newspaper business. I didn't pick up a camera again for another sixteen years, when my brother, on his return from a stint in the Peace Corp in Nepal, gave me his Minolta. I started out taking black-and-white available-light candid photos of people. My brother Sandy and I built our own darkroom, and we got pretty good at developing. I always went in with a great degree of anticipation to see what would magically appear in the developing solution.

In 1973 I went on a canoe trip in Quetico Provincial Park in western Ontario, part of a landscape photography workshop with Kryn Taconis, a Dutch-Canadian "Life Magazine" photographer. It was my first experience with color photography, and I embraced it with gusto. I got even more involved after my girlfriend gave me a bellows that extended the focal plane of my camera and allowed me to take close-up shots of flowers, ice crystals, lichen, critters, and more. It opened up a whole new visual world.

When I started working in the Grand Canyon, my whole focus shifted, and today images of the Canyon are all I shoot. I told Liz that my photos had been published in a coffee-table book, which I would be happy to show her in the morning. She said she would like that, said goodnight, and headed off to her tent. I went down to my raft and had a brief conversation with Eliza as she lay in her sleeping bag. She said the day had been quite enjoyable even though she would have preferred to keep the same people for the whole trip. I told her it was not my preference either, but felt the new folks would be just as enjoyable in a different way. Before I could finish the sentence, she had fallen asleep. So I settled under my sheet and felt my body relax. Listening to the growl of Granite, I allowed myself a few dreamy thoughts, took a couple of deep breaths that sounded more like sighs, and prepared for sleep.

My favorite rapid, running Hermit is like being on a liquid, high-energy roller coaster, where the first five waves just get bigger. The Fifth Wave always elicits exclamations of "Oh My God" as we look up at a rising, living mountain of water from the bottom of the swell. This photo was taken on an August trip when Rio Colorado was truly a river running red.

DAY NINE –
MONUMENT TO BASS CAMP

My alarm went off at 4:30, and the abrupt wake-up made me wonder whether the regular use of an alarm clock actually shortened people's life expectancy. I stretched, reluctantly stuffed my sheet, pillow, and sleeping bag into my waterproof black bag, put on my shorts and a fleece shirt, slipped into my sandals, grabbed the bacon, eggs, and fruit Carla had placed in my cooler last night, and headed for the kitchen, just twenty feet away. I lit the blaster to heat the coffee water, and one burner on the stove to heat the tea water. Each night, as we closed up the kitchen, one of our last chores was to fill up the coffee and teapots with river water. I kept the blaster down so as not to disturb the nearby sleepers. Upstream, the night was starting to surrender to first light. A gray streak at the horizon stretched across the river, topped by darker shades of gray, dissolving into blue black, then to black at the zenith. Polaris sat between the upstream cliffs, still holding on to its fading light. The early morning chill nipped at my bare legs.

On a trip in the late 'eighties, I was on cook crew and had volunteered to get up early to put on the coffee water. I had no alarm clock, and found myself waking up periodically, looking at the constellations as if they would tell me the time, until finally deciding it was the appointed hour. It seemed awfully dark, but I went up and lit the blaster. I then decided to put the bacon on early to help move breakfast along more quickly. I opened up the kitchen, sliced the fruit, made the juice, and set up the condiments. My cooking partner was still asleep, and I was getting perturbed, accusing him in my mind of being lazy and letting me do all the work. Finally I went over and woke him up. He checked his watch. It was 3:45, still an hour before we were supposed to put the coffee on. That morning everybody woke up to the smell of both bacon and coffee. To this day, some of those on the crew remind me of the midnight bacon party.

In addition to the French toast and the six pounds of bacon, I had a carton of frozen eggs, two cantaloupe, and two grapefruit. After washing my hands, I placed a clean Dutch oven on the stove, dumped the bacon in, and turned the heat to medium-low. It would take forever for the bacon to cook, and one of us just needed to check it periodically and turn it over to avoid burning it. I then grabbed my favorite knife out of the scabbard along with a medium-sized

Charly Heavenrich

bowl, and cut the melons and grapefruit into bite-sized wedges. Carla came up, gave me a hug, and started putting the condiments on the serving table. She said she would handle the French toast, and I told her as soon as the coffee was ready, I would put water on for the pasta, since we were scheduled for pasta salad for lunch.

I had great respect for Carla and her brother Albert. Both worked on the river and were incredibly competent and knowledgeable for their ages: Carla was twenty-seven and Albert twenty-one. I had first met Albert on a private trip in Utah where he had saved a woman's life from a near drowning. Carla was very attractive, very athletic, and very competitive, especially around Star. I've been an athlete my whole life, competing at the highest collegiate levels in baseball, and I don't believe I've ever played with or against two more competitive people than Carla and Star. Whether it's flipping plates to see how many they can do in a row, playing horseshoes, or leg wrestling, they both hate to lose.

The Canyon was now light enough to see details in the wall across the river. Upstream of the rapid, the river was deceptively calm, displaying a perfect reflection of nearly two billion-year-old rock. A still photo would not have revealed the chaos just downstream of such a peaceful scene. There was absolutely no visual evidence of what we would be running immediately after shoving off.

The bacon was cooking nicely, and we blew the conch for coffee and tea. Graham came up to grab coffee for him and tea for Chris. No one else seemed to be in a hurry to throw off the covers, so Carla and I filled the coffee cups of the rest of the crew and delivered them to their rafts. It's a nice little touch – coffee in bed. Seeing this, Antje, who was sleeping closest to the kitchen, asked what about her, in her perfect English tinted by a German accent. I asked her where her cup was and how she preferred her coffee. She said cream and two scoops of sugar. I brought it to her, and she smiled her thanks. Antje was a delightful, very independent businesswoman. She had worked for several years in Taiwan, and had opened her company's offices in Beijing. She was a frequent world traveler, outspoken without being overbearing, attractive, but clearly not looking for a relationship. After more than two decades as a guide, I have become familiar with the energy and signals (subtle and not so subtle) women who want to communicate their availability give out. I say this more as an observer rather than a common recipient of this energy.

One of the few times I got involved with a passenger, it turned out to be a less-than-favorable experience. We were on a string quartet trip in the early 'nineties, about two-thirds of the way through. One of the passengers had attended a workshop I had taught the year before, and after dinner one evening told me how much value she had derived from the experience. She said she wanted to show her appreciation, and asked if I would allow her to give me a massage. I never turn down a massage, especially on a river trip where I'm usually the one giving them, and told her it would be great. We found a fairly private place on the beach behind some tammies, and before she began I thought it best to be clear that while I was grateful for the massage, I didn't want it to go beyond that. She agreed and gave me a delightful massage – that did go beyond that.

A string quartet trip demands more work from the crew than a regular trip, and in the morning I involved myself in helping the quartet get set up for their concert. It wasn't until the day before my first trip the following season that I was told that she had been upset that I had "used" her and then ignored her. Evidently she had confided in a woman who was from

132

the company office, who had relayed her complaint to management. I was told about it at a debriefing before my first trip. I was told if I couldn't pull it off, I shouldn't do it.

In the old days, it was not uncommon for a passenger to hook up with a river guide. There is far less of that happening today, in part because there are more couples and families on our trips. However, I can't say it's a thing of the past either.

Slowly the rest of the passengers began showing up for coffee, tea, juice, and hot chocolate. Jim and Diane were the first of the new folks to show up, then Miriam, Elli, and finally Liz. She still had that "I'm not quite awake" look in her eyes, which only made her more attractive. After fixing her coffee, she asked me if it would be inconvenient to see the coffee table book. I told her it was easy, went to my raft and pulled it out of my ammo can. It was a book with a controversial theme. The text is an assemblage of vignettes from twenty-three authorities, most of whom had PhDs in some evolutionary science like geology and ecology. They were also young earth creationists, and the text was an attempt to establish credibility for their point of view, which involved a literal interpretation of the Creation story in Genesis. While those who embrace an evolutionary perspective on the geology of the Grand Canyon say the schist is close to two billion years old, young earth creationists, who don't accept evolution, and interpret the creation week as a literal twenty-four hour, seven-day week, believe the earth is slightly more than six *thousand* years old.

In fact, some say the actual date of the earth's formation was determined in the mid-eighteenth century to be October 23, 4004 BC. The Grand Canyon, the thinking goes, was formed in three stages: Stage One was during the Creation Week when the basement rock (the metamorphic schist) was formed. Then, during the next fifteen hundred real years, the sedimentary and igneous pre-Cambrian layers (known in part as the Grand Canyon Supergroup) were formed. Finally, a catastrophic global flood lasting a year brought all nine Cambrian layers to the area of the Grand Canyon. The first seven months of floodwater filled with sediment rushed into the area of the Canyon and laid down what would be known as the Cambrian layers of limestone, sandstone, and shale. During the last five months of the flood, the waters receded and carved the Canyon. While I am the chief photographer for this book, I do not embrace the young earth beliefs.

I gave the book to Liz, told her a bit about its background, and returned to the kitchen, where it was time to serve breakfast. Sue gave her morning talk indicating this would be a whitewater day, and reiterated her comments of the night before that she would start the day with the same paddleboat crew, but later would switch out some if others wanted to be in the paddleboat. Nathan and Jim B said they wanted to go, and Timmy said he would love to go in the ducky. Ralph wasn't happy when Sue said we would get the duckies out after all the big water. I assumed it was because he was concerned for the safety of his son. Timmy, on the other hand, didn't even try to conceal his excitement. Ever since Michael had helped him with his self-rescue at the Little Colorado, he had become a superstar in the ducky. Now he had a smile on his face more often than not.

Cleaning up after breakfast, my thoughts turned to the big water we would be running. The water level would peak around eighteen thousand cfs. Granite would be big, fast, and chaotic. The "Oh my God wave" in Hermit would be mammoth, and Crystal would definitely be a right run. Because it was early in the day, we wouldn't have the maximum flows, but they would still be huge and fast. Liz came over and asked if the four of them could ride with me, and I said I would be delighted to have them. She asked if I'd ever flipped in Granite, and I said I hadn't. In fact, I'd only seen two flips there, and only one of them was on a CanX trip.

I was pleased to have the Israelis in my raft, not only because of Liz, but also because I was interested in learning more about what it was like living in Israel. I also knew very little about Judaism. Growing up, I always felt more comfortable with my mom's family, in spite of having a father whose family was Jewish. For reasons he had kept to himself, he had not exposed us to any aspects of Judaism, opting instead to allow my mother to raise us as Protestants. Given my father's personality, I had always assumed he did this to protect us from the discriminations to which the Jews had historically been subjected.

We took some extra time to rig the rafts with the attention to detail required on big-water days. I was excited that we would be running so many fun rapids, although in the early years, when we were doing twelve-day trips instead of the sixteen days on this trip, we used to run the entire inner gorge in one day. We would often begin at Nevills at mile seventy-six and run Hance, Sockdolager, Grapevine, Zoroaster, and Horn Creek, in addition to all the rapids we would be running today. That meant thirty-two river miles and eighteen rapids rated six or higher. By the end of that day, we were all drained, and still had to prepare dinner.

When the Israelis came down with their day items, I showed them how to pack the day bag, inviting them first to give me their sunscreen and cameras that I would put in the more handy ammo can at my feet. Liz had a video camera as well as her 35mm Nikon, which I put in the can. Roni, speaking first, said she and Doron wanted to ride in the front. I said that would be fine, except in Hermit where I would probably have three of them up front. Doron asked why, and I told her it would be better if I showed her when we got there. I had spoken with Sue at breakfast and offered to be the only raft taking photos. That way I could take shots of everyone except those in my raft, and since I had become pretty good in these picture runs, the chances were that my photographs would be better than the rest, especially those with point-and-shoot cameras. She agreed, so as soon as everyone had made it through Granite safely, I would take off and go down to Hermit to get set up.

We shoved off and floated slowly up the eddy, waiting for the rest of the rafts to untie. I looked for Eliza, and she was busy helping close up the almost-waterproof bags on the paddleboat. She looked up and flashed me a big smile. She had made a good connection with the three women on the crew, and I was glad for that. But she had spent less time with me than I had hoped. As an uncle, I have not been geographically near my nephews and nieces, and have felt that I should have done more to be a good influence in their lives. This trip was my chance to be an uncle and make a deeper connection with Eliza. While I was happy that she was having such a good time, I was also disappointed that we hadn't had any of those conversations I had envisioned.

The running order would be the same as yesterday, with Floyd leading and Michael sweeping. The paddleboat would run fourth, behind me. Roni was carrying on a nonstop dialogue with anyone who would listen, about her hike down, about sleeping in the Canyon for the first night, and about how wonderful she thought the Canyon was. I interrupted her to talk about safety. I told them this was a very big rapid and it would seem very fast, and very chaotic. I showed them their handholds, and told them to hold on tight with both hands. I talked about highsiding and how to anticipate from which direction the water was approaching. I also told them in the highly unusual event that one of them fell out of the raft and wound up in one of the micro-eddies along the wall in the first half of the rapid, that they would have to swim out into the current, no matter how big it looked. There would be no way for us to get back upstream to rescue them because of the size of the water. Finally, I talked about King George Eddy on the right below the wall. If any of them wound up there, and there were no rafts to pick them up, they should follow the current around to the far shore and then get out of the river and walk downstream, where a raft could pick them up. Furrowed brows and wide eyes told me I was scaring them, so I tried to reassure them that all this was necessary to say, but very unlikely to occur. Roni was the only one who seemed unperturbed.

Floyd let out a raucous cry that startled Doron. Chris, Graham, and Mary were in his raft, with Mary in her usual spot in the back. Star had Nathan and Kathy in her raft. We watched as first Floyd, then Star, slid down the glassy-smooth tongue and disappeared. I was focused on making my entry on the left side of the tongue, remembering in the early years that we entered on the right of the tongue. I didn't care to chance getting stuck in one of the micro-eddies along the wall, so I was being a bit more conservative. Even so, I knew I would be funneled into the thick of the chaos, and we would take our licks. Just before dropping in, I saw Floyd's raft at the end of the rapid, and Star slamming into the big wave two-thirds of the way down. "Hold on tight," I yelled. "Primal screams are absolutely encouraged!"

Roni let out a wild scream as the raft reared up, lifted by the left lateral at the entry. I pushed through and then turned my raft to the right to meet one of the waves coming off the wall. Then we were in the midst of monster waves charging us from all directions. I kept my focus in front of me, relying on my peripheral vision to let me know where to face the raft. By now all the Israelis were screaming and laughing. I yelled to lean left, but no one seemed to hear, and then we were slammed off-center by the biggest wave, turning my raft sideways. As we climbed up the first of a series of large tail waves, I yanked hard on my upstream oar to turn and face the waves backwards. "Equal opportunity boating," I yelled, as both Liz and Elli screamed as they were doused. I was on the right side of the current and had to work hard to avoid getting sucked into the eddy. Star was already there, so I decided to pull over on the left side to run safety for the paddleboat. My raft was heavy and sluggish with all the water it had taken on. "Bail," I yelled to my passengers, as I continued to pull hard on my oars.

By the time I found an eddy on the left side, Michael was entering the rapid. He had a great run, and the paddleboat was already celebrating with their paddle-slapping ritual, so I pulled out into the current and headed downstream towards Hermit. It took fifteen minutes of bailing before I said it was ok to relax, and we were then entertained by Roni who couldn't stop talking about how thrilling Granite was, and that she wished we could go back and do it again. Elli said she was fine until we had turned sideways, and then she got a bit concerned. Liz said she loved getting soaked, but Doron remained silent.

I told everyone we would hit one small rapid before coming to Hermit. Once we were there, I would tie us up to shore and then we had to hustle to get into place to photograph the rafts as they came through one-by-one. I told them that Hermit was my favorite rapid because it was just like a big roller coaster ride. Each of the first five waves gets bigger than the one preceding it, I said, and the tail waves were also capable of flipping the raft if we didn't stay alert. Doron asked me if I had ever flipped in Hermit, and I told her to ask me after our run. Then I quickly told them some stories of past Hermit runs.

One of our favorite guides was Jimbo, the last of the great hippie boatmen. He had been rafting since the early 'seventies, and had actually been the main character in an independent film, The Same River Twice, about a group of private trippers who had rafted the Canyon in the early 'seventies. Most of the time they were naked, and Jimbo was the primary advocate for enjoying wherever they were with his "be here now philosophy." As a river guide he was unique. He could take twenty minutes to clean a DO, and his only commands from the back of the paddleboat were "forward please," and "stop please." That was when he was in the back of the paddleboat. Jimbo was an equal opportunity paddleboat captain, constantly playing musical seats, rotating his passengers regularly, including the captain's seat. On that particular trip, when running Hermit, Jimbo decided to give no commands. Instead he had his folks ship their oars and go with the flow. They made it through without incident. I don't know any other guide that could or would do that.

I prefer being on the oars and haven't wanted to captain the paddleboat, in part because I'm a bit nervous about it, in part because I love the dance I have with the river when I'm rowing. *However, once, on a training trip, I did captain a very light, fourteen-foot raft through Hermit. The water was at a pretty high level and I was nervous as hell. My crew consisted entirely of river guides, all accomplished paddleboat captains. In fact, Michael was sitting directly to my left. We entered the top of the rapid and I felt we were a tad too far left to hit the middle of the fifth wave; so I called a right turn and an immediate forward. Michael said "perfect timing" to me, which made me feel good, but we were racing towards the fifth wave, and all I could do was urge my crew to paddle hard. We climbed up the fourth wave that was so big I thought for a moment I had miscounted. But as we careened down the backside of that wave, I looked up and saw a mountain of water. I think that's when I christened it the "Oh my God" wave. We climbed the massive mound of snarling, expanding water, and just as we reached the top, seemed to hesitate for an instant. Just an instant. But in that moment I felt like I was on the top of the world. As we cruised down the backside of the wave and enjoyed the larger-than-expected tail waves, I felt ecstatic.*

Roni was listening intently. "Oh my God," she said, "and we're going there?" I nodded my head, and looked back at Elli and Liz, who didn't seem nearly as enamored. As I moved the raft closer to the left shore, I told them they were going to love it. Downstream on river left, a long narrow beach bordered by tammies pushed out into the river which suddenly disappeared. The low growl of Hermit drifted upstream on a soft breeze. It was a different sound than we had yet heard, and I felt some anticipation as I told everyone we were going to pull over and tie up, and then head down by land to the Fifth Wave. I reached into the dry can for Tal's cameras and handed them to her. I asked Doron if she would grab the bowline, but Roni jumped up and said she would do it. I told her to wait until we were right at the shore before she jumped out because the river was deep here. She complied, and held on to the line until I could take it from her and tie us up to one of the obliging tammies. I then offered to help everyone off the raft. For a split second I locked eyes with Liz as I grabbed her hand. It was enticingly soft, and I wondered how my calloused hands felt to her. She shot me a shy smile and then averted her eyes.

Looking upstream, I saw the other rafts floating slowly towards us. I jumped back on board and opened my ammo can that was secured to the deck immediately to the left of my cooler/seat. I removed the wide-angle lens, and replaced it with my telephoto. Earlier in the day, I had put in a new roll of film. I closed the lid and jumped off the raft, telling everyone I would be walking quickly to get down to the rapid in time to set up. I still needed to establish my exposures. After all these years I still have not recorded my settings, so have to check them each time I do this picture run.

We walked along a narrow sandy trail cut in the grass by thousands of human footsteps, crossed a warm, clear stream coming out of the Hermit drainage, ducked through a grove of willow saplings, and emerged into a sandbar strewn with river-polished boulders. The vibration of the rapid was now rising out of the ground, through my sandals, up my legs, and into the core of my body. The roar sounded like standing next to the railroad tracks with my eyes closed while listening to a speeding freight train. I stopped for a moment and told Elli, since she wasn't taking photographs, she could head straight to the river and watch as the rafts entered the top of the rapid. Doron, Roni, and Liz said they wanted to go where I was going, so we picked up the pace. A row of tammies blocked much of our view, except where I intended to set up for the picture run. A twenty-foot clearing opened up where the fourth and fifth waves had formed. The decibels were so high we had to yell to hear each other. I pointed out a good spot to Liz for shooting, and then walked down near the river directly across from the fifth wave. I pointed my lens towards the back of my hand and took a reading. I wanted to expose for the skin tones of the people instead of the water that was made brighter by the sun's reflection. I set my aperture at f-11 and my time at a five-hundredth of a second, checked to make sure my motor drive was set for multiple shots, and focused on the middle of the wave train.

While waiting for the first raft to appear upstream, I thought about my trip I had taken down the river with my parents. They had chosen to ride through Hermit with Sandy, and he had looked smooth, confident, and in control as he slid effortlessly over the fifth wave. How could I fault my parents for not riding with me when he was so strong?

Roni yelled they were coming, and I looked up to see Floyd slam into the left lateral at the entry and then gain speed. I picked him up through my lens and waited until he reached the top of the fourth wave. I took one shot there, and then waited again until he reached the very bottom of the trough before the fifth wave. I pressed down on the button to engage the motor drive and watched as the raft climbed to the top. He was standing up leaning as far forward as he could while pushing on his oars. The wave crashed on top, and for a split second Floyd, his raft, and his passengers all disappeared. Then the orange tube broke through sending water in all directions. The front of the raft dipped, and continued downstream. I could hear Floyd's laughing voice above the roar.

Each boat made a great run. The paddlers were working together in perfect harmony, a task made easier by fear. Eliza was in the front left, digging and smiling all the way through. Having been raised in the Northwest by a fisherman father, she was comfortable on water, and clearly having the time of her life.

After Michael's run, I checked my camera to see if I had any frames left. I was on #35 of a thirty-six-exposure roll. So I quickly took two shots of Liz as she approached me. She smiled, the afternoon sun highlighting her curly black hair that contrasted so with her alabaster skin.

As we walked back to the raft, Roni raved about the other runs and said she couldn't wait to do it too. When I told her it would look three times as big when we were in it, she laughed and said, "let's do it!" When we got back to the raft, I put away the cameras and said I wanted three people up front. I wanted all the weight I could find up there while still being safe. Liz and

Elli said they would come up front, and Doron could ride in the back. She seemed fine with that arrangement. I showed the three how to position themselves up on the front tube, and where they could hold on. I also showed Doron where to sit and where to find her handholds.

Then I coiled up the bowline and shoved off. "Let's get wet," I shouted, and pulled out into the middle of the river. Again I said things would get very fast and very big once we entered the tongue. I also said all the rafts would be there in case we needed help. If the boat should flip or someone ended up in the river, they should point their feet downstream, and to avoid taking in any water, they should turn their head to the side while taking a deep breath. I told them to breath at the top of the wave, not the bottom. Finally I said, "Let's have some fun," and set up for my entry.

The entry at Hermit had recently changed because of a flash flood, and I wanted to hit the middle of the lateral wave coming off the left shore. From the fifth wave, this lateral looked small, but as I pushed into it, the raft lifted up at a forty-five degree angle, and all three passengers on the front tube disappeared for a moment in a rush of water. We accelerated as we were funneled into the main current, and I counted as we hit each wave. As the numbers got higher, so did the waves. Three was big, and four was huge. I fought to keep the raft pointing straight downstream as we crested the top of four and slid down its backside. Now we were in the deep trough, and directly in front of us was a writhing, growing, living liquid mountain. From the front of the raft I heard a chorus of "Oh My God!!!"

I looked at the top of the wave to see how it was breaking, turned the raft slightly to the right, and then pushed as hard as I could. My right foot pressed against my ammo can on the floor in front of me, and my left braced against my cooler. I pressed my left leg against the ammo cans in my foot well, and this gave me a solid base from which to maneuver. My handholds are my oars. As long as they're in the water, I have a purchase. At times the oars slice through nothing but air, and that is when I could go flying.

The girls were as far up on the front tube as they could go, screaming at the tops of their lungs. As we climbed the fifth wave, I looked back to make sure Doron was in a safe position. She was plastered against the bags, and holding on tightly. In a second that lasted an hour, we were carried up the front of the wave, crested at the top as the wave broke over us, settled for an instant, and then the front tipped downward and we slid down the back side of the wave. I let out an exhilarated "Oh My God!" and then yelled that we weren't through yet. Before the flash flood, the tail waves had been smaller. Now they were big and steep, and the distance between them was narrow. If we began our celebration too soon, we could lose momentum, slide off the side of one of those waves, and possibly flip.

Amidst continued shouts, we rode each of the tail waves, passing the other rafts that had set up on the left and right sides of the current. Finally we settled into a calmer stretch, and as if on cue, we all shouted, "Oh My God!" Liz was beaming, Elli was laughing, and Roni was out of her mind. Even the normally quiet Doron was vocal.

Our adrenalin pumped through us for a few more minutes, and finally I asked Doron in the back and anyone in the front to bail. We had taken on an immense amount of water, and it took about ten minutes to empty it out. Then we all settled into a calm float. The next major rapid would be about three miles away.

Roni reminded me that I would tell them if I had ever flipped in Hermit, so I said yes, I had.

We had just picked up a new group of passengers at Pipe Creek, I began. We were delayed because one of the passengers had fallen on the way down the Bright Angel trail and had gouged a huge chunk of flesh below his knee. We actually discouraged him from going on the trip because of the potential for infections. The river was muddy and if an infection spread to the bone it could be very serious. He had come in with his wife, son, daughter, and father, and had waited five years since his last trip in the Canyon so he could bring his son. There was no way he was not going on the trip. So we cleaned up his wound, covered it with gauze, attempted to make it waterproof by taping plastic around his leg, and, with the help of another passenger who was an attorney, wrote up a waiver for him to sign. Then we headed for Horn Creek. His wife, son, and daughter chose my raft. The kids were both quite small, and the wife was less than thrilled about being on the trip. The only reason she had come along was that her father-in-law had paid for the trip, and her husband had really wanted her to go with the kids.

We ran Horn Creek and Granite successfully; but Hermit was a different story. I made a good entry, and raced into the current, hitting each wave squarely. The fifth wave was huge, a little bigger than usual, and we climbed it in perfect position. Just before we reached the top, the wave exploded, crashed down hard on us, and flipped the raft so quickly I didn't realize it until I found myself in a gigantic washing machine on the cold water rinse cycle. As soon as I reached the surface, I looked around for the kids and their mother. The kids were fine, and I told them to hold on to the safety line that was wrapped around the raft until the rest of the crew could come to help out. I found the mother, who was worried about her kids, and in a bit of distress herself. I assured her the kids were fine, and helped her to the raft. By then other rafts had surrounded us, and everybody was hauled out of the river. The kids thought it was a great adventure, each exaggerating their experience to one-up their sibling. The mom, who had asthma, took a while before she could calm down.

In spite of a very challenging first day, the trip progressed smoothly after that, we kept the wound clean, and on the last night, the mom actually said she was glad she had come.

Roni asked me if I was scared on my next trip, and I told her maybe I should have been. My next trip was two days after that one had ended. Again we picked up new passengers at Pipe Creek. Two couples, one from France and the other from Switzerland, joined me on my raft. As we pulled out, Lilliane, a widely traveled, friendly woman from Geneva, asked me how many trips I had done. I told her it was my fifty-first trip. "Oh good," she replied. "Then you'll be safe." The kiss of death.

Horn Creek and Granite were big and fast, and we managed to run them successfully. The water level was five thousand cfs higher than just two weeks earlier, and the river a deeper red-brown. Rapids looked less friendly. The shadows in holes looked more ominous. I was running sweep on this trip, and we decided not to do a picture run. I couldn't see anyone else's run, and later found out they had all cheated down the left side. Cheating Hermit was like an oxymoron to me. Why would I want to miss the fifth wave? Hell, I didn't even know how to cheat it. When I came to the head of the rapid, I silently wished I had learned.

I had just enough time to see the fifth wave looking bigger, wider, and uglier than I had ever seen it. I told my passengers to hold on tight, and ran down the gut. The first four waves were big and fun, and I was in the perfect position as I entered the fifth wave. It was enormous, but I had a good head of steam and as I began to climb the mountainous wave, I pushed as hard as I could on my oars. The raft rose up and up, and just as we were peaking a wave hit us from the right front and lifted the raft up, as if twisting it over to the left. Just as quickly, and with even more power, another wave slammed into us from the left side and turned us over in corkscrew fashion. Again I was in the giant washing machine, only this time it was more violent.

I don't know how long I was under the water, but when I finally surfaced, I was right next to my raft. The two men were floating near the raft, and I found Lilliane underneath, sputtering and afraid. I grabbed her hand and pulled her out. She was in a bit of a panic, so I talked to her calmly, telling her she was okay and help was on the way. Hermit is a pretty safe rapid in which to flip because there are no rocks, and the rapid has no bends. Suddenly Lilliane yelled, "Jeanne, where is Jeanne? She can't swim!"

I looked around and couldn't see her anywhere. Maybe she was also under the raft. I took a deep breath and swam under, coming up in the forward compartment. No Jeanne. I called her name. No reply. I swam back out and asked if Lilliane had seen her. She said no, concern carved into her face. By this time our kayak guide had come up. I said we were missing one woman, and asked if he had seen her. He said no, and then said I'd have to go under one more time. For some reason, that was a really hard thing to do. With some anxiety I took a breath and went back under the overturned raft. I swam to the rear compartment hoping I wouldn't find her there trapped in the rigging, always my greatest concern in the event of a flip. She wasn't there. Then I became disoriented, and instead of swimming out to the side, found myself pushing backwards down the middle of the overturned raft. I almost ran out of air before I found the edge and popped up. I was a bit freaked, but my concern for Jeanne took precedence over my own feelings.

It turned out that she had been picked up by another raft farther upstream, and she was fine. She later told me she found out she could swim – if she really had to.

Elli took a deep breath, let out a loud sigh, and thanked me for waiting until after the rapid to tell those stories. Liz looked at me and smiled softly. Roni decided that our run was definitely better. Doron said nothing, but allowed the corners of her mouth to turn up, and her eyes sparkled.

Below Hermit the river slowed to a crawl amidst spectacular metamorphic cliffs. Upsteam, the retreating, stair-stepped, red Cambrian layers contrasted sharply with the polished, iridescent, dark schist. We had one medium-sized rapid, Boucher (pronounced Boo-shay), to run before encountering our next major rapid. Louis Boucher was a French Canadian who had come to the Canyon in 1891. He established a camp and home in Hermit Canyon at Dripping Springs, and was responsible for the construction of the last trail into the Canyon in the early 1900s. Originally called the Silver Bell Trail, it is now know as the Boucher Trail that links Boucher Creek to Hermit Canyon. There is a camp in an eddy in the middle of Boucher rapid. Parking there is akin to parking in the North Sea. There is no way to sleep on your raft, unless you're unconscious. *On one of my trips, in the mid-eighties, we camped at Boucher when there was a lot more beach area than there is today. Just before heading downstream to run Crystal, a friend of mine on the trip conducted a silent ceremony designed to call in an eagle, a powerful totem for her. Less than five minutes after launching from camp, a golden eagle appeared overhead. I have not seen one in that part of the Canyon since.*

* * *

On a more recent trip while camped at Boucher, I experienced the consequences of being stubborn about putting up my tent. Because of lower water and concerns about our rafts chafing against rocks overnight, we had to park the rafts forty yards downstream from our campsite. After dinner a weather system rolled in. Assuming it would also roll out just as quickly, I stubbornly refused to go down to my raft and get my tent. I just didn't want to walk through thigh deep-water to retrieve it. As the night descended, the rain came, accompanied by some thunder and lightning. I assumed the storm would pass through. It didn't. The night wore on, and still the rain persisted. Finally, I looked for some shelter and found a small area with enough of an overhang that I would be protected from most of the rain. I'd like to emphasize most. Unfortunately it was on a pile of driftwood under the overhang. That didn't make sleeping a comfortable experience. It turned into a long night.

We passed Schist camp on the left, a peaceful place with plenty of soft sand, and continued our calm float. Liz returned to the back of the raft with Doron, while Roni regaled her mom with nonstop descriptions of her experience in Hermit. Finally we heard the soft rumble of another rapid. After Horn, Granite, and Hermit, Boucher seemed like small potatoes. Except for some adolescent squeals and protests about getting wet, our float was peaceful. As soon as we emerged from the rapid we entered a very calm stretch of river – Crystal Lake. The next mile-and-a-half had a very slow current, the river hemmed in by ancient walls and slowed down by the next major rapid. *Crystal had once been just a minor riffle along the way to bigger rapids downstream. Then, on December 3rd, 1966, a warm rain began to fall up on the North Rim, on ground already covered with six inches of snow. Three days later the snow, combined with fourteen inches of rain, generated a runoff dropping sixty-five hundred vertical feet through a twisting thirteen-mile course before being flushed out into the Colorado River. The runoff was estimated to be forty-four feet deep, and carried boulders fourteen feet in diameter, weighing 50 tons. The debris narrowed the river channel from a width of two hundred eighty feet to one hundred feet, and created a major rapid.*

Because of its location and configuration, it is considered the most dangerous rapid in which to flip. Even today I get nervous above Crystal. There are two sections to it: a short but very intense upper section with fast current, large waves, and huge holes, and then a large rocky island sixty yards downstream where the current splits into three segments – one on either side of the island and the third right over the mine field of boulders.

On my third Canyon trip back in 1980, I scouted the upper section by hiking down to the head of the rapid and standing on those boulders that had been pushed out in 1966. I then climbed up a hill overlooking the rapid to get a look at my run downstream. The day was still and hot. I sat down and tried to memorize my run while attempting to ignore my pounding heart. Unfortunately, I wasn't the only life form occupying the rock at that time.

A colony of red ants were also scouting Crystal, and apparently I had taken up too much space. Instead of just requesting that I move a bit, one ant decided to take matters into its own pincers. Known also as Fire Ants, their sting can be compared to that of a wasp or bee. It is not only very painful, it could also lead to some temporary numbness.

The stinging ache in my upper leg made the prospect of running Crystal even less appealing. But it was time. I limped back to my boat, secured my gear, took a large swig of water, dunked myself in the Colorado River, checked on my passenger, untied my boat, and shoved off with an advanced case of cotton mouth.

Perhaps it was the ant venom clouding my brain, or maybe it was my inexperience. Okay, it was my inexperience. Whatever the cause, I got disoriented immediately after entering the rapid. I was so focused on what was right in front of me that I had forgotten to look downstream. By the time I did, it was too late, and I was too close to a monstrous hole that I could swear was smiling at me as I frantically tried to swing my raft to the right to hit it straight.

Not a chance. My angle was wrong, and I hit the wave with the right front of my boat. Easy pickings for this huge wave that effortlessly lifted my boat up and turned it over.

Normally, when a boat flips, the passengers are ejected away from the boat. As mine was reaching its point of ejection, however, my right foot wedged between a strap and the box it was securing. The boat was coming down on top of me! Somehow, before the boat finished its 180-degree turn, I managed to release my foot from its shackle. But instead of being thrown away from the boat, I found myself submerged, floating directly under it.

I looked up and saw the ghost-like outline of my craft floating directly overhead, as if it was a shield protecting me from the harmful effects of fresh air and sunshine. For a quick moment panic reared its ugly head and stuck in my throat. In that moment of impending panic I recalled a scuba course I had taken in the early 'seventies. The first thing the instructor had said was, "There is nothing that can go wrong under the water that cannot be resolved under the water." I realized in that moment that I needed to find air. The nearest air was in the spot previously occupied by my feet – the foot-well of my overturned boat.

So I pulled myself up into that air chamber and took a deep, refreshing breath. And then something unexpected happened. Instead of getting out from under my boat, as I should have, I became fascinated with my situation. My first thought was that I could hear myself breathing in my rubberized and liquid air chamber. It was a strange sensation to hear something we all take for granted – breath. I then recall thinking, "This is amazing! Just yesterday I washed my hair in this river and frosted my brains; now here I am totally submerged in 50 degree water, and unaware of the temperature! How amazing the body and mind are."

At that moment I was reminded why I shouldn't stay in that floating air pocket. Suddenly I was being pulled, as if going down a water slide; and then my legs started bumping up against rocks. It was the rock island, and I was in danger of becoming bruised or shredded meat.

"I'm outta here," I thought, as I pulled myself upstream until I was free of the raft, and my life jacket raised me up to glorious daylight and fresh air. I first checked to see if my passenger was okay, and found her holding on to the upstream side of the boat as she had been instructed. Then I noticed apples and oranges floating all around me. Oops. I had failed to properly secure the lid on the fruit cooler, which was in the back of my raft.

I looked around for help and was relieved to see one of our other boats coming to the rescue. It was Johnny, and he was working hard to catch up to us with his own boat weighed down by several hundred extra pounds of river water. He finally reached us, pulled my passenger and me in, and with me holding my boat, pulled both boats into an eddy.

One by one, the rest of the crew arrived and helped return my boat to its proper, upright position. Fortunately, the only thing missing was a spare coffee pot. Had it been both pots I would have been in serious trouble, as this crew was very serious about its coffee.

As I sat on my cooler seat, each of my crewmates came over to check me out and gave me a hug. Then one spoke up and said, "You know Charly, there's something we forgot to tell you. We have a saying down here. In the Canyon, there are only two kinds of guides: those that have -- and those that are gonna" (flip). And then someone else joined in and said, "And those that are gonna again!"

Crystal Lake was actually still the Colorado River, but with very little current. A mild upstream wind forced me to work harder on my oars, and I decided to turn the raft and use my legs with my pull stroke rather than strain my arms by pushing against the wind. We still had a good mile to go before pulling over to scout Crystal. Doron surprised me by asking if I had any nice stories to tell about Crystal. I told her that by coincidence I did.

On one trip, one of my passengers, named Paula, was the type of person who had no filter between her brain and her mouth. Whatever happened to be on her mind was immediately transferred to their lips. A vibrant, perky woman in her twenties, she had an irrepressible enthusiasm for life and a non-stop, usually one-way conversation going on at all times. Her zest was infectious and everybody enjoyed her energetic approach to everything she did.

The day we ran Crystal, Paula was in my boat. Having already run three major rapids in the preceding eight miles, her adrenaline was flowing and she couldn't wait to see this gigantic rapid that everybody had spoken about with such respect. When we scouted the rapid, we realized that the water level was too high to "go big." It would have been just plain foolish and irresponsible. A flip at the top of the rapid could lead to severe consequences and put a serious damper on an otherwise enjoyable trip. We decided to enter with the back of our rafts angled toward the right shore. On most of our runs we entered facing forward making it better to see the river and where we were going. But pushing was a much weaker stroke, so on this run we would sacrifice a little convenience for more power.

With Paula in the front yelling encouragement, I rowed out into the middle of the river, and finding my entry, adjusted the raft for the set-up. My heart was racing and my mouth was dry, sure signs of adrenaline coursing through my system. Then I turned the raft with the rear facing towards the shore, to the consternation of Paula, who was looking forward to running straight into the maelstrom. The current moved agonizingly slowly until we reached the top of the rapid. Then everything sped up.

Pulling as hard as I could, I felt the raft enter the rapid, slicing through the lateral wave with surprising ease. That was it. Had I missed my mark, or had my raft been at the wrong angle, we could easily be in the land of the giants facing serious consequences. Instead, we took on hardly any water and cruised downstream to the right of all the chaos.

"That rapid was boring!" Paula shouted, frustration clearly revealed in her voice.

My first reaction was to be angry. My run was perfect. I had done what needed to be done, and yet here was a dissatisfied passenger who had expected more excitement – much more. Then I realized that I hadn't done an adequate job of describing the run. I told Paula why we ran the rapid the way we did. I also told her we would be going through some more rapids and assured her we would be "going big" in some of those. She seemed satisfied, although she did get a last word in wishing we had at least flirted with disaster. "Ignorance is bliss," I thought. "Until it isn't."

Roni asked if we would be doing the same run, and I told her with a smile that I hoped so.

I had a lot of other Crystal stories, like the time I kissed the left wall and nearly flipped; or the time the trip leader kissed that wall and did flip; or the time the owner's husband flipped in the entry and wound up in the rock island, and had to very reluctantly jump back into the river to be rescued. Then there was the whole 1983 saga when the river was up to ninety-two thousand cfs, and there was actually a fatality. A 37-foot motor rig with a rookie on the stick had decided to make his normal run, entering slightly right-of-center. He miscalculated both the speed and the power of the river, and went straight into a mammoth wave at the entry. Someone on the shore took pictures of the mayhem. In a sequence that lasted less than a minute, the photos show the huge craft enter the wave, disappear, surface in a writhing, twisting death dance that eventually stripped the boat of all its passengers and gear, and finally its tubes. One passenger died from a heart attack that was probably brought on by hypothermia. But telling those stories would have served no purpose. What I do remember vividly was on one trip early in my career rowing a sluggish, very heavy baggage boat filled with water and no passengers to bail. Getting into the rescue eddy downstream took all the energy I could muster. My forearms were screaming as I strained on the oars to break across the powerful current, and all I could think about was "please God, don't let me miss the eddy. If I did, my crewmates might think I wasn't good enough to work down here.

Finally the low growl of Crystal, carried upstream on a soft breeze, announced its presence. Perceptions change and expand on a river trip. Air is invisible, yet I could see the wind as it drew moving lines on the water. It raced up the river transforming the dark grey surface to black. I was momentarily transfixed as I awaited its arrival, and knew exactly when the first burst of damp, cooled air would slap me in the face, as the cold river water had in Hermit.

Downstream, on the right was a small beach area, actually more hard-packed dirt than sandy beach. A line of tammies spread out upstream, behind, and downstream of the open area. We pulled over below in an eddy just big enough to accommodate all our rafts. As I was tying my bowline to a tammy branch, I invited the Israelis to come with me to check out the rapid. Roni and Doron said they would come. Liz and Elli stayed behind. I waved to Mary, who was also staying behind. She was in the back of Floyd's raft, and shot me a warm smile. As I did every night and morning since she had hurt her foot, I had worked on her after breakfast that morning. She wasn't in any real pain, unless she put weight on her foot. We were pretty sure she had broken it, but she was still glad to be on the trip.

I passed Chris and Graham on my way to the rapid. Graham made some snide comment about people actually paying to be scared. Chris giggled, but seemed quite subdued. By now I was quite familiar with the run, and it would have been fine with this experienced crew to run Crystal without scouting. But Sue felt it would be valuable to let the paddle boaters see their run. While it would be very dangerous for so many people to be in the river should the paddleboat flip, the run was very straightforward, and with an experienced captain like Sue, the chances of something going wrong were slim. Still, we would approach the runs with a flip in mind, and set up for a rescue.

After a few minutes, I had seen enough and started back to my raft. Graham had his arm around Chris, who seemed to be crying. I asked what was wrong, and Graham said as soon as she had seen the rapid, her fears really surfaced. He asked if it would be possible for her to walk around the rapid. I told her it would be fine, if that's what she needed to do. I said there was a very small but real possibility that no raft would be able to get to the eddy down below, and if that were to happen, she would have to walk downstream to catch one of us. After thinking about it for a moment, she remembered her stiff British upper-lip, and said she would ride through. I told her she would be very safe in Floyd's raft, and gave her a hug. I could tell she was embarrassed by her emotional reaction.

Fortunately all the runs were flawless, and the drama was quickly forgotten. Chris had a smile of relief on her face as I pulled into the rescue eddy to wait for the paddle boaters to switch. A beaming Tyler replaced Eliza, much to the chagrin of Miriam, who wanted him to stay with her, and Nathan took Timmy's spot. Then Eliza and Timmy got in the duckies that Michael and Star had inflated. Each put on helmets and wetsuits provided by the company, and then paddled around the eddy for a minute or two. Timmy had come such a long way on this trip, especially since Michael had helped him master the self-rescue in the Little Colorado. He was smiling a lot more, and interacting with the other passengers with ease. Ralph had not changed much, but at times I caught him watching Timmy and almost smiling. The son was teaching the father.

Our next rapid, Tuna Creek, was less than a mile away. When I mentioned the name, Roni said it was such a strange name for a rapid and asked what it was from. I told her "tuna" was a Mexican word for the sweet, magenta fruit of the prickly pear cactus. Tourists know the fruit from prickly pear jams that are abundant in the southwest. I said I had attempted to make some jam one year when I was visiting a friend in Sedona. I followed the recipe exactly, except I had cut the sugar in half in an attempt to keep the calories down. I hadn't realized I needed that much sugar for the liquid to gel. So instead of jam, I wound up with a very colorful and tasty syrup.

I have been fortunate in having very few passenger injuries, and none in the major category. But at Tuna Creek on a trip in the 'eighties, Joanne, a vibrant sixty-something from Michigan, had been my first victim. Distracted by our conversation and not paying attention to my entry into Tuna Creek, I took a line that was too close to a hole at the top. I clipped the hole, and Joanne, who was in the back and not holding on, face-planted into the black bags and then fell into the river. She was back in the raft within seconds, smiling and not complaining about the two black eyes that were forming. Eventually we nicknamed her raccoon eyes, for the mask that she would wear for the remainder of the trip.

Tuna Creek rapid is a long, wave-filled ride followed by a sharp ninety-degree bend to the left with large waves rushing out to meet us as we turn the corner. Lower Tuna used to be called Willie's Necktie Rapid after Willie Taylor, who almost drowned on a 1950 trip when he fell out of his boat and two rescue ropes wrapped around his neck. Coming out of Lower Tuna, we were faced with 100-Mile Rock in the middle of a narrow section of the channel. One guide had called it Nixon Rock, because it was a major obstruction; the rock was always in the way and never did anything. We can run either left or right of the rock, and then have to avoid smaller rocks in the channel, sometimes called Spiro Agnew Rocks because they hide in Nixon's shadow. Both Eliza and Timmy had managed to run the rapids successfully, and Timmy was getting kudos from every raft. Eliza paddled up to my raft and asked for some gorp. She, too, was clearly having a blast. Her brother and parents, my brother Ned and his wife Lulu, had been my assistants on previous trips, so now her family would have a lifetime of stories to share.

The river had narrowed and the current had picked up speed, carrying us along a metamorphic alley with naturally sculpted schist and granite that would make any human sculptor envious. In this part of the canyon the sculptures were still primitive, taking on unpolished but sensuous forms, like unfinished sculptures awaiting final cutting and polishing. Later in the Canyon, we would encounter finished sculptures that would invite our caress.

We were about to enter the Gems, a series of rapids named after semi-precious and precious gems. The first, Agate, was barely noticeable, but the next, Sapphire, had been a thorn in our sides.

Once when one of our rafts clipped a large hole on the right side of the current, a returning passenger riding in the back of a raft and not holding on correctly slammed into the river bags and wound up in the river. The guide pulled her in quickly and she complained of pain in her ribs. We assessed her, were unable to determine the extent of any injury, and recommended that she be flown out by helicopter for x-rays. She talked with her husband about this option, and decided to remain on the trip. Soon after it ended, however, she filed a lawsuit against the company – the company's first – claiming that someone had said the guide shouldn't have been "over there." I was really upset, as were many others on the trip, especially after hearing the company had settled out of court because it would have cost them more to go to trial.

The waves in Sapphire and Turquoise were big, and by now both Roni and Doron had become accomplished high-siders, complete with loud shrieks and broad grins. Liz and Elli usually managed to remain dry, but in Turquoise I spun my raft around and they received a good dose of chilled river water. They took it well, and Liz gave me a big grin that distracted me for a moment. For the first time, I thought I noticed a subtle sadness encircling her eyes, as if something wasn't quite right in her life.

After running Turquoise we entered a long, straight stretch bordered by broken-up schist and a widening channel. Here the Canyon opened up temporarily, letting in more sun to beat down on us. A new form of jet-black metamorphic rock, called Brahman schist, dramatically reflected the summer sun. It was so black I found it hard to believe that any light could escape from it. I told everyone to keep their eyes out for bighorn sheep, because I had often seen them in this stretch.

Two miles downstream, the river seemed to disappear into a massive wall on river right. Ancient pink granite intrusions crisscrossed through the schist, topped by an eroded, horizontal layer of the Tapeats sandstone. I knew that this wall heralded Ruby Rapid, with waves that would douse all of us. Sometimes on this stretch I would encourage a passenger to sit up on the front tube, like riding a bucking bronco; but decided not to stress out the moms on this run.

We pulled over for lunch upstream of Ruby and fixed cold cuts amidst animated conversations about Granite, Hermit, and Crystal. Timmy and Nathan were down by the water playing with the Israeli girls. Chris was carrying on a lively conversation with Mary, and Tyler was capturing cicadas and bringing them over to show us, like a cat with a mouse in its mouth. The new group had made a quick transition and had become part of the tribe.

After lunch we resumed our charge through the inner gorge. Ruby was a riot. I entered on the right side, broke through a standing wave and cruised around a right-to-left bend where I was greeted by several very large waves. With Roni and Doron riding the front tube, we sliced through each wave, getting drenched in the process.

The last of the gems, Serpentine, was next. The first time I ran it, I had no idea there was a huge pourover on the right side of the current. I didn't see it until I was right next to it, and it scared the hell out of me.

A couple of years ago I was entering Serpentine when a gale force sheer wind struck me from the right rear, blowing me towards the left shore. I was fighting the wind with as much strength as I could muster and making no difference whatsoever. Meanwhile, the photographer in me wanted to throw out an anchor, grab my camera and get some shots of one of the most ethereal river scenes I had ever witnessed. The entire rapid looked like a time exposure of spray flowing downstream. Each wave looked like the gossamer wings of a gray-white dragonfly. But I had no anchor, and where I was being blown was anything but gossamer. The raft bounced over barely submerged rocks on the left side of the rapid. The next day I would be frying in the sun patching six small holes, while everybody else enjoyed a long hike to a cooling waterfall.

Serpentine had a similar series of large waves, and we again were drenched as we slammed into each one head on. Then, suddenly we were in calm waters. We had rafted through the gems, and were less than two miles from camp. Downstream, we could see the Canyon widen, and on the right side, layers of sedimentary rock tilted unsteadily skyward. These were layers of the Grand Canyon Supergroup, rarely seen at the river. The layers had been laid down, then lifted – sometimes two to three miles – tilted, and eroded away, so they were usually hidden by the layers that had formed above them.

As we approached these layers, the sound of another rapid got the girls' attention. Doron said she thought we were through the gems. I told her we were, but we still had some more rapids to run before we emerged from the inner gorge. What they heard, I told them, was the last small rapid before camp. Before we ran it, I pointed to a well-camouflaged metal boat sitting on rocks about twenty feet above a beach on river left. This was the "Ross Wheeler," the only boat to survive an ill-fated river trip in 1914. It had been abandoned at the beach, and a later river runner had hauled it up above the high water line. Initially it still had its oars and some of its gear. Over the years, looters had taken everything that wasn't bolted down.

We ran our last rapid of the day, and passed the remains of a turn-of-the-twentieth-century cable car used by William Bass to transport tourists and horses across the river so he could take them to his mining camp in the drainage over the hill. Between 1890 and 1930, Bass brought over 20,000 people down and across the river. Just beyond that was Bass Camp, one of the most popular camps in the Canyon due to its spacious size, grove of shade-providing tammies, and quiet eddy where bathing was convenient.

We set the kitchen up in the shade of one of the tammy groves, and told people to relax until dinner. That would give them two-and-a-half hours to allow the adrenalin of the day to subside, and enjoy a leisurely afternoon. We then enjoyed a dinner of pork chops and stuffing, cucumber salad, and carrot cake that I had happily offered to bake. I grated a few carrots into the Betty Crocker mix and added some crushed pineapple for flavor. While I was mixing the cake, Liz came over and said she hadn't expected such fine cuisine, especially the baked desserts. I wanted to ask her about her life in Israel, but Doron came over and pulled her away. She excused herself, gently touching my arm before turning away.

The moonless night sky sparkled out of a black velvet ceiling. The soft sound of the river was like a lullaby singing us to sleep. As I lay in my bag, I could smell the musky aroma of river mud uncovered as the Colorado dropped. Eliza was already asleep on the back hatch. It had been a very good day. As I drifted off, I thought about Liz with her tight curls and mysterious eyes. "It's time I found a girlfriend," I said to myself.

The Grand Canyon hides its beauty and diversity in its many side canyon. After a short hike off the river, Elves Chasm surprises visitors with a wonderland of maidenhair fern, yellow columbine and cardinal monkey flower in a verdant oasis nurtured by soft cascades. And this is just one of six levels we can enjoy.

149

DAY TEN –
BASS CAMP TO 118

I woke up again to the sound of the blaster. The pre-dawn air felt cool and damp. Across the river, the promise of first light tinged the south rim. I pulled my sleeping bag up under my chin and found Venus shining like a welcoming beacon in a featureless landscape. The sound of Shinumo Rapid competed with Floyd's snoring. Even that made me smile. Eliza was sound asleep, as were the rest of the crew, except Michael and Star, who were in the kitchen. The menu called for breakfast burritos, a combination of scrambled eggs, ground chorizo sausage, and cheddar cheese rolled in large tortillas. We keep the sausage and eggs separate for the non-meat eaters.

Soon after the coffee conch, breakfast was served, and Sue announced our plans for the day. She said we still had some really fun rapids to run before emerging from the inner gorge and into a much calmer stretch. After a leisurely morning at camp, we would float less than a half-mile downstream and pull into the mouth of Shinumo, hike up the creek a hundred yards to a pool and cascade, and play for a little while. Then we would head for Elves Chasm, eight miles away, have lunch, and go to another pool surrounded by narrow walls and lots of greenery. There, the more adventurous would have the option to climb up to other levels. Sue emphasized that no one had to go beyond the first pool. She said there would be quite a bit of exposure, so anyone with a strong fear of heights should be forewarned.

Elves Chasm is one of the most magical places in the Canyon. There are six unique levels, each one with its own ecosystem and vegetation. A deep, green pool sits less than fifty feet from the river, below a trail that leads to the first level. After a short hike up a trail strewn with travertine-covered boulders, a maneuver across a narrow opening between two boulders, and crossing a small creek, passengers are treated to a slim waterfall tumbling down fern-and-columbine-covered boulders into a clear, cold pool ten feet wide and thirty feet long. From there a glance up reveals the next of five more levels, each one requiring a different climbing technique, each level presenting unique vegetation displayed around and above pools and cascades.

I visited the upper levels for the first time, In 1979 on a private trip with my brother Sandy and six of his friends. I had hoped to interact with my brother a lot, but he had his girlfriend with him and she was his priority. I had even butted heads with her earlier in the trip: while rowing through Unkar Rapid I asked her what she could tell me about reading water, and she let me know that she wasn't going to tell me anything that I could discover for myself. I later found out she had spent the entire summer teaching "newbies" how to read water and was burned out.

When we arrived at Elves, Sandy decided that we would all go as high as we could go. When I entered the first level, I was struck by the energy I felt and became quiet and withdrawn. The others, including Sandy and his girlfriend, had the opposite reaction. They were laughing and kidding around, making jokes, jumping into pools, engaging in water fights, speaking loudly. For some reason, I was upset. How dare they have fun in this sacred space? Couldn't they feel what I was feeling? I wanted to tell them what I was feeling, but was intimidated, and kept it to myself. I now call it a case of spiritual arrogance. The Canyon brings out the playful child in all of us. When I think about my reaction, I'm both embarrassed and amused.

Graham asked if he and Chris could ride with me, and Mary had asked the same of me last night. It would be good to have the three of them back in my raft. I had been close friends with Chris and Graham since 1970, and was feeling a bond with Mary. We had come to enjoy our twice-daily physical therapy sessions, and I was relieved to see that she was having a great time, even though she couldn't go on any of the hikes.

Since we were going to take our time getting out of camp – a ploy to allow the sun to get into the cascade and pool in Shinumo – I found my coffee table book and took it over to Liz, who hadn't had enough time to look through it at our camp at Monument. I found her sitting on one of the polished rocks next to the river, taking some close-up shots. I asked her if she was still interested in checking out the book, and she smiled shyly and said yes. I left it on a flat rock on the beach and headed back to the kitchen to help break it down.

I then headed for the groover, located downstream beyond a thick grove of tammies. It was in an open area surrounded by schist, and offered an unobstructed view across and up the river. As I sat there, I thought about a calendar I had wanted to produce, but had never gotten around to it. It would be titled, "Unparalleled Murals in Your Bathroom," and would have images of the views from the groover. It was still a good idea, but I doubted it would ever happen. I have thousands of great images of the Grand Canyon, but except for my DVD and slide shows, I'm not particularly interested in doing the marketing required to sell my photographs. I'm waiting for someone who loves marketing and selling photographs to come along some day and offer to partner with me. If not, I'm happy sharing the Canyon with people in the various ways I do.

After a leisurely early morning, Carla announced she would be giving a geology talk, especially for those who had hiked in. I love to hear other guides' interpretations of the Canyon, so I joined most of the passengers in the shade of the former kitchen. Her talk was concise and easy to understand. After describing the different kinds of rock and the deep and complex history of the Canyon, she finished by suggesting two mnemonics to help remember the upper Cambrian layers. The first letter of each word represents the first letter of each layer in descending order: Kissing Takes Concentration, However, Sex Requires More Breath And Tongue; or, Know The Canyon's History, See Rocks Made By Time. K for Kaibab, T for

Toroweap, C for Coconino, H for Hermit Shale, S for Supai, R for Redwall, M for Muav, B for Bright Angel, and T for Tapeats.

Things were warming up on the beach, so we quickly adjourned to the rafts. Nathan and Timmy claimed the duckies, and Sue told them to stay behind her through the rapids. If for some reason either one found himself ahead, she told them to pull into an eddy until the paddleboat could catch up. Sue was the mother-ducky, responsible for telling the duckiers how to run each rapid, and making sure they were safe. With two kids in the duckies, she must have felt she needed to be a bit more motherly.

We floated just a half-mile to Shinumo, where all the rafts pulled into the mouth. The creek was shallow, warm, and clear. At the outside of the mouth, the sediment-laden Colorado swirled and mixed with the clear water, producing writhing modern-art. The sound of the rapid, just below the mouth of the side canyon, was fairly loud, in spite of the wider Canyon.

We walked up the creek bed to a pool fed by a ten-foot cascade charging over a carved-out slab of schist. The pool had been formed after river runners had built a mini-dam of river stones. It allowed us to swim and play under the cascade, and gave anyone strong enough to stay upright a wonderful shoulder massage. To do so, I had to lean against the water in a position that made me look like I was sitting in a slightly reclining chair.

Sounds of playful joshing, laughter, and directions for taking photos could barely be heard over the din of the cascade. The pool was slightly circular and about fifteen feet in diameter. Tyler caused a mini-tidal wave as he jumped in and swam behind the falls. A couple minutes later he emerged from under the cascade, a big, kid-like grin etched on his face. Miriam took several pictures, happy to see her son having so much fun. Roni and Doron, dressed in conservative bikinis, posed for their moms in front of the cascade, and then followed Tyler to the rear, where they, too, emerged from the cascade. Roni's laugh vibrated off the walls. The water drowned Doron's out. Just downstream from the pool, several guides and passengers relaxed on the polished schist, enjoying the warming sun.

In the early years the pool was deep enough that, after climbing above the cascade, we could jump into it. Over the years, flash floods brought down debris that had filled in the pool, thus necessitating the artificial dam. Recently I was on a trip with some very wilderness-smart passengers, including my U.S. Congressman. When we walked up to Shinomu, I was surprised to see the old pool depth had returned. It had to have happened sometime in the prior month, because it hadn't been deep on my previous trip. I convinced my congressman to climb up above the cascade, and then led him to a spot about twenty-five feet above the pool. I told him we used to jump from here, but it had been a long time. The distance to the pool wasn't daunting, but the wall on the far side of the pool, which jutted out over the pool most certainly was.

I'd learned long ago not to think too much before jumping After I pointed out the best place to enter, I stepped off the slick, polished rock. The wall reached out for me as I headed toward the pool. It was deep enough that I didn't touch bottom, and surfaced with a big grin on my face. After a little hesitation, he did the same. His smile upon resurfacing was reward enough for me.

Too soon Sue announced it was time to go, and was greeted with a chorus of complaints by four kids who had discovered Disneyland and weren't ready to go back to school. When I arrived at my raft, Mary was sitting on the shore in the shade of the willows. She said she had seen three different kinds of lizards and a flock of big horn that had come down to the river on the far shore.

I helped her onto my raft and asked Graham if he would untie my bowline. He seemed quieter than usual, and as he was coiling the line, he suddenly turned his back to the raft and began to cry. "There was nothing I could do for her," was all he said. Even though we had run Crystal yesterday, Chris's terror was clearly still weighing heavily on Graham. He was a no-nonsense, bright engineer, but I have seen the softer, more sensitive side of this man. During a phone call many years ago he had been the first man to tell me he loved me. At that time, none of my brothers or my father had mentioned that they loved me. That is not the case today. I wanted to offer him a hug, but refrained out of concern for putting him on the spot. So I waited for him to compose himself and secure the bowline. Without another word he stepped into the raft and sat on the front tube facing the river. I then began pulling out into the current to run Shinumo Rapid.

To run it correctly, I had to pull out into the current a short distance. I knew from past experience that as soon as I moved across the line where the creek flow met the river current, the stronger Colorado would force the back of my raft downstream. I pulled hard on both oars, with more than twice as much effort on the left, or downstream, oar. This held my raft at close to a forty-five-degree, upstream angle, and allowed me to float out into the current far enough so I could face downstream and enter the rapid safely. I focused on hitting each wave head-on to minimize splashing Chris and Graham, but sometimes the timing was such that they were doused anyway. The channel took a sharp two hundred-degree bend to the right. The current thrust us to the left, and I had to pull hard to keep us off the wall. We entered a long riffle as the Canyon opened up some more. At the end of a long straightaway, the river turned left and again I had to pull back to avoid being forced over a pourover, this time near the right shore.

After one more bend to the right, the channel again began to narrow. Ahead on the right was Hakatai Canyon. Hakatai was derived from a Supai name for Grand Canyon, meaning any large, roaring sound. I had hiked this canyon only once. It could have been twice, but on my first attempt I had been asked to lead the rafts to the pull-in, and I missed it, thinking it was farther downstream. I was embarrassed by my failure, and stayed away from the rest of the rafts until our focus turned to running the next big rapid.

My one hike in Hakatai had certainly proved memorable. No one on the crew had done it, so we were all excited and curious to explore an unknown side canyon. To get into the drainage, we first had to climb over a fifteen-foot, polished schist wall that looked more like a sculpture. Once in the drainage, we helped people up and over another short wall before we were slowed down by another maneuver along a polished wall and up a flood-carved, dry water slide. One guide climbed up to help people at the top, while another stood in the incised dry channel, and a third stayed below the wall to volunteer a hand for stability. It took twenty minutes to get everyone around this crux point. After that, we proceeded on a flat river channel with a narrow, carved-out schist floor, the reminders of past debris-flows lying in boulder-strewn gravel beds. I got into a conversation about snakes with Nora, a thirteen-year old princess from the east coast, and Greg, a thirty-something man searching for himself. Both told me they were scared of snakes. I told them that snakes were really quite beautiful creatures that had been portrayed in the movies as deadly demons. Besides, we probably wouldn't even see a snake on this hike. They said that was fine by them.

We continued into this narrow slit in geologic and human history for another forty-five minutes, and then the rains came. At first it was a sprinkle, but a glance at my other crewmates told me that we were in the wrong place at the wrong time. We announced it was time to return to the rafts. We were walking in a potential death trap, imprisoned in a natural wonder by sheer cliffs on both sides, and a hard-rock floor. Even a little rain over an extended period of time could lead to a flash flood. As guides we needed to exit this canyon as quickly and safely as possible without communicating our own anxieties. We were at least forty-five minutes from safety, and the rain was starting to fall harder. Minor rivulets of running water followed familiar channels to the floor beneath our feet. We quickened our steps, and I continued my conversations with Greg and Nora, monitoring my voice to detect any hint of the concern that was rising along with the water beginning to run beneath my feet.

By the time we arrived at the crux point, there was a long line of people waiting for help to get around the corner, like gawkers on a one-lane road. One guide was at the top of the incised slide, and another stood below to help each passenger edge around the corner and down to the canyon floor. With fifteen people, it was imperative that they move quickly because there was no place to get high should a flash flood erupt. I went up to see what I could do, and stepped down into the cut to help move the line along. The rain came harder, and a small, but insistent stream was now flowing over my sandaled feet. After a few minutes Greg and Nora arrived at the head of the line. Greg stepped down next to me, and then I saw it - a small rattlesnake coiled in an alcove on the right side of the channel. It was two feet away from Greg. I changed positions, moving between Greg and the snake. It wasn't a brave thing to do because I knew we were still far enough away from the snake. But I hoped the visual of my body as a barrier to the snake would ease Greg's concerns.

At the same time, Greg spotted the snake. He had no reaction, just nodded his head and continued around the corner. Meanwhile, Nora was leaning forward to step down when she spotted the snake. She panicked, slipping and fell forward into my arms. I told her we were safe from the snake, and said she needed to keep moving. The trickle was now licking at my ankles. My anxiety was rising, and I had a scared kid on my hands who was not thinking about flash floods. Meanwhile, the snake remained coiled in the corner of the alcove, undoubtedly sensing the rain and its own need to find a safe haven. I wondered how we could rescue the snake, but decided we had enough to deal with just getting everybody out. The snake could take care of itself. Or not.

The last passenger was helped down to the next flat spot and we continued moving toward safety. The storm was now overhead. Flashes of lightning lit up the darkened rocks as thunder, following immediately after each flash, caused the earth to shudder. Again we were slowed by the next climb, a twelve-foot scramble up slick rock made slicker by the rain. Finally, we inched along the last wall, and found the beach and our rafts.

As we floated past the opening to the side canyon, the early stages of a flood brought a change to the color of the Colorado. Ten minutes later, as we floated through a rain-soaked, now gloomy river channel, a barely discernable rise in the level of the river, along with deeper red sediment, told us we had just cheated death.

A mile-and-a-half below Hakatai waited the last big rapid in the inner gorge, and the most mysterious to me. Waltenberg had a rating between six and nine, depending on the water level – the lower the water, the higher the rating. At higher water, which was what we had now, the run was just plain fun. I would tell people it would feel and look like we'd be diving into the bowels of the earth; and then all of a sudden, it was like the Red Sea parting. Somehow we'd magically find a slot where there only looked like there was a massive hole, and we'd slice through, sometimes without getting wet. Well, we got wet this time, but still found that mystery slot, like the invisible bridge across a deep chasm in the Harrison Ford movie "Temple of Doom."

Sue had taken a very different path, choosing to lead the duckies down the right side, missing the big stuff. From the smiles on their faces, I would say Timmy and Nathan had thoroughly enjoyed their runs.

We still had two more small rapids to run before entering a calm stretch. The last rapid, 113 Mile Rock, was dubbed Rancid Tuna Sandwich Rock by a commercial trip in the early 'seventies. Apparently a rafter wrapped his boat on the rock, and while waiting for rescue, made himself a tuna fish sandwich. Help had arrived before he could finish the sandwich, which he left on the rock.

Just below the rock, the river entered a channel bracketed by the ledge-forming Tapeats sandstone. The more exposed, weathered edges of the sandstone had darkened with age, while the less exposed undersides retained their desert-tan hue. Currents in this stretch swirled chaotically, bound by eddies on both sides. The only sounds were of oars dipping in and out of the river, the occasional trill of the Canyon wren, and Sue's voice as she instructed the paddleboat crew. After running in the intense energy of the inner gorge, this calm, peaceful stretch of river gave everyone permission to kick back and relax.

We floated by two camps on the right – upper and lower 114. Upper 114 had a small eddy just large enough for five rafts. The camp itself was ringed by granite outcroppings and backed by a series of Tapeats sandstone ledges. We could see the rim and some of the Cambrian layers both up and downstream.

It was at this camp that my stubborn resistance to erect a tent again caused me to reconsider my choice. A light mist began falling just as we had begun dinner preparations. During dinner I assured everyone that the rain wouldn't last. It would surely move on. After dinner, most of the passengers erected their tents. I insisted the rain would end. The guides, except for me, erected their raft tents, actually waterproof shells with one center pole, allowing them to sleep on their rafts. I "knew" the rain would end, but two hours into the night, I was the only one getting wet. I tried waiting it out underneath a narrow overhang. Crouching there with my raingear on, I felt increasingly foolish and stubborn. Finally I peeked under the shell on the trip leader's raft and sheepishly asked if I could sleep on his cooler top. These were the old coolers that were narrower and shorter than the ones we use today. He invited me to join him for a slumber party.

After laying out my bag, and contorting my body to fit on the cooler that was too small even for me, Bill told me that he hadn't had the tent out of its bag for at least three years. He warned me it might leak. Sure enough, within a few minutes of his warning, a slow drip started landing right on my temple. For the rest of the night, I was tortured by that drip, and decided that at future camps putting up a tent would be far less inconvenient.

*   *   *

My fondest memory of Upper 114 came during my parent's private trip. For years they had slept in separate bedrooms – because my dad was such a restless sleeper my mom had argued. During our trip they shared the same ground cloth, and a natural intimacy unknown to them in their past together. When they woke up at Upper 114, they helped each other roll up their egg carton foam pads and discovered a guest. A scorpion had spent the night under the tarp, perhaps seeking some warmth from the fall chill. Their laughter warmed my heart.

*   *   *

More Recently, Lower 114 had offered an evening's entertainment like none I had ever experienced. On the periphery of camp was a large Datura bush with dozens of unopened flowers. The white, trumpet-shaped blossoms were the preferred restaurants for the nocturnal Sphinx moth. Its proboscis could be nine inches long or more, and the moth would fly with it extended. A few of us were casually looking at the bush around dusk when we saw a moth disappear into one of the open flowers, emerging a few seconds later having satiated its appetite for the nectar. I ran to get my camera and tripod, and returned to await future visits. As we stood there, for the first time I saw one of the flowers, then another, open up. Our surprised exclamations attracted the attention of others on the trip, and pretty soon the entire group was standing around taking bets on when the next flower would break free from its bonds and open up for the visiting moths. Someone said, "If we were home, we could be watching television right now." I said that we were watching television – The Discovery Channel.

*   *   *

On a September trip, I experienced one of the strangest and most energetic windstorms at this camp. I had found a campsite away from the crowded camps of the passengers and was enjoying the unusually warm, still air when it began. A sound unlike any I had ever heard roared out of nowhere from upstream with a blast of wind that blew sand everywhere and into everything, including my bed. This was followed by an eery silence, and then another roaring blast from upstream. And it went on all night. Once I tried to time the next sandblast hoping to have enough time to pee into my peebottle. Instead, I had my butt exfoliated. This went on all night. In the morning, I woke up covered in sand. While few people got much sleep, we all marveled at the unusual nature of the storm.

*   *   *

Directly across from Lower 114 was Garnet Canyon. A group of river guides had gone up there during one recent off-season and had worked on eradicating the tammies before they could become unmanageably prolific. They had cut down all the trees in the drainage for a couple of miles, and had applied a poison to the stumps, except where the stumps were too

156

close to water. My hike was less than two months later, and the supposedly eradicated tammies had already grown back, some as high as four feet. This is why ecologists make such a big deal when new non-native species of plants first show up. In the Southwest today, there are many miles of river where the non-native tammies have migrated all the way to the shoreline, and are so thick boaters can't even get out of their boats. With deep taproots that soak up precious water, and prodigious annual seeds that are carried by water and wind, they have become the scourge of the arid desert southwest.

We were still in a narrow stretch of river, but as we floated around a bend to the right, the Canyon opened up, and we were in what I called "Tolkein land." Alternating slopes and cliffs leaned back towards the north and south rims. At the tops of the Tapeats layer, dark streaks hung over the cliff edges, as if black, molten wax had been poured over the edge and now rested in vertical relief. I don't even know why I invoked JRR Tolkein, since I hadn't even read his books. It's just what I felt this area looked like. The fact that we were on our way to Elves Chasm may have had some influence.

I aroused my passengers by telling them that somewhere downstream on river left rested an image of Don Quixote, sitting on a horse, waving his partially opened umbrella at windmills. I challenged them to find it. When Chris asked for more information, I said the image was hatless, and only part of the horse was evident. Graham said something about a needle in a haystack, and I said that people with intelligence would be able to find it. He started to take out one of his cigarillos, and I reminded him there was no smoking allowed on my raft. He then said something about paying good money to sit in a rubber dingy with a tyrant. And smiled.

Just upstream of mile 116, Mary pointed to a section of the Tapeats on the right shore that was highly unusual. It looked, she said, like the rocks had been bent up at a ninety-degree angle. Bent, but not broken. She wondered how that could be. I told her it was called the Monument Fold because it lay below a point called Explorers Monument that honored past explorers of the Grand Canyon. I said she was right, it had been bent, and was indicative of a very slow process whereby the partly exposed schist had risen, likely due to plate tectonics, over a very long period of time. We think rocks are solid, and of course, at our level of awareness, they are. But under a strong electron microscope, we could actually detect movement at an atomic level. Most rocks do fracture from earth activity. But there are many examples of curvaceous layers in the Canyon, especially in the Tapeats, Muav and Redwall formations.

When we came around the bend just past the fold, Chris spotted Don Quixote. What followed was a husband-wife conversation with Chris clearly seeing a man on a horse with an umbrella, and Graham insisting it looked nothing of the sort. When Mary took Chris's side, Graham became silent for several minutes. Finally he said it was a stretch for him, but he could see how I might have come up with such a ridiculous image. In a very light cliff face on river left, just downstream from the opening to Elves Chasm, weathered erosional features offered an image that I had interpreted as Don Quixote. He had a light head, what appeared like a cape falling around his shoulders, was sitting astride a horse, but all that was visible was the horse's mane, ears and face. The Don also held an object in his left hand that looked very much like a partially opened umbrella pointing diagonally upward. I jokingly said it was my discovery, and I was seeking official status from the national naming board.

Arriving at Elves Chasm brought an end to our nonsense. Fortunately, no other groups were in the eddy. At times we'd pass by Elves if another large group was there. Most of the commercial companies only went to the pool at the first level. It's a beautiful and playful place to go, so no one feels cheated – unless they know what's above that first level.

In the early days of my rafting in the Canyon, we almost always went to the upper levels. In those days we did a lot of Sierra Club-sponsored trips. Every year, the same woman would show up for one of the trips. She drank to excess and was a bit overweight, but insisted on going on every hike. In today's litigious climate, taking her to upper Elves would be frowned upon, especially if she were to be injured; but back then, we had a different perspective. Our entire orientation was to give our passengers the best possible experience of the Canyon. To us, that meant going off the beaten path. So we lifted, and pushed, and coaxed her to the top, and then back down again. It was during those trips that I observed how much more people, including me, could do, with just a little support. If someone said they wanted to go somewhere, chances are we'd comply, unless it was sheer stupidity or clearly irresponsible. Today we still bring a "whatever it takes" attitude to our trips in the Canyon. Regrettably, there's more concern about the potential for litigation. Coupled with the relative lack of wilderness experience of the majority of our passengers, the concern is understandable.

We pulled in and Graham handed the bowline to Carla, who was already on shore. I warned Chris and Graham about the travertine. It was either very sharp from chemical erosion, or very polished and slick from thousands of grinding footsteps. I helped Mary over to a crystal-clear pool lined with brilliant electric green mosses, and found her a shady spot in which to relax and enjoy the five layers of life. Then I went back to the lunch boat and helped the rest of the crew set up a table and prepare lunch. The taco salad was eaten with gusto, and Sue and Floyd said they would clean up while we took the rest of the folks up to the first pool.

Going back to my raft, I pulled out my backpack, water bottle, flute, camera, and tripod, and headed up the trail with Carla. The rest of the crew would follow. As I passed them, I urged Chris and Graham to go on at least the first part of the hike. I guaranteed them they would appreciate it. Chris laughed self-consciously, and Graham shot me a skeptical glance, his way of saying he might appreciate the view but not necessarily what it would take to get there. Liz was still filling her water bottle as I walked by her, and I smiled self-consciously.

The trail into Elves was neither steep nor difficult, but it did have some foot polished travertine, so it was important to watch people, and give them a hand if they needed it. We walked up a rough trail cut in granite, stepped over and on slick white travertine, negotiated a small step up with some exposure to our right, and found what looked like a well-worn trail. That led us up some slick travertine formations to an angled conglomerate rock that required a step up to a larger conglomerate rock, with a foot of space between the two. It's odd how intimidating that short distance could be to folks who were unfamiliar with hiking in this environment. So Carla stepped across the chasm and sat down on the upper rock, while I positioned myself on the lower rock to hold people's cameras and water bottles, and give them directions and a hand if they wanted it. Some did, some didn't. But we quickly left that behind, climbed around another huge boulder, walked a tightrope edge with just a few feet of exposure, and crossed over a small pool. After climbing some Tapeats ledges, we came around a corner and were met by an oasis of maidenhair fern and monkey flower in front of a narrow pool fed by a stringy waterfall.

The water trickled down a two-step channel, hugging large boulders that had been placed there in the past by massive floodwaters. The rocks were hanging gardens of maidenhair fern, cardinal monkey flower, and in springtime, an explosion of yellow columbine. We wasted no time getting into the water, which, although cold, was still warmer than the Colorado. Carla led us past the sheet of water dripping from the rocks to a narrow cavern behind the falls. Climbing up slippery rock, she appeared above the lower falls, and waited for Nathan, Eliza, and Roni to come up. Liz had waded into the pool and had her video camera in hand waiting for Roni to jump. The view was spectacular, with narrow limestone walls splaying out as if encouraging us to notice the sun-drenched walls across the river. Slippery moss-lined rock bracketed her on both sides as she stepped down onto a wet, slick platform just a foot from the edge. The pool below was at least ten feet deep, and several passengers stood in the shallow end encouraging Carla to jump. She showed Nathan where to step, talked about pushing away from the wall, and then demonstrated. The rest followed, and that began a nonstop parade of suddenly childlike men and women reconnecting with their youth.

Chris and Graham arrived with Floyd and Sue, and we played for about fifteen minutes, jumping into the pool, exploring the cavernous room behind the falls, splashing each other, and looking for treasures in the bottom of the pool. Everybody, it seemed, had brought their cameras, and were taking photos of all the jumpers. I needled Graham a bit, trying to get him to go up, but he said the Queen wouldn't approve.

Sue announced a continuation of the hike for those who were willing. She again described the kind of moves we would be making, beginning with a climb up the Tapeats that included crawling under an overhang. When she pointed out the location forty feet above us, several people changed their minds. Eliza, Nathan, Antje, Jim, and Liz said they wanted to go. Of course, Roni wanted to go, but Elli asked her to stay with her. The look on Roni's face told us how she felt about that. Star would lead the hike, and Carla, Michael, and I would go as well. I decided to take my flute, camera, and tripod, even though it would make some of the moves more difficult.

Telling the rest to enjoy their time at the pool, we took off. Climbing up the Tapeats was easy. The sandstone was so coarse it was like planting our feet on sandpaper. We got up to the overhang and crawled along like soldiers on their bellies through an obstacle course. We had a forty-foot drop to our left. We edged along a narrow shelf, stepped down to a small ledge with nothing but air below us, climbed over a large boulder, and arrived at the second level. On a recent private trip, a woman had fallen to her death at this point. Evidently she had lost her footing on a slick, polished travertine boulder as she was stepping up to the second level and fell right on her head. I didn't think it was necessary to broadcast that.

In another *cul de sac* floated a pool fed by water dropping over a boulder that had wedged between narrowed walls. To get to the next level, we had to climb up a cut in the rock formed by sedimentary layers that had eroded away, block by block to form two walls coming together in a corner. We used convenient ledges as stair steps in our climb.

The third level was in the Muav layer, and consisted of a forty-foot water slide feeding into an elliptical pool of water with some partially submerged boulders at the bottom. So far, no one had needed a hand. We were climbing quickly, and taking time at each level for photographs.

We continued up the Muav steps, made a short climb onto a ledge that hosted a hanging garden of prickly pear cactus, and walked through a small jungle of bear grass with razor-sharp leaf edges. Emerging from the jungle, we came to another pool about fifteen feet below us, and a climb that required some agility and strength. We had to lift ourselves up between the wall on our right and a massive, undercut boulder on our left. A good climber would have no problem, as there were reasonable handholds. We let each person try on their own. Nathan went first, and it was obvious he had done this before. Michael lifted him up to the first handholds, and then he did the rest without any assistance. Eliza struggled at first, but managed to make it unaided. She looked down at me and winked. Jim needed some help getting started, and Carla, who had climbed up first, gave him a wrist-to-wrist lift at the top. Antje swore a few times in German, and finally requested some help. Michael gave her a foothold by interlocking his fingers together, and told her to put one foot on his shoulder before Carla helped her up the last bit. I then climbed up to replace Carla so she could lead to the next level. I reached down and took Liz's camera, and Star and Michael helped her up far enough for me to grab her wrist and help her up the final piece. She wasn't wearing perfume, but as she brushed up against me on her way past, I breathed in her femininity, and swallowed hard.

Michael and Star were in no hurry, so I walked with Liz to the next climb, a fifteen-foot conglomerate boulder covered in travertine that rested against the left wall. A shallow cavern led to a moss-covered wall with a buildup of calcium carbonate-encrusted humps. Liz took some time to take some close-ups, and I was curious how they would turn out. From a conversation we had had about my coffee table book, I already knew that she had a creative eye, and was interested in out-of-the-ordinary perspectives.

When she was ready, I showed her how to climb up the rock, followed behind her to make sure she felt safe, and stepped off the rock onto the last level. It was like walking into a gigantic greenhouse in the desert. Columbine, monkey flower, and maidenhair fern spread along the floor and up the walls. Everywhere drips falling from small ledges above splattered on rocks and into gardens below. A shiny wet wall eighty feet high told us we were at the end of this hike.

I found a flat, dry spot near one of the drips, and took my flute out of its protective case. I hadn't played it yet on the lower, but this was such a peaceful, quiet place, I felt it would add to the experience of being here. Even though I was still self-conscious when playing the flute, I wanted to hear its voice reverberating in this boxed-off canyon. Nathan was following a spotted toad as it hopped from pool to pool. Antje, Jim, Eliza, and Carla had found comfortable rocks on which to lie. Liz was working on capturing some reflections in a pool. I took a deep breath and began to play. I could almost see the notes floating through the air. The sound was deep and rich. Liz stopped to listen, and I saw her aim her camera in my direction. I was in a spectacular place being photographed by a beautiful woman. While I played, Michael and Star arrived, and they too found comfortable spots to relax. We stayed there for another half hour.

The climb down was easier than the climb up, and we stopped to take a quick plunge into the first pool before heading back to the rafts. When Liz emerged from the pool, her white blouse hugging her body, I thought of those enticing commercials showing a sensuous, beautiful woman emerging from the water.

Many flash floods had occurred in the drainage, and each one had altered the landscape. Unimaginably powerful floods occasionally carried massive boulders away. In the early days, an archway of boulders that had since disappeared in a flood had guarded the entrance to the first pool. Other times it was the water that was relocated. In the early 'nineties I took a photo that showed the water flowing around an outcropping on the rock face above the first pool. The aerated flow looked like long white hair, and indentations in the rock looked like eyes and a mouth. Another feature on the rock was perfectly placed to be a nose. It was most certainly the Elf of Elves Chasm. The flow has since relocated, and the Elf seems to have abandoned his home.

On the way down to the rafts, I told Liz to follow me. I took her to a pool of crystal-clear water, and told her the five layers of life story I had told people at Saddle Canyon in the upper Canyon. I then set up my tripod and took some shots of the features in the pool, while she sought her own images. It was fun for me to share some of the Canyon's secrets with her, and I enjoyed watching Liz discover what attracted her eye. When she seemed satisfied, I led her back to the rafts.

As I was untying my bowline, Sue called me over and said she was concerned that I was spending too much time with Liz and not paying enough attention to the other passengers. I told her I thought she was right, and appreciated the feedback. I said I would be more focused for the rest of the trip. As I went over to untie my raft, I felt like a chastened adolescent, embarrassed at having been caught with my hand in the cookie jar. At the same time, I forgave myself for being human. After all, this was the first woman in any of my trips that had so captured my attention.

We all jumped in and pulled out, rowing across the current to run on the far side of a pourover in the middle of the river. Chris spoke about what an amazing place just the first level of Elves was for her. She had actually gone up and jumped off the falls. I was surprised by this, congratulated her, and said that I hoped someone had taken a photo so we could look back on the event in years to come. Graham said he had. When I asked him if he had jumped, he said he was already too close to the grim reaper, and wasn't interested in accelerating their meeting.

We rounded a bend and entered a calm stretch called Stephen Aisle, named after a Christian Moor from Morocco who was one of only four out of four hundred men who had survived a Spanish expedition to Florida in the early sixteenth century. The river stretched downstream for two miles, bounded by the ledges of Tapeats sandstone. The sun had climbed above the shaded Tapeats, presenting a dramatic contrast to the pastel-tinted cliffs above. On our left, the bleached bones of a cottonwood tree twenty feet above the river spanned two cone-shaped rocks. The tree had been deposited in 1957 on the last flood to exceed a hundred thousand cfs.

We were floating in a very still place. No one spoke, so the only sounds were the oar blades entering and leaving the water, and the occasional squeak of the oarlock. I focused my attention on my dance with the river, carefully dipping my blade just below the surface, leaning into the oars and pushing the handles forward, pressing down on the handles to retrieve the blades from the river, feathering the blades and sliding them over the top of the calm water.

We pulled over at a sloping beach in a larger eddy at mile 118. From here we had an unobstructed view both upstream and downstream. The ledge-forming Tapeats sandstone, now at river level, gave off the impression of intimacy, while the soaring Cambrian cliffs above reminded me of the enormity of this place. People could walk quite a ways out into the river here before the water got too deep. Even though they were in an eddy, the currents can be surprisingly strong and unpredictable. Recently a man drowned after falling into an eddy at night. No one knows what actually happened, but it is likely he went down to the river to pee, slipped, and fell in. It's also possible that he had a heart attack. His wife told park rangers he had experienced some chest pains during the day, but they hadn't told anyone. Four days later they found his body five miles downstream.

After setting up their tents on a flat spot near the Tapeats wall which offered convenient ledges for hanging up wet clothes, the Israelis went down to the river to bathe and wash some clothes. Several others joined them.

Dinner, prepared by Michael and Floyd, was grilled steak and chicken, ranch beans and coleslaw, and brownies for dessert. Sue's dessert talk about the next day's plan called for two hikes and sixteen river miles, including several good-sized rapids. She thanked everyone for another wonderful day, and I could see that she meant it. We all felt so fortunate to be doing this work. Without passengers, we couldn't be paid for doing what we loved. Without passengers eager to explore, we wouldn't love it as much as we do.

As the sky began turning from day to night, I set up my tripod and got some good shots of an extraordinary sunset. The clouds burned a brilliant fuscia, reflecting off the river upstream in a display of beauty that brought tears to my eyes. The setting sun painted a streak of gold across the upstream rim. Through my lens I noticed breaks in the brilliant clouds that gave the appearance of eyes looking down on us. The Elf perhaps?

The sound of thunder brought people running for their tents, and we spent the next half hour helping people set them up. Liz and Elli were not willing to sleep outside, and had already put up their tents. I had encouraged them to sleep outside to see the amazing canopy of stars, the Milky Way, and shooting stars, but evidently my powers of persuasion needed some work.

Instead of putting up my tent, I took my bag and found a spot underneath a Tapeats ledge. It was pretty stifling there, the rocks still radiating the day's stored sun, and I wasn't totally comfortable thinking about the very real possibility of scorpions in the vicinity. Sensing some movement, I turned on my headlamp to see one scurrying away. That was it. I picked up my stuff and took it out on the beach. I went back to my raft where Eliza was sleeping, found my tent and took it over, just in case a real storm came in. Much of the rain in the Canyon, especially during the monsoon patterns of July and August, offered what I called the "Grand Canyon tease." Lightning, thunder, and what seemed like the beginning of a storm lasted just long enough to get people out of their sleeping bags to erect their tents. Then the rain would disappear and the sky would clear up for the rest of the night. Except when it didn't.

On nights like this, when there was the possibility of rain, I usually lay awake looking up at the clouds, trying to decide whether to put up my tent or not. Most of the time I would finally fall asleep.

I can't remember a time when I have slept straight through the night. But waking up has its own rewards in the rotating canopy of stars. It's always a treat to see the familiar shapes of constellations and the occasional shooting star. Of all the nights I've spent in the Canyon, one night stands out above all the rest, and it was at this camp. Early one morning I woke up and rolled over to see the stars. Instead I was treated to the most spectacular night sky ever. Cotton-ball clouds dotted the entire sky between both rims of the Canyon, and a bright gibbous moon provided backlighting to each cloud. I recall seeing blue behind the clouds. My eyes were only open for a few seconds, but the surreal image has been burned in my mind.

*Yes, there are rattlesnakes in the Grand Canyon. We're fortunate when
we happen upon one, which doesn't happen very often. In this case, I was
rigging my raft preparing to go downstream for a big hike when the trip
leader told me to get my camera. For thirty minutes we were all treated to
what we thought was a mating dance. Turns out it was two alpha males in a
territorial dance. Some times we're in the right place at the right time.*

DAY ELEVEN –
118 TO OWL EYES

During breakfast of sausage, hash browns, and eggs to order, I sat with the Israelis and asked how they were doing. Doron was still half asleep and said she was having a good time. Roni gushed about Elves Chasm and said she hoped there were more places like that on the rest of the trip. Elli said she was still feeling the effects of her hike down the Bright Angel trail, especially in her calves. Liz said she could feel the muscles in her shoulders from the climbs in Elves. She hadn't done anything quite like that, and appreciated all the help we had given her. Although I normally would have offered to work on Tal's shoulders and Elli's calves, after getting admonished by Sue I decided to hold off. Instead, I suggested the two friends work on each other.

I asked Elli if she had been born in Israel, because her accent didn't seem much different from many American Jews I knew. She told me she had grown up on the east coast and had moved with her family to Israel when she was thirteen. Her daughter Roni was born in Israel and was twelve, as was Doron. We talked a bit about life in Israel, and I was a bit surprised when Liz told me she supported the prime minister, Ariel Sharon. She seemed politically liberal, and my impressions of Sharon were that he was quite reactionary. She said the conditions in Israel today required a leader that would stand strongly for security, and Sharon represented that best. I also learned, in spite of the violence I had read so much about, life was fairly normal for most Israelis most of the time; except they were surrounded on three sides by people dedicated to their elimination. Since Sue had told us we would be getting out of camp more quickly this morning, I said I hoped we could talk more during the trip. She seemed open to that.

I took my plate over to the dish line and joined in. When I got to the first bucket, I cleaned off my plate, and then found the DO that had been used to cook the sausages. The bottom was caked with debris that would take forever to clean, so I found the coffee pot with grounds still in the bottom, and covered the bottom of the DO with the grounds. The acid would eat away at the baked-on sausage residue, and in five minutes I could clean the DO easily. Every time I've done this I think about the effect of coffee acid on people's stomachs and nerves.

I walked over to the kitchen area, collected all the dirty dishes and utensils, and carried them over to the dish line. Chris, Mary, Jim B, and Miriam were standing at each of the buckets, scraping, washing, rinsing, and disinfecting. So I dropped off the dishes and began carrying yellow bags to my raft. Tyler came over and asked if he could help, and I told him I would need six more bags. I asked him to bring me at least three that were small so I could get four rows across my back deck. After complying, he asked if he and his mom could ride with us, and I said I had room. He smiled and went back to his mom with the day bag.

Eliza was still packing up in the back of the raft, so I had to wait before strapping in my bags. I asked her where she planned to ride today. She said she would be in the paddleboat unless more than six people wanted to paddle. We didn't have as many people on this trip who wanted to be that active, so the regulars, like Jim B, Jim, Diane, Nathan, and Timmy, were given more opportunity to paddle. I told her the river would be getting mellow after today, and then some of the neophytes would probably jump on. She said either way would be fine with her. If she didn't ride in the paddleboat, she would want to be in one of the duckies. I could tell she wouldn't be riding with me very often, if at all.

We would have an easy two-mile float to Blacktail, another camp that held many memories for me. It was at Blacktail that I had played that competitive game of paddleball with my dad. Less than a year after that trip, he was diagnosed with a brain tumor which ten months later would lead to his passing. Whether we camped at Blacktail, or just floated by it, I always remembered that time with my father.

The nearest thing to a slot canyon in the Grand Canyon, Blacktail has been a concert venue on every string quartet trip, offering the perfect combination of close walls and a hard-packed floor. The entry to the canyon is a wide, gravel-strewn channel bordered by sandstone ledges. In the past, pockets of water had forced us to climb around on the ledges. Today those pockets are covered by several feet of gravel and cobble from recent debris-flows. As we walk up the canyon, the walls close in, in some places resting less than fifteen feet apart. Large boulders dot the landscape, and the quartet usually plays in a small open area surrounded by natural rock seating. With close, hard walls, and relatively solid flooring, the acoustics are spectacular. Often, a resident canyon wren will accompany the stringed instruments.

On one of my trips in the mid-eighties, we had run into a very rowdy group of testosterone-poisoned men at the Little Colorado. After drinking out of a five-gallon bucket of rum and cokes, they had tried to join our Frisbee-playing group. One inebriated man actually attempted to dive through the floating disc. We were on the same schedule, so we would see them on a regular basis. They had joined us for the concert at Blacktail, and my most vivid memory was of that Frisbee-diver. The quartet was aligned in a circle playing one of the classical standards, and this six-foot three inch twenty-something was sitting on a small ledge, his right leg crossed over his left, an open beer can resting on his right knee. His eyes were soft, his face relaxed, mesmerized, it seemed, by the magic of musical vibrations in a magical place.

Our pull-in to upper Blacktail was in an eddy protected by an outcropping of polished black schist. In 1999, we camped here during the wettest trip I had ever been on. It had already been raining for two straight days, and waterfalls were spilling over the edges of the Canyon upstream and downstream. The air was supersaturated with moisture that permeated everything. It continued to rain all that day and night, and when we woke up in the morning the kitchen had a mini-canyon running down the middle from a small waterfall that had originated behind the camp. We served French toast while many of our passengers complained about the rain. After all, they came here for fun in the sun. It took us most of that day to convince them they were seeing an incredibly unique and unusual Canyon. Once the rain ended the air became crystal clear, the colors vibrant, and clouds hung below the rim, a phenomenon usually seen in the winter. Mist rose from the river, often hiding our bright yellow rafts. Looking downstream, there were times when I could only see heads or upper bodies. It was hauntingly beautiful.

Sue announced we would take a short hike in the canyon so we could get downstream by lunch and take a longer hike in the afternoon. She led the group through a sand bar dotted with water-polished cobble and sparse vegetation, down a short slope into the gravel-strewn drainage. Ahead was a narrow canyon cut out of the Tapeats. There was no evidence of water. In all my trips, there had always been pools and little rivulets disappearing and reappearing in the gravel floor. Willow and tammy saplings in the drainage all bent towards the Colorado – testimony of a recent flash flood or debris flow.

Sue stopped at a particularly narrow section about a hundred yards in from the entrance. Sandstone ledges towered above us on both sides. We were standing on what appeared to be a fresh deposit of fine gravel and cobbles. She spoke briefly about the Great Unconformity, two geologic layers that were not contiguous in time. The Tapeats sandstone had formed in the Tapeats Sea around 530 million years ago. The layer on which it rested, Vishnu schist, had formed 1,800 million years ago. The difference in age at the contact point was far greater than that of the Cambrian and Nankoweap gap that we had seen in the upper canyon. It represented one billion, two hundred seventy million years of missing earth history. Sue went into some detail about how that could happen. She explained that after the bottom layer, the Vishnu schist, had been formed, the next 1.27 billion years experienced the deposition and erosion of two mountain ranges and multiple sedimentary and igneous layers. Only then had the Tapeats Sea encroached on land to form its ledge-forming sandstone. Tyler and Graham both walked up and placed their hands on the contact point. The look on Tyler's face, captured by his mother, was one of incomprehensible wonder. Graham said it made him feel quite like an adolescent in comparison. Then we continued walking into the canyon.

I stopped at a limestone boulder and talked about the fossils that we used to see at the top of that rock. Now, because of a massive flash flood, instead of standing on the right side of the channel, the boulder rested thirty feet away in the middle of the channel, and the top was upside down and rotated 180 degrees. The fossils were no longer visible. I estimated the boulder weighed at least two thousand pounds.

Sue suggested we continue our walk in silence. She said we would be stopping in an area that had hosted the string quartet concerts, and would remain there for about half an hour. It would be a good time, she said, to reflect on their experiences on the trip. As people found comfortable spots under overhangs and on flat boulders, I continued down the canyon, still fascinated by the absence of any water. I went to the back of the canyon where I expected to see a pool fifteen feet deep and forty feet long. Instead the canyon floor was a gravel bed. At the end, a small seep dropped weakly into a tiny pool. Above this, a chock stone was wedged into the notch of the two walls. That stone was about six feet above the all-but dry canyon floor. It used to be more than fifteen feet above the pool, and had been a barrier to seeing the upper part of the canyon.

For years I had wanted to climb up this slick wall and check out the rest of the canyon. But

I found it difficult to ask anyone to help me. Finally, I decided to bite the bullet and attempt the climb on my own. It turned out to be easier than I had thought. After swimming through the pool, I managed to climb up the right side, crawl under a large boulder, and stand up on a slick ledge just below the chock stone. There were no solid handholds on the stone, and I felt the fear of falling, but convinced myself that if I did, I would find a refreshing pool to catch me. I made it up and over the stone, and explored a bit of the upper canyon. On the way back, my terror returned as I carefully lowered myself over the stone. To allay my anxiety I whistled under my breath, and felt relieved when my feet contacted slick rock, and I was able to lower myself back into the pool. As I walked back to camp, I felt a new exhilaration from having gone beyond my edge with no help from others.

*   *   *

Not long after I severed part of my pinky finger, I decided to do a ceremony here, honoring the value of that part of my body and letting it go. So I found a piece of wood the size of my departed finger, threw it into the pool and said goodbye. Then I played my flute. I was surprised at the sadness I had felt. Since it was the first digit on my baby finger, people often minimized the loss, saying it was the least significant part of my body. I remember thinking that it was still a part of my body, and saying goodbye to it did bring up the feeling of loss. After my finger healed, I played a round of golf and was surprised to learn that it's the outside fingers that provide the grip strength. My first round was pitiful. Fortunately I don't need that lost digit to play my flute.

I had brought the flute with me on this hike, and played some notes on it. The sound was somehow different from what I had remembered when the pool had been there, but it was still rich and resonant. I sat with my eyes closed and just listened to the sound of the water dripping into the forming pool. From time to time, the resident Canyon wren would sing.

When I heard Sue rounding up the folks to return to the rafts, I left my ceremonial spot and rejoined them. Coming out of this shaded cathedral, we were quickly reminded that we were still in the desert. The sun seemed brighter, and the heat more intense. Getting back to the rafts, many of us dunked our bodies in the river to cool down. We would be floating on slow water for much of the day, punctuated by some fun rapids. Unless we had some unexpected delays, we would get to Stone Creek around noon, have a quick lunch, and then go on a long hike into a spectacular, open, side canyon.

Approaching my raft, I looked over at an eroded sand dune. This was the location of the game of paddleball I had played with my seventy-one-year-old father.

I looked around at our community of adventurers, watching how easily they interacted with each other, even those who had hiked in just three days earlier. Eliza was joking with Star and both looked so natural, their hair bouncing freely in the desert sun, their skin natural and darker than at the beginning of the trip. No one seemed to be sunburned, and most, except the kids, were wearing long sleeved shirts to cover up.

As she stepped into the raft, Miriam diverted my attention as she handed me the purple bag and her camera. She asked if she could ride in the back, and I gave her a hand as she gingerly stepped on the frame and over the yellow bags on my rear hatch. I asked Tyler if he would untie my bowline, which he did with a contented smile. I showed him the sailor's knot that would make it easy to unfurl the line when we reached our next destination. He pushed me off the beach and hopped aboard. The raft shuddered as it accepted two hundred-twenty pounds of man-child. He told his mom he wanted to stay up front to talk with me, and she smiled and nodded her head.

As we floated into a small rapid at the mouth of Blacktail, we also entered Conquistador Aisle, a three-mile stretch of river bordered on both sides by Tapeats sandstone spread out under a spectacular backdrop of the remaining Cambrian sedimentary layers. The Redwall Cliff, the most prominent feature above the Tapeats, towered over us. Sunsets in this section of the Canyon were always spectacular, with the Cambrian layers ablaze reflecting the brighter long rays of the spectrum.

On my 1979 private trip I had spotted a herd of eleven bighorn sheep on the slope grazing above the Tapeats. After managing to find a small eddy, I tied up my raft, grabbed my camera, and climbed up to the top of the Tapeats. I peeked carefully over the edge, and there they were, less than fifty feet away. I was so excited that I had trouble holding my camera steady. There were eleven ewes, some nonchalantly munching on desert delicacies while others stood at attention, alert for any danger. The largest ewe stood regally on top of a large boulder, her head held high. Most of them seemed to be posing, offering a full side view.

Tyler asked if he could row, and I was happy to oblige. He seemed at ease on the oars, although it took him a few minutes to adjust to the open oarlocks. He had learned to row while on Carla's raft, and the oarlocks there were pins and clips, so the oars remained in one position. He also was a bit big for my setup. Every few strokes, the oar hit his knees. I realized it would be a mistake to have him rowing anything but a small rapid.

I took the oars from him just above 122-Mile rapid, and then gave them back once we were through. While he rowed, a broad grin swept across his face. He was having a ball, and I couldn't help but fall in love with him. I asked him what grade he was in, and he said seventh. I then asked him what was his favorite class. Without any hesitation, he said biology. He told me he loved to explore in swamps and marshes, and he was very excited by all the lizards, toads, and cicadas he was seeing on the trip. In fact, at camp, Tyler was constantly coming over to show one of us a critter he had caught. He was destined to be a naturalist, of that I was certain.

Again I took the oars to run Forster Rapid, rated a six. It had some good-sized waves at the top, made an "S" curve around a large peninsula, and then disappeared into a gentle bend for two miles. The Tapeats was more broken up here, marking the end of Conquistador Aisle. The river was a little wider, and the ledges gave way to a slope covering up the Bright Angel shale. In some places, the slope was a wall of debris made up of boulders, cobble, and soil. Much of it had come from slides from above. We were now in an ecosystem in which barrel cactus could thrive, a lot more on the north side than on the south. I told Tyler to keep his eyes peeled for big horn, and within minutes he had spotted a gorgeous ram drinking from the river, and then a small herd with two ewes and three little ones. Since they have few predators, the big horn are seemingly oblivious, and certainly unconcerned, with our presence. That's so long as we remain in our rafts. As soon as we step out of the raft, they scatter.

A slight upstream breeze whistled by my ears as we floated around a wide-sweeping bend. The current ran fairly close to the right shore. To our left, an expansive eddy traced its current along a narrow sand beach. A steep slope rose behind the beach and in the distance I could see a stand of bedraggled cottonwood trees several hundred feet above the river. Cottonwoods drink a prolific amount of water, and there was no water evident around these trees. Until recently, they had stood proud and tall, their foliage bright green and full. A five-year drought had obviously affected the underground source of the trees' drinking water, and now they looked like they were barely surviving.

These trees heralded the presence of Fossil Rapid, rated a six to seven. It was very similar to Forster, except bigger, with a very long wave train at higher water that dragged the end of the "S" out for quite a ways.

On one of my trips, the paddleboat had fallen behind the other rafts and had entered this rapid last. They unexpectedly flipped, and it took quite some time to pull everybody out of the river. One passenger was unaccounted for. I had pulled over to the left shore, and the trip leader signaled for me to run upstream with a throw rope and see if I could locate the man. I scrambled over large, broken-up, weathered sandstone and limestone boulders along the shoreline, being careful to avoid stepping on the crypto-biotic soils and small desert blossoms. The August sun beat down on me mercilessly, and I had forgotten to bring water with me. Emergencies are rare on these trips, so when a potential one does occur, we all get very focused. I've been trained in wilderness medicine, but I have never wanted to use the training. The fact that I've rarely had to, makes me feel even more uncertain – use it or lose, and all that. I had a first aid kit, but that wouldn't help alleviate my growing thirst. After a half hour of searching and finding nothing, I was concerned that maybe he had gotten trapped under a boulder. Then I saw folks downstream waving, and my trip leader tapping the top of his head in the signal that says all is well. The passenger had floated farther downstream before being picked up.

The tail waves in Fossil were perfect for a long rollercoaster ride for the duckies and the paddleboat. Timmy and Nathan were by now very accomplished kayakers, and they had negotiated each of the rapids thus far. We had at least one rapid ahead of us, and maybe two or three, where Sue might decide to pull the duckies. But for now, the kids were having a blast – until a no-name, very short but intense rapid we call boat sucker. It's really only one wave, a lateral wave that comes off the right shore, and then turns into a combination of a hole and a whirlpool. Sue called the boys over and gave them instructions about how to avoid the hole. Neither one did. First Nathan, then Timmy, entered the rapid and flipped instantly upon hitting the hole. Nathan's ducky reared straight up and fell backwards, ejecting him into the right eddy. Timmy leaned forward as he encountered the wave but was just a little askew and his ducky flipped over, ejecting him into the same eddy. This was fortunate, because directly below the hole, the current charged towards the left shore into some Tapeats ledges that could be dangerous for a swimmer. Both surfaced with their paddles, and Nathan popped back into his ducky and paddled after Timmy's, which was floating in the eddy. With a big smile on his face he towed the errant ducky back to the bigger, older kid, who laughed as he struggled before getting back into his craft.

We were now floating next to the Tapeats, and the current rushed close to the left wall. Around the bend we passed a camp on the right just upstream of Randy's Rock. *Randy was a commercial guide in 1976 who had fallen asleep at the oars. Actually he was sleeping while a passenger rowed his twenty-two foot snout rig. The raft slammed up against a huge piece of*

Tapeats that had calved off into the river. A narrow channel flowed around to the left of the sandstone, and the river pushed up against the right side of the "rock." The raft was pinned on the rock by the strong current, and initial efforts to free it were unsuccessful. The trip's leader swam out to the rock, and, with the help of one of the passenger who had managed to climb up on the rock, cut away as much gear as possible. They salvaged the meat cooler and picked up a lot of stuff floating in the river as they traveled downstream. Other stuff was dropped off by passing motor rigs. At their takeout at the end of the trip, the company owner thought the guides were kidding when they informed him that they had lost one of his rafts.

*   *   *

The camp had been the scene of some outrageous antics on a recent summer trip. At the load out, one of the guides had thrown in a roll of vizqueen he then loaded on his raft and carried downriver. After setting up camp in the early afternoon on a warm, sunny day, he borrowed several sleeping pads from the rafts, laid them down two astride, and then covered them with the vizqueen. He then recruited two water throwers and announced a new game. The objective was to get a good running start and dive headfirst onto the pads. Just before the body hit the pads, the water throwers were instructed to spray the pads with their water. He then retrieved the dish soap from the kitchen, soaped up his front-side for lubrication, and demonstrated. The key, it turned out, was to get a really good running start. Some were better than others, but all had a blast. At first I held back, taking on the role of water thrower. For some reason I was a little reluctant to throw myself into this activity. But it just looked like so much fun, so I decided to go for it. I backed up to get as good a running start as possible and launched myself towards the pads. The water throwers were a bit tardy, so my slide was unspectacular. I got back in line, and the second time found myself being launched into the river. For kicks I tucked and performed a 360-degree roll. Soon others were doing twists and flips. At the end of the game, as I was helping roll up the vizqueen, I looked over at the guide and smiled. He smiled back and said he was just doing his job. Then he really smiled.

A half-mile below Randy's Rock, we entered another surprising environment. The river turned sharply to the left and then back to the right. On the left shore, a localized fault had pushed up the overlying Tapeats, revealing a jet-black schist. The color was due to a black mineral in the sediment called hornblende. With the sun getting closer to the zenith, the reflection off the schist was so bright I had to put on my sunglasses. The rock was smooth, polished, and sculpted into many sensuous forms. Some looked like crowds of people clustered together. Others were individual, abstract sculptures with interpretations as diverse as the beholders floating by. We were now in the Middle Granite Gorge. It would last for just four miles before we would enter a new, softer formation that would again open up the Canyon.

In those four miles, we would run two large rapids. The first was Specter, sometimes referred to as sphincter. It required a run along the right wall because of a rock bar emanating from Specter Canyon on the left. Just above the entrance to the rapid, a large schist outcropping stood ramrod straight, like a sentinel in the middle of the river guarding the entrance to the palace.

In 1984, this outcropping was only a foot out of the water, hiding much of its mass like a black, polished stone iceberg. We had pulled over to hike Specter canyon, and were having lunch when someone shouted that Georgie was coming down the river. Georgie was Georgie White, a short, slim, seventy-one year old woman in a leopard-skin leotard and white hardhat. Georgie was a hard-nosed woman who didn't pamper her people. She was known to serve hardboiled eggs and sausage cooked in its own can.

*   *   *

In 1983, Georgie approached Crystal when it had peaked at 92,000 cfs. Georgie had one, and only one, run – right down the middle. Clad in her trademark leopard-skin leotards, she clipped on her hardhat, grabbed her safety strap, gunned the motor, and ducked. The triple-rigged craft plunged into a mammoth wave right at the entry that completely swallowed the raft. In no time, the vibrating raft started spitting out passengers and gear. When it was all over, the only person left was – Georgie. By the end of the day, helicopters had removed all her passengers from the Canyon. Georgie's only comment was: "They don't make passengers like they used to."

*   *   *

On our '84 trip, we watched as Georgie floated towards the head of Specter rapid. Some guides made bets about whether she would run over the polished stone. I didn't believe that she would. She did. The right side of her outrigger raft (she was running a triple rig with a raft on either side of her main raft) rose up and then settled back down, and Georgie ran right down the middle of the rapid and disappeared. A few minutes later, an upset private boater rowed up to us saying that he had been enjoying a peaceful float down the river when Georgie had roared up, shoved him out of the way with her raft (he said she had run over him), and told him "Georgie doesn't get out of anyone's way." That was Georgie.

Specter could be very big, with the first two waves being the most threatening. The first wave could stand a raft straight up, cause it to lose momentum and angle, and the second wave, coming diagonally off the wall, could be number two in the one-two punch, resulting in a knockout.

Before running Specter, I asked Miriam to come up front, because I wanted more weight up there. I had Tyler sit on the right side, figuring if I needed to high side, it would probably be on the right side because of that second wave. I considered cheating the rapid by pulling backwards on the left at the entry to miss the first two waves, but rejected that idea and set up to hit the big ones. I floated just to the left of the outcropping, which was now three-and-half feet out of the water, found the current coming off the right wall, and pushed into the first wave. We hit it straight on, sent millions of water droplets flying everywhere, and rose to the top of the wave. I held my right oar in the river and pushed hard on my left to turn into the diagonal wave, and then flowed into the tail waves along the right wall. Tyler and Miriam shouted wildly as we cruised into the eddy on the left to run safety for the remaining rafts.

To the right of the current loomed a schist wall, with small alcoves carved over the eons

171

by abrasive river currents. In each alcove swirled a micro-eddy. If anyone wound up in there, it would be hard to make a rescue.

On a trip in 2000, a ducky wound up in there. The duckier was a Liberal member of the English Parliament, and a great guy. He was tall, slightly overweight, intelligent, witty, and committed to improving the quality of life for his constituents who lived in the poorest district in England. Earlier in the trip he had taught us cricket, using a paddle as the bat. He was also willing to take risks. After being in the ducky for a couple of days, he was feeling pretty cocky (his words). We told him about Specter, and he said he thought he could run it successfully. This was before he had set eyes on it. The first wave rolled him over so fast he said at first he hadn't realized what had happened. He came up in one of the micro-eddies, performed a self-rescue, and then spent ten minutes getting out of the eddy. By the time we arrived at camp, he was exhausted and, he told us, chastened. The river, he said, had taught him a lesson about arrogance.

After running Specter, we settled into a relaxing float, ignoring for now the challenges of Bedrock Rapid a mile below. Chris and Graham were laughing at something Floyd was saying, Liz and Elli had found comfortable positions in the back of Star's raft, and for the first time, Doron and Roni were in a different raft. They had chosen Michael's boat, and were engaged in a free-for-all water fight with Diane and Jim on Carla's raft. Soon, the paddleboat, with Eliza, Antje, Jim B, Kathy, and Mary, joined the fray, and all semblance of a peaceful float disappeared. I was already a ways downstream, so we continued on a sluggish current down a narrow corridor, like walking in an alley between two high-rise buildings.

Like House Rock in the upper Canyon, Bedrock rapid was formed from debris coming out of a canyon on river right. The rock bar extended into the middle of the channel funneling all the water towards a house-sized chunk of granite. Our run had to be to the right of the rock, and because of the rock bar, we would have to start farther out in the river and wouldn't have a lot of room for error. If we missed the cut to the right, we risked almost certain danger in the racing channel to the left of the rock.

On a motor trip in the summer of 1973, an enthusiastic but inexperienced trainee, Myron Cook, was at the helm of a thirty-seven foot motor rig, while a veteran guide was said to be sleeping under a tarp. Some suggested he might have had company. Cook, oblivious to the reality downstream, was enjoying the calm stretch after having survived Specter. It was only as he approached the head of the rapid that the veteran heard the rapid. He emerged from his retreat in time to look up, see the bedrock, and yell, "Go right!" Too late. The raft slid sideways up on the rock, hesitated as if considering its options, and then flipped.

Fortunately there were no injuries, but most of the sleeping gear and food were washed downstream. Other rafters eventually arrived to help right the raft and provide enough gear and food to complete the trip. The only casualty was the veteran river guide: the incident cost him his job. The rookie must have learned from his experience, because he went on to become a highly respected veteran. In fact, I ran into him on my last trip.

Flips are inconvenient because it takes time to re-flip the raft, especially if it's a thirty-three to thirty-seven foot motor rig. In the old days, guides would have to de-rig the large craft to turn it over. Sometimes, they had to call in a helicopter, at great and unwelcome expense to the company. Occasionally a passenger is traumatized. After I flipped in Hermit on my fifty-first trip, my Swiss passenger, Lilliane, told me if she happened to be in another flip, she would not get back in the raft.

I told Miriam and Tyler this story, and Tyler then asked me if I had ever flipped in Bedrock. I told him I hadn't, but I had had some very exciting experiences. With an excited grin he asked me to talk about them.

On one July trip I was enjoying a peaceful float above Bedrock when a major thunderstorm unexpectedly blew in. It rained so hard I couldn't see the end of my raft. In the near darkness, with Bedrock looking closer and closer in my mind, I became anxious about how close I might be. We were actually a half-mile away, but I didn't know that. So I pulled over onto a beach on the right to wait out the storm. As it began to let up, I realized we were at a short side canyon called 130 Mile. The entrance was very narrow, only about twelve feet from wall to wall. Fifty feet in, a chock stone topped by a tamarisk tree rested between even narrower schist walls. Behind that the canyon opened up a bit, and seventy-five feet beyond, the canyon ended in a sixty-foot wall bearing a travertine slide which, at the moment, was channeling a flash flood towards us. A half dozen of us, dressed in yellow, blue, and green raingear, were able to stand on the downstream side of the canyon entrance and watch the flood pour over the chock stone and flow past us into the river. The flow was less than two feet deep, and we had to be careful not to stand too close to the edge as the rushing water constantly undercut the banks on both sides. The sediment-rich flood water soon carved its own niche in the green river. Less than a minute after the beginning of the flood, the right side of the river had turned an iron-oxide shade, while the left side stubbornly stuck to its green shade. All the way up and down the channel waterfalls poured over the top and plunged down schist and granite cliffs that would hold on to some of the moisture to nurture current and future vegetation.

Thunderstorms in the desert are usually sudden, swift, and ephemeral. They arrive on a warning of strong, usually upstream winds, disgorge a large volume of water in a very short period of time, and then disappear, like a sprinkler suddenly being turned off. They leave their residue, temporarily shining rocks and cliff faces, dampening beaches and humans, before surrendering to the overwhelming arid reality of the desert. Some storms also leave a residue in my memory.

Tyler was fascinated and said he hoped we would see something like that on his trip. I told him I did, too. I'd been blessed with only a few storms that gave us such a show. I said it didn't look like that would happen today, as the sky was mostly sunny, and the clouds that were floating overhead were not the thunderheads that foreshadowed an impending storm. It was about eleven in the morning, and by then we could have expected to see the presence of those beautiful white, cumulo-nimbus clouds beginning to build if a thunderstorm was imminent.

We pulled over into a small eddy on the right just above Bedrock to scout and spend a few minutes playing in the Doll's House, a sculpted outcropping of schist and granite that had been named after a place in Cataract Canyon in Utah that contained sculpted rock formations. While the guides and the paddleboat crew went down on the rock bar to scout the rapid, many of the passengers climbed into, over, and around the Doll's House. As I went down to scout, I passed Liz, who had grabbed her camera and was heading to the granite outcrop to find some unusual perspectives. She smiled and quickly looked away as she walked by.

As I scouted Bedrock, I noticed that at this high water level, we would have a bit more room to maneuver than lower water afforded. The deeper water allowed us to start closer to the right shore. On the other hand, the greater volume meant a faster current and less time to make our cut. At lower levels, we have less room but more time to maneuver.

Sue decided to have Timmy and Nathan carry their kayaks across the rock bar and not run the rapid. Both were disappointed, but didn't put up much of a struggle. I asked Tyler to go into the rear of my raft so I would have more weight back there. Since I would be pulling backwards across the right-to-left current, his extra weight would actually help the raft track more consistently and give me an advantage against the current, so long as I held the right angle. The main reason I had wound up left of the Bedrock the second time was I had lost that angle, and the current had surfed me so far left I had no option but to go in there. If I left both Tyler and Miriam in the front, their weight would actually work against me, because they would be pushing the front of the raft down and allowing the strong current to grab hold of the raft.

If done correctly, the run through Bedrock should be anti-climactic. We had to decide whether we wanted to run inside or outside a pourover at the entry on the right side. The inside route was safer, but there was a better chance of scraping over rocks. In a self-bailer, with its hard plastic skin, that usually wasn't a problem. But with my Avon bucket-boat, my thin rubberized floor could easily rip on submerged rocks.

I chose the outside route, set up at a forty-five degree angle to the current, and waited until I was close to my entry on the left edge of a pourover. Some guides like to use momentum and set up farther out in the current. But that requires more precision, and I've never felt comfortable with momentum. As I approached my marker, I pulled hard on my oars, using the power in my legs to begin the stroke. On the third stroke we dipped down and broke through the outside of the pourover. I continued to pull hard to get to the right of a second pourover. If I didn't get right of it, I could be surfed to my left towards the rock. This time I made it, actually overdoing it a bit, and sliding over a couple of shallow rocks in the process.

Once below the rock, I pulled hard to the left to catch a small eddy so that Tyler could get a photo of the paddleboat. The current passed right in front of us, so it was a good spot for an action photo. Bedrock is usually an easy run for the paddleboat because they have such great momentum with all those engines. With an experienced guide like Sue, it would be very unlikely that something would go wrong. But we were set up just in case. Floyd had tied up to the Bedrock and was up on top of it with a throw rope in case anyone fell out of his or her raft. We could hear Sue's voice above the roar of the rapid, as Antje and Jim B in the front led the way. They took just a few strokes and then stopped, having gone as far as they needed to remain right of the Bedrock.

After Michael cruised by, a big grin on his youthful face, we pulled back into the current. This wasn't an easy matter, since the current was very strong, and it pushed us toward the right shore.

We were now out of the Middle Granite Gorge, and into the Bass limestone we had last seen below Hance. The diabase sill, a lava formation that looked like a textured, greenish-black vertical cliff, had also surfaced just below the limestone. At the contact point of these two layers sat a partially metamorphosed formation of asbestos, whitish rock with green flecks. The Canyon was again widening, allowing in more light and warmth. We were close to midday, and my belly told me so. We had one more big rapid to run, Deubendorff, a little over a mile downstream, before pulling over at Stone Creek for lunch and a long hike.

The river widened below Bedrock. We floated on a slower current near the right shore, ran a small but noisy riffle, and entered Deubendorff Lake, a half-mile stretch of calm water created by the debris flows downstream that had formed the rapid we were about to run. We passed a camp on the right that had been the scene of the Great Raven Caper.

On a trip in 2001, while we were enjoying breakfast, an impatient raven decided to visit an absent passenger's campsite. It was drawn to a closed ziplock baggie filled with shining metal things – bracelets, anklets, toe rings, and the like. The raven picked the baggie up in its beak and flew directly over our heads, as if to say this is my beach and I can have anything I want. The offended passenger cursed the bird as it flew downstream to the opposite shore, settling on a lava rock. It then proceeded to check the bag out for any delicacy, which to the raven was anything even close to organic. They're very intelligent birds, except when it comes to their diet. After finding nothing edible, the raven flew off, leaving the shiny things scattered around.

I had noted the location of the rock, and thought I would row over there on the way downstream. When I got there the next morning, I had no trouble locating the bag with all items accounted for. The passenger was very grateful.

The roar of Deubendorff now drifted into hearing range, and soon we were floating past another camp called Galloway, named in honor of Nathaniel Galloway, a pioneering river runner in the late nineteenth and early twentieth centuries. He literally turned river rafting around by choosing to face downstream when entering most rapids. The standard technique was named after John Wesley Powell, who had his oarsmen face upstream while he manned a rudder and shouted commands, as any good ex-Union officer with one arm would do. In 1896 Galloway began a solo trip in Green River, Wyoming, and finished in February, 1897 in Needles, California. In 1909, he joined Julius Stone, and Seymour Deubendorff, who was the first to flip in the rapid that would bear his name. Here is what he wrote in his journal:

"...I followed into the high waves and rougher water. In the very trough of one of these waves a rock lay in my path, which I struck squarely with the stern of my boat. This capsized me and when I rose I struck the gunwale of my boat with my head, cutting quite a gash. I swam to one side, and rising again came up free from the boat. I then swam for shore and was carried down stream 250 to 300 yards, most of this time under the water. I would catch my breath in the trough of each wave. Everything came out all right; even my cap was picked up. The boat was jammed in the stern and fore curtain torn. One of my extra oars was broken off above the blade. I bruised or sprained my knee in the river."

Deubendorff's notes reminded me of a trip when I thought I was following a seasoned guide down the left side of the rapid. I was mistaken. The left side was a minefield of boulders and pourovers. In one particularly violent pourover, the rear of my raft flipped up, and one of my passengers, who hadn't been holding on well, flew up in the air. On the way up, his head collided with his wife's, causing a serious gash above his left eye. We thought it was deep enough that he should have stitches and offered to call in a helicopter. He declined. As a devil-may care adventurer, he said he was used to these kinds of assaults to his body. Anyway, he thought the scar would look good on him. We made sure his wound was kept as clean as possible, and he suffered no ill effects.

175

In 1999, we had a prodigious amount of rain, and Stone Creek had flashed big time. Two weeks after that flood we had camped just upstream at Galloway. I had heard about the flood but had no idea how big it was until I hiked downstream to check it out. The drainage had a small creek fed by a waterfall about a quarter-mile in. Prior to the flood, the creek bed had been choked with willow saplings, small tammies, and other vegetation. When I turned the corner and had my first look at the drainage, I couldn't believe what I saw. The entire drainage was like a moonscape with a small creek meandering down the middle. It had been scoured of any vegetation. Not even a blade of grass remained. It was as if a gigantic road grader had roared down the drainage, its voracious blades gobbling up anything in its path.

The run in Deubendorff is fun at higher water, and more difficult at lower water. This time we had higher water. I would run third behind Floyd and Star. We were all clustered together with Star's raft just in front of me. I smiled at Liz and winked, forgetting that I had my sunglasses on. She smiled back and raised her fingers. To give Star some space, I pulled upstream and watched as she floated into the rapid. Then I entered on the right side of the tongue, passed just to the right of a big hole, breaking through a wave that reared up to challenge me, and entered a chaotic stretch of waves charging at us from every direction. Tyler and Miriam had a great time throwing their weight around in response to my directions. We raced into huge waves coming off the table rock, a ledge at lower water, and I pushed to the right to find the main part of the current. A hundred yards more and we slammed into some big waves, turned sharply to the left, and sailed through the tail waves. I turned the raft so the rear faced the right shore and pulled hard to get into the eddy so we could watch the paddleboat and Timmy and Nathan make their runs. It was a big rapid for anyone in the duckies, but we had received permission from Kathy, Nathan's mom, and Ralph had given us his grudging permission. We were ready for any rescue. I had my throw rope in my hand. If they flipped at the top, they would get a big, wet ride, but they shouldn't be in danger otherwise.

We shouted words of encouragement that no one but us could hear, as first the paddleboat with Eliza anchoring the front right, then Nathan, then Timmy, entered the rapid. Sue had them run farther right than we had, and they were doing great. At one point Timmy's ducky turned sideways and looked like it would flip for sure; but he managed to reach out with his paddle to brace against the wave and miraculously stayed upright. We cheered lustily as they floated by us, smiling from ear-to-ear. The paddleboat cruised into the eddy next to us, and Eliza sent me a thumbs-up and big grin before throwing water at me with her paddle. I responded by splashing the front of the paddleboat with my oars, and Tyler joined the fray by using the bailing bucket to douse everyone. Then we headed to shore.

We all pulled over at the beach that was now a shadow of its former self, having lost two-thirds of its sand, caused in large part by the operations of the dam. This was the beach where I had once roasted in the sun while patching the six holes in my raft after getting blown down the left side of Serpentine.

While we ate lunch, Sue described the hike we were about to take. Anybody who didn't want to go far could opt to go about a quarter-mile to a wonderful waterfall and pool that would eventually have some shade. In the meantime, they could take up one or two of our umbrellas to provide artificial shade. I told Mary I thought she could get up there with some help, and suggested she do that. She seemed open to whatever I said.

For those who wanted to hike more, Sue said there was an up-and-over trail that would take us into Stone Creek canyon, a wide-open valley with some of the Grand Canyon Supergroup formations usually not seen at the river. Sue said people could choose to go long or short, with several shady areas near small cascades where they could get wet. Because the '99 flash flood had stripped much of the vegetation from the drainage, the canyon was more wide open than ever, and we would be walking right up the drainage. We hadn't been able to do that prior to the flood, having instead to follow a trail through thick vegetation while meandering from one side of the creek to the other. Miriam and Jim B opted for the first waterfall. Mary said she would hang out by the river. Everyone else decided to do the up-and-over. Sue issued a warning for those who wanted to go long. We had to be back on the rafts by four o'clock, so those going long would have to be prepared for a very quick pace. The long hikers on the way back would sweep up those who planned to meander.

I told Sue I would be willing to go with the long group, as did Star, Carla, and Michael. Floyd said he would go medium, as did Sue. Liz, Roni, Doron, Diane, Jim, Nathan, Kathy, Timmy, Eliza, and Antje said they would go medium or long, depending on how they felt. Chris, Graham, Kathy, Elli, and Tyler said they wanted to meander. Tyler said he was excited to find some more lizards, and hoped to find a snake or two.

We announced the hike in ten minutes, told people to fill up on water and dunk themselves in the river, and we broke down the lunch table. Finally, Star and Carla announced the first wave would be leaving in two minutes, and we all grabbed our packs with a first aid kit, extra water, and some snacks. I added my camera and tripod, and before heading out grabbed my umbrella and set it up for Mary near the water, along with a Crazy Creek chair. She asked me if I had had any unusual experiences at this camp. I told her I had – a snake Dance between two Grand Canyon Pink rattlesnakes. She got very excited and asked if I would tell her more about it. I looked over at the line of hikers moving up the trail and decided it would be easy to catch up with them after telling Mary the story.

On August 4th, day nine of a trip down the Colorado River in 2005, we were camped at Stone Creek. I had heard past reports of snake sightings here but had personally never seen any. After dinner, as dusk was removing the brilliant warm rays of the sun, one of our passengers reported a possible snake sighting near the "groover." I pointed out the location to Mary, downstream from the main camp area behind some rocks that provided some privacy while still allowing a spectacular view of the Canyon. A couple of us went down to investigate, came up empty, and turned our attention to sleep.

We returned to the camp and were making a game out of staying up until at least eight o'clock when word came from upstream that a rattlesnake had been sighted cruising close to a campsite. We grabbed our headlamps and hurried to the area where the affected passengers were gathered. A Grand Canyon Pink rattlesnake, three feet long, moved slowly over the soft sand, inconvenienced by the bright lights of curious humans, but intent on continuing its hunt for a late-night snack. We watched as it headed away from the beach into some basalt rocks, still radiating heat from the day. We thought it would disappear under one of them. Instead, it changed directions and moved towards the nearest campsite, not too far from where we stood – ground cloth, thermarest, and sleeping bags laid out awaiting human warmth. When it continued its march and cruised right through the campsite, we decided to relocate it.

Grabbing two buckets and a paddle, the trip leader softly hoisted the snake onto the handle of the paddle and carefully dropped it into one of the buckets. I placed the second bucket on top, being careful not to harm the snake, and we walked up a sandy trail leading into the Stone Creek drainage. Once in the drainage we removed the second bucket and watched as the snake casually emerged, thrust its body away from the bucket, and slithered away.

Mary asked if the snake had been injured and I told her no. Several of the passengers had been curious about the snake's behavior and we told them it hadn't rattled, didn't seem perturbed, and probably wouldn't be a further bother. We said good night, and headed back to our respective campsites.

Mary said she would never have risked moving the snake, but I told her it wasn't a big deal, and then said to her that this was "the rest of the story."

In the morning I heard a few comments about the snake sighting during breakfast, but most people were focused on the food in front of them and the events of the day to come. Then I heard Tom, the trip leader, shouting to me to bring my camera. He was in the area of the groover, and without questioning I grabbed my camera and headed downstream. When I arrived there, Tom simply pointed to a group of polished boulders twenty feet below, about thirty feet from the river's edge. I pointed out the spot to Mary.

Once I had seen a postcard with two snakes intertwined in a very provocative mating-dance, and I had envied the photographer fortunate enough to be in the right place at the right time. I never thought I would find myself in a similar position. But there they were, two Grand Canyon Pink rattlesnakes swaying in an eternal dance of procreation. Both had the typical "V-shaped" pit viper head. The larger of the two sported a thicker body and a light brown cast. Dark brown borders laced its entire back in jagged elliptical rings. The smaller snake had a similar pattern with more of the usual pinkish cast common among these unaggressive cousins of the Western Diamondback.

I was only fifteen feet away and able to fill my lens with the swaying, undulating images of these two magnificent creatures, aware that I was witnessing something that few others had had, or would have, the privilege to see. Before long the entire group, twenty passengers and six crew, stood around mesmerized as the snakes continued their stirring movement. At times they mirrored each other's postures while swaying sensuously, at other times the snakes intertwined like clenched fists, demonstrating a strength not seen in any of their normal movements. In a ritualistic pattern, the snakes would separate and move to opposite corners, feigning indifference, only to return to the dance floor to resume their foreplay. At all times they seemed to be fully aware of each other's presence.

Comments from the gallery ranged from the sacred to the profane. Several wondered which was the male and which the female. I watched through my lens, waiting for the telltale stroking of the female's chin, an action the male would use. Both snakes seemed oblivious to the transfixed voyeurs while clearly being aware of each other. At times the snakes would rise up in unison, fully two-thirds of their bodies swaying back and forth as if connected to a beat unheard by us. Other times one would travel across the other, and then suddenly they would become entangled as if ecstatically charged. We watched in awe as one would rise up, its body forming a variety of sensuous shapes, and the other would follow suit.

Our lovers moved toward the river, and I moved with them, positioning myself with a direct view as they continued their dance, bracketed by polished igneous and sedimentary boulders. I silently wished for my tripod but didn't want to leave for fear that the music would stop. I considered asking someone to retrieve it from my raft, less than a hundred feet away, but it didn't feel right to deprive them of this spectacle, even for a couple of minutes. I felt incredibly energized, and could have stayed there all day, but knew we would have to leave shortly. Would we be there for the "moment of truth?"

Finally the snakes made our departure easy. They broke off their dance and slithered slowly away to neutral corners in the shade of nearby boulders. Was this just teasing behavior, or the beginning of a protracted dance resulting in new life? We would never know

After the trip, I was informed by my friend Dr. Larry Stevens, who knows more about the Grand Canyon than anyone possibly could, that snakes mate in the Spring, not in August. As a result, my Mating Dance turned out to be two males doing their Alpha Dance. Still, it makes a great story.

After making sure Mary was comfortable, I took off to catch up with the rest of the hikers. By now they were over the first ridge and out of sight.

I walked up a cobble-filled slope and at the top looked up the drainage that was slowly filling in with vegetation. I could see the first waterfall standing tall without the greenery that used to feed off its spray. I call the waterfall Stone Creek Woman, after a short story written by Terry Tempest Williams.

On the private trip with my parents in 1986, we had camped at Stone, and I had walked up to the waterfall after dinner. The night sky was hidden behind a blanket of clouds, removing any distracting light and pulling me inward. The air was still, like a held breath. The heat was stifling. A grove of trees drew a semi-circle in front of the falls and removed any light from the darkening sky behind me. Sitting on a rock near a shallow pool in front of the waterfall, I inhaled the pungent combination of desert organics mingling with alkaline water. A cool, moist breeze off the waterfall caressed my dehydrated skin, causing me to shiver in the still heat of the summer night. My eyes were drawn to the top of the falls, transfixed by the sound of water flowing from above. Suddenly I saw her – the woman in the waterfall. The nearly invisible stream of water split around an outcropping, turning an aerated gray-white, flowing like a grandmother's long tresses. As soon as I saw her face and hair, the cool, light mist shifted from in front of me, turned warm, and pulled me towards the waterfall. I was aware that I was being embraced by an old soul. Terry called the waterfall Stone Creek Woman, and many years later I had the chance to tell her I'd met that woman.

I could see Jim B and Miriam near the falls, relaxing under Sue's huge red umbrella. Scanning the trail leading above and to the right of the falls, I found the snaking line of hikers halfway to the top. I crossed the drainage and climbed up a foot-carved trail in the greenish, crumbly diabase (lava), continued along a narrow path with nothing but air to my left, and stepped onto a more stable path ground into the slope by curious river runners eager to see what lay beyond the next hill. It didn't take me long to catch up with the group. They had slowed down to make a short climb over limestone blocks. At the top of the trail the canyon spread out in front of us, marked by a naked streambed that had previously been choked with catclaw acacia, six-foot-tall barrel cactus, bear grass, and more. In the distance, my favorite cliff stood proudly in the midday sun. It was one of the best examples in the Grand Canyon of the Cambrian layers we had floated through in the upper Canyon. The early afternoon sun highlighted the cliffs from the Kaibab down to the Redwall, and presented a stark contrast to the pre-Cambrian Grand Canyon Supergroup that languished in the shaded foreground. The canyon walls funneled my eyes towards a notch in the distance. It was a visual conundrum because we would be gaining elevation as we hiked towards that notch – yet there was an illusion that the notch was below us.

I dropped down onto a trail scattered with flecks of green Bright Angel shale, a second waterfall flowed below and to my left.

Several years ago, a forty-two year old emergency room surgeon had stepped off the trail to photograph that waterfall. A very experienced hiker, she must have been more focused on the view through the camera than on where she was stepping. She slipped on some loose rocks and fell, tumbling down the slope and then thirty feet over the waterfall. The guides on the hike immediately went into rescue mode. One ran back to the rafts to grab rescue gear and the satellite phone, while others climbed down to assess the woman and attempt to stabilize her. She knew she had broken her back, and had no feeling below her waist.

The guides carefully placed her on a backboard and set up a line to bring her to an open area where a helicopter could land. They had to lift her, hand-over-hand, up the waterfall. Within two hours of her accident she was in a helicopter and on her way to Phoenix. The doctors said if she had arrived a half hour later she wouldn't have survived. Two seasons later, we saw her again on a string quartet trip. She told us she was determined to finish what she had started. Although she was paralyzed from the waist down, she had retained her positive attitude and finished the trip. This was by far the most serious accident suffered by passengers with the company for which I work. Most are minor and don't interfere with their enjoyment of the trip.

The trail followed the creek bed until we came to a small cascade. Some of us took off our packs and stood under it, allowing the water to rain down on us, saturating our clothing and cooling us down. We would be dry in fifteen minutes. A second cascade a half an hour later served the same purpose. Chris, Graham, Jim and Diane decided to remain there, where there was both water and shade. I looked around for Liz, but didn't see her. Perhaps she had found an interesting spot to express her photographic creativity.

As we continued, we alternated between hiking on a well-worn trail, and up the creek bed whenever the trail disappeared. After another half an hour, we arrived at a cul-de-sac that ended in a twenty-foot waterslide. We took a break and Sue described the rest of the hike. She said we would go up and over a cliff directly above us, scramble up the side of another water slide, navigate a large boulder field, and wind up in a narrow chasm with a beautiful, forty-foot water slide and shallow pool. The day had turned hot, and no one seemed eager to leave such a beautiful, shady spot. So Sue said we could relax here, and then head back to the rafts and get to camp a little earlier.

I took a container of salty gorp out of my pack, and Star had a container of sweet gorp. The salty gorp had a mixture of peanuts, roasted almonds, rice crackers, raisins, and dried peas. The sweet gorp included dried banana chips and M&Ms, almonds, peanuts, raisins, and other dried fruit. Sue took out her portable water filter and told people they could fill up their water bottles if they needed. I found a comfortable shady spot, leaned back against my pack, and closed my eyes. The next thing I knew, Sue's voice was announcing time to leave.

The hike back was all downhill, and pretty effortless. The beauty of these hikes is that we get two in one. The scenery coming in looks different than the scenery going back. There are plants and rock outcroppings that may be hidden when looking in one direction, but are in plain view when looking in the opposite direction. Wildlife, especially birds and lizards, may scamper across my path and disappear into the underbrush and not be seen by the person directly behind me. I walked with Tyler for part of the hike, and told him he'd make a great river guide because he was so curious about life in the natural world. As we walked down the creek bed he was constantly looking for evidence of life, stopping to watch tadpoles in an isolated pool and chase lizards. With each discovery, his face would light up. He was a delight to be with.

We gathered up the stragglers as we walked by them. Chris and Graham had enjoyed a "stress-free afternoon," as Graham described it. They had been in no hurry to get anywhere, and had enjoyed hanging out in the shade talking with Jim and Diane, and meandering when the mood struck them. There are so many ways to experience this place.

Mary had again enjoyed her stationary experience of the Canyon. She said she had seen several motor rigs running through Deubendorff, but no oar trips. This bode well for our next campsite, Owl Eyes, being available. Sue had decided to have a longer day on the river tomorrow, but she still wanted to spend the morning at Deer Creek and offer people another long hike. We could have remained at Stone, but by going a couple more miles downstream, we would have an extra half hour to get closer to another great side canyon the next day. Being a trip leader requires more thinking and planning. Since we have so many options down here, the plans are always flexible and depend on the energy and interests of the group, as well as weather conditions and the presence of other trips. We attempt to minimize contact with other river trips to provide as much of a wilderness-type experience as possible. Some attraction sites are more coveted than others, so it's very likely we'd see other groups at Deer Creek the next day, and Havasu the day after that.

We shoved off and floated a fairly calm stretch bordered by the diabase/Bass limestone cliff. This was a stretch where it had been common to find bighorn. I told Miriam and Tyler to keep a lookout because I had a sense we would see some rams.

On the right side of the current, a noisy wave beckoned me over. I set up to hit the biggest part and got everybody wet. We all laughed. You didn't have to be a kid to be a kid down here.

Just downstream and hidden from view was the mouth of Tapeats Creek. A small eddy sat in front of an equally small beach, sometimes used for the kitchen when we camped there. *In the early 'eighties, my brother Sandy was on a commercial trip that had decided to park their rafts in the mouth of the creek rather than in the eddy. They strapped their rafts together, side-by-side, with the swift current rushing against the upstream raft. The creek disappeared into a deep gorge choked with monkey flower, watercress, horsetail, and willow saplings. In the middle of the night, as the guides slept peacefully on their rafts, a flash flood came charging down the drainage, spearheaded by a mature cottonwood tree. The tree slammed into the upstream raft, flipping it and dumping much of the guide's personal items into the creek. For the next hour, guides were engaged in recovering their rafts and attempting to find lost gear. One guide lost all of his personal jewelry. The guide had failed to secure the lid before drifting off to sleep. Because of that experience, we don't park in the mouth any more.*

* * *

On my parents' private trip in 1986, we hiked up to Thunder Falls, a spectacular cascade coming straight out of the wall and falling over a thousand feet down a channel choked with trees and boulders. Although it was around eight miles round trip and included a twenty-five hundred foot elevation change, my seventy-one year old father came along. The start of the hike was a steep trail that climbed four hundred vertical feet before coming to a narrow trail that gradually declined back to the creek. After crossing the swiftly moving creek in knee-high water, we traversed a beautiful canyon rich in vegetation, particularly thick groves of cottonwood trees and forests of prickly pear cacti. After one more creek crossing, we climbed a trail that bordered a thundering cascaded river, arriving at the base of the falls flowing out of a water-drilled hole in the Muav limestone. Spray from the falls nourished an oasis of trees, mosses, spearmint, and grasses, along with several varieties of cacti. There were moments on the steep, narrow trails where we had to watch my dad closely, but he just put one foot in front of the other, and was a wonderful model for us all.

We now had just over a mile to camp. I pointed to a formation a couple miles downstream on the right, and asked Tyler if he saw anything unusual about it. He studied it for a couple minutes and then said something looked out of place. I told him he was right. Pointing to a dark, diagonally slashed Tapeats cliff about forty feet above the river, I told him that had been the downstream bank of the old Colorado River channel. A major prehistoric earthquake had caused a massive rock fall that had filled in the channel, forcing the river to find a new path. We would be floating through that in the morning, I told them, and it would be the narrowest part of the river in the Canyon.

After running one more short, wet rapid, I guided the raft to the left shore. Suddenly Tyler pointed to the open, rolling field several hundred yards off the river. He had found a herd of big horn, all rams. As he scanned the field, he kept finding more, eventually counting thirteen. I didn't think his smile could get any wider. We pulled into our camp, a long, narrow beach backed by a steep dune dotted with clumps of desert grass. The camp was called Owl Eyes, for the eroded shapes in the Kaibab cliff at the rim. Two convex openings on either side of a sharp prominence looked surprisingly like the eyes and beak of an owl, especially when the hollows were in shadows.

This was one of the two beaches that I photographed on every trip to help sediment scientists track the progress of beach erosion. Various elements contributed to this erosion, including people, river sediment, different flow levels, wind, and flash floods. We set up camp quickly, with the kitchen close to the rafts. The water would be going down overnight, so we weren't concerned about losing anything to rising water. After the kitchen was complete, we set up the horseshoes and invited people to find partners. Star and I challenged all comers. It wasn't fair, because Star is a great athlete, having been a basketball star in college, and now a collegiate coach, and although I only played horseshoes on the river, I managed to hold my own. Both Star and I can be very competitive, and neither one of us would have been happy if we had lost. But the games were fun, and offering another opportunity to be playful always enhanced the trip. Several of the passengers, including the Israelis, provided an enthusiastic cheering section as dinner was being prepared in the glow of late-day light.

I interrupted my game to help with dessert, a ginger cake. Floyd and Eliza were on cook crew and were happy to have me take this off their hands. I asked Carla if she could give me some extra ginger, which I grated, and a spare can of beer, which I used to moisten the mix. The menu called for butterscotch to be poured over the finished cake, but I mixed it into the batter and added a few more coals to compensate for the added moisture. After putting the DO on the coals, I went back to the horseshoe pits, but found that Carla had taken my place, so I hopped on my raft and pulled out my adopt-a-beach camera and note sheet and walked downstream to take a picture.

I climbed up a fifteen foot wall of Bass limestone, scrambled down a sandy slope covered with lizard tracks and the hoof prints of a large big horn, climbed over a small limestone outcrop, took my photograph, and jotted down my notes. When I finished, I sat on the rock and surveyed the camp, the river, and the Canyon walls. People were playing horseshoes, drinking beer or wine and enjoying the game, or just relaxing at their campsites. The world outside had disappeared.

The Grand Canyon was carved by abrasive, sediment-filled water over many millions of years. The Deer Creek Gorge offers an example of the power of water on a smaller, but no less spectacular scale in one of the many side canyons. Not even the 570 million year old Tapeats Sandstone could resist the cutting power of the creek.

DAY TWELVE –
OWL EYES TO LEDGES

When I opened my eyes, I knew we were well past first light and into sunrise. The shadows of the owl's eyes in the golden Kaibab looked like the mystery behind a mask. I wanted to go back to sleep but knew we were close to breakfast, so I stretched my legs, torso, and arms, put on my shorts and shirt, packed my sleep stuff away, and carried everything to my raft. Just then, Floyd blew the conch and announced that the pancakes and sausages were ready.

Most of the passengers had been hovering around the serving table waiting to refill some of those calories expended on the hike in Stone Creek the day before. Liz and Elli were in line, but Roni and Doron were absent. When I asked about them, Elli said they'd rather sleep than eat this morning. She said they'd set aside some food for them. Chris and Graham were relaxing with their morning tea, in no hurry to stand in line. Tyler was down by the water watching the school of rainbow trout that had been drawn in when Floyd had rinsed the bowl with the pancake batter in the river. There were at least two dozen, all around the same size, lying in wait for their breakfast.

Sue stood up, and with a warm smile in her voice, talked about the plans for the day. For those who were ready for another adventure, she and Carla would be leading an "up-and-over" hike beginning less than a mile downstream. The hike would start with a pretty significant elevation change, then follow a fairly level trail downstream for a mile before another significant elevation change. This would bring the hikers to the top of the ridge overlooking Deer Creek valley. She said only those who were willing to push themselves should consider this hike. The other options were to float down to Deer Creek and hang out near a waterfall, or hike up and into the side canyon above and behind the waterfall.

She asked who was interested in the up-and-over, and Eliza, Liz, Tyler, Diane, Jim, Nathan, and Antje raised their hands. We would float to the Piano Rock Eddy to drop off the seven passengers plus Sue and Carla. Floyd and Star would tow the paddleboat and Carla's raft and the rest of us would float down to Deer Creek, where people would have a better idea about their choices for the hike. Chris and Graham, and Mary, who was feeling better but not yet ready to hike, were going to be my passengers. Sue said we would be going on a second hike into another spectacular side canyon in the early afternoon. She also announced we would be getting out of camp earlier this morning to accommodate both of those hikes. I had planned to offer some stretching, but decided to wait and offer it at camp at the end of the day.

We were now in the section of the Canyon with an abundance of great hikes. Besides Stone Creek, there was Tapeats Creek with Thunder Falls, Surprise Valley, and a great up-and-over hike; Deer Creek with several options to accommodate a variety of hiking levels; Kanab Creek, Olo Canyon, Matcatamiba, Havasu, and National Canyon – all in just over thirty miles. Each of these attraction sites could take an entire day and more.

We broke down the kitchen and began loading our rafts. Graham offered to bring me my quota of yellow bags, and Michael told him to make them all big ones. I always asked for some short bags so I could lay them on my rear hatch so they didn't hang over the edge of my frame. Shorter bags often belong to people hiking out or hiking in. The packing list that each passenger received before the trip had a lot of what I call "if come" items. "If" a storm comes in, and the temperatures drop, they would need fleece and rain gear. "If" they want to be a fashion statement, they would need more colorful clothes. "If" they intended to read, they'd need books. On most trips, half their items would remain in the bottom of their bag and never be used. But when those items were needed, they were, well, needed.

We were ready to shove off, and passengers began picking their rafts for the day. The up-and-over hikers went with Carla and Sue. After massaging and wrapping Mary's foot, I helped her into my raft. She and Chris would be in the front, and Graham in the back. I looked over at Carla's raft and saw Eliza helping her with some of the rigging. For a moment I allowed myself to visualize being on a trip with Eliza as part of the crew. I imagined that I would feel protective at first, experience some nervousness for her in the big water, and enjoy celebrating large and small successes. How great it would be to have another Heavenrich on the river.

I thought I caught Liz looking at me, or in my direction. She had on a blousy lavender shirt under her life jacket, and was wearing no hat. Her skin had darkened slightly in just four days on the river. She was the most attractive passenger I had ever seen. Of course she wouldn't be available. For years I'd fantasized about meeting the love of my life on one of these trips, and having someone like Liz along just heightened that yearning.

Mary interrupted me with a question about the morning hike. I told her she would only have to go about a hundred feet and she'd be in heaven, and asked her to be patient because I wanted it to be a surprise. I enjoy watching people's faces light up when they first see the waterfall at Deer Creek.

Graham again coiled up the bowline and shoved me off the shore. I floated for a moment in the eddy while he scrambled to the back of the raft. I then pulled out into the current and continued across to the far side to avoid Helicopter Eddy, a small rapid with a whirlpool-like eddy. On my first few Canyon trips this eddy scared the hell out of me. A shallow rock bar forced the river towards the left shore and a very loud, circulating body of water. If I ever lost my angle I could be surfed right into that maelstrom, and it would be almost impossible to get out without flipping. I'm no longer cottonmouth-nervous before running this rapid, but I definitely stay focused.

As I entered the rapid I pulled back on my oars and watched as we approached the yawning jaws of the eddy. Chris was gripping her safety lines and Mary seemed mesmerized. An outcropping of Bass Limestone protruded into the river on the upstream and downstream edges, containing and channeling the racing eddy. At the downstream edge, large waves came out to greet us, and then we were past it. As the sound of the eddy receded, a new sound floated upstream. Just above a very narrow channel, water wrapped around a large boulder in midstream. It sounded bigger than it was because of the cliffs on either side. I pointed out the old Colorado River channel on river right about forty feet above the river. A massive pre-historic landslide had filled in the old channel, so the river did what it always does when presented with an obstacle: it surrendered, backed up, and eventually carved out a new channel. The river didn't seem to notice that it was carving its way through granite and schist.

Just downstream of the noisy rock, we passed through Granite Narrows, the narrowest place on the river at a mere seventy-six feet wide. This was the path the river had taken when blocked by that landslide. It was narrow because the granite was so hard. I told Graham, Chris, and Mary about the challenges this narrow section had been back in the highwater year of 1983, when the volume exceeded 90,000 cfs. Once past this narrow slot, the very strong current flowed towards the right wall. It took several minutes of hard pulling to avoid slamming into the wall before we got through this short stretch.

Ancient cliffs rose straight from the river, blocking out the warmth of the sun. The current slowed to a trickle, and the sound of the short rapid upstream faded. Once again, the only sounds were of the oars rhythmically dipping into the river, and the occasional descending trill of the Canyon Wren. On our right, behind a still eddy, a large opening in the granite revealed a bat cave. I told my passengers this was known as the Christmas tree cave. A sculpture of salt resembling a Christmas tree hid in the rear of the cavern, formed from the evaporation of salt-laden moisture dripping out of the overlying rock. This had once been an active bat cave with a large population. Unfortunately, the curiosity of rafters hiking into it had disturbed their reproductive cycles. When bats are gestating and in a state similar to hibernation, any distraction, like human visitation, will cause them to abort. Now the only evidence of bat habitation was the mound of guano lying on the ground inside the cave. I mentioned that in the 'seventies and 'eighties there had been a palm tree just below the entrance to the cavern. Each time the park service removed the tree because it was a non-native species, another would miraculously take its place. The third time the palm tree was removed was the charm, at least for the park service, because no palm replacement has appeared since.

We drifted for a while, and as the Canyon again began to open up, we pulled up to the beach next to the other rafts, and another of the Grand Canyon's amazing gifts appeared. First the sound of roaring water, then the sight of a 125-foot waterfall disappearing into a shallow pool less than one hundred feet off the river. Deer Creek Falls, mile 136 on our 226-mile river journey. I was as impressed as those who were here for the first time.

One year at this location, I had a memorable experience with two women, Carol and Marilyn, two sixty-ish best friends who had come on the trip together. Carol was a tall, casually overweight woman who didn't seem particularly comfortable in her body. At first she resisted my invitation to join Marilyn and the rest who had already hiked up and behind the falls. The thought of a four-hundred-foot elevation change seemed daunting to a woman who said she didn't have a good relationship with her body. I gently encouraged her to give it a try.

The trail, cut into orange-pink Zoroaster granite by millions of passing steps from two- and four-legged visitors, rose at a steep angle.

"I can't do this," Carol insisted after only a few steps. Her pulsating carotid artery signaled an accelerating heart. I admit that I felt impatient. Then I reminded myself to walk in her shoes. I knew what Carol could do more than she did.

"Yes you can, Carol," I said softly. "Let's just take one step at a time."

She tightened her jaw muscles as she decided to trust me. With each step, the past receded and the future beckoned. Soon we were looking down on the milky-green river, swirls of sediment in solution looking like chaotic brush strokes on a moving canvas.

I helped Carol up a course sandstone wall shaded by a grove of overhanging catclaw acacia trees. We emerged into the desert sun and proceeded along a narrow trail, up a steep rock fall, and arrived at the top. A smile had replaced Carol's worry lines. Just before reaching the rest of the group who were relaxing on what we called the patio, Carol looked at me. "It was worth it," she said. Seeing a surprised and pleased Marilyn, Carol rushed over to give her an exuberant hug, while she shared her adventure.

The "patio" at Deer Creek is a timeless place. Negative ions from rushing water surrounded the passengers resting in the embrace of ancient rock, opening them to unimagined dreams. Large blocks of Bright Angel Shale lay where they had fallen, in varying stages of decomposition, testament to the earth's recycling process. Steep, narrow walls provided cooling refuge from the desert heat. Young cottonwood trees rose out of the carcasses of fallen ancestors. The song of the creek played softly as it nurtured wild watercress and wilding humans. For a short while, there was no time.

Deepening shadows finally called for movement. As everyone prepared for the return hike, Carol approached me and, noting Marilyn's fear of heights, asked me to help her friend in the dangerous narrows of the side canyon.

On my first river trip in Cataract Canyon in 1976, my best friend, who was a guide, and his crewmate, were very accomplished boulder-hoppers. On our first hike together they told me if I wanted to go with them, I had to keep up. No offers to teach this flat-lander the techniques that would assure my safety and spare me from the terror I went through my own terror learning to trust my body and negotiate the challenge courses. As a result, I became very empathic to the fears and concerns of others who found themselves in the same circumstances. I offered to support Marilyn on the return hike. She expressed relief and gratitude, saying she had barely made it past the narrows coming in.

I started by making two suggestions. First, if she became fearful, she should focus on her breathing. When we get into fear, I told her gently, we get out of our bodies and into our heads. We stop breathing. By taking the time to breath, we bring our attention back into our body, which makes it more likely that we can proceed, and less likely that we'll have an accident because of the tension that has built up. And second, I told her that with each step, she should feel her feet massaging the skin of the earth. This way, she would feel more connected to her body and to the earth. On the trail Marilyn revealed one of her fears: she was a poet seeking her voice, thinking about her first public reading right after the trip. She admitted to a fear of being rejected, concerned that her poetry would be considered inadequate.

The trail narrowed and the walls closed in. Marilyn hugged the coarse sandstone wall like a woman with something to lose. A hundred feet below, the sound of rushing water reverberated off the chasm walls. Marilyn's toes edged closer to the wall as her heels hung precariously over the chasm. "Breathe!" she said to herself, straining to regain control and get

188

back into her body. I wanted to reach out and offer a helping hand, but our agreement was if she wanted help she would ask.

I believed this was a choice point in Marilyn's life; an opportunity to overcome the kind of physical obstacle from which she had habitually retreated. This time she had no choice. The rafts were down below, and the only way out was through.

After taking several breaths, she took a tentative side step to the left, but it only served to validate her fear. I was less than a foot away, but she later told me my words had been all but drowned out by the sounds of rushing water and her heart pounding in her ears.

"Breathe, Marilyn, breathe. Feel your connection with the earth. Take one more step. That's it. Keep breathing. Just a couple more and you're there." I wondered if she could understand the breakthrough opportunity this experience offered. I knew if she took advantage of it, it could change her life in many ways.

Another step. This one appeared easier, although her racing heart might disagree. Then another. A couple more just to be sure. The trail widened and the chasm receded to a more comfortable distance. Marilyn's shoulders relaxed. Her white knuckles disappeared. She sighed, and her face softened. A tear traced down her right cheek.

Emerging from the shaded side canyon and rounding a bend in the trail, Carol took a moment to look over the edge to the muddy river below. Our eighteen-foot rafts seemed like child's toys, she told Marilyn. From the safety of the trail, Marilyn smiled and said she would take her word for it. Soon another challenge loomed ahead. Marilyn's steps grew tentative. Below her was an "improved" trail of angled boulders, steep, and strewn with contorted rocks. Her body tensed up. I imagined she was thinking, "Not again."

Three hundred feet below, the sediment-laden river flowed inexorably toward its destination. I talked about the lesson of the big horn sheep, which always managed to find unseen toeholds while moving from one stable platform to the next. "Momentum. That's the lesson of the big horn. Start on a stable platform and keep moving until you come to another stable place." As I said this I demonstrated, stepping confidently from one rock to the next, stopping when I reached a flat surface. "It's just like walking down stairs at home. Only there are no 90-degree angles here."

Tentatively Marilyn bent her knees, hoping to bring the safety of the earth a little closer. As she reached down with her left hand in a search for security, I felt a bit perturbed. Controlling my impatience, I said. "Marilyn, you are strong enough and have enough balance to do this."

She looked at me with an expression of surprise. "No one has ever told me I was strong enough," she said. I felt my eyes moisten, as emotion rose into my throat. After a moment she straightened up and stepped down. Soon she was walking with more confidence. Something had shifted. A smile appeared. I couldn't wait to reward her courage with a 360-degree rainbow in the pool below.

The date was September 11, 2001.

We were the first raft to arrive at Deer Creek. I jumped off the front and tied the bowline up to a chock stone wedged into the cliff face. I told Mary that she could find a shady spot near the rafts, or I would be happy to help her walk to the waterfall where I said she would be more comfortable. I grabbed my umbrella and one of the paco pads on the front hatch and helped Mary off the raft. I then told Chris and Graham to grab their daypacks and make sure they had water, a camera, and some reading material if they wanted, since we would he hanging out for around three hours. I also removed the six-gallon water jug from the front of my raft and carried it into the shade for others to fill up their water bottles, both before and after the hike.

Graham picked up the paco pad, Chris grabbed the umbrella, and we headed up a trail to our left. Mary leaned on my shoulder, favoring her left foot. The sound of a small rapid to our left was overwhelmed by a deeper sound from our right. We maneuvered around some fallen chunks of sandstone, ducked under the branches of some mature tamarisk trees, and emerged into open air. With a narrow creek in front of us, we stood in awe of a one hundred-twenty-five foot waterfall shooting out of a narrow chasm, plunging into a pool bordered on two sides by granite cliffs. The creek was filled with watercress swaying in a gentle current.

Mary was mesmerized by the waterfall, and almost tripped on a small rock as she gingerly stepped into the creek. She was able to walk slowly without much pain, and we only had twenty yards to go before she could relax on the paco pad and read her book. The entire area was in shade, but by the time we returned from our hike, it would be in the sun. Graham placed the paco pad against the granite cliff to the left of the waterfall and I told Mary to enjoy the peace while she could. She lifted her eyebrows in a question, and I said there would probably be others from our trip coming shortly, and it was quite likely that other trips would show up as well.

Deer Creek was one of those attraction sites that every river trip wanted to visit. Many of the motor trips just took their people to the waterfall. At times there could be a real traffic tie-up of parked boats with oar and motor rafts ranging from fourteen to thirty-seven feet jammed into a small eddy, and dozens of people milling around. Fewer commercial motor trips hiked their people up to the patio, and even fewer offered them the up-and-over hikes from Tapeats or the Piano Rock. Still, it was a rare trip when we had Deer Creek all to ourselves.

I walked over to the pool and felt the cool, moist spray blowing out from the falls. The pool was no more than forty feet wide, and it narrowed as it approached the falls. In the past, when the waterfall had reached farther out into the pool, an outcropping to the left of the cascade used to be a favorite jumping-off spot. A recent flash flood had changed the path of the water that now fell close to the wall. The gale-force wind coming off the cascade as it plunged into the pool made it difficult to approach the falls. In the early 'nineties, I had been able to swim behind the cascade. It was claustrophobic, bordering on suffocating, so I didn't remain there very long. Recently I was challenged to swim under the cascade and touch the wall behind. I hesitated and then declined. Later, while no one was around, I decided to go ahead. Taking a deep breath, I dove under the water, made a sharp turn to my left, and swam deeper. I was surprised at how silent it was under this thundering cascade, and how easy it was to see the wall and touch it before pushing off and returning to the surface. I was so exhilarated I did it again.

Finally, I asked Chris and Graham if they were ready to get their hearts beating a bit harder. Graham said he'd rather save his heartbeats for his old age, thank you. Chris said she was ready. We said goodbye to Mary and headed back down and to the right of the creek bed. I found the trail going up. After a short elevation change we left the granite and entered the Tapeats sandstone. I had to slow myself down to accommodate the pace of my friends. When I hiked on my own, I usually did it for the exercise value, in addition to being out in nature. Now I was working, and my job was to be supportive of people at their level of stamina and strength. Chris and Graham were used to flat surfaces near sea level in a humid environment. Here, except for the river, there were no flat surfaces, we were two thousand feet above sea level, and as soon as we got a short distance away from the river, we could feel the arid desert sucking us dry.

We stopped to catch our breaths, and I pointed to a part of the trail that disappeared into some trees. To the left and below the trees was a verdant, marshy slope bathed in green. I pointed out some poison ivy on the left side of the trail. I said that my brother Sandy, whom they knew, had fallen in that patch, and the poison ivy had been so potent he had to be flown out of the Canyon. Graham said if they had known about a helicopter ride, they might have left on the third day, because Chris had been feeling so uncomfortable. I told him he wouldn't have enjoyed the ride after he'd received the bill, about fifteen hundred dollars an hour. He said they'd better make it quick then.

We continued up the trail as the rest of the rafts were tying up next to mine. Chances were the first wave would catch up with us before we reached the patio. We passed through the arboreal section being careful to stay as far right as possible to avoid the poison ivy. "Leaves of three, let them be," I quoted from an old warning.

The trail turned up and to the right requiring a short climb up a Tapeats wall. The sandstone offered good grip as I helped Chris find footholds and handholds. Although she was a bit soft in her body, I could tell the Tai Chi she had been studying was making a difference in her strength. I think she let me help her only out of English courtesy. Graham, a short, stocky, former rugby player, also made the climb look easy.

Tree limbs offered good handholds and suddenly we emerged from our shaded trail into the summer heat. The trail now led back upstream, and except for a large rock here and there the path was clear. We were now a couple hundred feet above the river, and could see far up and downstream. The narrow slit around Granite Narrows seemed barely wide enough to allow a raft to float through. The whitewater at Helicopter Eddy stood out in stark contrast to the milky-green river. Far upstream, the pine trees on the North Rim looked no bigger than shrubs.

The path turned sharply to the left and we started to climb a part of the trail forged out of an improved rockslide. The park service had sent trail maintenance crews, often staffed by volunteer river guides, down the river during the off-season to replace and anchor dislodged rocks and remove debris along the trails. We stopped in the shade of some overhanging rocks for a water break and let our breaths again catch up with us. I told Chris and Graham about a private trip that had turned into a bit more of an adventure than I had anticipated.

Half of us on that trip were doing the Tapeats Creek, Surprise Valley, Deer Creek up-and-over. When we arrived at Thunder Falls, an incredible cascade emerging from a cave in the Muav, we decided to climb up to the source. The climb was scary in some spots, especially where the narrow ledge disappeared for a couple of feet, and all that was below us was air and a thousand feet of white water plunging down rocky steps. We had stayed longer than planned, and a storm system came in suddenly. By the time we had arrived at the patio, it was getting late, and we still had the narrow path through the gorge, and then the outside trail to negotiate in the dark. It had started to rain and no one had thought to bring a flashlight. I had to lead three women, none of whom had been to the Canyon, back to the rafts safely.

By the time we had made it through the gorge it was pitch black. We talked to each other a lot on the way down the rock fall. I felt a huge responsibility for the well being of these women. At the same time, I was inwardly excited by the adventure of it all. I have always wanted to accomplish something really heroic, and am often very moved when I read about people doing extraordinary things. On the way down the rock fall I led with my feet, literally. I was familiar enough with the trail that I felt confident in my ability to get us all down safely. With each step, I felt with my sandal-clad foot for the next step, and then communicated that to the women. Help with flashlights finally arrived just as we were nearing the bottom.

We continued the climb, finding convenient stair-steps on the way. I suggested that they use small steps whenever possible to minimize the demands on their heart and lungs. The higher the step, the more of our big leg and butt muscles we used, and the more blood that was needed to feed oxygen to those large muscles. Graham said with his short legs, every step was a large step. Chris said it was even truer for her.

After one last grunt we stepped on to a narrow, well-worn trail that led out towards the river. As we walked around the corner, Chris gasped, impressed by the view and the drop-off to our right. I offered to take a photo of them with the North Rim and river upstream in the background. I asked them to step down to a flat spot near the edge. Chris was nervous about it, but I told her she could put Graham closest to the outside. Her laughter broke the tension.

We entered the shadows of the gorge and walked along another narrow trail. Water flowing for eons had carved this gorge as easily in geologic time as a flash flood cuts into sand today. We were walking on a sandy trail through a narrow alley of scalloped sandstone walls. The space between the walls still carried the memory of the water that had created the gorge. We arrived at a crux point in the trail where a step one foot to our right would send us into the void below. Both Chris and Graham faced the wall and took short side steps along the narrow trail. To provide the visual of relative safety, I walked outside them on a narrower ledge one step below. If either one of them had lost their balance, it was unlikely that I could have prevented them from falling. It was more likely that I would also have been catapulted down to the unseen creek more than fifty feet below.

We made it to a wider part of the trail, with more distance between the chasm and us. The trail continued to meander below steep sandstone walls. Our ceiling was a desert blue sky dotted with puffy cotton ball clouds. The sound of Deer Creek rushing through the gorge drowned out any other voices. Twice we came to a bend in the gorge and could see down to the bottom. A narrow creek flowed over and around boulders. Maidenhair fern clung to mini-grottos unperturbed by the prospect of the next killing flood.

As we walked along, I pointed out two-hundred-year old Paiute pictographs - tiny hand prints in white and red on walls, protected by overhangs. These were adult hands, yet they were even smaller than my hand, as their meager diet could not support larger features. Mixing crushed hematite, a soft, iron oxide-rich rock, in water, and then blowing the liquid through a hollow reed around an outstretched hand or leaf had created the red dye. Smearing white clay on one's hand and imprinting it on a wall had created the white pictographs. While relatively young, they were a reminder of those who had come before.

The Paiutes believe the spirits of their departed reside in the Deer Creek gorge. While they would prefer that we not venture down there, they realize times have changed and have requested that we treat the gorge as a sacred place and have our passengers treat it with respect. Other tribes have requested the same about the Grand Canyon as a whole.

We were now at or near the top layers of the Tapeats, and could see light green and purple flecks from the Bright Angel shale that was often intermixed in the sandstone. The Muav, Bright Angel, and Tapeats layers had all been formed during the same time period. When the ocean was deeper, more Muav would form, when it was shallower, it could be the Tapeats or the Bright Angel.

I invited Chris and Graham to peer over the edge again and pointed out a large alcove and rock garden blanketed by a carpet of maidenhair fern. Rising out of the middle of the lime-green fern bed was the blackened skeleton of a dead redbud tree. It had been here to greet us with its scalloped green leaves and dainty lavender flowers since my first trip in 1978, and I don't know how long before that. The same flash flood that had changed the flow of the waterfall had also claimed the redbud. I hoped to find new growth each time I passed this way.

A hundred feet more and we got our first glimpse of the patio. In the foreground a narrow ribbon of creek cut into flat rock, plunging down a twelve-foot cascade into a shallow pool, then down a thin chute into a deeper pool with a rounded boulder the size of a compact car in the middle. On the far side of the gorge, a series of descending shelves ended five feet above the pool. I told Graham that was where we could climb down into the gorge. "What do you mean, we?" he replied. I told him only if he wanted to go down there. His eyebrows practically touched as he shot me a frown.

The creek, passing over the flat rock through the shaded patio, was like our own private water sculpture. A flat ledge on our left offered plenty of room for relaxing. On the other side of the creek, the carcass of a very old cottonwood tree lay slowly deteriorating, offering fodder from which younger offspring rose. The creek flowed out of another narrow gorge about ten feet high. At the end, a six-foot cascade plunged into a pool we called the Jacuzzi for the massaging benefits it offered. To the left of the pool, a grandmother cottonwood tree displayed her scars from the assault of debris in countless flash floods. Exposed, gnarly roots embraced various-sized boulders. Brilliant rich pink roots swayed sensuously in the current. Above the cascade, open sky hinted at an expansive valley and the source of the creek.

Sounds of voices down the gorge signaled the arrival of the rest of the rafters. The up-and-over hikers wouldn't show up for at least another hour. I walked through the creek and climbed up a short ledge to another ledge still blessed with shade. After dropping my backpack, I reentered the creek bed and walked toward the Jacuzzi. Watercress patches lined the shore on both sides, along with six-foot high Hooker's primrose with its yellow-orange flower. The nectar vesicle rested as much as nine inches below the opening of the flower, and only one creature had a proboscis long enough to harvest the nectar: the Sphinx moth, which days earlier had entertained us so much by disappearing into the datura flower.

I removed my shirt and sunglasses and carefully approached the cascade. Large stones placed by enterprising hikers at a narrow neck in the creek had created a mini-dam and pool. Cool, clear water lapped at my calves. The bottom of the pool consisted of loose stones and small rocks, forcing me to make sure of each step. I reached into the cascade with my left hand and wondered if I really wanted to subject my body to the cold water. To hell with it. I stepped behind the cascade and walked forward. The force was strong, so I took a small step forward and then leaned back into the water, making sure the flow was on my shoulders, upper back, and neck. I stood there for a couple minutes as my body shook amid the roar of rushing water washing over me. When I finally stepped forward, I felt a refreshing tingling all over my body. They pay me for this!

I returned to my pack, took a big swig of water, and then, using my pack as a pillow, lay down to "meditate." I closed my eyes and focused on the sounds of rustling leaves in the cottonwood above me mingling with rushing water and the voices of satisfied people.

In my dream, I was enjoying a rainstorm. Then I opened my eyes to see a smiling Eliza shaking her drenched hair all over me. The hikers had arrived and Eliza had immediately climbed down to the Jacuzzi to cool off. I asked her how the hike was, and she said she loved it. She hadn't tested her legs very much to that point, and there were some significant inclines they had to navigate. She also said it was fascinating to look upstream and downstream from the elevated trail they were on, and it had given her an even greater appreciation for the immense scale of the Canyon. Sue had taken them to an Indian site that she said had probably been used for ceremonies. It overlooked Deer Valley, and Eliza said she was impressed with the strip of green that bordered the creek bed. Carla had also pointed out one of the two sources of the creek, an oasis high up in the Redwall on the right side of the valley. I told her that was the location of the throne room. When she asked what that was, I told her legend had it that an alien race of obviously large beings had built a throne out of very large slabs of sandstone. I promised I would show her photos of an average human being dwarfed by the throne, like Edith Ann in her rocking chair. For some reason she didn't believe me.

I stood up, stretched, and walked over to the edge where I could see the Jacuzzi. Liz, Doron, Roni, and Elli were all in the pool. Doron and Roni were climbing up a water slide to the right of the pool, and Liz had just emerged from the cascade. Her sky blue blouse clung again tightly to her petite body. She looked up, saw me watching her, smiled, and waved. Elli turned and smiled as she disappeared behind the cascade.

Sue announced we would be returning to the rafts in a half hour, so I grabbed my tripod and camera, crossed the creek and walked towards the pool. I was tempted to take some photos of Liz, but it felt like an intrusion, so I stepped over a slippery limestone boulder and found the trail into the valley. The first thing I noticed were the burned-out remains of giant cottonwood trees that had been destroyed in the 'eighties by a camper's out of control toilet paper fire. Less than a week after that fire, I had come into the valley from above on an up-and-over hike through Surprise Valley and Tapeats Creek. The floor of the valley for twenty yards on either side of the creek bed had sprouted a vibrant carpet of bright green vegetation, nurtured by summer rains and ash from the dead trees. There were still a good number of trees alive, although most had charred trunks.

The creek channel was choked with vegetation, much of it bent downstream by recent flash floods. An exposed, ten-foot bank on the far side of the creek offered testament to the power of those floods. I walked through a small prickly pear forest with the fruit and seedpod, called tunas, ripening on the top of the cactus. Right now they were a light shade of purple. Within a month, they would be a deep purple, ready for harvest to make prickly pear jam, or they would become a snack for the resident deer.

I noticed some color to my left and found a fishhook cactus hiding under a desiccated bush.

It had a crown of flowers, thirteen in all, ringing the top. In the desert, flowers tend to be loners, and don't have to compete for attention. In this area, noted by the absence of any color but gray, the soft pink blossoms were another form of eye candy. I set up my tripod, took several shots, and then walked back to the pool to see if Liz and the girls were interested in my find. Only Liz remained, lying on her back on a small ledge by the edge of the pool. I enjoyed the view for a moment and then called down to her that I found something she might want to photograph. She took a moment to stretch, then walked back up the creek to retrieve her camera. I met her on the trail and took her to the flowers.

She didn't say a word, but took her time looking at the flowers from every angle. Finally she took one shot, from an angle I hadn't noticed. This lawyer had a creative eye. We walked back to the group as they were preparing to return to the rafts. Tyler was down in the creek, intent on finding as many critters as possible. At the moment he was stalking a chuckawalla, an angry looking, wrinkled, gray lizard with a waist twice as wide as its shoulders. Like a puff adder in the ocean, this lizard's primary defense is to scurry between two layers of rocks and then puff up its body to become wedged in place. Its tail has several knuckles that break off when captured; the missing portion eventually grows back. The chuckawalla was feasting in a garden of watercress. When it opened its mouth to feed, its bright red tongue stood out in stark contrast to its wrinkled gray face.

On the way back up the trail, I pointed out more pictographs, also handprints, on the rounded underside of a partially broken-off ledge across the gorge and twenty feet up. There must have been other ledges beneath it when they were painted because there didn't seem to be any way to get up there now. In recent years, the park archaeologist has accompanied men and women from the Paiute, Hopi, Navajo, and Hualapai tribes through the Canyon to visit sacred sites. Many of them were older and several were overweight. She told me that when a group of Paiute elders discovered those pictographs, they immediately went back down to their raft, changed into ceremonial dress, and came back up to perform a ceremony to honor their ancestors.

Recently, at a guides' meeting, we heard from several tribes that considered the Canyon part of their history and sacred. Many echoed the same feeling - they would prefer we not go there. Knowing this wouldn't happen, they all requested that we let our passengers know it was sacred to them with the hope we would all treat it in that manner.

As soon as we reached the bottom of the trail, most of us headed straight for the pool and waterfall. I called Chris and Graham over and invited them to join me. Both declined, but I told them they would be in for an amazing treat, and all they had to do was walk into the pool. Except for the spray, I assured them they wouldn't get wet above their shins. Graham said something about knowing where I slept, but after putting down his camera, both he and Chris followed me. It was around eleven o'clock and the sun shone on our backs. I went to the edge of the pool farthest away from the waterfall and started to walk directly toward the plunging water. Soon we were feeling the water droplets carried out on jets of air. Chris was the first to see it: a three hundred-sixty degree rainbow surrounding us. It made my heart beat faster. Chris laughed with delight. Graham looked me in the eye and said, "Brilliant. The wonders never cease."

I told them I had brought my seventy-one-year-old mother here after hiking up to the patio, and upon seeing the rainbow surrounding her, she looked like she had just seen the face of God. I told them this was a gift for pushing up the trail.

We still had almost twenty miles to go before camp and another hike in store, so Sue corralled us back to the rafts. She wanted to float a half-mile to Panchos for lunch. It's a great campsite with an overhang to protect us from rains. There would be plenty of shade and a flat spot close to the rafts, so we could serve a fairly quick lunch and then make some miles. Mary was already in my raft when we arrived. Floyd had hung out with her, Miriam, Jim, Diane, and Kathy. When I asked her how it was, she said "heavenly," except for the two boatloads of people that had temporarily interrupted her peace. The groups had stayed for only forty-five minutes before departing.

On the float to Panchos we passed a long beach on the left that I had dubbed "Howling Wolf Camp" for the prominent rock outcropping that resembled a wolf baying at the moon. It was at this camp the night of September 11th that I helped Marilyn discover the metaphor that her fear of heights represented for her. We had pulled a medicine card from a deck of fifty-two cards, each one a different animal representing a theme based upon the observations and mythologies of Native Americans. Each card came with a description of what the animal represented, and consistently provided people with a fresh perspective that helped them gain insight into some issue on which they were focusing. We explored the connection between what had happened on the hike and her desire to be more open and expressive with her poetry. She realized that her fear of exposure on the hike was a physical manifestation of her fear of exposure as a poet. She also realized that, as she had on the hike, she could feel the fear and do it anyway, and that's what she decided to do.

Graham motioned towards the left shore as he reached for his camera. Two bighorn rams were drinking from the river, both with big curls that marked them as elders. The ram with the slightly smaller curl showed great deference to the Alpha male, waiting to drink, staying a respectable distance away, and trailing behind as they both walked casually away from the river. As we floated by, they seemed unconcerned about our presence, and Graham was pleased with the photo opportunity.

We pulled into the beach at Panchos, and I pushed my sand stake into the soft mud in front of the raft, then slipped my bowline through the carabineer on the stake. We called it a big toothpick, and it was very useful at a beach like this where there were no trees or rocks on which to tie the bowline. To our left, Tapeats sandstone formed an overhang that curled from left to right away from the river, bordering a sand-filled hill. On one of my trips, my Aussie friend played his didgeridoo underneath the overhang. The vibration of the didge seemed to rise out of the earth, filling my body with a primordial rhythm that pulled me deeper into my own roots.

Lunch was prepared and consumed quickly. Sue said she wanted to make a quick stop at Matcat, a spectacular side canyon at mile 148. We were currently at mile 137, and on a swift current could get there before three o'clock if we didn't encounter any upstream winds.

On our float to Matcat, short for Matcatamiba, a Havasupai family name, we would run several medium-to-small rapids. We passed two large camps, the Football Field and Back Eddy, often used by motor rigs because the river remained deep all the way to the shore. We floated through a riffle and watched as the Canyon widened a bit. Slopes replaced the Tapeats on the right, denoting the location of the old river channel that had been blocked by the landslide, which forced the channel through the granite at the narrows above Deer Creek. The sound of Doris Rapid floated upstream. It was named for the wife of Norm Nevills who had pioneered commercial boating in the Grand Canyon. Doris was the organizer, food manager, cook, and politician in the Nevills household. Ironically her maiden name was Drown, and she had fallen in the rapid in the 1940s, survived, and was rewarded with a rapid named after her. And she kicked my butt in the highwater year of 1983.

I was running my small Miwok with my sister-in-law and her neighbor in my raft. The river was running around 60,000 cfs and the current was fast. We were having a lively conversation about sex and I must have been distracted because I had failed to notice that this once small rapid was now very large. We hit a surging wave charging at us from the left. I noticed it too late to turn my raft to face the wave, and over we went. Even as I was being ejected into the river I couldn't believe that we were flipping. We were quickly rescued by one of the other rafts, and there were no injuries, except my bruised ego, especially when my brother Ned unceremoniously removed his wife from my raft. She had also been in my raft earlier when we had flipped in Crystal.

This time I encountered no such difficulty, nor did I in Fishtail, another half mile downstream. This rapid was easy to run because I could pull to the right and miss all the bigger water. A rock bar on both sides of the river had pinched down the channel funneling the water into a big hole at lower water, and a powerful wave at higher water. We had the higher water, so I kept the raft in the current and at the top it looked like we were headed right for the big wave. However, I knew we would just catch the right side of it. Chris let out a loud squeal, certain we were going in. Both she and Graham were doused by the wave, but no other damage was done. Graham looked back at me as he brushed water off his face. He thanked me for cooling him off and requested more warning the next time so he could climb to the back. He looked back at Mary, who was bone dry and smiling broadly.

The current over the next four miles would be mellow, with just a few small riffles to interrupt the peace. I suggested that we float this stretch in silence and enjoy the scenery without any conversation. Everyone seemed open to the idea, and I watched as they found comfortable positions lying on one of the tubes using the baggage as a pillow.

I settled into a comfortable rhythm. Holding the oars in front of my chest, I would begin each stroke by leaning forward and then pushing out with my arms. By leaning, I engaged my stomach muscles to get the stroke started. In this way I already had some momentum and I could finish off the push without putting undue strain on my shoulders. At the end of my stroke, I pushed down on the oars, lifting them just out of the river, rotated the oars so the blades were almost flat to the water, and then pulled my hands back toward my chest. In the really calm stretches I enjoyed trailing the oar blade on the very top of the water, carving a line on liquid paper.

The sound of birds, primarily yellow-breasted chats and flycatchers, floated across the river. A downstream breeze made rowing even easier and helped move us more quickly toward Matcat. I could remember many trips in this stretch where I had strained against very strong upstream winds, slowing me down to a crawl and testing my grip strength. It was always nice to have a downstream breeze, although we couldn't count on how long it would stay with us. In the Canyon, guides say to never trust a downstream wind because it will turn on you.

Chris and Graham looked relaxed as they watched the sky float upstream. Both had busy lives with work and family obligations, and I was glad they had taken the time to experience life at four miles an hour. They were great friends, and I smiled thinking about being able to reminisce with them in the future.

We were making great time, and I interrupted the silence to announce that Kanab Creed Rapid was on the horizon. Kanab Creek was rated only a three, but it had been the perfect size rapid to initiate a willing rookie.

One of the more memorable times was when a three-generation English family came on a river trip. Grandfather Anthony was a former ranger on Mt. Kilimanjaro in Kenya. His two sons, Richard and Chris were successful businessmen. Both stood over six feet tall. Richard's daughter Charlie was seventeen and quite independent. And Chris's wife Libby was slim, attractive, and quiet, choosing to defer to her husband, brother-in-law, and father-in-law. As we approached Kanab, I asked Libby if she would like to row through the rapid. She looked startled at first, but then a smile lifted her face and she said yes. Her husband asked facetiously if I really wanted to do this, and I said absolutely. Libby asked when, and I told her this was a good time. She was tentative at first, trying to figure out the mechanics of facing downstream while rowing. I sat on the bags behind her and showed her how to do it. We still had about a half a mile to the entrance of the rapid, and with each stroke she gained more confidence. As we reached the tongue, I told her to trust the current. It might look like the raft would be forced into the wall on the left, but I assured her that wouldn't happen. The walls of the Canyon were closing in, narrowing the river channel and increasing the speed of the current. Kanab was a very long rapid giving Libby lots of opportunity to gain confidence. The farther we traveled, the more erect she became. A wry grin was molded on her face. The men in her family were silent, maybe for the first time.

We were about to enter the Muav Gorge, a long stretch of river with Muav limestone cliffs rising directly out of the water, few campsites, and the absence of sunshine. Some guides called it the refrigerator of the Canyon, especially during a rain and early and late in the season. A large side canyon had provided the debris that had created the rapid. Kanab is a Paiute word for the ever-present willows in the Canyon. Maj. Powell had decided to end his second exploration of the Canyon here in 1872, much to the delight of his crew.

When I first came into the Canyon, I had some preconceived notions about what was "normal" down here. I assumed that most of those who would want to raft in the wilderness would be male, and relatively young. Well, my mother Annie was neither male, nor young. In fact, we celebrated her 71st birthday on her trip.

Annie had received an artificial knee in 1985, just ten months before our eighteen-day private trip. Like many of us, young and old, she had some deep concerns about her mobility and sense of freedom in her later years. That concern surfaced during our trip.

We were camped just upstream of Kanab at about mile 143. In the morning, we were planning a long hike up Kanab to a place called Whispering Springs. Just the name conjures up images of still waters and peace. It was an eight-mile round trip hike requiring many crossings of a very slippery, muddy creek

My brother Sandy was concerned about my mother's ability to navigate the slippery creek, not to mention the large boulders she would have to scramble over. Because of her recent surgery, her leg muscles were still weak, and that made hopping from rock to rock impossible. So after dinner the night before the hike, Sandy told Annie he didn't think she could handle the hike, and probably should stay behind.

All of a sudden those fears of being unable to go where she wanted and do what she wanted were right in her face. The tears that slipped out of her eyes were indicators of the turmoil going on inside. In the morning, before the hike, I went up to her and asked if she would like to try the hike. At the very least, we could go partway into the canyon and explore it a bit.

That appealed to her, so after breakfast a group of us, including my father, set out to see just how far we could go. This would be his third long hike in three days, having gone up to Thunder Falls in Tapeats Canyon, and the patio at Deer Creek the two previous days. He was a gamer all right.

It was slow going hiking up Kanab. We had to be careful while crossing the creek because it was so slippery. And there were many big boulders we had to climb around and over to make progress. Annie developed a new method of boulder hopping. I called it "sit and slide." She would get herself up on a boulder, and then slide down; get up on another boulder, and slide down. It wreaked havoc on her pants, but it worked.

It took us an hour to cover a mile, and the prospects of making it to Whispering Springs were fading. One man in our group, Steve, wasn't feeling well and decided to stop and hang out. Thinking perhaps the rest of us might want to actually make it to our destination, he asked Annie if she wanted to stay with him. Her reply? "No!!! I'm going to make it, or die!"

Well, she didn't make it; and she didn't die. We managed to get about three miles into the canyon when others from our group showed up on their way back to the boats. At that point, we had about four to five hours of light, and since we needed at least an hour on the river, we decided to turn around.

It turned out what was important for Annie was to be able to find out for herself what she could do. She could have made it to Whispering Springs had we had more time. That was enough.

I entered the tongue of Kanab, a rapid that stretched for almost a half mile, as we watched the walls close in. On the left side, a narrow slope rose up to the base of the Muav. The slope on the right side was much higher, reflecting the elevation difference between the North and South Rims. The Canyon was tilted from North to South, reflecting the geologic reality of Canyon country. Earth activity had tilted the Colorado Plateau, causing the North Rim to rest one-to-two thousand feet higher than the South Rim.

We floated past another side canyon in an inlet hiding behind a young cottonwood tree. The inlet used to be devoid of debris, but now was choked with an island of large boulders that had been flushed out of the canyon during substantial flash floods. It was called Olo, a shortened Havasupai word meaning horse.

The entrance used to require a climb up a knotted twenty-foot rope. On my first trip in 1978 we had camped at Olo, and my best friend, Gary, had unexpectedly awakened me early in the morning and told me *to follow him. I watched as he climbed up the rope, placing one foot at a time in loops. When he reached the top he effortlessly pulled himself over the edge. I was a little nervous, concerned that I might not be able to get to the top. It wasn't as hard as I'd imagined, and I felt pretty good once I joined my friend. Then I found out it was just the beginning. Gary scrambled around a pool along a narrow ledge, and I followed. After negotiating around the pool, we walked to the front of a waterfall, actually more of a seep, on a twenty-foot travertine wall. This climb was more challenging because we had to scramble up the center of the slick wall with no solid handholds at the top. I had to transfer my weight to my hands and hope I didn't slip. I did.*

On my first try I lost my grip and as I began to fall, I pushed off the travertine with my hands and my shins. Fortunately there was a pool of water below. Except for a lot of blood where my shin had been scraped, I was relieved to learn that I had suffered no injuries. I washed off the blood and went back, and this time was able to make it up and over. We were now in a narrow, sensuous, mini-Muav gorge with a thin line of water moving slowly between small pools. We rested near a pool twenty feet wide and fifteen feet deep. The water was so clear I thought I could reach in and pick out one of the pebbles lying on the bottom.

*   *   *

In '86 we again climbed up the rope into Olo, only this time both Sandy and I did so under the watchful and innocent eyes of my parents. As I approached the lip at the top of the rope, I took a minute to slow my breathing and relax before pulling myself up. I looked down on the raft holding both my parents. They were smiling. I'm sure the possibility of a fall had not entered their minds.

We were now less than two miles from Matcat. The Muav cliffs rose directly out of the water pinching the channel down even more. Muav is another Paiute word meaning pass or divide. The color of the limestone was a rich pewter. This was a formation described by geologists as thin-bedded with inter-bedded layers of clay; a close examination would reveal small pebbles. As the walls rose and receded from the river, the iron-oxide veneer that had painted most of the cliffs in the Canyon replaced the natural color of the Muav.

I could now see the entrance to Matcat. The wall on river left angled down to the opening. Sunshine bathed the downstream wall just inside the canyon. I pulled over in an eddy a quarter mile away to wait for the rest of the rafts to catch up. Floyd and Star were already there. Miriam and Tyler were in Floyd's raft, and Timmy, Ralph, and Kathy were in Star's. Soon Sue joined us with the Israelis and Antje in an international paddleboat, and Jim and Diane in the duckies. Sue asked Floyd to carry one of the duckies, and when Carla arrived, asked her to carry the other one. I invited Diane into my raft, and Star took Jim. The pull-in to Matcat could be a little tricky, and Sue didn't want anything to go wrong.

She then headed for the mouth of Matcat, and the rest of us would go in one at a time. After she disappeared around the corner, Floyd shoved off and we watched as he floated with the back of his raft facing the left wall. Just before he reached the opening, he started pulling on his oars, and we lost sight of him. I then pushed off and did the same.

The eddy in Matcat had a strong current that flowed counter-clockwise around the wall. Each raft had to be anchored to something solid, and as I pulled in, I saw Sue up on the right side and Floyd on the left. Each had climbing pieces trying to find little notches in which to anchor them, attach a carabineer, and then a bowline or stern line. This was always an exciting time where raft guides could scramble around on slippery walls doing their thing. One at a time, the remaining rafts floated in. I was up on the right wall anchoring down my stern line when Michael came in with the Israelis. I stopped for just a moment to find Liz, but she was busy putting her daypack on her back and wasn't paying any attention to me.

Within fifteen minutes everybody was off the rafts and on dry land, preparing for the hike. Sue described the two options, wet or dry. The wet hike would go right up the drainage, and was more of an adventure hike. We would have to do some scrambling and help the passengers with a few moves, like a chimney move with feet on one wall and backs against the other. Nathan said he could show us how to do that.

The dry hike would involve a little exposure, but was fairly easy. Sue and Michael would lead the dry hike, and several passengers opted for that. The rest of us started up the wet route. A small stream flowed between pebble-dotted limestone shelves through another narrow Muav gorge. We walked through a stomach-deep pool, and scrambled up and over a chock stone. I noticed Liz carrying both her new Nikon and a digital video camera, and offered to put them in my pack so she would have both hands free. She declined, saying she would probably want to take some pictures on the way up. I thought about insisting, but didn't.

The next stretch was on very slick limestone made even slicker by a coating of algae in some spots. We stepped up on a two-foot shelf as the canyon undulated to the right and then to the left. After walking around a small pool, we came to another bend in the channel with a deeper pool in front of a rise in elevation. To get past the pool and up the rise, it was best to lean with both hands on the left wall while placing our feet on the opposite wall near the pool. Liz was holding both cameras in one hand, and attempting the maneuver with the other hand. I was about to offer to hold the cameras when her left foot slipped and she fell into the pool. I heard one of the cameras strike the rock and reached down quickly to grab the cameras from her. Both were wet.

I helped Liz out of the pool and asked her if she was hurt. She said no, but something was wrong. Suddenly she seemed very young, almost frightened. She asked if the cameras were all right. I said I couldn't be sure until we could open them up, but first we had to negotiate the rest of the gorge. I put the cameras in my backpack and we continued on. There were two more spots that required moves, the last being over a chock stone about six feet above the canyon floor. To negotiate that, we had to place our feet on the left wall, and our back on the right wall, and inch our way up to the same level as the rock. Then we could scramble over the rock. Floyd was standing in front of the rock to offer support and comfort for those who had never done this before. Carla was above the rock offering a wristhold to anyone who needed it. Nathan was also there with words of encouragement.

This was a great hike simply because it was so different from most of our hikes and it involved people doing things they didn't know about and never imagined being able to do. In addition, it's a spectacular canyon, formed in a narrow Muav gorge, the gray-white walls washed clean by repeated flash floods.

After everybody had made it beyond the last boulder, we scrambled up the Muav wall that receded just enough for us to have thin stair steps. The creek was now below us, and the heat practically stifling after time in the cool, wet gorge. Up ahead, the walls curled from right to left. Maidenhair fern hung from the walls and trailed along a damp limestone floor. It looked very much like an amphitheater, and was one of the very best locations for our string quartet concerts. On many trips, I would bring my flute up here and enjoy the near-perfect acoustics.

Sue said we would be hanging out here for a short time, so I asked Liz to follow me to a place in the sun where we could check out her cameras. She was very quiet, and her eyes were moist. I asked her if she was all right and she said she wasn't hurt, but was concerned about her cameras. We looked at the Nikon, and I could see moisture in the lens. Water had definitely gotten into the camera. She tried to turn the camera on but was unsuccessful. I suggested we take the roll of film out and open the camera and allow it to sit in the sun. After it had a chance to dry, we could check to see if it still worked. She agreed, and I first removed the battery, then put her camera inside my backpack, opened the back and pulled out the film. Keeping the film inside to minimize any light, I slowly rolled the film back into its canister. I told Liz that when she returned to town, she could take the roll in and see if any of her shots could be salvaged. I then unscrewed her lens, and placed the camera on a rock in the direct sunlight. Because of our short stay here, I said we would probably have to continue drying out the camera at camp.

Tears rolled down her cheeks. I wanted to hold her, but didn't feel comfortable offering. There wasn't anything I could say, so we just sat on the rock and watched the camera, hoping it would be okay. In just a few minutes, Sue announced we would be returning to the rafts and heading to camp. Everybody took the dry route back, following a very narrow trail with a sixty-foot drop to our right. We took our time down-climbing a couple of ledges, and were back at the rafts in fifteen minutes. It took some time to get everybody to their respective rafts, which were parked in single file in the narrow channel and eddy. The Israelis had to scramble across five rafts to get to Michael's. Then, one by one, we pulled out of the eddy and into a short rapid.

Still in the steep Muav gorge, we floated down a long straightaway. On the left, at a sharp bend to the right, a young cottonwood tree guarded another camp, Matcat Hotel, which was the location of one of the more exciting storms I had experienced in the Canyon. *Michael had been the trip leader on a July trip in 1999, and we had planned a long stay at the amphitheater in Matcat. Real thunder convinced us to evacuate the side canyon to avoid any dangers from a flash flood. We had barely left the mouth when a monstrous storm rolled in from upstream. This was unusual because most storm systems rolled in from downstream. By the time we had reached Matcat Hotel, waterfalls were forming over the nearest rim eight hundred feet above us. One waterfall plunged over the rim directly across from our camp. While Michael was celebrating the rain with a mud dance, we watched as a long stream of water plunged from the top and attempted to reach the river. It never arrived. The winds were strong, the parched desert air dry, and the water was blown back up and evaporated, like virga, moisture from rain clouds that evaporates before it touches the earth.*

While this was going on, another waterfall came down right into the middle of camp. It was a small cascade and no one was at risk, but we were then treated to a microcosmic demonstration of the carving of the Grand Canyon. At first the flood followed a meandering path down the sandy beach; but as the water began to cut a ditch deeper and deeper, the path straightened out. At the same time, Michael decided to enjoy the water by standing directly underneath it as it plunged over the edge. Only later did he admit that wasn't very smart, since rocks and other debris often get carried in the water. When the flood finally subsided, we were left with a big ditch about eight feet deep and fifteen feet across.

After floating around the bend, I told everyone that in about a mile we would be running Upset Rapid, and I thought it would be a good idea if they put on their raingear. It was late in the afternoon, we were in the shade, and we would be getting drenched in the rapid. No one argued. Chris opened up the dry bag and found mesh bags for her, Graham, and Mary.

While they donned their gear, I told them a story about my second run through Upset. *My first had been a left-to-right run that was similar to House Rock and Bedrock rapids. This time we would run down the left side. The rock bar pushing out from 150 Mile Canyon on river right forced all the water towards the left wall. The tongue was narrow, and the water was very low. When we scouted the rapid, my crewmates showed me the lateral wave at the top that we would break through. It was crucial, they emphasized, that I hit the very top of the wave to run far enough left to avoid the hole at the bottom of the rapid. I was to run third, behind Gary, who had introduced me to rafting in the Canyon, and Carlos.*

We pulled out and moved into the current. Gary made his entry and started racing in the current very close to the wall. Just above the hole, I saw his raft slide up on an angular rock leaning against the wall. My heart jumped into my throat as in one fluid motion he leaped out of his raft, pushed off the rock, re-entered his raft, and cruised to the left of the hole. Carlos made the same entry and wound up stuck on the same rock. Only he couldn't push off the rock; and I was following close behind. Instinct took over. The roar of the rapid receded as I focused on the raft in front of me. I was sure I was going to hit it, but brought my left oar in so that the blade touched my left tube, missing Carlos's raft by inches, and somehow managed to slide to the left of the hole. I was too relieved to celebrate. All I did was exhale.

Mary asked if we would be doing the same run, and I told her no. With the water much higher, we wouldn't have to be as far left. It would be, I said, a very exciting, very wet run. Graham asked how the rapid got its name. I told him during the 1923 US Geological Survey trip in 1923, Emery Kolb had flipped his boat there, and the leader of the trip promptly gave it the name Upset. Graham suggested we not repeat the experience. I told him I would do my best.

At least I would know which way was left and which was right. *The first time I ever captained a paddleboat in Upset, I was still inexperienced as a guide, and with no previous experience on the paddleboat, felt tentative. We made a good entry, and as we approached some big waves coming off the left wall, I intended to call for a quick left turn to face into them. Instead I called for a right turn. Nancy, the real paddleboat captain, immediately shouted, "No! Left Turn!" Not my finest moment. I was quickly returned to my own raft.*

Upset turned out to be as I had predicted: big, fast, and wet. We entered on the slice of tongue which quickly disappeared into a jumble of waves rushing at us from the left wall. Chris and Graham were up on the front tube greeting each wave as it crashed into us, sending water over their heads and dousing me. I told them their job was to keep me dry, but couldn't hear Graham's response as I slammed into another wave, pushed hard on my left oar and raced into the frothing fury of the last big wave. The raft slowed, almost stopping before rising up and through the wave, finishing the rapid in some smaller tail waves.

As we floated below the rapid, Chris thanked me for recommending rain gear. Her experiences of being chilled in the Roaring Twenties were evidently still on her mind. Camp was now a little over an hour away, and except for a few small riffles and one small rapid, we would be on pretty calm water. We passed a rusted metal plate attached to a large boulder on river right. When Graham saw it and asked about it, I told him it was a memorial for Shorty Burton, a motorboat guide who had drowned in the hole in Upset on a trip in 1967. His motor rig flipped and his life jacket snagged on something. Graham thanked me for not mentioning that story before the rapid.

We passed a small spring dripping off a hanging garden about twenty feet above the river. If the sun had been on us, I would have maneuvered the raft under the runoff. We were still in the depths and shadows of the Muav Gorge. Late afternoon rays of the sun were beginning to paint their warm light, inching towards the rim. This was a section of the Canyon where I beseeched the rain gods to open up. With steep walls, and several layers, flash floods were always spectacular. *At the Ledges Camp where we were headed, we had the pleasure of watching the formation of several waterfalls on a previous trip. The cascade first appeared at the top, would disappear for several minutes into the first shelf, then dramatically reappear as another forming waterfall a level lower. This would happen four times as the water reached each descending layer before finally flowing out into the river. On one trip, we were enjoying dinner next to a small seep that dripped enough water for people to wash their hair. Maidenhair fern covered the travertine-coated wall, and a small marsh with cattails and grass had grown up on the limestone bench to our left. Suddenly the drips turned into a deluge, as a flash flood erupted without warning. Since we were not at risk, we enjoyed dessert to the song of the flood.*

Ledges is a unique camp comprised of several levels of Muav limestone and a bit of sand. Parking the rafts required a soft landing and quick action, since the rafts would remain partially in the current. Floyd pulled in first and jumped out of his raft with his bowline, then had Tyler hold his rope while he waited for Star to pull in. One-by-one we floated up against the next raft and quickly found places to tie up, using climbing pieces wedged into Muav cracks. We then linked our rafts together using the straps attached to each frame. This was a defensive maneuver in the event that a climbing piece should be dislodged or a rope became loose.

We set the kitchen on the first ledge just to the left of the rafts. People were told there were plenty of campsites up a short trail to the left, as well as behind and above the kitchen area. Directly across the river rose a limestone cliff. Behind the camp, the stair-stepped Cambrian layers reached for the sky. Eliza and I were on cook crew, and the menu called for lasagna, tossed salad, and garlic bread. Sue called us over to Floyd's raft for a crew meeting, actually an excuse to crack a beer and celebrate another good day on the river. The Canyon has always been a place where bright, sometimes counter-dependent men and women enjoyed a level of freedom not available in mainstream life. Partying has always been high on the agenda, and passing the bottle a primary form of bonding, especially after a big water day. But I think alcohol in the desert is an oxymoron. It's an especially arid environment where dehydration is one of the main physical concerns. And the typical river guide's diet piles on more with caffeine from coffee, Mountain Dew, and Pepsi or Coke at breakfast, the same during the day, and then alcohol at night. I consider it a testament to the adaptability of our bodies that they put up with such abuse for so long. Of course, that is a personal choice, and I don't pretend to feel better because I don't indulge in those things. The only concern I have, beyond the well being of crewmates whom I love, is that after a couple of beers, or a couple of mixed drinks, I feel shut out. I'm not passing the bottle, and have noticed over the years that I get left out of the conversation. It's still a challenge to be a non-drinker in an environment where it is so prevalent.

In the old days it was normal for some guides to drink during the day, and not unusual for some to smoke pot. I remember trips where the crew convened at the groover for a "safety talk", a euphemism for sharing a joint. Today Park Service regulations forbid drinking alcohol during the day, and allow drinking in moderation at camp only after the kitchen has been set up. And no drugs. Each river company has their own random drug-testing policy, and guides who refuse to quit smoking pot have either left the river or have been fired. A lawsuit contending violation of constitutional rights was filed in an attempt to overturn random drug tests, but it hasn't gone anywhere.

On this night, everyone had a few beers. I sucked down a bottle of water. Afterwards, I told Eliza that this would be dress-up night for the cook crew and encouraged her to be playful. She said that would be no problem. While Carla "shopped" for dinner, I returned to my raft and opened up my clothes bag. In the early years I had just stuffed my clothes in my black bag. That guaranteed crushed and wrinkled shirts, so I had created my own drawers, actually plastic shopping bags. One "drawer" contained my presorted and color-matched short sleeve shirts and shorts, one my colorful sun pants, one my sarongs, and one my extras. I selected a black corduroy vest with green and red patterns, and a sarong with black edges and a brightly patterned combination of light blue, green, red and white. I then used a spare water bottle rainbow-strap-tie fashioned in a full Windsor knot.

Eliza selected a sleeveless lavender dress, pearls, and a light blue scarf tied around her forehead. We were quite a pair. Preparations for the lasagna called for a team effort. Michael brought up the charcoal, set enough coals in the fire pan for two DOs – about fifty in all – soaked them in fluid and lit them. At the same time, Chris, Jim B, and Miriam volunteered to help. I asked Jim to chop up the onions while Eliza grated the mozzarella cheese, and Miriam opened up all the cans of mushroom pieces, spaghetti sauce, spinach, tomato paste, and crushed tomatoes. Chris was given the responsibility for the tossed salad, chopping up the red cabbage, cucumbers, lettuce and tomatoes. I set out the hors d'oeuvres: marinated mushrooms, calamata olives, roasted red peppers, and crackers. After placing the hors d'oeuvres on the serving table, I blew the conch and announced their availability.

I then mixed the eggs, ricotta cheese, spinach, and seasonings in a bowl, sautéed the Italian sausage, and then added half the mixture. Now we were ready for the line. After oiling both DOs, I asked Eliza to ladle the tomato sauce, Miriam layer the noodles, Jim B the sausage mixture into one DO, and the mixture without sausage into the other for those who didn't want to eat meat. My job was to sprinkle the mozzarella. In less than five minutes we had two very full DOs ready for baking. I heated both lids, covered the DOs, and took them over to the fire pan. I spread twenty coals around the tops of both lids, and arranged ten on the fire pan. I also found three beer cans, crushed them to a third of their height, and laid the first DO on top of the cans. The second DO had legs, so I placed that on top of the first DO. It would be a good forty-five minutes before the lasagna would be ready.

I told Eliza to take a break and said we would have to prepare the garlic bread about fifteen minutes before dinner. She went down to the raft, and I went looking for Liz to see how she was doing and take another look at her cameras. She and Elli had set their tents up near the remains of that seep. Something had caused the water to change directions and the seep was now dry. A rust-colored residue still clung to the travertine, and all that was left of the marsh were the dried-up skeletons of grass and cattails.

Tal's camera was still in her backpack, so I had her remove it and checked to see if it was functioning. It wasn't. I told her the electronics were probably fried, and hoped she had insurance. She said she did, and was at least glad it hadn't happened early in the trip. She thanked me for my concern and gave me a hug. It felt good to feel the warmth of her body against mine. Her damp hair smelled of fresh shampoo. I could have remained in that embrace for a long time, but started feeling awkward, and told her I had to get back to the dinner.

I could still feel the softness of her body as I returned to the kitchen. Somehow garlic bread wasn't at the top of my focus at the moment, but it served as a good distraction. Eliza came up and asked what she could do. I asked her to slice the three loaves of French bread lengthwise while I chopped and sautéed the garlic. We carry a quart container of peeled garlic on our trips, and use it liberally. I like to experiment with different flavors, so I asked Eliza to grab a block of cheddar cheese and grate it for me. While the garlic was sautéing I placed the grill on the stove and lit all three burners. As it was heating up, I poured some canola oil on and spread it around. Then I spread the garlic and butter on the bread, and when the grill was hot enough, I placed the bread, wet side down, on the grill. Eliza cleaned off the serving table and set up the tossed salad, the Italian dressing, and tongs. I asked her to check the lasagna. She thought it was ready. She removed the coals from the lids of both DOs and brought them over to the serving table, then found serving spoons, and set out the Parmesan cheese in a bowl.

Meanwhile, I turned the bread over, spread the grated cheddar, then turned it face down to melt the cheese. Using a spatula, I made sure to scrape under the cheese and turned the bread over again. This time I cut the bread into bite-sized pieces and put them in a small pot. It was obvious that people were hungry because they were milling around the kitchen area. Eliza made a lame effort at blowing the conch shell and then announced that dinner was ready. She pointed out the DO with sausage and the one without.

While people were serving themselves, we went down to the dish line to wash some of the pots and pans. I thanked Eliza for her help, and she thanked me for inviting her on the trip. It continued to be, she told me, an awesome experience. I asked her how she felt about the prospect of being a river guide, and she said she hadn't thought too much about it. She did, however, gain a lot of respect for the demands of the job, and for the skills of the guides on the crew.

Once most of the folks were eating, we went up and served ourselves. Sue was talking about the next day, saying we would be making our lunches in the morning because we would be spending around four hours at Havasu. She described the canyon as one of those really magical places that offered something for everyone. We would have a quick breakfast, make our lunch, and float on a flat stretch about five miles to the canyon. The pull-in would be similar to the Matcat entry, and we would drop our passengers off on shore before tying up the rafts. People could hike as little as a quarter mile, to a pool we called the motor pool because so many motor trips took their passengers there. Others could choose to meander up the creek and find other spots to play, read, and relax. Still others could elect to go on a forced march three-and-a-half miles to Beaver Falls, a spectacular, wide, twenty-foot cascade that plunged into a beautiful turquoise pool. She said she would remind folks of their options in the morning.

Dessert was Pepperidge Farms cookies, and they disappeared quickly. Nathan, Timmy, and Tyler spent extra time around the cookie jar. This was a messy meal, and we had to dump out the first wash bucket because it looked so gross. We had a lot of dishwashing assistance, and were able to close up the kitchen before dark. I invited Eliza to follow me behind camp to see a roasting pit I had just discovered, after more than twenty years of camping right underneath it. We scrambled up the Muav steps and climbed over several boulders before coming to what looked like a small landfilled hillock. The top was flat and covered with small debris. It was such an innocuous spot that I had literally walked right by it for years on my way to climb the wall behind without noticing it.

It had been used in the spring, most likely by the Paiutes, as an agave-roasting pit. Wood would be burned in the bottom of the pit, underneath a layer of rocks covered by wet agave leaves. The agave heart would then be placed on top of the leaves. Dirt then covered up the pit for up to two days while the agave steamed. After retrieving the hearts, there would be a feast. It didn't look like much now, but it had served a very important purpose in its day.

Dusk had descended on us and we headed back to the rafts. I decided to find a camp spot away from the rafts, so I gathered my stuff and headed for a shelf beyond where a lot of the folks were camping. I took my flute with me, and after laying out my pad and bag, removed it from its PVC case and began to play. The sound of the music floated out over the river and mingled with the soft voice of the current. I played for about fifteen minutes, and then put it away. Someone shouted "more," but I was ready for sleep. I had told Eliza that I would get up and put on the coffee water, and would wake her when it was time to make breakfast and lunch.

The sky was clear, and the Milky Way was bright, although the rims seemed so close I only had a narrow section of sky to enjoy. We hadn't been threatened by rain, but the monsoons could begin at any time. Hopefully we wouldn't have rain while we were in Havasu. While it was a relatively easy place to get to high ground, it would be a shame if folks missed the opportunity to play there.

Havasupai means "People of the Blue Green Water." A hike into this unexpected land of rushing water and greenery, as diverse as wild Arizona grape leaves and Cottonwood trees, is like a journey through Alice's mirror. Farther up the creek are waterfalls and the Supai Indian reservation. On September 3, 1990, a hundred year flash flood of immense proportions, 22,000 cubic feet per second, ripped out seventy-five percent of the trees, and shattered ancient travertine pools. Since then we have watched as the natural cycles ebb and flow. The Great Blue Heron seems to enjoy the scenery.

DAY THIRTEEN –
LEDGES TO NATIONAL CANYON

My alarm beeped me into the day just after four in the morning. I took a moment to come fully into my body and allow my eyes to adjust to the darkness. Then I took some deep breaths, feeling the cool moistness of the air. I stretched, reaching overhead with my right arm and pushing my right leg in the opposite direction, and then doing the same with my left side. My bed was a limestone shelf with three feet of headroom and a limestone ceiling. I could hear the soft dribbles of the re-channeled seep fifteen feet away and a damp chill hovered around me. The air tasted slightly salty, and there was a distinctly organic aroma from the dead marsh nearby. I put on my shorts and a fleece shirt and walked to the kitchen, passing the tent where Liz was asleep with Doron. I took a deep breath and continued down a short trail, found the lighter, opened the propane valve, and started up the blaster. With a fairly quiet river and hard rocks all around, the sound of the blaster on high would surely wake just about everyone. I decided to give people more time to sleep by keeping the flame and sound low. I also started the fire under the tea water.

A breakfast of hot cereal, orange juice, and bagels would be easy and quick to allow us to get out of camp and spend more time in Havasu. I washed my hands, decided to let Eliza, my breakfast partner, sleep in, and opened up the rest of the kitchen. After making the orange juice and putting it on the serving table, I found the bagels and oatmeal in the "plates" box where Carla had put them last night as protection from nocturnal predators.

In 2002 I had hiked up behind this camp before breakfast to show two of the string quartet members the roasting pit that I had only discovered earlier in the year. We decided to continue higher even though breakfast was being prepared and the climb had some risk. One was the leader of the quartet and up for any adventure in the Canyon. This was the first trip in the Canyon for the other man, and his first time rafting. He had not done any boulder hopping or climbing. The cliff face we climbed was covered in crumbling salts, and there were few solid handholds.

When I'm nervous I tend to whistle under my breath to keep breathing and stay in my body. I was whistling all the way up, and once I reached the top, decided we should find

209

another way down. We explored for fifteen to twenty minutes, picking our way carefully over and around small pools surrounded by grasses and cattails. When the conch blew, I said I would try to find a different way down. Everywhere I looked had more exposure and even fewer handholds and footholds. With some anxiety I resigned myself to risking the original route. I looked around for Derek and couldn't find him. Finally I called his name, and heard a response from below. The neophyte had already down-climbed. When I asked him how he got down, he pointed to a drainage filled with boulders to the right of our route. It was an easy way down, and would be an easy way up in the future. So much for experience.

With the bagels sliced, I heated up the griddle and put water on for the oatmeal. The coffee water was boiling, so I turned it down, poured in the bag of Macy's French Roast coffee, stirred it, and covered the pot. In the early days, the crew would buy their coffee from Macy's, a local Flagstaff coffee shop with unbelievable pastries, and serve the passengers Folgers in a can. Now everybody gets the real deal. I let the coffee settle for five minutes, strained it into one of the Gott coolers, and placed it on the serving table. Then I poured the tea water into the other cooler and placed that next to the coffee. Also on the table were the condiments, granola, orange juice, and cocoa. Instead of blowing the conch shell to announce coffee, I took out my flute and played some notes. Graham was the first to show up, complimenting me on the wake-up call without his usual British humor. Several others said it was a nice way to start the day.

Eliza came up, gave me a sleepy hug, and asked what she could do. I told her the bagels were all hers. All she had to do was put a little butter on each one and toast them on the griddle. I poured the dry oatmeal into the boiling water, stirred it, added a little maple syrup, some raisins and cinnamon, turned off the flame and covered the pot. I told Eliza I was going up to pack my sleep kit, and she smiled and said to take my time. So far she hadn't spent any time on the oars, and that was a bit of a red flag. Usually, anyone who is really interested in this work would want to spend as much time on the oars as possible. I was tempted to say something, but decided to just watch.

I walked up through the fragmite grasses that stood about six feet tall, stepped onto the Muav bench with several tents in front of me, said good morning to Miriam and Tyler, who were rolling up their sleeping bags, and stopped to ask Mary how her foot was. About the same, she said, and I told her I would work on it again during breakfast. She had a walking stick that helped her be more mobile, and as usual had no complaints along with a warm smile. Liz was just emerging from her tent and gave me a sweet good morning grin. Doron was still asleep, and I told Liz she'd better wake her up because we would be calling breakfast any minute and it would be a quick one. I asked her if she had checked her camera and she frowned and said it was definitely dead. I told her I was sorry. She said she was disappointed that she wouldn't be able to take pictures in Havasu. I said she could still take pictures in her mind. She smiled and headed to the serving table.

It took me five minutes to stuff my pillow, sheet, and sleeping bag in my black bag, and carry everything down to the raft. Eliza said breakfast was set up, and I asked her to go ahead and blow the conch. It was hardly necessary, since people were already helping themselves. While I organized things on my raft and applied some sunscreen, Sue asked who was interested in the "forced march" to Beaver Falls. She reminded people that they could hang out at the big kids' pool, meander and find a spot to hang, or take the three-and-a-half mile hike to Beaver.

The Israelis said they would meander, as did Miriam and Tyler, Chris and Graham. Diane, Jim, Timmy, Nathan, Kathy, and Antje opted for Beaver. Mary had said earlier that she would be willing to go to the first crossing with some assistance. Sue then talked about what we would do once we pulled in. It would, she said, be like the pull-in at Matcat, except that as each raft pulled in, the passengers would be dropped off before parking the rafts. This meant they had to be ready with their water, cameras, and lunch.

While she was talking, we set up a deli-lunch on the prep table. In addition to sandwich fixings, people could choose from apples and oranges, dried fruit, nuts, Cheetos, and granola bars. Each would have a brown bag in which to carry their food. Carla told everyone to carry their lunches in their daypacks.

I invited Eliza to hike with me, telling her I wanted to point out some things I thought she would find interesting on the way up. She said that would be great and went over to make her lunch.

We made a last call for both breakfast and lunch, and while the rest of the crew cleaned up, I went over to work on Mary's foot. The swelling had gone down, but she still felt a sharp pain on the top of her foot just below the ankle – a pretty good sign that it was a non-displaced fracture. She told me she hadn't had this much attention in a long time, and was thoroughly enjoying it. I said I wanted to hear more about her work as an internal consultant at a large paper company, and suggested she ride in my raft so we could talk during the long float after Havasu. As I refitted her portable cast and wrapped an ace bandage around it, she said that would be great.

Timmy asked if he and his dad could ride with me and I said yes. I told him he could row if he wanted, and he quickly said yes in a manner that made it feel like a gift. He seemed so much more relaxed, and was quick to smile. Ralph hadn't changed much at all, except I had noticed him watching Timmy with an expression that I interpreted as a father's pride. I believe he was surprised at how competent his son was in the ducky, and even if he couldn't relax, he was happy that his son was having a good time.

As soon as the rafts were loaded and the groover taken down, we shoved off. It was seven-thirty, and even though we were deep in the shade of the Muav gorge, the temperature was already rising.

Below Ledges we ran one small rapid, Sinyala, named after a prominent Havasupai family whose patriarch was Havasupai chief, Judge Sinyella. He had provided much of the knowledge that had gone into a fascinating book written in 1928 by Chrislie Spier for the American Museum of Natural History.

Just below Sinyala dripped a delicate waterfall, more like a series of droplets falling into the river off a travertine slide. In some years the slide would be a hanging garden covered with ferns, mosses and other greenery, while in dry years it was bald, as if someone had removed its wig. I maneuvered the front of my raft inches away from the wall so my passengers could enjoy a momentary shower of water that had been warmed as it flowed over rocks heated by the sun.

The source of the water was high up in the Redwall, a place we called Pete's Pocket, or the more poetic Slime Canyon. I'd been up there once, and it was such a surprise to be hiking up a rocky trail and come upon a wetlands complete with algae-covered pools, cattails, and a variety of grasses. The water had originated on the rim, as rain and melted snow held in shallow pockets. After filtering through five porous layers of sedimentary rock, reaching the impervious Muav layer, backing up to form underground lakes and ponds, it eventually ate its way through the Redwall to feed this perennial marsh.

We passed Last Chance, a name given by river runners to note the last reasonable camp before Havasu. (There were theoretically three more campsites in the mile above Havasu – Last, Last Chance; Last, Last, Last Chance; and No Fucking Way.) *In my early days, we had always tried to camp at Last Chance to get an early start so we could spend the better part of the day hiking and hanging out in Havasu, the side canyon everyone called the Garden of Eden. One night, we were awakened by jarring thunder, and the arrival of rain. Within minutes a flash flood began jetting out of a hidden amphitheater just above camp. Our rafts had been parked in a small eddy directly under the stream of water. Suddenly five naked boatmen and one boatwoman were scrambling to relocate our rafts out of harm's way. Pulling rafts upstream while walking over sharp Muav limestone slabs made the task more painful. In the morning we woke to find a collared lizard struggling to climb out of the water. Shear walls of soft sand kept thwarting his efforts, so we intervened with natural law and rescued the little critter.*

We passed Last Last Chance, then Last Last Last Chance, and finally No Fucking Way, and one-by-one pulled in to the eddy at the mouth of Havasu. It was exactly the same as the pull-in at Matcat, except the eddy at Havasu was shallower and we had more space to tie up the rafts. After unloading all our passengers on shore, we rowed our rafts to the back of the parking lot, tying up along the left wall and strapping our rafts end-to-end so that the last raft was within reach of the shore. This way, we could walk over the rafts to get to shore, and our passengers could walk back to their rafts without having to swim through the eddy. A water jug was brought off one of the rafts so people could fill their bottles before the hike, and refill them after the hike. Life jackets were strapped together on shore, and we took off to hike into Havasu.

We had to climb a short but slick shelf, polished smooth by thousands of hands, feet, and butts. Before heading in, I invited Eliza to follow me and I walked around the corner to the edge where we could look down on the rafts thirty feet below. The blue-green water flowed out of Havasu and disappeared into the Colorado. At the edge of the downstream eddy line, the two currents mingled in a sensuous, merging dance, like new lovers tentatively exploring a first embrace. Directly in front and just below us, I pointed out an overhang over thirty feet above the creek. I told her that in 1983 the Colorado was so high it had backed up a quarter mile into this drainage. There were oar marks on the underside of that overhang from rafts rowing up the creek. The water had been that high. Eliza just shook her head.

We quickly caught up to the rest of the group hiking along a narrow shelf on a well-worn path looking down on Havasu Creek. Iron-oxide pigment had painted the limestone wall across the creek a light reddish-brown, offering a perfect accent to the color of the water it contained. A hundred feet up the creek, a ten-foot cascade of water plunged over boulders, choking the channel. We walked by an ocotillo, a distinctive "marker" plant (a plant indicating a new eco-system) looking decidedly like the skeleton of a previously healthy plant. A cluster of awkward-looking thin poles stretched fifteen feet toward the sky, half-inch spikes encircling each shaft from bottom to top. The desiccated remnants of a red-orange flower clung to the top. It appeared lifeless, but like other desert plants, was merely waiting for the next sprinkling of rain. When that happened, this ugly gray shaft would be transformed by hundreds of light green florets dancing around the shaft, drinking in as much water as possible. And in a few days the leaves would disappear, and the ocotillo would resume its dormancy. Until the next rain.

We scrambled down a worn travertine path, stepped onto a Muav shelf, itself polished by thousands of feet, and crossed the creek where it was only mid-thigh deep. Havasu was awash in lush vegetation, from velvet ash trees, to wild Arizona grapevines, dinosaur-aged horsetail with its silica-based skin, willow, acacia, mesquite, grasses, datura, and much more. Until 1990, we would walk along the trail and not be able to see the creek for the lush vegetation, even though we could hear its rushing water, which might be ten feet away. Vegetation was so thick that female guides used to sunbath naked on a smooth rock in the middle of the creek. It was called Hag Rock after the female guides of another river company who had proudly taken the name of boat hags.

On September 3, 1990, a flash flood estimated at 22,800 cfs, came roaring through the Supai village. Picking up speed and debris as it raced toward the river, nature's fury took out everything in its path, ripping out seventy-five percent of the trees in the drainage, gouging out huge chunks of the creek bed, removing travertine terraces that had formed deep blue pools over many decades, and lowering Mooney Falls, a 175-foot waterfall a couple miles below the village – several feet. This was a tenfold increase in the creek's normal volume and a thousandfold increase in its power. Fortunately no one was killed, but the canyon had been significantly altered.

When we stopped for a look just two weeks later, Eden had been stripped of much of its greenery at and near the creek, and huge piles of debris, including trees with their root balls still intact, had been pushed into corner pockets like matchsticks. Some of the trees lay bent but not broken along the creek bed, and grape leaves were already pushing up through the dried sediment. Nature's cycle hadn't stopped, but the Garden of Eden had undergone an extreme makeover. Before the flood we couldn't see the creek. Now all we could see was the creek, like a beautiful woman whose clothes had been stripped off, revealing her naked wonders.

Some of my private trip friends no longer care to go into Havasu, because "it's not the way it used to be." True, and change is part of the natural order of things. I'm fortunate that I can watch the canyon recreate itself. Since that flood I've taken one shot upstream and one downstream from the same point on each trip, just to see the subtle and gross changes that occur in nature over time. Exactly a year later, a second flood came roaring down, and although it was smaller, it still carried away more vegetation and destroyed the freshly forming travertine dams.

A quarter mile off the river is one of the favorite stopping points for many motor trips: the motor pool, or the big kids' pool. Before "the flood," it had been separated by a travertine shelf and velvet ash trees, with a diving pool on one side and a shallower wading pool on the other. The diving pool was deep enough to allow people to dive off the Muav cliff next to it, something we don't allow on the Colorado because we can't be sure what's under the surface. Much of that pool has been filled in with sediment, and a gravel bar has replaced the trees and travertine shelf. The wading pool has been a bit inconsistent. On one trip it might be waist deep, on another hip deep, and on still another, over my head. All in the same season.

Flash floods have taken the lives of hikers in the Canyon, but to my knowledge, no passengers on commercial trips have been killed by floods, although there have been plenty *of near misses. One CanX trip became stranded in Havasu when an unexpected flash flood ripped all its rafts out of the "parking lot" and washed them downstream. The downpour that commenced after the flood made everyone miserable since all their raingear was on the washed-away rafts. Two large motor rigs that were moored downstream of the entry to Havasu transported passengers and crew from several trips nine miles to Tuckup Canyon, where they all spent an adventurous night trying to stay warm.*

To get beyond the motor pool we had to walk through the wading pool and climb through a small cave formed by travertine. The opening was about seven feet in diameter, and led from the pool to a trail that continued up the canyon. After the '90 flood, park rangers had to cut through trees piled high above the upstream opening, at least sixty feet above the level of the creek.

From there it is a bit over three miles to Beaver Falls, a wide cascade plunging into a deep, crystal clear pool. At the far end of the pool, water flowed over travertine dams to continue its journey to the Colorado through a series of pools and dams, some with trees encased in travertine rising out of the creek. Two miles up the creek from Beaver is Mooney Falls, named for James Mooney, an early twentieth century miner who had used too short a rope trying to down climb the 175-foot waterfall. He fell to his death, and his travertine-encased body was recovered ten months later.

On many trips we would hike up to Beaver and enjoy an hour or so swimming and eating a picnic lunch. In the early years the hikes were more like forced marches because of the rapid pace set by the guides, especially if we wanted to get to Mooney. The trail to Beaver followed the creek on the right side (looking downstream). At approximately the halfway point, we made the first of four crossings. Just before arriving at Beaver, we had to climb up an improved trail on creek right blasted out of the Muav. After ascending fifty feet to a trail that continued upstream, we climbed a frozen flow of travertine. At the top was a dizzying view of a deep pool a hundred feet below. Upstream the creek meandered through dense brush and trees until it reached the pool fed by Beaver Falls. We had to descend a steep trail to a flat bench about fifty-five feet above the first pool. In the past we used to jump from this spot into the pool below. At that time it was around forty-five feet. The extra ten feet made a huge, often intimidating, difference.

After walking through a small forest of prickly pear cacti, we scrambled down a dusty chute, walked up a narrow trail bordered by deep green grass, and arrived at Beaver. It had changed a lot since I had spent the night there on my 1979 private trip. The flat, grassy mattress next to a shallow pool where I had slept, was now a wide, deep pool. Next to the big pool, what used to be dry land was now under water. Where we used to walk casually to the edge of the pool, we now had to balance along a narrow travertine shelf with water rushing over it. Directly under Beaver was a subterranean cave we called the Green Room, for the green light bouncing off the bottom of the pool reflecting on the ceiling. To get into the Green Room we had to jump in front of the falls into a small eddy between two cascades, dive down and go straight in.

On my first try I jumped in, panicked, and came up directly under the largest cascade. As I was being tumbled around, I struggled to get my bearings. The tumbling water was mixed with a lot of air and I had trouble finding any resistance to swim out of there. It was like the difference between the resistance I felt with my oar blade in the water and the absence of that resistance when my blade was flailing in the air. I was scared that I would drown, and it took me longer than I would have preferred to get away from the danger.

I finally made it in, but remained nervous for many years, until one trip when I just decided to overcome the fear. On the way up, I was so pumped I felt like I was gliding over the path. It felt effortless. When I reached the pool I quickly jumped in, swam to the side of the cascade, climbed up and plunged in. Without coming up for air, I swam directly under the falls and came up in an air pocket. There was still enough room to get all my body out of the water, even though the travertine-covered ceiling was getting closer and closer to the water. I was told there was a tunnel that led from the Green Room to the far side of the pool, but I wasn't about to go that route. In fact, on one of my trips, one of my crewmates came back with his chest and back completely abraded. He had gone into the tunnel only to find it had narrowed so much that he had to exhale underwater in order to get out of there. Exhaling underwater? Not a chance.

Sue told us we had a little over four hours, enough time to take people up to Beaver. Eliza and I had decided to meander. We scrambled through the tunnel and I climbed up on top to take my photos up and down the creek, then caught up with her. She told me she hadn't done any trail running for quite some time. We walked another fifteen minutes and she mentioned trail running again. I said we could try to run to Beaver if she was up to it. I hoped she wasn't because I was wearing sandals; but she said hell yes, so we decided to go for it.

We lightened our load, drank a bunch of water, and then took off, a sixty-one year old uncle leading his nineteen-year old niece. I set a pace I thought I could sustain, and we ran. The trail alternated between soft sand, hard packed earth, and boulders. Much of it was fairly flat, with some up and down stretches, sometimes weaving between small boulders, other times running through a field of soft grasses that caressed my legs. When we came to the first crossing, I dunked myself in the creek to cool down, then took off again. We spoke very little, but I felt a camaraderie with her I hadn't known before.

Eliza's dad, Ned, had been a good, competitive athlete. Early in life she didn't seem to have either of those traits, preferring dance, and the musicals and plays her mom enjoyed. Then, around the fifth grade, she took up track, and turned out to be quite fast. She started to enjoy the competition, and became a decent distance runner.

I fully expected her young legs to come flying by me at any time, but she seemed content to follow. I won't say I wasn't feeling a tad competitive, wanting to reaffirm my youthful condition in spite of my age. We crossed the creek three more times, and after a short run through a forest of horsetail, walked up the creek about a hundred yards before climbing up the Muav stairway, then walked near the edge of the cliff, finally coming to the travertine-covered slope. Many millennia ago there must have been a lot of water pouring over this section. Even today I could imagine the flow that left this thick deposit from carbonate-infused water. I told Eliza we would walk up to the top of the slope, and then I wanted her to close her eyes and take my hand. After some hesitation, she let me walk her up to the lip that looked down on that deep pool, with Beaver in the background.

When she opened her eyes, she gasped at the natural beauty laid out before her. Stately cottonwoods lined the creek for as far as the eye could see. Cascades plunged into deep pools, turning the blue-green water into white chaos. Directly below us, an Olympic-sized pool stretched out its welcoming arms. We stepped through a narrow opening in the travertine and descended a thin trail to limestone ledges above the fifty-five foot jump spot. I didn't point it out because I didn't care to be tempted. We continued through the prickly pear forest toward Beaver, its foaming white cascade shining in the summer sun. After negotiating a steep drop though a narrow slit in the wall, we emerged into the sunshine with Beaver roaring in the background, walked up a sandy trail cut through lush desert grass, and traversed a travertine ledge that lay just underwater. Trees provided an oasis-like setting, with sunlight and shadows dancing on the water's surface. It had taken us an hour and a half to get up here, and it would be another half hour or more before the rest of the group would arrive. Eliza said the run felt great, and gave me a high-five. I smiled, saying a silent "yes!' at being able to make it all the way without stopping or being passed by her.

I set my backpack on the shore, told Eliza to keep her lunch inside her pack to stymie the ravens that were already cawing for food, removed my shirt and sandals, and stepped into the pool. I had a spectacular view of the cascade framed by swaying limbs of trees rising out of the pool. The tree's roots were embedded in underwater travertine ledges. The cool water felt refreshing to my overheated body, and I pushed out and under the water, swimming like a frog to the side of the cascade. The sound of the thunderous falls echoed in my ears as I surfaced less than five feet from the turbulence. I climbed up on a ledge and walked over to the side of the falls, immediately recalling my first attempt to enter the Green Room. I knew there was an underwater ledge just below me, so I jumped out and swam under the chaos of the cascade to the far side of the pool.

When I emerged, I saw Eliza coming over, and invited her to follow me up to the next pool. We scrambled up a graduated wall of heated rock, walked around the edge of the upper pool, climbed a Swiss-cheese-like travertine wall sprouting vegetation, eased to the side of the upper cascade that was about half the size of Beaver, and stopped by the edge of the creek. I told Eliza we had to get to the other side while being careful not to get sucked over the cascade. I jumped in and took three strokes, grabbing on to a ledge on the far side, scraping my leg on some sharp travertine under the water. I would have to treat it when I got back to the raft to avoid infection. Eliza was very comfortable around water and had no problem getting over. I then led her to the edge of the upper pool six feet below, jumped in and swam across to the right side of Beaver. After waiting for Eliza, I stepped onto a small flat spot and jumped eighteen feet into the pool. Eliza followed me, and we repeated the climb and jump two more times before taking a break for lunch. Once everybody else arrived, Nathan, Antje, and Michael joined us in climbing back up and jumping. The rest spread out to eat and enjoy some fun in the sun. We were definitely in the Garden of Eden.

No one wanted to leave when we announced that it was time to go. The return hike was a lot easier and seemed to take less time, probably because it was a slight downhill grade. As we stepped out of the river at the last crossing, *I told Eliza about a snake encounter I'd had here with one of my passengers, a woman who was so afraid of snakes she wouldn't even look at a photograph of one. I had volunteered to give her some snake aversion therapy at no extra cost, and as luck would have it, we had more snake sightings on her trip than usual. It's actually unusual to see any snakes. I also had given her my traditional "snakes are actually beautiful creatures that serve the useful purpose of keeping the rodent population in check" speech. Besides, I told her, she probably wouldn't see a snake on our trip. None of that seemed to make any difference.*

We were hiking up to Beaver, and I was in the sweep position at the rear with my friend Ash. He was telling me one of his aboriginal tales from his homeland in the Northern Territories of Australia when he tapped me on the shoulder and pointed to a rattlesnake just to my right. The snake was only interested in getting away from me, so we both went on our way. When we returned to this spot on our way back from Beaver, the snake was still there, again caught out in the open, and futilely attempting to crawl up a steep slope. At that moment Beverly showed up. I went over, took her by the hand, told her she was very safe, and then asked her to check out the snake. She very courageously looked for some time while crushing every bone in my hand. But she looked. That night, at camp, I read her the snake card from the Medicine Cards book. The snake was representative of transmutation in the shedding of its skin, and Beverly said she could relate to just about everything I had read. The next morning her son came up and asked what I had done to her. He said she seemed to be totally changed.

We had rounded up the meanderers as we finished our hike back to the rafts. Tyler came out of the drainage with a Northern Whiptail lizard he had captured. He looked like the family cat, so proud that he had brought home another mouse. He just wanted to show it to us, like it was a one-of-a-kind event. He was like that with everything he captured. He set it gently off to the side of the trail, and called Miriam to head back to the river. The Israelis had found the ideal swimming hole with a four-foot cascade that dropped between two large boulders. At first Roni didn't want to leave, but she knew it was time.

After we counted heads to make sure all were present, we pulled the rafts up to the rock ledge where the passengers got in. One-by-one we pulled out into the current to begin our nine-and-a-half mile float through the remainder of the Muav gorge. The river ran slower in this stretch, with only small rapids and riffles to break up the calm stretches.

After a full day of hiking and playing in Havasu, my passengers were relaxed, enjoying a silent float underneath looming cliffs that blocked all but a thin strip of blue sky overhead. The chance to sit back, or lie back, and watch ancient walls floating upstream as if on a conveyor belt provided an unusual visual treat, and a reminder of how little we needed to feel comfortable.

On this stretch on an earlier trip I got into a spontaneous competition with one of the women on the crew. We raced our rafts all the way from Havasu to National, almost ten miles. I don't know how it started, but I was positioned downstream of her when she began to row harder. I decided this woman was not going to get by me, so I matched her stroke for stroke. When she slowed down, I slowed down. As soon as she sped up, I sped up. I assumed she would give up after awhile because she had injured her shoulder; but no, she kept it up the entire distance. I was a bit surprised at how important it was for me, approaching sixty at the time, to stay in front of this twenty-two year old woman. We didn't stop until we arrived at camp, and never spoke about it. It was stupid, but it was fun.

Over the years, on quiet stretches like this, I have introduced many of my willing passengers and crew to the Medicine Cards, a deck of fifty-two cards, each one a different animal, each animal offering personal insights into issues that already exist or might arise during a trip. The insights come from the descriptions of what the animals represent from a Native American perspective, often determined through observation, tradition, and mythology. For example, a hummingbird once flew in and rested for a few moments on one of my gloves as I was rowing.

He then slipped his beak between two of my fingers, seeking nectar. Because it was such an unusual occurrence, I read the card for Hummingbird and learned that it was reminding me to seek and experience joy. That's what the hummingbird represented, joy.

I asked Timmy if he would like to row. He thought about it for a minute and said okay, in an unenthusiastic pre-teen tone. But a subtle curling up of the corners of his mouth conveyed how he really felt. I changed places with him in the front of the raft, smiling at Ralph, who just couldn't seem to break gravity with his facial muscles.

It took Timmy only a few strokes to get into the rhythm of rowing. I wondered what else he hadn't tried in sports or other physical endeavors simply because he hadn't been encouraged and supported. I suggested that he feather the oars a little to get a feel for that. At first it didn't go well, so I sat behind him and put my hands on top of his. We pushed the oars forward, pressed down to lift the blades just out of the river, then I gripped the back of his hands and rolled our hands forward to rotate the blades. We then leaned back and pulled on the oars to complete the elliptical cycle, and repeated it a couple more times. I then let go of his hands, and after a couple more strokes, he smiled. I ruffled his hair. His eyes sparkled, but for the first time, I noticed him squinting. I chalked it up to the sun's reflection off the water.

A mile from our camp, we passed Tuckup Canyon on the right. Originally called Tucket for the name of a mining claim, over time the name had become corrupted. Several miles up the canyon a wall of near-psychedelic petroglyphs known as the Shaman's Gallery displayed garish images unseen anywhere else in the Canyon. It was said to be a difficult hike, and I had yet to go there.

Just upstream of the camp, the river took a sharp bend to the left and then immediately to the right, flowing around a rock bar formed from debris pushed out of Tuckup. A noisy but small rapid got Timmy's attention, and I saw him grip the oars tighter. I told him to push to the right of center to avoid the small hole, and then straighten the raft to hit the waves straight. I heard his child-like glee for the first time, a high-pitched giggle, as a wave splashed over the left side of the raft and drenched his father. Ralph looked back at Timmy and tried to smile.

The camp on our right was at least a hundred feet deep and two hundred yards long. A rocky beach made offloading the rafts a challenge. We had to be careful to avoid slipping on wet rocks. From the middle of the river we could see a large port or window up at the rim, one of several in the canyon.

It was in this area in 1999, on my trip with the Swiss and French couples, that Jeanne, the non-swimmer who had learned in Hermit that she could swim, first complained of pain in her lower back. She had had problems before, we were told, and during the trip it had flared up again. We made the decision to call in a helicopter and found that our satellite phone couldn't make contact from Tuckup, so we loaded up the rafts and floated down to National, two miles downstream, where the Canyon was more open and we could make contact with the satellites to call out. Within an hour the Park Service helicopter had found a hard packed area large enough to land, and within thirty minutes had taken off with Jeanne and her husband aboard. The evacuation left me with an immediate sense of loss and sadness. On that trip we had to say goodbye to two very sweet people who were having a wonderful experience together. My sadness may have been rooted in a realization of my own vulnerability. As a guide I have become good at saying goodbye, at least to the outside world. To cover up my sadness, I have learned at times to put on a happy face, even when I don't feel like it.

The two-mile stretch below Tuckup was fairly straight with a slow current. If I could custom order a rainstorm in any part of the Canyon, this would be it. Sheer cliffs that rose impressively in receding layers from both sides of the river dwarfed us. A hard storm here would create mystical waterfalls pouring over the edges more than two thousand feet high, disappearing into descending layers only to reappear as new waterfalls until finally plunging into the river, immediately transforming it into the historic Rio Colorado. It's such an awesome sight, and one I've seen too rarely.

The sound of a motor coming from upstream invaded our ear space. Two large rigs, each with fifteen passengers, floated up to the paddleboat and stopped. It was the company that Sue's husband, Scotty, worked for, and she knew both of the guides. They talked for a few minutes, and then one of the guides opened up his huge cooler and pulled out five blocks of ice. Carla had rowed over to them and she took the ice and put it in her cooler. At camp she would distribute it to the lunch cooler and the meat cooler, both of which were low on ice. The two motor rigs resumed their journey, their passengers waving as they floated by. I imagined that some were wondering why anyone would want to go on such small, slow rafts, while maybe a few others were wondering why they hadn't selected a trip like ours.

I pointed to a side canyon on the left a half-mile downstream, and told my passengers that it was our camp. National was a very large canyon with two campsites, one a long, narrow beach fronting an equally long, narrow eddy in the upper part of a small but long rapid. The other camp rested hidden from upstream views by a forest of willow saplings at the end of the rapid. A large eddy provided a calm location with a wide-open downstream view. The T-shirt logo of Wilderness World, my first river company, was of a soaring eagle with its wings outstretched. It you lay down in the upper camp on your back, and traced the lines of the north and south rims silhouetted at night against a grey sky, you would see that image.

As we passed the opening to the side canyon, I instructed Timmy to push to the left and pointed to the eddy in the middle of the rapid where we would pull over. Again he gripped the oars and I saw the muscles in his jaw tighten. Like many inexperienced rowers, he was too eager to get into the eddy, concerned about missing it. I told him to slow down and let the raft float almost to the point where we would camp so he didn't have to work against the upstream flow of the current. As we edged into the beach, I congratulated him on his superb rowing, then grabbed the bowline and sand stake and jumped onto the shore. Just upstream of National there was almost no beach on either side of the river. But here, flash floods and debris flows coming out of the side canyon had pushed out so much debris and soil that our camp was wide open and at least two hundred yards away from the wall that lay behind our camp.

I pounded my sand stake into the hard-packed beach and clipped my bowline onto the carabineer. Mary started to unhook the yellow bags in the back and roll them towards Ralph and Timmy in the front. They handed the bags to me, and I set them on the beach. I told them there were plenty of campsites in the dry sand above the high water line, and the water would be going down overnight if they wanted to sleep closer to the river. Ralph grabbed his yellow bag and went off to claim his camp.

Floyd pulled in with the Israelis on board. Liz was in the front, looking very relaxed. She smiled as she handed me the bowline, which I attached to my sand stake. I then went over to her and encouraged her to sleep outside her tent, something she hadn't done yet. She smiled shyly and nodded. When Roni stepped off the raft, I asked her if she was ready to sleep under the stars. She looked at her mom, and then said she didn't know. So I invited them all to a pajama party under the stars. Roni thought that was such a cool idea and accepted. I hoped they would all do it, because the rotating canopy of stars was such an amazing visual treat. If I woke up inside a tent, all I had to look at was the tent. If I woke up under the stars, I would be treated to the Milky Way, satellites traveling to and fro, shooting stars, and the constant rotation of the earth changing the position of my friends, the constellations. A conversation with Liz under those celestial bodies wouldn't be all that bad either.

After setting up camp, the crew got together on Floyd's raft for some refreshments before moving on to dinner. We'd had a great day, and Sue again complimented us on our work. Tomorrow we would be running the last major rapid, Lava Falls, and covering a lot of river miles. The water would be fairly high, which usually meant a left run. But that was tomorrow. I looked around at the people on this crew and felt very fortunate to be working with such competent, playful men and women. I felt a lump in my throat as I considered my good fortune at being in this amazing world with such great companions.

Carla left to shop for Star and Michael, who were on cook crew. I offered to set up the dessert, but Star said she wanted to do it. The menu called for ginger beef, couscous, tossed salad, and chocolate cake with cherries. I looked out over the camp and noticed only two tents had been set up, Tal's and Elli's.

Nothing in my experience has rivaled the challenge after learning about September 11th while in the Canyon. Only it wasn't on the 11th. In fact we didn't even notice the lack of overhead flights on the 11th. September 12th was another ordinary, extraordinary day. We floated through the Muav Gorge under imposing flint-grey limestone walls rising straight out of the river. The steep cliffs prevented the warming sun from reaching the river, and passengers were bundled up to ward off the chill. I was content in shorts and a t-shirt as I generated my own heat from rowing.

For the first time on any of my previous trips, we had passed by two of my favorite side canyons, Matcatamiba and Havasu, stopping to camp at National Canyon at mile 166 on river left. Again our camp was surrounded by steep, imposing walls. The song of the small rapid in front of camp reverberated off the wall across the river, and the late day sun brought warmth and light to our nesting activities. As I was preparing dinner, guides from another river company walked up from the camp down below and struck up a conversation with Christa, the trip leader. Other members of the crew joined in. Their conversation was unusually subdued. Normally when river guides get together it becomes an excuse to party.

Suddenly the other guides departed. Christa motioned for the rest of the crew to come over. She wasn't smiling. "We just learned that yesterday the World Trade Center was bombed and a hundred and forty thousand people have been killed." She was close to tears. The news had come from some hikers in Havasu.

Oh my God. A hundred and forty thousand people! How? Why? Nothing like this had ever happened while in the Canyon. In fact, for the past twenty-three years I had said that World War III could break out and we wouldn't know about it down here. Not any more. We were suddenly in new territory.

Our training did not include what to do if the country were attacked. We were on our own. Many questions required answers. But we didn't even know all the questions. Should we tell the passengers? Would it destroy the rest of the trip for them? If we didn't tell them and they found out from another trip, would they feel betrayed? Who might have family in harm's way? Would we be able to get a helicopter down to take them out? Who would the Park Service consider flying out? Was the information accurate? Someone noted there had been no overflights for two days. All air traffic must have been grounded.

We decided our first priority was to verify what the hikers had reported. Christa would get on the satellite phone and call the office. In the meantime, we should proceed with dinner and talk again after she had more information.

We had a great group of people who had become very close. As I resumed my cooking, I watched them interact. They had spent twelve days together and were like an extended family at a reunion. Some were playing a game on the beach using buckets, trying to get them to land inside a bulls-eye target drawn on the beach. Others were sitting in small groups talking and laughing. They were like innocent children totally unaware of the drama unfolding outside the Canyon. It was one of the great gifts about being down here. No interference from the outside world. For me that had been shattered.

After dinner we all gathered in a circle to hear Marilyn read a letter from her son. It was the kind of letter every mother wants to receive - loving, supportive, and indicative of their special relationship. Christa was having trouble with the satellite phone, and had been unable to maintain contact with the office, so we still didn't have enough information from which to develop a plan.

There was no moon. The only visible lights were two small lamps in the middle of the circle illuminating curious, respectful faces. Listening to Marilyn read her son's letter moved us, and enhanced the love that everyone felt. When she finished, I asked her where her son was now. With a mother's love in her smile she said, "He just moved to New York City." I looked at one of my crewmates as my heart sank. For the first time in my life, I felt the burden of knowledge.

Finally Christa was able to make contact and get more accurate information. What she heard was verification of the attack and an estimate of six to seven thousand deaths. We had three passengers – Marilyn, Carol, and Mark – who had relatives in the city. Marilyn's son had called in and was safe, as was Mark's wife. Carol's husband had called, desperate to speak with her. Her brother had been in the North Tower and was missing.

We contemplated all the scenarios and our options. No point in telling people tonight. Nothing could be done until morning. Carol, whose brother was missing, was the only person the Park Service would take out, if she so desired. In the morning, Christa would tell Marilyn first, since we knew her son was safe. Then she could be available to support Carol, and finally, Mark would be told. Then we would bring the whole group together and tell them. Carol would be given the option to fly out.

The Canyon had never seemed so dark. I had never felt so alone. I wasn't sure I would be able to sleep. Several of us stood together in unbearable silence. I wanted a hug, but didn't ask. Finally we drifted off to our rafts and the long journey to daylight.

In the morning, I watched as Christa and Marilyn took Carol by the hand and led her into a grove of willow saplings at the back of camp. I could see Christa through the trees as she spoke. After a few minutes they all emerged, Carol wiping tears from her cheeks.

As the group assembled in a circle I wondered how they would react. Even though this news was devastating, I sensed it would be okay. We were, after all, in the Grand Canyon,

221

in the womb of the earth. We were safe, in the company of a family of newfound friends. It was, I thought, the best place to be.

Christa spoke. Some people burst out in tears, others held them back with trembling chins. Still others wanted more information. Carol was faced with a decision. Should she fly out? If she did, would she even be able to find a flight back to New York? She decided to stay. Marilyn expressed surprise and admiration for the courage of her decision.

The next four days were magical. The Canyon embraced us. Rather than tearing the trip apart, the news brought us even closer together. We arrived early at camp that afternoon, one I had never camped at before. A flat, muddy, island had risen out of the falling river just in front of the camp. It became our playground. The soft mud was perfect for sinking into. Up to our knees in the mud, we could lean forward and back at angles impossible to hold while standing on solid ground. Someone started a water fight, and others began chasing friends with mud in their hands. It was good to hear shrieks of laughter erupting, finally breaking the tension and grief of the devastating and incomprehensible news. Carol didn't join in the frivolity, but remained connected to the passengers. Marilyn stayed nearby, and periodically I would see them hugging.

In Judaism, when a family member passes away, those closest perform a ceremony known as "sitting Shiva." For four days, they sit and reflect on the person and receive condolences from well-wishers. We had four river days left on the trip. Four days to sit and reflect in one of the most powerful and grand places on the planet. Four days to appreciate the beauty of the natural world. Four days to love and support one another. Without planning it, Carol was sitting Shiva for her brother, who, it turned out, was one of the victims of the bombing. As she would say after the trip, it was the best place to grieve.

I went for a walk behind camp into the side canyon. The floor was strewn with the remnants of past floods, from well-sorted gravel to medium-sized boulders. Catclaw acacia bordered the dry channel, and steep Muav cliffs blocked out the day's fading light. Water in small pools and narrow channels appeared and then disappeared under the debris. I came to an amphitheater-like setting with a limestone stage polished by an infinite number of floods. The string quartet loved to play here because of the acoustically friendly hard walls and floor. A narrow creek, less than a foot wide, gurgled over the hard rock. I could remember passengers and crew spread around, sitting against supportive boulders and walls, or lying in contemplative poses, as we listened to Brahms, Mozart, PDQ Bach, and Albert Schnitke.

Finally I came to a small pool in front of a narrow Muav gorge. It was here that I had one of my scarier times during a hike into the upper part of the canyon.

It was a spectacular hike several miles into the Redwall. To get there we had to swim through a deep pool, chimney up a slick limestone slide, and then climb up a wall using a rope placed by one of the more adept climbers on the crew. Coming down, I was with two other guides who had decided to climb down a crack in the wall without a rope. I had never done it before, and was not very confident in my abilities, but decided to try it if they would talk me down. We removed the rope used by the others, and both of them climbed down with a fair amount of ease. Of course it helped that they both had long arms and legs. Being vertically challenged, I wouldn't have that advantage.

My first move was to lower myself to a ledge about six feet below the top. As I gripped an angular rock at the top and started my descent, the rock moved. My heart wound up in my throat. I froze, waiting for my handhold to desert me. After a few seconds, I released my locked breath. Fortunately the rock had held, and after some deep breathing to calm my heart and get back in my body, I was able to reach the first shelf. From there the ground looked much closer, and with some verbal help from two guides telling me where to place my feet, I was able to reach terra firma and return my heart and breathing to their natural pace. One of my favorite lines is "if you want to go where you've never been before, you have to go where you've never been before." Pushing my edges allows me to step into the shoes of my passengers when they are on their own edges. It can be both humbling and freeing.

I returned to camp in time for dinner and filled up my plate with salad, couscous, and a veggie burger Michael had prepared for me. I then went over and sat next to Doron and the rest of the Israelis. I asked her if she was going to join Roni and me for a pajama party. She smiled shyly, just like her mother, and said she didn't know. I looked at Roni, who smiled and nodded her head. I knew they would both be there. I also asked Elli and Liz, and both were non-committal. Liz gave me a look that seemed like a wish. Then Roni asked if I would tell her a story. I told her about one of the most amazing thunderstorms I'd ever been in, right here at National.

In the early 'nineties we camped at the upper camp in anticipation of our runs through Lava the next day. The level would be around 14,000 cfs and would make for a very exciting run down the challenging right side. That night after dinner, we enjoyed some spontaneous music compliments of one of the crew who played his guitar and sang a bunch of old folk songs, and then set off to bed.

Around midnight a thunderstorm rolled in. Since it was August, this wasn't unexpected. Its duration, however, was. It lasted all night. The thunder gods must have settled right over us. The clashes were so loud and so close, we could feel the ground shake. Lightning flashes were so bright we could see the Canyon walls lit up as if millions of strobe lights had been triggered simultaneously. The smell of ozone permeated the air.

As the evening progressed, it had become obvious that I was not going to get much sleep. The storm had settled in, and would remain directly over us as a reminder of some of Nature's other sources of power, besides the river. At times the microsecond flashes of lightning had spotlighted waterfalls shooting out of sections in the Canyon wall directly across the river from our camp. The carved and polished chutes that spewed huge volumes of water were testimony to the persistence of Nature that had formed, and continually re-forms, the Grand Canyon, from millions of similar experiences through eons of time. After a while the rain let up, but the thunder and lightning stuck around the entire night. I didn't get much sleep, but it was worth it to be in such natural fury.

When we emerged from our tents in the morning, the Colorado had turned a brilliant red and National had begun to flash. It was a gentle flood that allowed us to walk up the drainage and observe it from the side. Instead of fourteen thousand cfs, the Colorado was running twenty-two thousand, a level that would add to the drama and challenge at Lava Falls.

Roni asked me to tell about what happened at Lava, and I told her I would do that at camp tomorrow. She pushed me as a twelve-year-old intent on getting her way can, but I resisted. I make it a point not to talk about dramatic events until after we were downstream of their location. Before heading to the dish line, I pointed out to Roni where I would put my sleeping bag. The light had faded, and the first stars, two of the brightest – Vega in the constellation

Lyre, and Arcturus in Bootes – turned on their lights. I laid back for a moment to find the outline of the eagle against the deepening gray sky, said a silent hello and thanks to my former Wilderness World crewmates, and then went to wash my dishes and help close up the kitchen. Carla and Star were in another competition and laughing continuously. They had a plastic plate on the serving table, and were trying to see how many times in a row they could flip it over by flicking it with the back of their fingers, and catching it with the same hand, before it hit the table. As soon as Star hit a new high, Carla would take over. They hated to lose.

We closed up the kitchen, strained the dishwater into the river, filled the four dish-line buckets with fresh water, filled up the coffee and teapots, and made sure the garbage was closed up. Star and Carla were still attempting to beat each other, so I said goodnight and went to my raft to brush my teeth and gather my sleeping bag and pad. I carried them to a flat spot on the sand about forty feet from Liz and Elli's tents, laid out my large ground cloth and anchored it with small rocks at the corners. Then I set out my sleeping bag on one side of the tarp, and looked over at the tents. There didn't seem to be any activity in the dark tents, and I assumed that meant I wouldn't have company tonight.

So I did some stretching, lathered up my feet, legs, shoulders, and arms with lotion, and lay back to look at the stars. The moon had risen but was hidden behind the Canyon walls, providing indirect but still fairly bright light that caused the sand to glow and the tents and vegetation to stand out. I felt some disappointment that not even Roni and Doron were joining me in enjoying the night sky, but also thought it might be a blessing, since I assumed that as energetic as Roni was, we might be up pretty late. Then I looked up and saw Roni, followed by Doron, carrying their sleeping bags and thermarest pads. I smiled and welcomed them to their first night under the stars. After they settled into their sleeping bags, I asked how much they knew about the constellations. Not much, Roni said. Did she want to learn? She was game, so I started to point out how to find several constellations using the Big Dipper as a convenient and easily identified source. Before I could show the first one, I noticed that both girls were asleep. I smiled, then glanced at Tal's tent, exhaled deeply, and lay back on my pillow to enjoy the show.

The night before running Lava Falls, the last major rapid in the Grand Canyon, we experienced one of the wildest thunderstorms in my memory that resulted in an extra 8,000 cubic feet per second of water in the river. By the time we arrived, Lava was roaring. On her 46th trip, one of my crewmates flipped for the first time. No one was injured, and now she, and her passengers, have a story.

DAY FOURTEEN –
NATIONAL CANYON TO PARASHONT

I woke up thinking about Lava Falls, the last major rapid we would run on this trip. Every guide who has worked in the Canyon has his or her folder of stories that range from the sublime to the ridiculous, from exhilarating to frightening. Lava has a reputation that is carried by most passengers for the entire trip, even though it comes a hundred and seventy-nine miles after we begin. Some think it doesn't deserve such a reputation. I'm not one of them.

I rolled over and saw that Doron and Roni were still asleep. Both were mostly out of their sleeping bags, with Doron half off the ground tarp. I'm always surprised when I wake up out of a deep sleep in the morning, because it seems like it takes me forever to doze off on these trips. I actually wonder about the quality of my sleep down here, since I wake up so often throughout the night. Still, I almost never feel sleep-deprived during the day. I took in the Canyon walls around me, and recalled the *morning of September 13, 2001 when we talked to our passengers about the attack on the World Trade Center. We didn't know about the attack on the Pentagon until we emerged from the Canyon four days later.*

That morning we had heard thunder and were treated to a rainbow spanning the narrow Muav gorge just upstream of camp. Then a lightning bolt flashed directly under the rainbow. Color seemed to have infused every atom of air. The river was a bright red-brown, the air a celestial gold, and the Canyon walls a combination of the two. It was as if, in the midst of our sadness and shock, the Canyon was reminding us to be present to the beauty and life all around us.

I left my sleep stuff for later so I wouldn't wake the girls, and walked over to the kitchen where Graham was filling up his cups of tea. I asked him how he was feeling, and he replied as good as could be expected for a proper Englishman in the colonies. I told him that no one had ever accused him of being proper. He cocked his head while pouring milk into his tea. He said that after that crack he wasn't sure if he and Chris would grace my raft today, but he would have pity on me and come along. I thanked him for the honor.

Star asked me if I'd blow the coffee conch, which I did, and then went down to my raft to get my greens and cup. Eliza was still asleep on the back deck of the gently rocking raft. She was snuggled into her bag with only her head out. Like all my siblings, she looked younger than her twenty-three years. Asleep, she conveyed an innocence and trust that moved me. I looked across the river at the dory rock, one of the markers the dory guides used to tell them where in Lava they would be running. Although I didn't know what the factors were, I had been told about the rock that rested directly across from camp, just off shore. The rise and fall of the river had been predictable enough that they would know what Lava would look like when they arrived there.

In twenty minutes breakfast was called. I served up some scrambled eggs, passed on the Canadian bacon, selected two toasted raisin muffins, and made a cup of green tea. I sat down near Diane and Jim, told them I was fascinated with their work in Antarctica, and wanted to hear more about it. Jim said he was a manager with the National Science Foundation responsible for hiring employees over the long Antarctic summer. Diane was an artist who did administrative work and took advantage of the absence of distractions down there to paint. We talked about the kinds of jobs someone like me could do, and Jim told me I should contact him after the trip to see about the possibilities. It would be very interesting to spend a few months down there during the off-season. I imagined myself involved in some ground-breaking explorations, but knew most jobs would be menial. It would, I thought, give me a perfect opportunity to write and share my interest in personal and spiritual growth.

Sue interrupted our conversation by asking for a show of hands for those interested in the paddleboat. She had announced the night before that anyone who wanted to run Lava in the paddleboat should let her know at breakfast. If there were more volunteers than spaces, she would choose through a lottery. Tyler, Timmy, Jim, Jim B, Eliza, and Antje indicated their interest. Perfect. No need for a lottery. I finished breakfast, and as I was getting up, Diane asked if I still had room in my raft. I said I did, and then went to wash my dishes and help break down the kitchen.

I went back up to gather my sleep kit, and as I was stuffing it into my bag, Liz walked by and asked about the pajama party. I said I was disappointed that she hadn't joined us, and that it had gone very well. In fact, I had expected to be kept awake late into the evening by Roni, but she had been the first to fall asleep. I told her I had been giving a star talk when I looked over and both kids were asleep. She smiled and said she'd love to know more about the stars, and I promised to do that. She blushed a little as she left to take down her tent.

Back on my raft, Eliza helped me load up on bags. I told her how I wanted them strapped down, and she focused on that. Again we would be rigging the gear with a bit more focus, making sure it was a little tighter, with no loose ends. When we were finished, Floyd called everybody over to a flat spot in front of the rafts where he had created a model of Lava Falls. He'd drawn two lines representing the left and right runs. Between the currents he had scratched out a trench to represent the ledge hole, and had placed a rock just downstream of it. He'd also fashioned waves to the left and right of the ledge hole, and a big rock on the far right at the bottom of the waves. He said that the ledge hole had been created by some boulders emanating from Prospect Canyon on river left. It was fifty-to-sixty feet wide with recirculating waves that would almost always cause a raft to flip. He also stated a preference for not going there.

As he described the entrance to the right run, he mimicked a look of terror on his face, and after talking about being crunched in the "V" wave, two lateral waves that folded together, said we probably wouldn't be doing that run. I looked over at Chris, and she didn't seem amused by Floyd's antics. The Israelis were clustered together, and they also had serious looks on their faces. Liz looked over at me and I gave her a big smile to reassure her. Then Floyd described the left run with more humor and lightness, saying we would enter to the left of the ledge hole, hit some big waves, and float to the right or the left of the "chub rock" directly below the ledge hole. On one of my recent trips I had gone sideways over that rock and had gotten a small gash on my shin from highsiding into one of my ammo cans. Unfortunately, two other river companies had been watching my run.

Floyd finished his description by pulling Herby, his squeaky rubber hamburger-in-a-bun, out of his shirt, squeezing it a few times, and throwing it into the ledge hole. Herby would show us the correct run, he said. That broke some of the tension. In the past I would minimize the dangers of a rapid like Lava, but I've learned that it's important that people take it seriously. And the ledge hole is definitely a place where no man or woman should ever go. I've seen a couple rafts go in there.

One of my crewmates told me about going in the ledge hole in a paddleboat. The river was clear, and he said when he realized they were going into the hole, he had taken several deep breaths and quickly found himself deep in the hole looking up at the flailing feet of his passengers. Instead of swimming to the surface, which would have been my first thought, he dove down to the bottom of the river and was flushed downstream, coming up near the bottom wave. Another crewmate had flipped his canoe at the entry on the right run, and was swept into what we call the corner pocket. He had great difficulty finding anything to grab onto that would help get him out of there. He finally realized his only way out was down. Down was through a small space between the "cheese grater," a large piece of lava just offshore, and the boulders on shore. At the time, he really didn't know if there was a channel that would spit him out into the eddy below, or if he would drown. He was spit out.

*　　　*　　　*

On one of my trips with Michael, we had camped at National and were talking about Lava the night before. Michael mentioned one of our paddleboats had recently gone in there, and then he said, "What's the big deal? All you have to do is read the river." I swallowed hard when he said that. When we arrived at Lava, we pulled over to scout from the left side, and I volunteered to do a picture run. Michael, the trip leader, pulled out first, pushed out past the middle of the river and suddenly realized he was too far right. I watched as he pushed very hard to get to his line on the left. He was making progress but for some reason stopped rowing for just a few seconds. Realizing he wasn't far enough left, he made an extra effort. I waved frantically for him to get farther left, but he wasn't looking at me; he was looking at the ledge hole right in front of his raft. He continued pushing and got as far as the corner when the raft dropped violently into the far left side of the ledge hole. His raft rose immediately on its side and was about to flip when a big wave reared up and slapped him back, preventing the flip. One of my photographs shows him in the ledge hole, and in the upper left corner of his raft is a hand and arm of a passenger who had fallen out. It was coming from the river still clinging to the safety line.

After the rest of the rafts had finished their runs and I went back to my raft and made mine, we all stopped for lunch on some ledges down below the rapid. As I approached the table, Michael came over to me and said, "Now don't give me any of that karma crap." I just smiled.

Diane and Chris said they wanted to be up front, and Graham was glad to join Wild Thing in the back. After leaving National, we embarked on the longest "calm before the storm" stretch of river in the Canyon. Most of the thirteen-mile segment was calm and slow, with only riffles, small rapids, and huge, snaking eddies, often accompanied by upstream winds. The narrow currents were often obscured by the winds and it became a game of feeling the river and staying in the downstream flow. Nonetheless, it's a beautiful stretch with spectacular, widening vistas as we emerged from the Muav Gorge and entered the land of lava. The first signs of lava would be more than eleven miles away, and there was plenty to enjoy beforehand.

Just below National, on the left, is officially Hualapai land. The name was Anglicized by Lt. Joseph Christmas Ives from Ja Whala Pa'a, meaning Pine Tree Mountain People. We would finish the trip by taking out at a beach called Diamond Creek and driving through the Hualapai Indian reservation.

On our left was a camp I'd stayed at only once, and it practically cost one of my crewmates the sole of his foot. Stuart and I were on cook crew, and linguine was on the menu, along with a baked dessert. We had prepared the dessert – cherry cobbler – first, to get it out of the way, and had just dropped the pasta into the boiling water when Stuart headed for his raft to grab a beer. In an instant I became a solo cook, as Stuart stepped right on scalding sand where the pan holding the charcoal had rested. I can only imagine how much pain he was in, and for a while it looked like we would have to evacuate him. If it hadn't been for the thick calluses on the bottom of his feet, there would have been no doubt. We treated him, pampered him, and decided to see how he looked in the morning. His calluses were thinner, but he had avoided serious injury, and we decided to keep him on the trip. The dinner, by the way, was a hit.

Chris was having a conversation with Diane about her artwork, and Graham was surveying the shoreline looking for birds and bighorn. We were floating in the shade but we could already feel the desert heating up. Bright green grasses lined both sides of the shore, reflecting in the glassy stillness of a quiet river. A mile-and-a-half below National was Fern Glen, a relatively short side canyon that had been used as a venue for some of the string quartet concerts.

On one of those trips, Peggy pulled out Bag 51, a black bag that contained some of the most atrocious bridesmaids dresses and leisure suits imaginable. I don't know the details, but evidently Peggy's family had some connection to the invention of polyester. The clothes had been donated over the years by people embarrassed that they had once been seen in them. Everyone had found an outfit, and I looked particularly good in a shiny green crinoline dress complete with a pearl necklace and painful earrings fashioned from carabineers. It was all in great fun, until three motor companies arrived to enjoy the concert. It just happened that I had been asked to be the official photographer for the musicians, so there I was in all my female glory, walking around in front of these amused strangers. I got to put on a fashion show as I bravely accepted my responsibilities, as we say, "for the company." It takes a real man to wear a dress, you know.

229

*   *   *

I told Graham about a training trip at Fern Glen. The senario was this: a man had fallen from a dry waterfall and was suffering from head injuries and broken bones. After assessing the volunteer, who was actually still recovering from ACL surgery, we "packaged" him for transport. First we stabilized his neck and spine with a collar, then carefully placed him on a backboard and strapped him in. It's one thing to work with a dummy, like Resusi-Annie in CPR, and quite another to work with a live person. Our challenge was to lower him over fifty feet to the canyon floor below so he could be transported to a location where we could bring in a helicopter. It was a great learning experience, and one I hoped I would never have to replicate. Teams were set up for safety, anchoring safety lines, securing the victim to the backboard, and lowering him down. One guide acted as the scene leader responsible for the big picture, like a coach on a sports team. Other guides led the various teams. We learned that in a rescue situation there was only one scene leader, and everybody else's job was to minimize his/her time stress. In other words, our job was to avoid taking actions that would cause the scene leader to waste time, or hurry unnecessarily. Haste makes waste, especially in rescue situations, and there's always a tendency in an emergency to rush. That's where mistakes are made, and lives lost or imperiled. We also learned that too many chiefs can make decision-making quite challenging. And with everyone being a river guide, we definitely had too many chiefs.

Three miles below Fern Glen we crossed the Mohawk-Stairway fault, named by George Billingsley, the father of one of my crewmates. Billingsley was the man who had helped map the geology of the entire Grand Canyon. It only took him thirty-plus years.

The morning that we had informed people about 9/11 we stopped at Mohawk Canyon on the left, a route that had been used by the Paiutes and Hualapais to cross the Colorado to fight each other. Christa had decided we needed time to play, so we pulled over and spent a relaxing day letting go of the tension built up after hearing about the attacks. The side canyon walled off less than a mile up, and as we were hiking, a Great Horned Owl flew low, directly overhead, and landed on a shelf for all of us to see. It was highly unusual to see owls during the day, and to have one so close was amazing. I knew that in the Lakota tradition Owls were harbingers of death. As we approached the owl, it flew farther up the canyon, alighting on a shelf five feet off the ground. This time it didn't fly away as we drew near, sitting and watching with a wary eye. We did the same. Unfortunately, in my desire to get a close photograph, I scared him off. My selfish act had interfered with others enjoying this majestic bird.

Just before Mohawk we passed by a stack of limestone blocks sitting well beyond the angle of repose. It sat on an eroded Bright Angel Shale outcropping at such an extreme upstream angle that it was hard to understand how it could remain standing. A small gust of wind should have been able to topple it. Every time I passed it I expected to see an empty space where it had once reigned.

Two and a half miles downriver we floated by Cove Canyon. There were two things that were significant about Cove: first, it was five miles from Lava Falls; and second, from Cove you could see one of the best-known, least-often-visited locations in the Canyon. Toroweap Overlook was a platform that had split off from the Esplanade member of the Supai Formation three thousand feet above the river. (Toroweap in the Paiute language means gully or dry wash, although Toro means greasewood, and Weap means canyon.) To get to the overlook by land required a sixty-five mile drive on a rough dirt road. *I made that drive for the first time on July 3rd, a few years ago while coming back from California. My car had no air conditioning so I had to keep my windows open. I drove the entire way in a cloud of dust and it took me six hours to clean all the dust out, including from my trunk and glove compartment.) When I arrived at the end of the road, I found a car with Texas license plates, two men, and an erected pup tent. I unloaded my gear and found a spot about ten feet from the edge to spread out my sleeping bag. The three-thousand-foot sheer drop was dizzying, and standing at the edge I felt a familiar body sensation in my groin, one I often felt when on high edges. To be neighborly, I went over and introduced myself to the men, who returned the favor by inviting me to share dinner with them.*

After spending the afternoon exploring and photographing the impressive vistas up and down stream, including a tiny stretch of whitewater that I knew was Lava Falls a mile to the west, I gathered some fruit and vegetables out of my cooler and walked over to help prepare dinner. While we were eating, one of the men pointed to my sleeping bag and asked if I actually planned to sleep there without a tent. I told him I was looking forward to having a canopy of stars overhead and the sound of the river below. He said they had never slept outside of a tent.

After dinner I said goodnight and went back to my camp. While waiting for the full moon to rise, I noticed a man off in the distance whom I didn't recognize, and for some reason his movements seemed suspicious. I finally decided he was looking for a good seat to watch the moon come up, but it was still unnerving. After the moon rose, I rolled over on my side and closed my eyes. Some time later I felt a tap on my shoulder. "Would you mind if I threw my bag over here somewhere?" It was one of the Texans, and he was quite tentative. "Not at all," I replied, "help yourself." I assumed he would find a spot a reasonable distance from me. But no. Within minutes I had a neighbor less than ten feet away. And then my mind went haywire.

Oh my God, I thought. These guys are probably gay and I'm going to wake up with a knife to my throat; they're going to rape me, cut my throat, and throw my body over the edge. I found my knife and put it under my ground pad, and tried to sleep. But my racing mind wouldn't let me. I was amazed, and afterward embarrassed, at how quickly I had journeyed to the dark side. Finally some reason returned and I realized this was a man who had never slept outside and needed to be nearby to have the confidence he felt from me to go where he'd never been before. Go to sleep, I thought. And I did.

The float from Cove becomes an exercise in anticipation. When would we see the first signs of lava? When would we pass Vulcan's Anvil? When would we first hear the rapid, and how would it sound? What side would we be running? Oh, and how many times will I have to pee before we get there?

The first signs of lava appeared on river right two miles upstream of the rapid. It's just before a corner that makes a big turn to the right, and the entrance into Lava Lake. A couple hundred yards downstream a fifty-foot volcanic plug reared its head out of the right center of the river. Vulcan's Anvil is considered a sacred site to both the Hualapai and Paiutes. The Hualapai contend one of their most powerful medicine men took his power from the Anvil in the early 19th century. *Until the early 'nineties, some river guides would throw a coin high up on the Anvil in a superstition that if the coin stuck they would have a good run in Lava. Beginning in the late 'eighties, other items began appearing on the Anvil. I once saw a broken ukulele discarded on an igneous shelf a few feet off the river. Representatives from the Hualapai tribe contacted the river guide's association and said we were desecrating a sacred shrine. It would, they said, be like dumping trash in the Sistine Chapel. They asked that we stop placing or throwing anything on the Anvil.*

Floyd's raft was already near the Anvil with Roni and Doron in the front, and Liz and Elli in the back. Even Floyd looked small next to the fifty-foot high volcanic plug. A garden of prickly pear cactus adorned the top like a crown of thorns. Carla's raft had Ralph and Mary in the front. They also floated close to the Anvil. Liz was looking up at the top, perhaps admiring the rock garden dotted with prickly pear cactus, and clumps of desert grasses. Sue guided the paddleboat into the calm shadow behind the Anvil, and I waved to Eliza as we floated past.

The current for the next mile would be almost nonexistent, a calm that heightened our nervousness. On one trip a group camped on the left banged drums while chanting "Lava, Lava" as we passed. Now, tension was actually heightened by the absence of sound. On some trips we would see the huge eroded delta coming out of Prospect Canyon on the left before we would hear the rapid. The first sounds rebound off the debris flow and are almost soft, not what one would expect from a rapid with the reputation of Lava Falls. It's not until we finally make the last turn around a point, to the right an eighth of a mile above the rapid, that we would hear the true voice of Lava, a low, gutteral roar that made stomachs turn, and bladders want to empty. If the water level was lower, we might run down the more dangerous right side. At higher levels, we usually ran left.

One of the passengers on a recent trip was a long time producer of a major Sunday morning newsmagazine. She had brought along a cigar-shaped video camera and wanted me to wear it on my head while running the right side of Lava. On the way down, while still in Lava Lake, I made some comments with the camera on while surveying the lava flows on river right. Because the small unit had only about four minutes of memory, she put it on pause until we were just above the rapid. She then turned it back on so we could hear the roar of Lava. She again put it on pause while two of the guides, one of whom was rowing Lava for the first time, hurried up to the scout rock to watch our runs.

Finally the rest of us pulled out into the current to run without scouting, a strategy guaranteed to heighten our anticipation. For some reason the camera was not turning on, and I was a bit distracted as my passenger fussed with it while I was setting up to enter this massive rapid.

On my previous two trips I had made two of the best runs I'd ever had, and I was looking forward to three in a row. As trip leader, I was the first raft in. As I slid down the tongue I hit the lateral wave off the ledge hole slightly askew, and my raft turned sideways. With no time to straighten out forward, I cranked hard on my left oar and ran the "v-wave" backward, and proceeded down towards the mountain wave. I assumed that the camera was capturing all this, but when I pulled into the eddy on the right to run safety, Lou informed me that the camera was still on pause. Later I told the rookie guide that I had run it sideways and backward to show her how not to do it. Her run was great.

Despite its name, the rapid was not formed from lava flows, although at least thirteen lava dams had formed over the past million years or so. A couple were as much as two thousand feet high and would have backed water over two hundred miles up into what is now Southern Utah. What remained of all those dams could be seen primarily on the North side. We would also be seeing lava flows and formations in the form of large boulders and monoliths for over fifty miles below Lava Falls. Some formations looked like geometric logs stacked on end. All along the way, we would see a black veneer painted on the face of the Cambrian walls, with viscous shapes forming into massive tapestries. In places we would see lava flows frozen in time, and with just a little imagination we could visualize red hot molten rock charging over the rim, racing towards a sizzling plunge into the river, sending plumes of steam skyward.

Lava cools into shapes depending on its viscosity, leaving sculptures shaped like fans, butterflies, angel's wings, and abstract paintings. Improbably, cacti and tamarisk thrived in small cracks and crevices on the tops and sides of lava rocks. They would begin with a windblown or bird-dropped seed finding a crack with just enough soil and water to germinate. Eventually this symbiotic relationship would lead to fragile but persistent roots breaking down the rock, like a non-encapsulated tumor spreading through the brain.

I've flipped twice in Lava: once as a baggage boatman with no passengers, and once with passengers. On my first flip, my brother Sandy had run the right side before me and was waiting below the bottom rock on the right in case I needed help. I did. I made a nice entry, slammed through the "V" waves perfectly, and set up to run the bottom wave. My angle was slightly off. The huge bottom wave turned me sideways and a smaller wave coming off the black rock we called the "cheese grater" attacked me from the side and flipped me faster than I could say "Oh my God." I came up near my raft and was hanging on to the side when I saw Sandy pulling hard to catch up. He needed to pull me over before reaching the next rapid, Son of Lava. He seemed to be working very hard, but he managed to catch up and pull us over into the eddy above the next rapid. As we were working to re-flip my raft, Sandy laughed and pointed to the rear of his raft. His stern line had wrapped around a floating log and had acted as an anchor, impeding his progress. It was a testament to his strength and boating skills that he was able to pull me over above Son of Lava.

*   *   *

My second flip was in the early 'nineties, on a trip with some passengers who had come from a New Thought Church in Portland, Oregon, where I had spoken. That time I came out of the "V" wave sideways and didn't stand a chance in the bottom wave. Again, up and over in an instant. This time we swam the bottom rapid before the raft could be pulled to shore. As we were working to re-flip it, one of my passengers came over and said, "I just want you to know I think it was purr-fect that we were in the raft together when it flipped." I was already irritated by what I considered my mistake, and her well-meaning comment definitely didn't sit well. She may have thought it was perfect, but I certainly didn't.

*   *   *

My most dramatic experiences at Lava were in 1983, on a private trip with my brother Sandy and some friends, and again in the early 'nineties on a commercial trip. In that high water year of 1983 we arrived at Lava when it was running around sixty thousand cfs. Our normal flows since the 'nineties have fluctuated between five and eighteen thousand cfs. In 1983 most of the rapids were either washed out or had become fairly easy, enjoyable wave trains. Not so for either Crystal or Lava, which had just grown in size as the volume had increased. By then I had run the Canyon six or seven times and felt comfortable on my oars, although certainly not highly skilled. My crewmates, on the other hand, were very experienced. Between them they had almost 200 trips and only two flips. The roar of the rapid was like nothing I had ever heard before: a herd of stampeding buffalo amplified, like a gigantic, out-of-control freight train. We pulled over on the right and climbed up the lava-strewn trail to the scout rock directly above the entry. Where there was normally a massive ledge hole in the middle we saw a mountain of water rising to a peak. The "cheese grater" was underwater, and water was recirculating back upstream at least fifty feet below the rock. The hole created by the water flowing over the cheese grater reached out to the middle of the river. There was no way in hell we were going to run right.

It was really tempting to run the wave off the ledge hole, but if we miscalculated and ended too far right, we would be in big trouble in that bottom hole. Normally our scouts would take less than fifteen minutes. Take a look, decide on the run, and get out of there. Not this time. The longer we looked, the more nervous we became. Especially our passengers. Normally my three crewmates kept very close counsel, saying very little. But this time I was surprised to hear words like, "that's a keeper," and "I sure wouldn't want to go in there," coming from their lips. We must have been on that rock for forty-five minutes before Claire Quist, a grizzled oldtimer with more trips than all of us, finally said, "Just put your left tube on the left lateral." It was what we were planning, but it wasn't obvious from the right side.

Because the river was flowing so fast, we pulled as far up the eddy as possible to allow us time to get across the river and set up for our runs. My little 13-1/2 foot raft felt like a toy in a storm, but when we saw the run from the left, there was a wide current taking us left of everything that wanted to eat us up and spit us out. The runs turned out to be anti-climactic.

*   *   *

Not so on my commercial trip in 1990. That was the trip with the major thunderstorm at National that had pumped an additional 8,000 cfs into the river from side canyon flash floods. Instead of running Lava at 14,000 cfs as we had expected, we arrived on 22,000. Our six-boat group pulled over on the right and walked up to scout. The river looked angry. It had turned from a mellow milky-green, to a raging red-brown. Shadows thrown by the morning sun made the holes look deeper and the currents more difficult to read. The right run was so big and the "V" wave seemed to be waiting with glee to swallow up its next victim. The wise thing to do would be to pull across the river and scout from the left side.

Running the right side of Lava had always been a "white-knuckle experience" for me. Our entry drops at least ten feet so we can't see the entry wave until we're right on top of it; and by then it's way too late to make any adjustments. We had to line up on current lines coming off a volcanic monolith, on the right shore a hundred feet from the head of the rapid. If we were too far right, the current could pull us even farther right and take us into certain trouble. That was the easy part.

Sitting in the middle of the river was the infamous ledge hole, a yawning depression with churning white water where no one ever wants to go – except Georgie. Remember, she only had one run: down the middle. As I understand it, she did the same run at Lava every time. She would set up in the middle of the river, grab her safety strap (she already had her hard hat on), gun the motor, and duck. Her "thrill boat" – one 33-foot "G" (for Georgie) rig with two smaller rafts lashed to each side – would then slam into the ledge hole, and if her passengers weren't holding on tightly, they would be swimming. I don't know how many swam Lava, but I do know Georgie had one unfortunate death on that run when one of her side rafts flew up and folded on top of her main rig, crushing the passenger.

Georgie used to bring in a helicopter just below Lava to take out some passengers and bring new ones in. When the Park Service helicopter landed to investigate the death, Georgie was in a hurry to have the body removed. The ranger who had come in later told me he said, "You just killed a passenger and now you want to hide the body so your new passengers don't see it?"

"That's right," was her reply.

Without the power of a motor, oar boats avoided the ledge hole like the plague. The current lines we had to follow didn't cooperate by flowing in a straight line. Oh no. Instead, they flowed off the monolith and snaked out into the middle of the river where we were treated to a few seconds of terror looking into the middle of the ledge hole. It took experience and inhuman self-control to trust the current to bring us back. More often than not, we would pull back on the oars – chicken strokes, we called them – just to make sure we didn't wind up in the ledge hole. And this was all before we entered the rapid. A solid run began by hitting a strong lateral wave coming off the ledge hole. If the angle of the raft was right, we would break through the lateral, and begin the race towards the "V" wave. If it was kind to us, we would break through with all our fingers and toes intact, heading for a mammoth wave in front of the cheese grater, and if our angle was square to that wave, we'd fly up and over in celebration of our good fortune.

Then there are the other possibilities. I've run Lava dry just one time, coming out of the "V" wave with no water in my raft. But on one run, the "V" wave slammed into my raft, turning it sideways, sending me sprawling, sliding towards a speedy exit from my raft. Only the oarlock prevented me from leaving my raft, but that took its toll by breaking my seventh rib. I felt that for the next forty-seven miles

It's said that the test of a good guide is not what happens when everything goes right, but how he or she responds when things go wrong. If that's the criteria, then I'm a good guide, because I've recovered many times in Lava. On one trip I found myself in a light self-bailing raft with no passengers. It had just turned out that way because we had a small group with couples who hadn't wanted to split up in Lava. The paddleboat captain told me after running the rapid he would pull over to the right shore hike back up with one of his passengers and ride through with me. I would photograph their run and wait for them to join me. I did my part, but they didn't make it to the right shore. So I hiked back to the raft and said, "looks like its you and me, babe. Let's go run a rapid."

Charly Heavenrich

I decided to enter backwards because there was more weight back there. I planned to break through the top lateral and get some momentum to meet the "V" wave on somewhat even terms. I was nervous, but a strange thing happened once I shoved off from shore. I became calm and focused. After all, it was too late to worry. I was committed, and the best thing I could do was focus on my entry. I knew the river was in charge. So I'd said my prayers to the river gods, expressed gratitude to the ancestors of the land and the earth mother, and surrounded my raft with white light, something I always did before running a major rapid. My job was to do my best and trust the river to deliver me safely through the storm. And as we say in the Canyon "shit happens, things get wet."

As I entered backwards, my right oar struck a rock and popped out of the oarlock. I uttered the words you don't want to hear coming out of a guide's mouth, "Oh, shit." I was heading for the "V" wave sideways with only my left oar to maneuver the raft in chaotic, powerful water. The current was so fast and strong I knew I only had a couple seconds before slamming into the "V" and meeting my maker. But a funny thing happened on the way to that wave. I missed it. Expecting to hit the brick wall any moment, I looked to my right and there was the "V" wave – to my right. To my right! What a pleasant and unexpected surprise. I had found the right slot on my entry, the run usually done by the dories with the deliberate intention of missing the "V" wave. Great! But I had precious little time to celebrate. There was still that gigantic wave at the bottom grinning in anticipation of a very light raft coming down sideways. With only one oar, and given the overpowering strength of the current, my only option was to push hard on the oar hoping to get turned around to hit that wave head on. As light as my raft was, I still risked flipping end-over-end.

My angle was still a bit off as I began my descent into the trough of the wave, but at the very last moment my raft turned just enough and we started up the fifteen-foot wave. I jumped into the front of the raft to add my puny weight. Right at the top, it stalled for just an instant, as if trying to decide: flip or not? go back or not? Not! The front end dipped down and I jumped back on my oar, pulled the other oar out of the water – the tether had worked – and finished running the tail waves. Better lucky than good. Later my crewmates congratulated me for finding the slot run. I smiled and said nothing

*　　　*　　　*

One of my good friends told me his Lava story when he flipped and swam the entire rapid, and then Son of Lava. That short but very intense rapid has a lot of current pushing against the left wall, and big waves rebounding off the wall. Brownell said he was swept against the wall and sucked down, down, down. His ears were popping from the depth, and he sensed he was going to drown. Instead of panicking, for some reason, he said, he relaxed and felt himself being lifted to the surface. The river is so much stronger than we are, he told me.

*　　　*　　　*

On my '86 private trip with my parents, we ran Lava in the rain. One of my screwball

236

friends, Bill, carried a packaged bar of Lava Soap up to the scout rock and had his picture taken holding the bar of soap with the rapid in the background. Again we were going to do a right run, and because it was raining, I had decided not to do a picture run. As I entered the tongue, a bolt of lightning flashed directly overhead and an immediate clap of thunder made my entry a truly grand one. It was the only day it had rained on the entire trip, and we wound up sleeping in a bat cave that night to get everyone out of the weather. Even my mom, with her recently implanted artificial knee, managed to climb the slick slope to get to the cave.

*   *   *

In March 1996, a group of sediment, and debris flow scientist were camped a quarter mile above Lava on the left. Around one in the morning some of them heard louder sounds, which they attributed to wind amplifying the rapid, and a couple had noticed that the river had risen a bit. It wasn't until early in the morning that many of them walked down to the rapid and saw that a massive debris flow had taken place the night before. Water was still pouring out of Prospect Canyon, and debris had pushed halfway into the ledge hole, pinching off any chance of them getting downstream. But then, why would they want to? They had come to the Canyon to measure sediment and examine debris flows. And here they were, witnessing the effects of the second largest debris flow, after Crystal in 1966, to occur in the Grand Canyon since the building of the dam. How amazing that must have felt.

Two days later the river had removed much of the debris, and a run had opened up. Since then our runs have been the same as before the debris flow, even though the rapid has been slightly altered. The right side is now bigger at lower water, and the currents at the entry are a bit trickier. And we've been running left a lot more. Change is happening all the time in the Canyon, and it's our job to adapt. Sometime, and I hope it's in my lifetime, I expect there will be an event, perhaps an earthquake, that will cause a landslide that will completely block the river, creating a temporary lake for miles upstream. Will the dam operators release enough water to break up the natural dam? Will the Park Service bring in dynamite? Or will they resist the pressure from the public and the concessionaires, and allow nature to take its course? I want to be around to find out.

*   *   *

So, back to the '90 trip with 22,000 cfs, I convinced Pete, the trip leader, to let me do a picture run, and he agreed so long as the paddleboat and one other oar boat stayed back and ran with me. That meant Pete would run first, followed by Christa (on her 46th trip with no flips), and Snooky. Before they took off, Pete gave his "fear of God" speech, saying the water was huge, and he couldn't hold on for his passengers. He finished with a strong message. "Hold on!"

On some Canyon trips a few passengers seem out of place; some are quite timid. Carol, riding in Christa's raft, was the most timid person I had ever seen in the Canyon. She had a shy and endearing smile, and usually deferred to her male companion, letting him do the speaking

237

and make the decisions. She had been drawn to the Canyon after seeing the multimedia presentation I had done at her church. When a large group from that church decided to see the Canyon up close and personal, Carol had decided to take a huge risk, go outside her comfort zone, and try something different. Very different.

Several of us hiked down to the river to find places to photograph the first three rafts. There we waited, all the while looking at the massive amount of water pouring over rocks, racing into monstrous waves, and wondering how anyone in their right mind could think this rapid could be run safely. It took at least twenty minutes for people to walk back to the boats, check their life jackets, tighten down the gear, drink water, go over the safety instructions, and relieve themselves. All this time, we were down by the middle of this gargantuan rapid that sounded like a freight train, and shook the very ground on which we were standing. After awhile, even the rocks on the opposite shore seemed to move – an optical illusion caused by looking at the moving water.

Finally the boats appeared upriver. The drop in Lava is approximately thirty-seven feet, with almost half of that right at the entry. Where I was standing was probably twenty feet lower than the rafts, which were approaching the head of the rapid at an agonizingly slow rate. I could see Pete standing in his raft, looking downstream to see the entry and determine whether he had to reposition the raft. Remember, we couldn't see the entry spot because of the significant drop, like a steep slide, into the first waves. From the scout rock high above the rapid, this first wave didn't appear too large. From experience I knew it was both large and powerful. I also knew the rafts had to be right on with our entry. Too far left, and we were in the hole; too far right, and we risked running up on rocks.

Pete's entry was great, and he had time to set up for the "V" wave knowing he must come out of it facing downstream with both oars in his hands (the powerful water often rips oars out of our hands and out of the oarlocks). Yes! He even had time to take a couple of adjusting strokes before running up the twenty foot wave at the bottom of the rapid. Perfect run.

I let out a sigh of relief at this run, more confident that all would continue to go well. Christa was now at the entry point. She hit the entry wave slightly askew, coming out of it sideways as she raced towards the "V" wave. I felt my jaw tighten, knowing that at her angle anything could happen. Christa struggled to straighten out her boat, with Carol hunched down in the back holding on very tight, just as Pete had said. She entered with a thud, waves totally engulfing her raft, obscuring her passengers. When she emerged from the "V" wave, she was again sideways, heading for the last big wave. As I photographed her, I could see she was using all her skills to turn the boat so it would be square to the wave.

And she almost made it. Almost. Her slightly askew boat rode up the wave, reached the top, and then slid down the back side. It was as if she were being swallowed by a whale, and then all of a sudden, the right side of her boat reared up like a breaching whale, hovered for a second as if trying to decide which way to turn, and then gave in to the river and came down with the wet black underside reflecting in the sunlight. Flip!

I then experienced one of the most frustrating and powerless feelings I've ever had on the river as one of my crewmates and four people I had come to love struggled to survive in the powerful river. There was nothing I could do but watch and hope that Pete, who was downstream, and Snooky, who was just entering the rapid, could rescue the five, who now must have felt as if they were in a giant washing machine. Then Snooky hit the "V" wave. I have a picture of her with her left oar high above her head, and in my next frame, she is in the river. The boat was fine; it just had no guide. The three men up front were plastered to the front tube, unaware that no one was on the oars as the raft eased over the mountain wave and slipped past the black rock. Nel, the cook, climbed over the black bags to take the oars, as one of the men yelled "Great run, Snooky."

"Uh, guys," Nel replied, "Snooky isn't here anymore." About that time she surfaced about ten feet away from the raft.

As I looked downstream, I saw Pete rowing out to intercept the overturned raft, and two people climbed into his boat. I spotted two others in the right eddy swimming towards the shore and safety. That left one person to rescue with no one in sight. Pete had to use all his strength in an attempt to pull his raft and the overturned raft into an eddy on the left side. But the current was too strong, and "Son of Lava" was just ahead. Pete later said he had to order his passenger to let go of Christa's raft so they could maneuver through the next rapid. Afterward they retrieved the overturned raft and pulled it to shore on the right side. Meanwhile, there were three of us who still had to run this monster. I was concerned about who the missing passenger was, and whether he or she was safe.

The paddleboat captain decided to run left, along with the other oar boat. In spite of clear evidence that it was a foolish option, I chose to go right. It could have been another case of testosterone poisoning, but I checked with my passengers and they were all for it. So we headed back to the rafts and tightened down everything an extra notch. I even put my sunglasses and visor in my ammo can, a sure sign that the potential for a flip was present. I would lead, and the other two rafts would follow down the left side. I told my passengers to have their weight as far up on the front tube as possible, and warned them to be ready to throw their bodies around if needed. I put the heaviest passenger on the right side figuring if we got through the "V" wave our biggest risk was the wave off the black rock, and that would be coming from the right, if I was still facing downstream.

I approached the black rock at the top and lined up on the current line. My grip tightened and I could feel my heart beating in my neck as the current carried me out into the middle of the river so I could take a good look at the ledge hole, then pulled me back from the brink and we started down the glassy tongue into the entry wave. My angle must have been slightly off, because all of a sudden my front end was facing upstream. "We're going through backwards," I yelled to my passengers three feet away. I don't think they heard me, but they definitely saw. After breaking through the waves above, I made one last hard pull on the oars, and the next thing I knew the light had disappeared and I was out of the boat and in the cold water rinse cycle, not knowing what was up and what was down.

Only surfers and river runners know what it's like to be in water that big. A few seconds can seem like an eternity, and panic is the last thing you need. I knew it would only be a few seconds before the tail waves and I would probably see light and be able to suck in some precious air. Sure enough, I popped up directly behind my still upright raft, and had so much adrenaline pumping through my system that when I reached for a strap hanging off the back of the raft and pulled on it, I flew over the tube into the back and quickly jumped back on the oars. Only one passenger was still in the raft, and she looked as if she had been thinking about grabbing the oars when she saw me emerge. "Oh, thank God," she replied, clasping her hands together in a gesture of relief. My other passenger was also close to the raft, so I pulled her in and still had time to set up for Son of Lava. Afterwards I pulled into the eddy where Pete and the rest were working to re-flip Christa's boat. I still didn't know the whole story, and what had happened to the fifth person.

The paddleboat and other raft soon floated in, their adrenaline still pumping. The paddleboat captain said he had only given one command – three times. "Forget the paddles, high side!" The laughter helped me release my self-judgment for nearly flipping and making that swim, plus putting my passengers at risk. Neither one of them had any issue with me, and I had certainly given them a story to take home.

The missing fifth passenger had been Carol, and only after some tense moments had she been located. Pete told me he was very concerned and looking for any sign of Carol or her lifejacket. He tied his boat to a rock on shore and looked around. Still no floating life jacket. Then he looked down at the side of Christa's boat and he said his heart stopped. Floating motionless under the boat were two legs, Carol's legs.

"Oh my God," he thought, "she's caught in the rigging." With great trepidation he reached down, grabbed a safety line on the side of the boat, and lifted it up. And there was Carol. At first she remained motionless, her eyes closed. Then she blinked her eyes, smiled weakly, and after a pause, said "Can I come up, now?"

She had been under the raft the entire time. Having heard Pete's FOG speech, she knew it was up to her to hold on! And hold on she did – through the remainder of Lava, almost into the eddy on the left side, then through son of Lava, and over to the shore on the right side. Ironically, she might have been seriously injured had Pete not instructed his passenger to let go of Christa's raft, because he then floated around one side of a barely submerged rock, and Christa's raft had gone to the other side. Had he continued to hold on to her raft, Carol might have been dragged over that rock.

Amazingly, she turned out just fine: no trauma, no hypothermia, not even a sense that what she had just done was almost beyond credulity. She had found an air pocket and ridden it out. We were dumbfounded, relieved, and thrilled. Lava had flexed its muscles, flipped one boat, and ejected two guides. And we were all coming back with a story. Especially Carol.

We floated around the last corner and heard the sudden freight train-like rush of Lava race up to greet us. Chris turned around and bit her lower lip. I knew there was nothing I could say to alleviate her anxiety, so I smiled and remained silent. This would be one of those "let's just get it over with" experiences for her.

The closer we got to the head of the rapid, the louder its volume. Initially we could see only some explosions of whitewater. Now we could see the entire chaotic rapid, and I felt my bladder calling out. I floated into a small eddy on the left just upstream of the current that fed into the rapid, and Graham jumped out and tied the raft to a large tammy tree. Grass covered the bank, and a thick grove of tammies offered shade for anyone who didn't want to hike down to the rapid.

I grabbed my camera and my water bottle and walked under drooping tree branches, crossed the dry channel coming out of Prospect Canyon, and scrambled up a boulder-strewn incline to the head of the rapid. The noise had modulated during the walk, dropping down as I walked through the trees, increasing as I emerged from the grove, again lowering as I walked through the channel, and finally increasing to a fever pitch as I stood on the remnants of the 1996 debris flow overlooking the rapid.

Graham appeared to my right, pointed to the ledge hole, and yelled "That thing is horrendous." I nodded and continued to watch the currents. Michael showed up and smiled a nervous smile.

The key to running the left side of Lava safely rested in our ability to read the currents and stay on the flow that funnels into a narrow tongue just to the left of the ledge hole. The spot above the ledge hole where the current splits was very clear from the scout rock. If we were to the left of that point, we'd be safe, barring some unforeseen left-to-right wind. If we ended up to the right of that point, we would be in the clutches of the ledge hole.

The paddleboat crew arrived en masse, and I gave Eliza a high five as Sue pointed out their run. With six engines, they could maneuver and change directions quickly. The entry wave at the bottom of the tongue was very large, and if the paddleboat didn't have sufficient momentum, or if their angle was off, they would be at the mercy of the river gods. *I had once seen what looked like a very good paddleboat run enter the tongue, hit that first wave, and stall, rearing up in the front and throwing everybody into the river, like a dump truck removing its load.*

*   *   *

On another trip my good friend Robert had been the captain, and the night before at National, Robert had admitted that he just didn't completely understand the left run. From my position on the rocks I watched as he pushed out into the middle of the river far right of the crux point. I silently exhorted him to move left, and as if on cue, the paddleboat turned to the left and started moving into position. Then, inexplicably, the crew stopped paddling. They were still too far right. Suddenly, Robert ordered his crew to paddle hard and they surged forward. I couldn't believe what I was seeing, and assumed that he had realized they were going into the ledge hole and was just trying to build up as much momentum as possible. He later told me he thought he was in the right position.

The paddleboat charged over the lip of the ledge hole and came to a screeching halt, on the downstream edge of the ledge hole, halfway out and halfway in. As I photographed I could see Robert launched from his seat on the back of the raft. Through my lens I watched as the four passengers in the front paddled furiously to keep the raft from being sucked back into the maelstrom. It remained suspended right on the far edge of the ledge hole for what seemed like eternity. Meanwhile, Robert and another passenger pulled one of the other passengers back into the raft. Finally the efforts of the paddlers succeeded in escaping the clutches of the ledge hole.

As I climbed back up to the surface of the debris flow, Art still had his video camera running, and I gave him a look of amazement. He asked me what run I planned to make. I spoke into the camera and said, "Not the paddleboat run." We walked back to my raft, put the cameras into the dry box, and shoved off. My entry was perfect, and I could see my crewmates on the left and right side of the current waiting for my run. I slipped down the right side of the chub rock and the raft shuddered to a momentary halt, and then continued on. A successful run. Over my shoulder I could see my trip leader shouting and pointing to the back of my raft. I looked behind me in time to see Art holding on to his head as he slumped against the bags.

My trip leader had seen it all. After our entry, Art had decided to get a better view of the rest of the rapid. As my raft slid just to the right of the "chub rock," it tipped down at a steep angle and hit hard. Art lurched forward, hitting the side of his head on the bags, perhaps striking one of the buckles, or maybe even the edge of the cooler.

I shouted to him to see if he was okay, and he didn't respond. So I pulled to shore in the eddy above Son of Lava, and helped Art to shore where I asked him to lie down and not move his head. With the help of others who showed up, we assessed him and found that he had a little numbness in his neck. The first response to any head injury is to stabilize the spine by holding the head very still, and check it to make sure there are no spinal injuries. This involved a careful palpation, or touching of the entire spine from the top of the neck to the tailbone. Art was uncertain about feeling in his neck, and therefore we could not "clear his spine." To play it safe, we decided to call in a helicopter to take him out to make sure he was okay. It was the first time I had been involved with somebody in my raft injured to this extent. I felt really bad about it, and was relieved when Art met us at the warehouse at the end of the trip. He had suffered no permanent injuries. Since I still had his video camera in my raft, we had photographed the helicopter scene for him. It immediately followed my comment about not going where the paddleboat had gone.

Graham and I remained behind while the rest of the group headed to their rafts. Chris and Diane had decided to pass on a closer look at the rapid and had remained back at the raft. The sun was high overhead and the heated black rocks magnified the temperature. I felt the effects of the cooling river on my face and the intense arid heat of the desert on my back.

After fifteen minutes, we saw Star pushing out into the current, followed by Floyd, Carla, the paddleboat, and finally Michael. Their runs were perfect, and I was able to get some great shots of the paddleboat with Eliza in the left front position. As I walked back to the raft, I hoped the pictures would provide some great memories for her.

I returned to my raft where Chris and Diane were putting on a brave face. I pushed off and looked for the current coming off the shore, then found the crux point where the current split. Making sure I was left of it, I lined up to put my left tube on a small wave, checked my position to be sure I was left of the ledge hole, and then pushed hard to get as much momentum as possible going into the entry wave. I said a silent "thank you" as I saw the ledge hole out of the corner of my eye and hit the wave square. Chris and Diane threw their weight into the front tube. We cruised to the left of the "chub rock" and I pushed right so we could get a piece of the big wave coming off the "cheese grater." The tail waves were large, and even Graham let out a yell as I pulled toward the left side.

Often, especially when the river is muddy, I'll pull over into the eddy above Son of Lava, where warm water flows from a spring directly into the river. As a reward for a successful run, I'll get out my shampoo and offer it to anyone in my raft who would like to wash his or her hair in warm, clear water. Hardly anyone passes up that offer. Because there might be endangered fish swimming in the eddy, I'll fill up a couple of buckets and let people rinse their hair in my raft. Then, when we're back in the current, they just bail the soapy water into the river.

They all took me up on my offer, and then we ran Son of Lava with all three in the front, and joined the rest on the ledges on the left for a tuna salad lunch. Everybody was still pumped up and talking about their Lava runs. Roni was practically shouting, saying she wished we could do it again and again. Liz had a wry grin on her face, and Doron seemed content to be an observer. Tyler was animated as he described his experience to Miriam, and Timmy and Nathan talked excitedly as they made mud sculptures.

As we fixed lunch, I asked Eliza to describe her run, and she said she couldn't really see much since she was in the front and constantly being hit by the waves. The rest of the crew were focused on putting out lunch, but I knew that Sue felt just a little relieved that we had made it below the last major rapid without any incident. We would still be running some big, fun rapids; but barring some highly unusual event, the rest of the trip would be comparatively relaxed. We would be celebrating tonight at camp.

We almost always stopped here for lunch after running Lava. It provided shade or sun, depending on what we needed and the time of year, and also was the location of one of the many river "mailboxes," which were actually ammo cans hidden away in secret spots known by guides who could leave and receive river news, and love letters. *On one of my trips we ran into another CanX group, an all-women's trip, at Deer Creek. We had a short interaction, and the women left. When we finally returned to the rafts, I found that Wild Thing had been kidnapped. I knew one of the women on the other crew had done this dastardly deed, and of course lost a lot of sleep worrying about the wellbeing of my companion. When we stopped at the Lava lunch spot, I was told that WT had been left in the mailbox. We walked several hundred yards downstream, and found her, along with an extra jar of peanut butter the head cook had asked them to get if they could beg one from another river trip. Mice had ravaged both. WT had her foot partially amputated, and clearly had been traumatized. I returned her to her rightful place on the rear tube of my raft where she had proudly ridden for the past several trips. (She even had a custom-made rain suit for big water and rainy days.) After the trip ended, a couple of the passengers took WT to their hotel, gave her a bath and a shampoo, patched her leg, and put a lavender bow in her hair. She's looking pretty good now.*

After lunch, the river below Lava widened, slowed down, and mellowed out. The eroding flows from various volcanic eruptions remained stark evidence to the power and majesty of the natural world. Extensive collections of murals seemed to show up around every bend, and down every straightaway. From lava grew sprawling gardens of cacti on soft slopes, and prickly pear and barrel cactus rising out of hardened monuments. Whole cliffs hundreds of feet high covered in a lava veneer harbored a variety of vegetation that had somehow found toeholds in impossibly vertical faces.

At low water, springs of crystal clear water bubble up out of subterranean wells. Catclaw acacia groves draw a line along gradual slopes representing the high water floods in 1957. That year, 125,000 cfs raced through the Canyon. But for the dam, 1983 would have seen around the same level or higher, instead of the 92,000 cfs that powered the turbines and shot out of the overflow tubes at a hundred miles an hour.

Just below Mile 183 the river took a sharp bend to the right, passing close to a wall of frozen lava displaying fascinating hexagonal, end-on views of columnar jointing, like a hundred feet of stacked wood seen from the end. This jointing was the result of contractions that had occurred when the molten lava cooled. Directly across the river in a large eddy that sometimes served as a lunch spot, Beecher Spring (named for a Hualapai family) fed a lush stand of tamarisk, and made a perfect home for a king-sized Grand Canyon pink rattlesnake we had spotted one day during lunch.

As we continued downstream we passed several fascinating lava flows that had formed in a variety of fantastical shapes – a fan (my favorite), a butterfly, and a long sequence of parallel lines split by a vertical crack. It looked like a gigantic backbone and rib cage. Diane took several pictures, saying that she could paint some wonderful cards from the various shapes. Graham was silent, but was also taking some shots. Some lava flows formed along walls sitting atop river cobble, indicating that the lava had filled in the ancient river channel, forcing the river to find a new path. The rounded cobbles, inter-bedded underneath the lava, were differentiated by size and nestled together in formation facing downstream, like a disciplined army preparing to march. Rounded rocks indicated movement in water over long distances, during which the edges were removed through constant collisions with other rocks.

The Canyon continued trending south-southwest. Soft Bright Angel Shale slopes pushed the rim back, opening us to direct sunlight and heat. A two-mile straight stretch of river channel revealed three volcanic cones on the rim at the end of the channel. Graham asked about them, and I told him they hadn't been active for quite some time, but had been the source of all the lava formations we would see for the next thirty miles.

The current was slow and wide here, encouraging a laid-back attitude for passengers and guides. A generator sat three feet above the river on a grassy ledge in a large eddy on the left. A short hose led from the river to the generator, and then a longer hose snaked up a sandy slope to a flat surface reinforced by rocks around its edges. Chris asked about it, and I told her it was the helipad used to fly passengers in and out of the Canyon. Most of those who left the Canyon by helicopter, I said, were from motor trips off-loading their passengers. They would then spend the rest of the day at the Bar Ten Ranch, a dude ranch on the north rim. There they would often be treated to Western hospitality in the form of a rodeo and a barbeque, before being flown to Lost Wages (Las Vegas), and a return to the insanity of normal life. Diane said she thought that would be too jarring a way to end such a peaceful trip. Graham uttered "from the sublime to the ridiculous" under his breath.

The motor rigs would then run without passengers to their takeout at Diamond Creek, forty miles downstream, or Pearce Ferry on Lake Mead, fifty-four miles away. I said I had been on only one trip in which our passengers had been helicoptered out. Some later told me they loved the view from the helicopter, but since then the Park Service had removed our permit to use the helipad and I'm glad we don't do it any more. I told Diane that I agreed with her that it was too abrupt a transition from the slow, peaceful pace of the river, to the frenetic world most of us inhabit.

There has been a controversy raging over the use of motors in the Grand Canyon, and helicopters to transport passengers. The helipad is on Hualapai land, and they receive substantial revenues for the use of the pad. Some of the river companies pick up new passengers who have been brought in by helicopter, and take them down to Lake Mead. If the helipad weren't available, motor companies would have to transport their passengers to Diamond Creek and pay to shuttle them through the reservation, or go all the way to Lake Mead. This would be very costly, so those companies opposed any change.

On the other side, helicopters are very disruptive to the peace and calm of the Canyon, and environmentalists may have a good case for eliminating motors on rafts, even though the change to four-cycle engines has reduced the sound and pollution significantly. I can do without the helicopters, but think eliminating the motors would result in a negative impact on the Canyon. Seventy percent of all the passengers who raft through the Grand Canyon do so on the big motor rigs. If these craft were eliminated and replaced by oar boats, I fear we would have an unbroken parade going downstream, because all oar boats go approximately the same speed. This would result in reducing the quality of the experience for all passengers. In addition, I find it comforting to have a motor rig waiting below a major rapid at high water, in case of trouble. It's also my belief that the majority of people who float through the Canyon acquire at least a passing understanding and appreciation of environmental and ecological principles, as well as the politics of water. Finally, motor rigs have a greater carrying capacity for ice, and when they have extras, we often benefit from that in the lower end of the Canyon when we're running low.

On this spot on the river a few years ago I was slammed by a waterspout. I kid you not. There I was, enjoying a lazy float with my two passengers relaxing in the front, when a strong upstream wind announced an impending thunderstorm. The river was very wide and about to take a sharp turn to the left. I looked to my right, and was shocked to see a water spout a hundred yards away. Out in the ocean it might be called a cyclone. This was nowhere near as big, but it was beautiful, a silvery funnel about twenty feet in diameter at the base, and fifty to sixty feet high. It was spinning in a clockwise direction, sucking up water like a super-saturated funnel-cloud. After a few seconds, the spout drifted off the river, and became a dust devil, swirling dust and debris through a high side canyon. We continued around the corner and suddenly the wind made a dramatic shift downstream. What a treat! Just as I was about to shout Yahoo! in appreciation for the wind's assistance, the spout reappeared, slamming into me from behind with fierce winds, and an infinite number of water droplets that felt like b-b's beating against my face. I had absolutely no control over my raft that had turned sideways and was being pushed downstream at a fast clip. My passengers were down on the floor, and the howling wind was so loud they couldn't hear me yelling for them to high side. My downstream tube was being pushed under water, and my upstream tube was rising. I leaned into the wind in the most unusual high side I'd ever done. But it wouldn't have made any difference if the spout hadn't suddenly dissipated. It was replaced again by upstream winds, a sharp drop in temperature, and heavy rains. Everything happened so fast, as it often does in the desert, that no one had time to don rain gear. My passengers were getting cold, as I'm sure were all the others, so we pulled over into an eddy on the left and found shelter under an overhang where people could find their rain gear and put on dry clothes.

On our right I pointed out a wall that contained some Paiute petroglyphs, and modern grafiti written by surveyors for the Bureau of Reclamation's Prospect Canyon Project in the late 1950s. In a century or so, I said with a bit of sarcasm, these would morph into archaeologically treasured petroglyphs.

The canyon just below us, Whitmore Wash, had its own share of history. I pointed to a slope just upstream of a side canyon and said that over a thousand feet of gas line sat naked under the desert sun, the remnants of the 1960 upriver run of New Zealander Jon Hamilton, who, along with others, became the first – and only – men to successfully go against the flow of the Colorado River. The gas line, brought down to the river from the nearest road on the North side, fed his hungry boats on the way to Lava Falls and beyond. Graham said he would have enjoyed that adventure, except for the deafening noise of the powerboat.

Whitmore was also the place where one of the motor companies used to offload passengers and replace them with fresh bodies who had come down from the Bar Ten Ranch by horseback.

The new passengers would then float the lower end of the Canyon while the old passengers would ride out of the Canyon on those same horses, clean up with a shower and a western meal at the Bar Ten Ranch, and then fly to Las Vegas. Three days later, the new passengers would finish their trip on Lake Mead, and the saddle-weary folks who had ridden out of the canyon would be back home.

I've camped at Whitmore numerous times. On one private trip, I hiked into the side canyon with my friend Bob. It was late in the afternoon, and the sun had dropped below the rim, offering us welcome relief. He was a very successful public employee in Boulder, responsible for some innovative ideas in public transportation. During the trip, he had turned fifty. We found a comfortable rock on which to sit, and Bob spoke to me about his father and the strain in their relationship. He said they hadn't spoken in several years. I told him I was sorry to hear that, and then said, "Maybe all it takes is someone willing to make that first step." A strong introvert, he didn't reply. He just sat there and thought about it for a minute, and we said no more. Five years later I saw Bob at a party and he told me he had taken that first step and had reached out to his father. He said he was very nervous and somewhat pessimistic about his father opening up, but pleasantly surprised when he did. They began having regular conversations, and several visits. Now, he was happy to say, they had developed a great relationship.

As we floated through a small rapid, I pointed out a "marker plant," the creosote bush. Most know the name creosote from the smell of the preservative, which was extracted from the plant and applied to railroad ties. It's called a marker plant because it represented a new eco-system, in this case the Mohave Desert, determined by the ph of the soil, the amount of moisture (less than 4" per year), and the average temperature, among other characteristics. The creosote bush has been around for a long time, and has its own natural selection process. As it grows and ages, it moves out from its center, releasing a chemical that makes other plant growth difficult. Some think the Angel Plant, a creosote bush a quarter mile in diameter located in the Mohave desert, could be as much as 10,000 years old, and perhaps the oldest living thing on the planet. The first signs of the creosote bush appeared upstream at mile 169 on river left.

For the next few miles the Canyon wandered through basalt (lava) flows,often remnants of larger deposits on both sides of the river. Sometimes the remnants overlay gravel indicating old river channel, other times they rest on Precambrian gneiss, and still other times on dark-brown dolomite beds at the top of the Bright Angel Shale. We were a lot more relaxed in this stretch, and we had become stretched out. I could barely see Floyd in the raft ahead of me, and I saw no rafts behind me.

Around mile 192 the river made a sharp bend to the left and a mile later back to the right. In a large eddy on the left, past a lava cliff and across from another lava cliff on the right, was 194, a camp I used to stay at often. For the first six years we were on a twelve day schedule, and we would stop at 194 at the end of day ten, then row twenty-six miles to 220, and finish the trip with a six-mile silent float at first light on the last morning.

I said there had been some very interesting things that had occurred at this camp, and Chris asked me to share some of them. *I told her about a trip in 1986, during the last year of my old river company, Wilderness World, before it was sold and became Canyon Explorations. The management had deteriorated, and crews were made up of any guides who were still available.*

On this particular trip, I said, the leader was burned out and on his last Canyon trip before moving on to other endeavors. Several members of the crew were extremely opinionated and expressed their opinions freely, especially in the first few days when the trip leader refused to lead or provide any direction. By the time we arrived at 194, this had all been sorted out, and in spite of some tension on the crew, everybody seemed to be having a good time. Dinner was clams linguine, and called for two packages of cream cheese, plus milk. Before dinner preparations began, a bucket was cleaned out and much of the remaining juice and booze poured in, aided by ice scored that day from a deadheading motor rig.

After a few drinks, the cooks threw away the recipe and creativity took over – inebriated creativity. Instead of two pounds, all the remaining cream cheese was put in the pot with the linguine – six pounds. The pot ran over with dairy. During dinner a whipped cream fight broke out, and all sorts of mayhem erupted. Soon pots became drums and spoons drumsticks. Any resemblance to the peaceful Canyon I knew had disappeared. In spite of the tension and the unprofessional behavior, everybody said it was the trip of a lifetime. Chris said she was glad she wasn't on a trip like that, and I told her that for me, it was the worst trip I'd ever been on with regard to crew interaction. But to the credit of the compelling nature of the Canyon, the people didn't seem to notice, or at least it hadn't interfered with them having a great experience.

Fortunately, I told her, that was an isolated experience, with every other trip not only having great crew interaction, but a clear intention to provide the best possible experience of the Grand Canyon for our passengers. She asked me if there was a trip that stood out in that way, so I told her about holding *a re-marriage ceremony at 194.*

Esteban, who was one of my passengers on the waterspout trip, had returned for his second trip, this time with his wife Mary Ann. Eighteen years earlier they had shared a meaningful experience hiking into the Canyon, and this would be like an anniversary. Sometime during the trip I got the crazy idea to have a re-commitment ceremony. At first they seemed excited by it, and had picked the day that we ended up camping at 194 for the ceremony. However, the closer we got to the day, the more nervous and uncertain they became, and eventually they avoided even talking about it. As in all marriages, they had had their challenges. Since the Canyon held such powerful memories for them, they had taken the suggestion of a re-commitment ceremony seriously. Both told me later that they didn't want to go ahead with it if they had had any reservations about the relationships.

Finally, on the day of the ceremony, they decided to go for it. Mary Ann went off with Sue, who was also leading that trip, and a couple other women who created a bouquet of wildflowers and a headdress in addition to fresh nail polish, sparkle, and lipstick. Meanwhile, Esteban received cello lessons from the cellist with the string quartet, hoping to play Pachelbel's Canon. The quartet played softly in the background to begin the ceremony. As Mary Ann came in with her attendants, one of the guides blew bubbles along the path, and the quartet played the wedding march. I read a piece on commitment, and Esteban and Mary Ann spoke of their commitment to one another. Then we had a party – a joyful, celebratory party.

As we continued downstream, another marker plant began to appear on the right. Teddy Bear Cholla looked soft and cuddly, especially when backlit by the sun. But it was actually a cluster of hard needles introducing us to the beginning of the Lower Sonoran ecosystem – hotter, dryer, and subjected to more intense sunlight. We passed 194 Mile Canyon, 196 Mile Canyon, and the last stretch before the Parashont camp narrowed, as the Muav cliff again approached the river. The shore was covered with groves of tamarisk and willow, and was home to many birds, like the yellow-breasted chat with its staccato song, white-throated swifts, black chinned hummingbirds, Say's phoebes, violet-green swallows, ravens, and many others. Parashont Wash, at mile 198 ½, had a very long drainage coming off the North Rim. It was the home of the Book of Worms, collapsed segments of Bright Angel Shale looking like the pages of a book, with fossilized worm tracks created by half-billion-year-old worms inching through the muck and mud.

In the July 1999 trip, the wettest trip I had ever done, we camped here at Parashont. The weather had changed and we had enjoyed three days of typical summer weather, with high heat and desert blue sky dotted with beautiful clouds. My friend Michelle, a meeting planner with a "whatever it takes" attitude, was my guest. The sound of thunder erupted up the drainage as we were preparing dinner, and then Parashont flashed, even though there were no clouds in sight. To be safe, we decided to put up a tent. Since I was cooking, I had asked Michelle to find a good spot to set up the tent.

Good thing, too. Soon after dinner the sky clouded up, an incredible thunderstorm rolled in, and like the one at National years before, settled in directly overhead. I've never seen such intense flashes of lightning, nor felt the ground shake so much as that night. While the storm at National was intense, this one was exponentially more so. The lightning was brighter, the thunder closer, shaking the ground with greater enthusiasm, and the rain beat down on us much longer. And I loved it! About one in the morning I heard a couple of my crewmates walking through water. The sound came closer, and then with a chuckle, one of them said, "Hey Charly, you're in a lake." I stuck my head out of the tent and discovered we were in a small depression with standing water almost up to our door. With Michelle's help we picked up the tent and moved it to higher ground. In the morning, we checked the other campsites. One had been set up near a cliff behind the kitchen, and water cascading off the wall behind them had created a mini-Grand Canyon directly under their tent. The tent was stretched over air.

As we approached the point hiding the camp, the cliffs on river right opened up and we could look into a wide side canyon all the way to the North Rim. The drainage was dry and the creek bed covered with small gravel brought down during the most recent flash flood. I angled my raft towards the right side of the current and pushed towards the edge of the eddy line, which I rode until I was slightly below the camp. Floyd and Star were already tied up and their passengers had started to unload the yellow bags. A grove of catclaw acacia trees covered the downstream end of the beach, and that would be where the groover would be set up, near the water, but hidden from view of anyone at camp. The kitchen would go directly behind the trees in a small clearing.

It had been a long river day, almost thirty-two miles, with some exciting moments in Lava Falls. As we were setting up the kitchen, Nathan came walking by doing his daily chores, carrying his and his mom's river bags to their camp. Kathy had selected a camp a ways up the drainage, and evidently this was the second of four trips Nathan would have to make. He had a Pepsi in one hand, and a yellow bag half his size in the other. He stopped and looked me in the eye, then he looked at the rafts. He again looked me in the eye, then looked to the campsite two hundred yards away. Once more he looked me in the eye, and with a straight face said, "I'm going to be eleven before I get all these bags to camp."

The evening would be dedicated to celebrating ABL, Alive Below Lava. We didn't have a lot of time to relax before getting dinner started, but we did get together on Floyd's raft to enjoy a drink and a few moments to relax. Dinner was white bean chili with chicken, along with cornbread and rice. We set out some tortilla roll-ups, a mixture of cream cheese and diced black olives spread on large tortillas and cut into triangles. Meanwhile, Floyd and Michael were making up a batch of gin and tonics for anyone so disposed. Graham had brought his own bottle of Glen Livet scotch, which was now empty, and he was in the process of introducing a new game. With our feet remaining in place, he challenged us, while holding the bottle with both hands, to travel as far as possible without allowing our hands to touch the ground. It proved to be a lot harder than it looked, but there was a lot of laughter.

Graham had brought with him a book of short essays from the British humor magazine "Punch." He offered to read out of the book and seemed pleased that people were interested. While he read, Chris could hardly contain herself with laughter, while the Americans stood stone-faced trying to figure out the humor. Now *that* was funny.

At dinner, Sue announced we would be sleeping later than usual in the morning. We would have around twenty-four river miles to float, there would be some good-sized rapids to run, and the current would be fast, so we wouldn't need an early start. Her announcement, supplemented by gin and tonics, was greeted with good cheer. The descending night was warm, we were very comfortable with each other, there was no rain in sight, and we still had another day to play in the Canyon. Life was very good.

*An afternoon storm lifted just at sunset, providing us with brilliant
lighting that contrasted sharply between the shaded desert landscape in the
foreground, the sunlit bluffs behind camp, and the still darkened sky.*

DAY FIFTEEN–
PARASHONT TO 222

My campsite was on a small spit of land at the head of the eddy and ten feet from the river. I was awake, but my eyes were still closed as I listened to the sound of the rapid. It seemed to be coming from behind me, but I knew the river was in front of me. I opened my eyes, and realized I was hearing the echo of the river off the wall behind camp. Sometimes I'll have that sensation at night and it gives me the feeling of actually being on the river. In my not-quite-awake, not-quite-asleep state, I've actually thought that somehow my raft had come loose and I was heading towards a rapid. My heart would be racing, and after I'd come back to my senses, it would take awhile before I could relax enough to get back to sleep.

I remember one time being camped at Kanab Creek sharing a tent with my girlfriend. We were close to a wall that stretched behind camp. In the middle of the night she woke up crying "Charly, we're in the rapid." I couldn't convince her we were on land until I took her hand and had her touch the hard ground.

I could hear Floyd and Sue laughing in the kitchen area, but stayed under my bag because I knew this was a sleep-in morning. I thought about the events of the trip, how enjoyable the passengers had been, and felt a little regret that this would be the last full day. At least I would have Liz back in my raft. At dinner last night she had asked if the four of them could ride with me the next day.

The smell of brewing coffee finally convinced me to stretch and get up. Tyler was up and already exploring. I watched him as he reached into the branches of an acacia tree. He brought his cupped hand over to me and with his Cheshire-cat grin, opened it up to show me his captive, a cicada that promptly erupted into cacophonous flight. He then invited me to see his primitive "fort," a series of dead branches leaning against a tree across an open stretch from the kitchen. He explained that it was not complete, but if we were to stay here another day, he would have used it for a tent.

Breakfast of blueberry pancakes and ham was a relaxed affair, and we took our time loading the rafts. Tyler and Nathan had asked to paddle the duckies, and they were busy putting on their wet suits and helmets. They had become good buddies on the trip, and I wondered if they

251

would remain in contact after. I doubted it. In spite of the warmth and comaraderie generated on these trips, relatively few people keep in touch. Besides, Nathan lived in Northern Montana, and Tyler in South Carolina.

Tal came over and handed me the purple day bag and her sunscreen. I told her I was looking forward to spending the day with her, and said maybe we could talk about creative photography. At least that would be a safe topic, I thought to myself. She said that would be wonderful, and smiled as she walked toward the groover. Her light blue, thigh length smock swayed as she walked. I watched her for a moment before switching my focus to strapping down the purple bag and stowing the sunscreen in my people box. Eliza came in and finished rolling up her clothes bag. She said she was going on the paddleboat, and we talked for a moment about the trip. She told me she had come to appreciate how demanding the job of a river guide was, and didn't think it was for her. I felt a quick pang of disappointment, then told her I was glad she had come on the trip and had found out for herself. I also thanked her for her help.

Liz and Elli came on board and walked to the back of the raft. I offered my hand to each of them for support, and enjoyed Tal's momentary touch, her soft hands seeming to linger for just a moment. Then Roni loudly asked if she should untie my bowline. I smiled and thanked her. Doron, looking half asleep, climbed in and immediately found a place on the front tube to lie down. I told her I'd warn her if she was going to get wet. She opened one eye, then just as quickly, closed it.

Roni shoved us off and hopped aboard with a big grin. We were on our way to our last camp on our last full river day. She asked me what the day would be like. I told her we had twenty-four river miles and a few fun rapids. In particular, I said, when we ran the last big rapid, I was going to have her and Doron sit on the front tube. Roni squealed with delight. Doron opened her one eye again and lifted her eyebrow, but didn't have enough energy to respond.

As we entered the current I thought about this last full day as an opportunity to soak in the full energy of the Canyon with the people on this trip. We had become a cohesive group, and were drawn to some more than others. The very fact that two-dozen people, most of whom were unacquainted before the trip, had formed into a cooperative, interactive tribe without any real effort was testament to what was possible in human relations. I believe we could take on sworn enemies at the beginning of a trip, and with the right kind of intention, have them leave the Canyon as allies.

For the next seven miles we would be in an ever-widening part of the Canyon, with both North and South Rims receding farther back, removing our sense of being in a canyon, at least as we had come to know it. Several faults zones either crossed the river or ran parallel to it in this area, creating a mixture of formed and forming side canyons. We had entered the lower Sonoron ecosystem around mile 194 when the first of the Teddy Bear Cholla had appeared. This was the most arid section of the Canyon, and vegetation was sparse. We passed broken-up remnants of basalt (lava) flows harboring their clinging cactus gardens. The cliffs of Cambrian rock were thicker here than in the upper part of the Canyon. I pointed out the Temple Butte formation, and told Liz and Elli that we'd first seen it as hull-shaped lenses in Marble Canyon. Here it formed a 420-foot cliff between the Muav and Redwall. I also told them that the Muav, less than five hundred feet thick in the upper Canyon, was 720 feet thick here. Liz asked how that could be. I told her during the formation of these two limestone layers, the ocean had been deeper in the area that was now the Western Canyon than it had been in the Eastern part of the Canyon; so more limestone had formed and less had been eroded. She thought about it for a moment and said she thought she understood. It was hard to take my eyes off her.

Below mile 200 I pointed to a brilliant red ring on the right wall surrounding a cave twenty feet above a short drainage. It was a hematite mine, I said, another form of soft iron-oxide rock that has been used by native inhabitants for body painting in community and healing ceremonies. Elli said she remembered reading about a recent discovery on Mars of what NASA scientists thought might have been hematite. This could prove to be evidence that there had been water there at one time.

One of my early crewmates, fair-skinned and red-haired, had discovered his own sunscreen in that hematite mine. Every time we would float this stretch, he would pull over, run up the drainage, and fifteen minutes later emerge covered in red. Too bad there weren't more such accessible mines in the Canyon, because Jimmy had to deal with melanoma later on.

We floated by 202, a great camp, especially in the cooler shoulder seasons of spring and Fall, when the sun would remain on the camp late into the day and rise to warm us. The camp fronted a very large eddy with a basalt remnant bordering the downstream edge. A small, eroded cave in the lava cliff would have made a great shelter from rain, were it not for all the scorpions and other crawlers already taking up residence in there. Hidden from view, a camera across the river took daily shots of the beach as part of the Adaptive Management process. Scientists used the data to determine how to more effectively operate the dam to minimize any negative downstream impacts, like the erosion of beach sand. It was all part of utilizing science to understand what was required to repair what the historic high flow/low flow operations of the dam had damaged.

I looked back upstream to see whether Sue wanted to pull over to hike here. A short hike behind camp would take us to some agave roasting pits that had been used by the native inhabitants as part of their harvesting ceremonies. Farther up the drainage, some fallen slabs of Muav limestone rested in a jumble against the left wall, adorned with Paiute petroglyphs. This may have been a ceremonial space, but because of the erosion, we couldn't find any evidence to prove it.

By now we could see the rest of the rafts near us. Chris and Graham were in a prone position in the back of Floyd's raft, and Timmy was rowing Carla's raft, smiling and rowing with little effort. The paddleboat was the estrogen boat today, with Miriam, Mary, Kathy, Diane, Antje, and Eliza on board. I was surprised to see Eliza in the captain's position, but not surprised to see her smiling.

Spring Canyon, at mile 204, came in from the North side, and was so named because of several springs in the drainage. In the late 'seventies there had been a big beach at the mouth, large enough for a camp. Today it is choked with tamarisk, horsetail, and other vegetation. The hike is beautiful, once you get through the several hundred yards of thick undergrowth and dense canopy. It's not the undergrowth and canopy that's the problem, but the snakes that have taken up residence there. *This I know only by reputation, but one of my crewmates said he was walking up the drainage when he discovered a rattler coiled to his left, then another to his right. Fortunately he stopped right there, because he also spotted one just in front of him, and unbelievably, a fourth one behind him. He was surrounded. Luckily he was able to back out without incident.*

The Canyon continued to flatten and widen until our peaceful float was interrupted by 205 Mile Rapid, also known as Kolb Rapid. The Kolb brothers, Emery and Ellsworth, were best known for their photographic studio, opened in 1903 at the head of the Bright Angel Trail on the very edge of the South Rim. They must have been in great shape, because they initially made their living by taking photographs of tourists riding mules and hiking down the trail. After taking the pictures, they would hike four miles down the trail to Indian Gardens, where there was water, and develop the prints; then hike back up and sell the pictures to the returning tourists. In 1911-12 they rafted the Colorado from Green River, Wyoming, where Powell had begun his trip, to the Gulf of California. Until Emery's death in 1976, one or the other of the Kolb brothers showed the film they shot on that trip in their studio. Emery had been a resident at the Canyon for over seventy years.

They wrote a book about their journey, and I received a copy of it in the early 'nineties from an unexpected source. I was in Astoria, Oregon to do a benefit for KMUN, the local public radio station. After setting up my projectors in the room, I went to dinner with my brother Ned. Upon returning, I saw a man near my projectors. He asked, "would you be the fella who's doing the slide show tonight?" I said I was, and he showed me a book and replied, "In the early 'fifties I visited the Grand Canyon and met Emery Kolb, who autographed his book for me. I thought you might like it." Such a simple yet profound gesture: a man passing a small treasure on to another generation.

Kolb Rapid is fairly long with some fun, big waves. Most people enter just to the right of a pourover that has drawn many unsuspecting river runners into its hole. From upstream it's not apparent, and the current can suddenly pull you in. After a quarter mile run in the wave train the river bends sharply to the left and then again to the right. If my raft were on the left side of the current at that first bend, I would have to work very hard to stay off the left wall at the next bend since all the current flows directly toward that wall. *Speaking of walls, in the high-water year of 1983, a 37-foot motor rig ran up on the wall on the right and flipped. I would not have wanted to clean up that mess.*

I woke up Doron and told everyone we might get wet in this rapid. When I heard some protest, I said my raft wasn't known as the wet raft without reason, and they should grab their safety lines and hold on. Instead of the usual run to the right of the pourover, I drifted down the middle of the tongue and aimed at a large standing wave. We hit it at the perfect moment when it was building to a peak, and sailed up and over without taking on much water. I then pushed hard to the left to catch the eddy near the top so I could photograph Nathan and Tyler in the duckies. It took some effort, but I was finally able to pull to shore on the left just below the entry. I jumped out and wrapped the bowline around a large rock on shore, grabbed my camera with the telephoto lens, and walked a hundred feet upstream to get ready for the paddleboat and duckies.

I had a great view of the river upstream. A few puffy clouds were starting to form over the South rim, and they stood out dramatically against the robin's-egg-blue sky. Both rims were so far back, they seemed insignificant. I looked down and saw the paddleboat picking up momentum as it raced past the pourover. Eliza was now in the right front digging with her paddle. She had a big grin on her face, as did Antje in the left front. Kathy and Miriam were in the middle and both were yelling over the din of the rapid. Mary and Diane were in the back, and everyone was beaming. I took a couple of shots of the paddleboat as it hit the first big wave, and then quickly swung my camera upstream to find Timmy on the oars beginning his entry. He looked very relaxed and confident, a far cry from his first few days when there was tension apparent in his face and body language. He hit the large entry wave straight on, seemed to stall for just a moment as his raft climbed the wave at an almost vertical angle, dipped over the top and continued downstream into more big waves. Nathan and Tyler followed close behind in the duckies, and both had great runs. I got some action close-ups of them. All three of those kids were fearless, and having the time of their lives.

I returned to the raft, and Roni said something about going in the ducky on the next trip. I looked at Elli, who cocked her head and shrugged her shoulders.

By the time we had returned to the current, everybody else was downstream. We cruised down to the first turn and I moved to the right side of the current, floated to the left and then, a hundred yards later, to the right. The right side of the Canyon was now a long, slowly rising slope covered with desert grasses, ocotillo, and cacti. The slope on river left was steeper, with a variety of vegetation, including more catclaw acacia trees. Again we noticed more volcanic flows. Suddenly Doron shouted that she saw some big horn. Sure enough, several ewes and lambs were climbing in single file up a narrow trail in a basalt cliff some fifty feet high and a couple hundred yards long. Elli said it was remarkable how agile and sure-footed they looked.

We passed Indian Canyon on the right and I mentioned it was the site of several cliff dwellings up the long drainage leading to and from the North Rim. *To river guides it was best known as the home of the Bundy jars, relics left by a ranching family that had lived up on the Arizona Strip, and had grazed their cattle in the canyon. There were several old jars, one with the bleached head of a now extinct Colorado River fish.*

For the next few miles the Canyon was hardly recognizable when compared to the steep cliffs of Marble Canyon, the Inner Gorge, and the Muav Gorge. The Canyon had become a wide river valley with willows, acacia, and tamarisk abundant on river left fronting hillocks that very likely covered old habitation sites. Basalt flows on the left and right added a stark black contrast to the greens of trees and cacti, and desert sand.

Liz leaned up against the yellow bags behind my cooler and we talked more about photography. After a while, she asked me if there was one thing that I had learned that I thought was the most important requirement to being a great photographer. I actually had to think about that, and was uncertain of my answer until I heard myself speaking it out loud. I said that for me at least, the most important quality was to be in love with my subject. I had, I told her, a deep heart connection with the Grand Canyon, and that was what had allowed me to capture its beauty. She seemed to like that answer.

Around river mile 208, we entered Granite Park, so named by Col. Birdseye in his 1923 USGS exploration. The name had come from granite outcrops in side canyons and the abundance of willow trees along the left bank. *In my early years, we had to put up with the auditory assaults of wild burros, escaped and abandoned survivors of the mining era. They liked to stand on top of hills in this part of the Canyon and scream at rafters invading their territory. The burros made a habit of going anywhere and eating everything. They were not only destructive of the fragile ecosystem; they were also competing with native animals for scarce food, and winning. So the Park Service decided to have them removed. In the late 'seventies, the Park hatched a plan to round them up and ship them downstream on large motor rigs. They hired some cowboy wranglers, who failed in their efforts. Then the Park proposed shooting the feral burros. In 1980-81, after a loud protest from animal lovers, Cleveland Amory, the president of the Fund for Animals, rounded up five hundred eighty animals and removed most of them by helicopter. The animals were then put up for adoption.*

Far off the river on the left rose a series of ledges, slopes, and cliffs of Muav Limestone (770 feet thick), and Temple Butte (420 feet thick). A small beach guarded by an aging willow tree had served as both lunch spot and campsite over the years. The willow had been photographed in 1891 on the Stanton trip, and currently proudly displayed its age and history of weather abuse in its bowed and broken branches. Ample campsites were hidden behind willow saplings, and a long rock island stretched out below the drainage. Until recently, a channel had flowed around the island from the upstream side, but debris flows had choked that off, creating a wetlands complete with cattails and many varieties of birds. In the 'eighties, one sighting of a Gila monster had also been reported in the area.

Across from the head of the rock island lurked a short but intense rapid. The river took a sharp right, then bent left, with most of the current plunging into a monstrous hole. No one in his or her right mind would go in there on purpose. *Except Tom, the middle school science teacher. At least once he had purposefully taken his paddleboat into the hole. Oh, he had given his passengers the option of not going in; but his enthusiasm was infectious, and they were all for it. I'm not sure they'd do it again, however, as the results were predictable. They flipped, and some of them met the bottom of the river. He later told us several members of that crew actually begged him to carry the raft back up and run the hole again.*

*   *   *

A few years ago I ended up in that hole, unintentionally I guarantee you. On the previous trip I had gone right of the hole for the first time. Just below the hole, the shore jutted out, and I had glanced off it. So on the next trip, I decided to run forward so that when I passed the hole, I could pull away from the shore. Only problem was, the volume was about 5,000 cfs higher, the current was stronger, and instead of feeding to the right of the hole, the current flowed into the right side of it. My trusting friend Greg was following me on his first right run, confident that I knew what I was doing, because all my previous runs on that trip had been spot on.

As I approached the hole, my two passengers were enjoying the shade of an umbrella, and were paying absolutely no attention because they, too, totally trusted their guide. At the last minute I realized I wasn't going to be able to push through the current to make it to the right of the hole. We dropped into it at an odd angle, and frankly should have flipped. The sudden crunch caused my passengers to meet in the center of the raft, but somehow we emerged from the hole right side up. Meanwhile, Greg had noticed the likelihood of me going into the hole. Up to the last instant he was certain I would do something miraculous. Didn't happen. Fortunately he was able to pull across the front of the hole and run down the left side of it.

*   *   *

On a trip in July 2000 we were having lunch at Granite Park when a group of dories came into view. I watched as they floated close to the right shore. Up to that time I had always worked hard to pull left against the flow of the current to break through the current that flowed into the hole. I watched as the dories floated, literally, from right to left, and barely dipped their oars in the water. I was fascinated by this run and decided to try it myself. It was effortless, and I wouldn't have had to take any strokes except that I couldn't totally trust the current to carry me away from the hole. It's different at varying water levels, so I'm still experimenting with that run.

I set up on the right side of the river as the rest of the rafts set up to make the traditional run down the left side. I still get a little nervous doing this run, because a screw-up could have disastrous results. I looked for the current coming off the right shore, and placed my raft on the left side of that current. The rear of my raft was angled toward the left shore in the event that I had to pull away from the hole. I took a couple of strokes when it looked like we might get pulled to the right, and then allowed the raft to float by the very edge of the hole. It was incredibly loud and big, like an ocean wave curling back upstream and crashing loudly into the depths of the hole. Doron looked like she wasn't sure we would be safe, but Roni just whooped and hollered with delight. I was looking forward to seeing the two of them on my front tube in 217.

At the end of the rapid, the channel again made a sharp bend to the right, and we passed by a summer lunch spot, one of the more difficult to set up. It was in the shade of some overhanging Tapeats Sandstone shelves at the top of a thirty-foot sand dune. Carrying the table, lunch box, and food up the loose sand was a workout, and in sandals could result in burns from the hot sand. But it was also one of few places in this stretch where there was any shade in the middle of the day. So we would use it when necessary.

Just above Little Bastard Rapid at Mile 212, we encountered some more river sculpting. At first the water-eroded shapes were very primitive, but sensuously smooth. Just below Little Bastard, which was a noisy but mild rapid except at low water, the most beautiful natural sculptures I have ever seen rested along the right shore. They looked like a choir of little people, polished a shiny gray-black by the ancient river's abrasive touch. Like a finely sandpapered hard wood, they called out to us to be touched. As we passed by them, Liz said she was very sad not to have her camera at that moment.

A half-mile below Little Bastard, we encountered a not-so-hot hot spring in an eddy on the left. The travertine-encrusted pool looked very much like the upper half of a pumpkin with its lid off. Appropriately, it was called Pumpkin Springs, and was often visited but rarely entered. The only thing that was hot about it was the uranium that leached into the pool from sources on the Hualapai reservation.

We had camped just below Pumpkin on a private trip in 1979. At the time there was a small tree in the middle of the sandy beach to which I had tied my 13 1/2 foot raft. In the morning, my raft was still tethered to the tree, but instead of floating, I woke up to find it high and dry, hanging at a steep angle, sitting on wet sand. From the back of my raft to the edge of the river was at least fifteen feet. That was how far the river had dropped overnight. That tree is now gone

*   *   *

On one trip we camped here and had to get up at 3:30, that's in the morning, to make up for the lack of miles we had made the day before in the face of some very strong upstream winds. We needed to be at our takeout, thirteen miles downstream, by 7:30, and the current was pretty slow. It was pitch black when we woke up, and heavy storm clouds hung over us like Snoopy on his doghouse. When we launched, I was behind the trip leader, who had placed a blinding lantern on the back of her raft. I pulled around her and rowed the next three miles in the dark, having to rely on sounds and the feel of my oars in the water to stay in the current. I loved it. Without the benefit of eyesight, I was forced to rely on two other senses. Eddies are silent, but speak loudly through my oars. As I approached an eddy, my oar would feel less resistance, and I would merely push hard on the oar to move me back into the current. As long as I felt equal resistance from both oars, I was in the part of the river I needed to be to move downstream. Riffles have a slightly louder sound, and small rapids even louder with a deeper voice. I knew there were no big rapids in this stretch, so when I heard the riffle or small rapid sound, I kept my oars in the water and allowed the current to carry me through. With no stars, I could barely see the end of my raft. The experience also taught me how much we could actually see just from starlight coming from trillions of miles away. In the absence of cloud cover, it's quite easy to walk around at night, if one is careful.

Just upstream of Pumpkin, a ledge of Tapeats Sandstone gave us another glimpse into the sculptures created by river currents. One sculpture – an upright, thin piece of sandstone shaped like the profile of a human head – even had a hole where the eye would have been. It could have easily been attributed to Miro or Picasso.

On a trip in 1991, we stopped below one of the tunnels near the sculpture, and helped each of our passengers up a rope. One was a delightful 73-year old woman, Marian, who was on her first vacation in decades after taking care of her elderly mother. She had come on this trip a couple of years after seeing my slide show in Michigan. She told me it had taken her that long to get up the courage. She thoroughly loved the experience. And we loved her. We helped her up the line and then offered her a chance to climb down into one of the holes. Roger Henderson, an old-time guide with a gruff exterior and a warm heart, climbed down first and offered his shoulders as footsteps for Marian. It was a long step to the floor of the tunnel, and Marian's laughter reverberated throughout the tunnel as she stretched down Roger's front. I did see her once back in Michigan, and she still had warm memories of the guides, the other passengers, and the trip. A teacher of nutrition, she was particularly impressed when we got out a ripe watermelon on the thirteenth day. During the trip a couple of the guides took her camera without her knowledge and photographed one of them mooning her. When she had it developed, she laughed and put it in her photo album.

*   *   *

Those same tunnels were the focus of a rather dramatic experience on a trip in 1988. At the beginning there was nothing to indicate it would be a trip with all the ingredients for an action-packed thriller – a beautiful, mysterious blond passenger, a handsome guide, a casual relaxing of the safety standards, an unexplained delay arriving at camp, tension among the passengers and crew, a séance with the missing passenger's mother and aunt, and rising fears of tragedy as night descended.

It was the last training trip for a trainee named Franco before he was scheduled to become a paid guide rowing commercial passengers. He rowed the baggage boat, heavily laden with gear and the repository of anything that couldn't fit anywhere else. It is the duty of the baggage boatman to take it all with a smile. For Franco that was easy, since he seemed to have a perpetual smile on his face, communicating his pleasure at being in the Canyon and his love of people.

While there were no incidents of note on the upper portion of the trip (from Lees Ferry to Phantom Ranch), Franco seemed to be in his own world much of the time. He didn't appear to be paying enough attention to the river, resulting in several poor entries into rapids, losing an oar every now and then, even bouncing off a wall or two. The trip leader didn't seem to notice or didn't care, perhaps because it was his last Canyon trip before he was to move on to other things.

Then "she" appeared. Kelly was tall, blond, beautiful, and already filled with wonder as she waited at Pipe Creek Beach with her mother and aunt. They were among several other passengers who had hiked down the Bright Angel Trail to raft the lower section of the Canyon. After the first day, it was obvious Kelly had the same curiosity about the wonders of life as Franco. Over the next few days, they became friends, taking hikes together or finding unusual viewing points from which to observe the Canyon. No hanky-panky, just the unfolding of a friendship.

On the last full day of our trip, we ran 205 mile rapid and pulled over on river right for lunch. Afterwards, as we prepared to head downriver, Kelly said she wanted to ride with Franco. Technically she wasn't supposed to be on his boat, since he was still a trainee and not qualified to row paying passengers. But the burned-out trip leader said it was okay since there were only a couple of rapids left, and how much trouble can you get into in medium-sized rapid like 217? It never occurred to him that an eddy would be their undoing.

As the guide on the sweep boat, it was my responsibility to make certain that all other boats remained ahead of me. When Franco signaled he was pulling into the eddy at Pumpkin Springs, I started to pull over as well. But the trip leader said it was okay and I should continue the remaining seven miles to camp.

Franco had seen an opportunity to show his passenger the unique shapes that had been sculpted by the pre-dam, sediment-laden Colorado in the sandstone walls bordering the river. As I continued to drift downstream, I glanced back to see both Franco and Kelly running along the sandstone heading upstream, life jackets still buckled.

Rowing downstream, I couldn't shake my uneasy feeling. Safety is our number one concern in the Canyon, and I didn't feel comfortable about leaving a paying passenger with a trainee, especially one who hadn't been paying enough attention. After running the rapid at mile 217, I decided to pull over at the bottom and wait for Franco to come through. I expected to wait no more than ten or fifteen minutes.

After thirty minutes, I started getting impatient. After forty-five minutes I ran out of conversation with my passenger, and I spent the next fifteen minutes watching the antics of a ruby-throated hummingbird. By now it was getting late. The sun was down below the rim, and even in June darkness descends quickly once the sun has set. After waiting and wondering for ninety minutes, I reluctantly decided to row to camp. It was early dusk, and would be dark within the hour.

When we pulled in to camp, the tension was palpable. The absence of Franco and Kelly had become a serious concern, especially to her mother and aunt, and the crew. To make matters worse, Franco had the stove and most of the kitchen on his boat; so the last evening's dinner, usually a hearty meal complete with baked dessert, was less than lavish, not to mention cold.

It was hard not to speculate. Some thought they had pulled over to celebrate the sensuality of the Canyon in a more personal way. Others were convinced their boat had floated away without them. Still others were certain a tragedy had occurred. Kelly's mother asked me if I would join her and Kelly's aunt, both very psychic women, in a circle to see if we could "see" something that might shed light on their absence. Even though I didn't expect to see anything, I actually visualized an empty boat floating calmly on the river. At the same time, I felt that both Kelly and Franco were safe but had gone through some kind of harrowing experience. Both women arrived at similar conclusions.

At this point it was late dusk and visibility was dropping fast. The trip leader called the crew together, and said he'd decided to send three guides back upstream – an overland hike covering seven river miles, in the dark. As exciting and adventuresome as it seemed at the time, it would be a very difficult hike. It would also have been very foolish. Fortunately, we were spared.

As three of us from the crew prepared for our hike, someone noticed a raft floating about a half mile upstream. By now it was almost dark, the gorilla was out (a rock formation across from our camp that takes on the appearance of a gorilla head after dark), and we couldn't see anything but the outline of the boat floating quietly and solemnly towards us. At first our fears were heightened as we failed to detect anyone on board. Finally we managed to detect Franco and Kelly, but they were like statues, just sitting there with no movement. Something frightening must have happened. Were they hurt? Was it at the Pumpkin, or at 217? My mind was filled with "shoulds" and "shouldn'ts." I should have stayed behind. I shouldn't have let Kelly ride on his boat.

It took forever for the boat to float into camp. With uncharacteristically grim expressions, Franco and Kelly disembarked and had a short and obviously serious conversation with the trip leader. A Grand Canyon journey begins with a group of strangers and ends with a family. As family we were all relieved that they both had arrived safely, and concerned about the cause of the delay. Franco was the first to speak.

He told us he had pulled into the eddy at Pumpkin to show Kelly the tunnels and rock sculptings upstream. On their way back to the boat, Franco said he had fallen into the river. The eddy at Pumpkin is very large, and deceptively strong. Franco said he was sucked under and pulled across the river. His life, he said, flashed before him; and later, Kelly would tell me she saw a look on his face that told her he was in serious trouble. Without his life jacket he probably would have drowned.

Finally Franco told us he had managed to drag himself up on land, on the other side of the river. As he lay there, partially hypothermic, Kelly remained on shore across the river. Realizing she needed to get to Franco to help him, she ran to the boat, untied it, and frantically attempted to row out of the eddy, no easy feat for someone with no rowing experience. The boat was very heavy, and the strong current constantly forced her back against the wall.

After much effort, she managed to break free of the eddy and worked her way across the river to Franco, who by now had warmed up. Even though he was exhausted from the experience, he had enough strength to head downstream, run 217, and make it to camp. Everything turned out okay and Franco came out of the experience aware of the need to pay more attention, and with a new appreciation for the power of the river. Kelly had a story. And that, as they say, was that. Except that's not where this story ends.

Kelly and I stayed in contact with each other after the trip, and one day she told me their story wasn't "accurate." Since she had pledged not to divulge the real story, I was left to wonder. Even so, there were several versions of the story circulating around the river community. Finally, in the name of historical accuracy, Franco realized he needed to tell it like it really was. So now you can hear the rest of the story.

Yes, they pulled over at Pumpkin, and yes, they hiked upstream along the sandstone to see the tunnels and sculpting. That's where the original story and the truth diverge. On the way back, Franco did not fall in. Instead, both he and Kelly, at her suggestion, decided to jump into the river and swim down to the boat. Because they were in an eddy, they had to swim against the upstream current. The strong currents pulled both of them across the river! Franco said his life did flash before him, and he was partially hypothermic when he pulled himself out of the water. It took awhile for Franco to recover from his swim, and when he did, he realized his swimming was not over.

His boat still rested peacefully near the Pumpkin, on the other side of the river, almost a quarter mile away. There was no choice. Someone had to hike upstream, jump into the river, swim across to the other side, and get to the boat.

It was absolutely the last thing Franco said he ever wanted to do. After being sucked under the water, after seeing his life flash before his eyes, subjecting himself to that possibility again was abhorrent to him. But he had no choice. He was responsible for a paying passenger, and he was responsible for a boatload of supplies, gear, and other commingled personal matter. Reluctantly he hiked about a half mile upstream, looking for as narrow and peaceful a crossing point as he could find. Nervously checking his life jacket, Franco recalled his harrowing experience of just an hour before. The thought of getting back in the water, knowing he had to reach the other side, made him feel queasy.

The swim across was not easy, and there were moments when Franco was aware of fear creeping into his consciousness. But he did make it to the other side. Practically devoid of energy, Franco managed to hike downstream to the boat, row it across the river to pick up Kelly, and get back into the current. He had no strength to row. All he could do was keep the boat in the current.

Today Franco is a regular guide in the Canyon. He still has that smile on his face. He still loves the Canyon and the people who come down there. And every time he passes the Pumpkin, he's reminded of the power of the river. Oh, and no one has to remind him to pay attention.

The stretch below Pumpkin is bordered by the shelves of Tapeats sandstone hemming in the river, with a slithering current contained on one side or other by wide eddies that love to snare rafts in the commonplace winds blowing upstream on many afternoons.

In the past we used to make regular stops in this section at one of two jumping spots. The first, called the diving board, is an overhanging Tapeats shelf twenty-five feet above the river. One raft would remain in the river just downstream of the jump in case the current swept the jumper away. It is an easy climb up to the flat rock, but not necessarily an easy jump. The more one thinks about it, the more difficult it becomes.

The other jumping rock is just downstream, in an eddy above Three Springs Canyon, at mile 215. In May 1978, on the last full day of my first Grand Canyon experience, we had just finished eating lunch and were in no hurry to get to camp. Only seven river miles downstream, it would be in the blazing sun for several more hours. So, we were relaxing on our boats in the shade of some overhanging rocks. Some people were sleeping, some reading, and some engaging in quiet conversations. It was a very peaceful time.

Without warning or any prearranged signal, all six of my crewmates climbed off the boats and began scrambling up the rocks providing our shade. Well, I was a member of the crew, and not wanting to miss out on any adventure, I followed. Being new to the mountain goat approach to travel, I was slower than the rest. As I reached the top of the rocks, I watched in horror as all six jumped, one at a time, thirty-five feet into the river.

Now it was my turn. Do you know how far thirty-five feet looks when it's your turn, and you've never jumped before? Take a two-story house with an attic and imagine standing at the peak of the roof looking down to the ground.

Tentatively I walked up to the edge and looked down. Suddenly fear gripped the pit of my stomach, and my legs felt like rubber. The message was clear – "Danger, you're in imminent Danger! Get out, fast!" Meanwhile everybody was down below, smiling, and waiting for me to jump.

"Come on Charly jump!" someone from way down below shouted. It was drowned out by the conversation I had going on in my head: "Oh my God, look at how far that is! And I've got to jump out past the boats (there were six of them, all lined up directly below me)? What if I don't make it past the boats? What if I do a belly flop? I'll be hamburger!"

"Come on Charly, jump!" Trust me, that wasn't helping.

I walked away from the edge for a moment, to collect my thoughts and decide if I really wanted to jump. I also hoped that when I returned to the edge, the distance would miraculously appear much shorter. If anything, it looked farther. The only thing shorter was the patience of those gleefully awaiting my jump. "Come on, Charly! We haven't got all day you know!"

I remember thinking no one had seemed in a hurry just a few moments ago. But I said, "Just give me a little time to get my act together, okay? I've never done this before." With absolutely no sign of compassion or empathy, one of my crewmates shouted back, "Look, Charly, either jump – or come down!" So, I jumped. And the moment my feet left the rocks, I wanted them back on the rocks.

Eternity passed in that second or two it took me to reach the water. Then my feet slammed into the water, jamming my sandal straps between my toes. Pressure built up between my ears as I plunged deep into the river. Suddenly, as if on a bungee cord, I reversed direction, and surging out of the water, let out a triumphant yell. But as I emerged from the cold depths

262

of the Colorado, I knew I had to do it again; and this time do it right. So I climbed back up the rocks, walked out to the edge, looked where I wanted to jump . . . and, I jumped. It was much easier the second time.

Now, when we do stop at Three Springs, I enjoy leading the way for others. On this trip we stopped and Eliza, Nathan, and Tyler followed me up. After the rest of us had jumped, Tyler inched up to the edge and looked down. We had all grown to love this man-child, all two hundred and twenty pounds of him. He was shy and very innocent for a kid who had helped his single mom through the trials of breast cancer from age four.

I could tell he really wanted to jump, and I knew exactly where he was – where I had been that first time twenty-seven years before. He stood up there for a good fifteen minutes listening to our encouraging words and getting oh so close before backing away, to think about it. I knew that wasn't helping, so I climbed back up and offered to jump with him, telling him he didn't have to jump. He insisted he wanted to, and then I showed him how to go, hoping he would follow behind. No dice. Still thinking about it too much. He was paralyzed. So Floyd finally climbed up to help.

He had us all in stitches as he told Tyler how ridiculous it was to even think about doing such a crazy thing. But, he said he'd go first if Tyler promised to go right after he got out of the way. Tyler's face formed into the perfect "isn't it a great day" smile, and agreed. So Floyd walked to the edge and nearly had a heart attack – and let everybody know. Then, to the tune of "What am I doing?" he jumped. And the next thing we knew, Tyler was air bound. The splash drenched us all. It was perhaps the biggest cannonball on record. But it couldn't compare to the size of the grin on Tyler's face when he emerged from the depths and swam back to his raft.

We pulled out into the current and approached 217, the last decent-sized rapid before our take-out. If we had run it on the first day, people would have been intimidated. Now it was just another opportunity to have fun and get wet. It has become a "breaker" rapid for a few of my passengers. I use it as an opportunity to help someone break through a belief they may have about their limitations.

Early on one trip, I decided that a young man from North Carolina would, if he so chose, be a good candidate. He had just graduated from high school and the trip had been his graduation gift from his mom. He was a good kid, and clearly enjoyed being in the Canyon. A few days before arriving at 217, I offered him the opportunity to row through the rapid. Of course, he had no idea what it was like, but he seemed to enjoy the challenge. Each day I reminded him he would be rowing 217, and each day he would smile a little bigger.

When the day finally came, I had him row the raft for about a mile before we arrived at the rapid. I then told him I was going to ride through the rapid standing on the front tube, and would give him directions if he needed them by pointing which way to turn the raft. It was a blast, for both of us, and several months after the trip, his mom sent me a letter saying what a difference that experience had made to her son. He was more confident, more outgoing, and more interested in doing other outdoor adventures.

217 was the perfect last big rapid: it didn't present any great challenges, yet it was big enough to give people that last thrill before leaving the Canyon. The rapid was long, and split in two sections, with a big right-to-left-to-right bend in the middle.

At that bend was a small hole on the right, and on one trip our intrepid science teacher and paddleboat captain decided to surf the wave in the hole in the paddleboat. The first time they almost flipped and had two swimmers. The second time they did flip, but recovered in time to catch the eddy. The third time they actually surfed for a couple of seconds before the raft raised up on its side, dumping half of them into the river. On their last try they all went swimming, even though the paddleboat stayed upright. They were exhausted when they got to camp, but still talking about it in enthusiastic tones.

As we floated around the corner, I told Roni and Doron it was time to take their seats on the front tube. Both were enthusiastic about it, and I showed them the best way to hold on, with one hand on the chicken line between their legs, and the other on a strap I had placed on the water jug behind them. I also told them to sit as far forward as possible and not lean back too far. Elli and Liz had bemused smiles, enjoying their daughters' excitement.

As we entered the tongue, I encouraged the girls to let out some screams. To the accompaniment of their excited voices, I pushed into the first wave coming diagonally off the right wall. The raft rose up the wave and for a moment the girls were perched high above us, laughing and giggling as the raft broke through the wave and then followed the current into several more rollers. Even after we had finished the rapid, they insisted on staying on the front tube. I looked back at Liz and Elli, who both gave me a warm smile of thanks.

The final stretch before 220 ran through another mini-gorge of lower Precambrian rock. *On a recent trip, passengers on the paddleboat talked the guide into letting them swim the short but squirrely rapid below mile 217. Several passengers, including Stephanie, a fearless and fit Kiwi, were sucked into the right eddy. I pulled into the eddy upstream of her to pick her up and, as I pushed towards her, urged her to swim to my raft. She was casually floating in my direction when all of a sudden her eyes grew wide and in slow motion she disappeared below the surface. An unseen current had gently grabbed her and pulled her down. It was unexpected and disturbing. She remained underwater for ten to fifteen seconds, although she later insisted it was more like twenty minutes. When she finally re-emerged, I pulled her into the raft. We have since become good friends, and she doesn't hesitate to remind me that I didn't jump in to save her that day. I reply that the rules of river rescue involve saving yourself first, other rescuers second, and the victim third. It's never a good explanation.*

After one more rapid, the gorge disappeared and the Canyon opened up again as we passed a campsite at mile 220. Until the last decade, the upper camp had always been one of our preferred camps. *It was at 220 that I had made my subtle pitch for the attentions of Kate Carr, a bright, attractive, strawberry blonde passenger on my first trip. All the passengers were honors college students who had just spent a semester in Flagstaff studying all aspects of the Grand Canyon They were part of a program appropriately called Grand Canyon Semester. The trip was the Grand finale, so-to-speak, of their semester. Kate was the oldest of nine children from a suburban New York Irish-Catholic family, and her obvious love of the Canyon had made her all the more attractive. We had spent a good part of the last afternoon sitting on a slope behind camp at 220, talking about things that people who love the Canyon talk about. I found myself hoping that we would continue our conversations after the trip ended. Unfortunately, that night she rowed across the river with another guide, who was to become her boyfriend for a short while. She went back to New York and finished college, and then returned to the Canyon a couple years later to work in the office of Wilderness World. That's where she met my brother Sandy. At the time they were both in other relationships, but over the next three years, they became good friends, and then in 1983, Kate gave a surprise package to a mutual friend who was hiking in to meet us on a private trip. The package included a pink negligee, shower cap, and slippers, which Sandy wore while running Lava Falls. In 1984, prior to one of our commercial trips, I went with Sandy and Kate, who were now dating, to the south rim of the Canyon. I took along a good friend, a travel writer who had come on the trip to write an article about rafting in the Canyon. Oh, and she also happened to be a romance novelist.*

The previous day I had gone with Sandy to a jeweler in Flagstaff, where he picked up something in a small white box. We went to Hopi Point on the south rim and enjoyed a great lunch, including a very expensive bottle of wine I had purchased many years before. Without explanation, Sandy took the white box out of his pocket, placed it at Kate's feet, and said, "Kate, I'd like you to take the plunge with me."

She looked at him, a surprised expression on her face and said, "Don't kid me Sandy. Ask me again."

Sandy then said, "Kate, I'd like you to be my wife."

She immediately replied, "When?"

I looked at my friend, who was as surprised as I was about this proposal. I'd had no idea Sandy was planning to do it. I felt honored that he had trusted me enough to share such an intimate moment.

They were married at this same point less than two months later. Of the sixteen siblings from both families, fifteen made it to the wedding. They now have three kids.

There are three camps that are part of 220 – upper, middle, lower. *On one trip, we got to know folks on a private trip that loved water fights. And they had water tubes that could spray copious amounts of water a great distance. With just buckets, we were better equipped for in-close fighting, so we were always at a disadvantage. They made the mistake of camping just below us at the middle camp, and in the morning, as we pushed off on our Dawn Float, two of the guides ran through their camp with buckets and doused the biggest offenders. It wasn't a silent start to our float, but it sure was funny.*

Less than a mile below 220 is Granite Spring Canyon and Rapid. The rapid is small and, at least in my experience, the canyon had always been dry – until October '04. *As we were floating to our last camp, we saw a huge storm south of the Canyon and knew that it could mean trouble for our take-out the next morning, because it was dumping directly over that drainage. As we approached Granite Spring, we saw the beginning of a surge of deep red water coming into the river. We pulled over and walked up to what moments before had been a dry wash. Now it was flushing rainwater and debris into the Colorado, instantly turning it red. A substantial volume of water raced down the drainage, its power eroding away the sand and vegetation. The flood undercut the banks and claimed small trees, bushes, and cacti. Boulders were revealed as the soil was stripped away. Mud waves formed as mud jammed up against some obstacle. The waves expanded until reaching some critical mass, and then collapsed only to rebuild again. Finally, after a half hour, the water subsided, and we hopped back in the raft, energized by the natural rhythms of desert canyon country.*

At the end of a straightaway with a couple more small rapids lay another camp, 221, on river right. *At this camp on a previous trip I had removed my shorts while bathing, and had placed them on a bush next to the river to dry. I had put on a colorful sarong for dinner, and after eating, decided to retrieve my shorts and put them on. When I did, I received one of the biggest shocks of my life. A velvet ant, really a wingless wasp, had taken up residence in my shorts. I found out the hard way. Oh my God, was I shocked.*

*   *   *   **

Another year we had camped at 221 on a string quartet trip I called my 60/60 trip, as it was my 60th trip after turning 60. Before the trip I had decided that I would do something to celebrate the occasion. I just didn't know what. That night at 221 we had a No-Talent Talent Night. Anybody could participate. I took a big risk and asked the lead violinist if he would play a duet with me – he on the violin, me on my native flute. I played notes. He played music. Fortunately, he was so good, it sounded like we had rehearsed.

Normally, we won't go farther than 222 on river left. It has two sections: a narrow beach in a small eddy along the river, and a bigger beach in a huge eddy just downstream. When the group is camped in the big eddy, the narrow beach makes a great honeymoon camp for any couple wanting some alone time. It was easier to park at the upper beach, and that was where we usually camped, until a recent flash flood washed it away.

In '02 I had a long conversation with Floyd at this beach. He had come up to me after dinner and asked me why I had never led a trip. I told him it was because for a long time I only ran one or two trips a year, and it just wasn't possible. I also admitted I was afraid to lead a trip because I would have introduced some things that I feared some guides would probably not have liked. Like having us determine our purpose as a team before beginning the trip. This is something that no one does, but it is part of my value system. If we focus on our purpose, it always makes the trip run more smoothly. I think that happens with individuals, but I don't know of any trip leader who looks at the collective purpose. Floyd said he thought I would make a great trip leader, and suggested I not try to introduce something new until I had a couple trips under my belt and had become more comfortable with the role. It was sound advice that I have taken up. I have since led several trips, and much to my surprise, have enjoyed that role.

We set up camp in the big eddy at 222, and enjoyed a delicious last supper of chicken cacciatore, garlic bread, fruit salad, and Mystic Mints for dessert. During dinner Sue announced the plan for the next morning. We would have a leisurely morning because we wouldn't be arriving at our take-out until nine. In the past we would enjoy a true dawn float where we would get up in the dark, and float the last few miles in silence, bringing closure to the trip while watching the Canyon wake up. More recently our dawn floats had been silent but not as early. Now, the Hualapais, who have their own thriving river business that takes people down to Lake Mead, have said they need the beach until nine in the morning, which is the time their trips are scheduled to launch. So Sue said we would have a continental breakfast with coffee and bagels, and enjoy a big spread at the take-out. We would still be floating in silence as a way to tie our experience together. I suggested that for those who found it useful, they think about the *gifts* they had received while on the trip. I described gifts as a new awareness about themselves or others, a new skill, a new ability, anything they could take back home and integrate into their lives. I also suggested they *give away* anything they had brought into the

266

Canyon they no longer needed – an attitude, a belief, a judgment that no longer served them. Give them to the river, I suggested.

After the dishes had been washed and the kitchen closed up, we gave the passengers an opportunity to express their creativity in a no-talent talent night. The only person who took up the challenge was Timmy. Jim had taught him some magic tricks, and he entertained us all for ten minutes with card tricks, a rope trick, and a sleight of hand with some coins. I was struck with how confident he seemed in front of a group of strangers, and how expressive his face now was. After he finished to a rousing round of applause, his dad came up to him and gave him a big hug.

It was pretty dark by now, and because we had such a big sky and a late-rising moon, I offered to give a star talk. Several folks came down, including Tyler, Miriam, Timmy, Eliza, and Mary, whose foot hadn't gotten any better, but didn't seem to be any worse. The night sky was awash with stars, and the Milky Way painted a white, diaphanous streak down the center. I started with the Big Dipper, and from there pointed out Polaris, the North Star at the end of the handle of the Little Dipper. I also showed them the rest of the polar constellations: Draco the dragon, Lyre the harp with the bright star Vega, Arcturus the bright star at the bottom of Bootes, and the Corona Borealis, the Northern Crown, with the brightest star Gemma (the gem in the crown). I then described the Summer Triangle, with Deneb in Cygnus the swan, Altair in Aquila the eagle, and Vega in Lyre. Finally I pointed to Saggitarius the archer, and Scorpius the scorpion. At that point I asked if everyone could see all these forms. Timmy, looking up at the sky, said all he could see was fuzzy things. Mary asked him if he was nearsighted, and he said yes, but his dad told him he couldn't bring his glasses on the trip. Then Mary said she was near sighted, and offered her glasses to him. He put on her glasses and looked up. "Wow," he said, "look at all the stars."

On the last morning of our trips we enjoy a silent float as we reflect on the journey we've just taken, and prepare to transition to life outside the Canyon. All who travel through the Canyon come out the other end changed by the experience. For some it is subtle, for others dramatic. The Grand Canyon is a transformative place.

DAY SIXTEEN –
222 TO DIAMOND AND THE WAREHOUSE

Each time I awoke at night at this camp, I watched the constellations arc over Diamond Peak, a prominent triangular-shaped feature standing out against the downstream sky, looking very much like the image of the movie logo for Paramount Pictures. In the dark it didn't look very imposing, but in the morning its 3,517-foot peak would loom over us as we floated past it. For those passengers who had started the trip at Lees Ferry, it offered a great visual demonstration of how far we had dropped in elevation. The top elevation of Diamond Peak is slightly higher than the elevation at Lees Ferry.

Our last morning always brings with it the recognition of change. The trip is about to end, and life beyond the Canyon waits along with news of what has transpired during our time insulated from television, newspapers, telephones, and the Internet. Most of the passengers from the 9/11 trip, connected by both tragedy and our Canyon experience, pledged to return as a group on a future trip. Several did.

The Canyon had profoundly touched some passengers on our trip, like Jane and Ben on the upper, and Chris and Graham. For some, like Mary, the impact was subtler, and would probably take some time to "cook." Others had had a great time and were ready to return to "normal" life.

During a breakfast of fruit, bagels, and orange juice, Sue talked about how the Dawn Float and the morning would unfold. She said we were only four miles from the takeout, and most of that time would be spent in silence. Once we arrived at Diamond Creek, we would, with everyone's help, proceed to remove everything from the rafts, load it all on the company's truck, clean the rafts, carry them to shore, and after they dried, deflate and roll them up. It's always amazing, Sue told them, to watch the entire contents of a sixteen-day trip being loaded on a truck. After the trip was broken down, the passengers would remove their personal gear from the yellow bags and place them into plastic bags. Then they would be treated to a delicious brunch before being driven back to Flagstaff.

Since we wouldn't be getting out of camp early, we took advantage of the extra two hours to begin cleaning our gear. We washed all the dishes, silverware, pots, pans, and utensils, made sure the tents were dry, and checked to see if there had been any damage. This would save us time back at the warehouse.

While we cleaned up, our passengers packed their dry bags for the last time. Tyler came up to me and showed me a lizard he had captured, and asked if I knew what kind it was. I told him it was a side-blotch lizard, and pointed to a dark mark behind its forelegs. He thanked me with a happy smile in his voice, and took the lizard back to where he had found it. Nathan and Timmy were again down by the river making mud sculptures. Diane and Ken were helping us wash dishes, and the Israelis had yet to break down their tents.

I walked over to Mary, who was sitting by the river, and offered to work on her foot one last time. She was only too happy to comply, so I took off her splint, removed the ace bandage, and applied some cream on her foot and gently massaged the top of her foot and her ankle. The swelling was down, and there didn't seem to be as much tenderness. I was encouraged that it may not have been broken afterall. We talked about her experience on the trip, and she said it had been beyond anything she could have imagined. In spite of not being able to hike, or because of it, she had received a unique perspective of the Canyon because she could just sit and watch things come to her. I told her I would be more aware of that on future trips.

We completed the cleanup and loaded the rafts, this time not being too concerned about tying everything down securely. Chris and Graham had asked to ride with me, along with Mary. Eliza was going on the paddleboat, and the Israelis would be riding with Floyd. Sue reminded everyone that we would be in silence, and we shoved off. As I floated out into the current, Floyd passed by and my eyes met Liz's. She smiled at me, a smile tinged with sadness. On one of our hikes we had talked about her creating some opportunities for me to come to Israel to speak. It would be great if that happened, because I felt so ignorant and a bit judgmental about the Israelis. But that would have just been a good excuse to spend some more time with her.

We ran several splashy rapids, and I challenged myself to keep my passengers dry. Graham took several photographs of Diamond Peak as we approached, and then floated by it. The last rapid at mile 224 was a noisy one that always seemed to provide one last dousing, albeit minor.

Just upstream of the rapid was a large eddy and a rocky camp on the left. I had stayed there in 1996 on a trip with a group of international change agents. On our last night, these trainers and consultants, who were so experienced in group work, had formed a circle and invited each guide to sit, one at a time, in the middle. To the obvious discomfort of each of us, our passengers took turns acknowledging us for the contributions we had made to the quality of their trip. Guides love being in the spotlight, but usually when they're in control. It was a wonderful form of thank you, and while we all appreciated it, we were unused to being put on the spot like that.

In addition to the more spiritual/personal aspect, the dawn float had a very practical element. Two, in fact. By getting to the take-out early in the day, we could avoid a lot of heavy work in the blazing sun; and, we could get out of any potential danger from flash floods, most of which occurred in the afternoon during the monsoon months of July and August.

After running 224, we entered a final narrow gorge about two miles long. The current slowed to a crawl, and the silence was palpable. I propped my oars under my knees and allowed the raft to float in the soft current. As the sound of the last feisty rapid receded, I thought about the trip and my own experiences. One of the gifts that I had received was the opportunity to share the Canyon with Chris and Graham, whom I had known since 1970, and to watch the Canyon weave its magic for them. Another gift was to spend time with Eliza, and acknowledge her for graduating second in her high-school class. I also thought about what I could give away to the river, and as I seemed to do on every trip, I gave away the need for approval from others. There were times on every trip when I had felt overshadowed by some of my more extroverted crewmates. The shyness I felt growing up had not gone away; it merely had been hidden under a bit of self-confidence and a bit of willpower. I still look around to see when I am, and am not, being noticed. Part of my own healing involves learning to accept my uniqueness and myself. These trips help me recognize, that compared to some, I have a relatively low-key personality. While I do a lot of things well, I usually do them quietly. Trying to compete with others, and trying to be more comical or more loquacious, just leads to frustration.

When the sound of the last rapid turned to a whisper, I removed my flute from its tube, and played some notes. My friend Ash, a very accomplished flute player, once advised me to play from my heart. So as notes floated out of my flute, I focused on feeling grateful for the opportunity to share the Canyon with another group of grateful passengers and awesome guides. Chris looked back at me while I played, and I saw tears in the corners of her eyes. The paddleboat floated by and Eliza gave me a thumbs-up signal. Sue smiled. Floyd was downstream and had also stopped rowing. The Israelis were all looking back upstream. The sound of the flute mixed perfectly with the awakening beauty of the lower Canyon.

On my last quartet trip, Tanya, a world-class cellist and human being with great flair and passion, played two Bach solos in this same eddy. We were all transfixed as she played with her eyes closed, feeling the vibrations of her strings. I could see the white water as she rushed through the rapids in her mind. It was one of the most riveting moments of any Canyon trip.

I knew the end was near when I spotted the orange ball suspended on a cable over the river. It had been placed there to warn helicopter pilots of the presence of the cable, which was used by sediment scientists to measure the amount of sediment carried by the river. They have to hand-crank a chair to get out to the middle of the channel. While there, they also measure how much sediment has built up on the riverbed. Before reaching the cable we passed other evidence of human activity, a solar-powered gauging station on river right that measures the flow of the Colorado, sending the data by satellite to government scientists.

As we floated under the cable, I turned the raft upstream for one last look and a silent goodbye, then declared the silent float over. Now it was time to turn our attention to the take-out and de-rig. I reminded my passengers that we would be taking everything off the rafts and stacking them in four locations near the truck, which should be waiting when we arrive.

Only twice during my time down here had there not been a truck at Diamond Creek when we arrived. The first time was in 1984, a particularly rainy year with an abundance of flash floods. We pulled up to an empty boat ramp and waited for two hours hoping that the truck had merely been delayed. No such luck. Finally we shoved off to float down to the lake. During the float we were accompanied by a thunderstorm with spectacular lightning bolts striking high up on Canyon terraces. We spent the night at Separation Canyon, the place where three of Powell's men had left his trip, never to be seen again. While there, we were entertained by a flash flood coming out of the side canyon. It was more like the slow advance of mud pressing its way into the river. In the morning we were picked up by a large jet boat that carried all of us, including our equipment, to Pierce Ferry where our truck was waiting. While driving away from the river, we were delayed by another flash flood roaring down a normally dry wash. We watched as mud waves, created by debris piling up against rocks on the floor of the wash, built and then disappeared, only to rebuild in a rotating earth dance. We watched in fascination as the surging flood undercut banks, felling whole trees. And we listened as the power of the river pulled up asphalt and bounced it across the road.

After the flood subsided, we drove through a small desert town and were delighted when the raft company manager offered to buy us lunch. I had been sugar-free for the past two weeks, and the only store open was a Dairy Queen. My irritation was magnified when Sandy asked me to hold his milkshake so he could call Kate, then his girlfriend. He met my frustrated response with, "Well it was you who decided to be sugar-free, wasn't it?"

As we floated into the eddy, we saw that the truck was there. Graham unwrapped my bowline, tied the end to the truck, and the derig began in earnest. Most passengers were happy to help. As we pulled up to the beach, someone would pull the raft partially up on shore, and each guide would begin to unload. I helped Mary off the raft and took her up to a shaded area where she could watch all the action. Then I returned to my raft, where Chris and Graham were waiting. As I handed gear and cans to a waiting passenger, I directed them to the appropriate piles: one for company equipment (oars, paddles, life jackets, stove, duckies, first aid, filter, buckets, back board, tables, plates, tents, rain fly, propane tanks, blaster, yellow sleep kits, purple day bags); one for garbage and human waste; one for passenger gear; and the last, and often the largest pile, for guides' personal stuff (bags, life jackets, straps, carabineers, ammo cans, leftover sodas and beer, umbrellas, sand stakes, etc).

I asked Chris to untie the tether on my oars, and take all four of them to the right front side of the truck. I then asked Graham to unbuckle each of the frame straps, making sure he kept the straps on the frame rather than on the raft. Then I removed all the ammo cans from my foot well and hatches. The guides' gear was thrown in a pile to the right of the truck, the garbage to the left side of the truck near the rear, and the rest of the CanX gear off to the right near the middle of the truck. Sue had jumped up on the truck to help stack everything. The coolers and frames went on first, followed by all the "schnadle" (small items like buckets, throw ropes, safety cushions, grill, and filter). Within an hour all but the rafts had been loaded on to the truck. The rafts had been stacked on one another, and we would deflate them after drying for a few minutes, then roll them up and carry them to the truck.

Meanwhile, the passengers found their yellow clothes bags and removed all their personal gear to be placed into a plastic bag, or in their backpack for those who'd hiked in. Then they assembled under the shaded structure where a feast awaited them, complete with crabmeat, shrimp, chicken, brie, fresh fruit, juice, sodas, chilled cappuccino, and more. After I rolled up the rafts with the rest of the guides, we headed for the same feasting ground. The transition to the world outside the Canyon had begun.

On one June trip, probably the hottest I'd ever been on, agitated red ants had stung most of the people. I alone on the crew had escaped. We had almost finished the derig and only had one more raft left to roll up. I was in the process of doing that when I felt the unmistakable sensation of many little feet on the top of my left foot. I looked down to find dozens of red ants swarming over my foot, Only then did I realize that I was standing on their anthill. Unfortunately for me, they were not pleased, and three of them stung me to let me know. I quickly walked toward the river to stand in the cold water when I heard to my right what I thought was a cicada. Instead it turned out to be an agitated rattlesnake lurking within striking distance. Its rattles were clashing as a warning that I was treading on shaky ground. Fortunately there was already a meal in its mouth, a lizard that hadn't been quick enough. I proceeded to the river and after standing in the cold water for five minutes I joined the rest of the crew for breakfast, and then grabbed some ice, which I applied to my bites for the next hour as we rode back to Flagstaff. I could feel the venom crawling up my calf, and focused my attention on not allowing it to get into the lymph nodes in my groin. The sensation seemed to stop at mid-calf, and by the time we reached the warehouse the pain had changed to a frustrating itch.

Diamond Creek is on the Hualapai Indian Reservation, twenty-four miles up a less than ideal road to Peach Springs on Old Route 66. The drainage is often subject to violent flash floods after strong rains during the monsoon season. Some are more extreme than others.

In 1984 two fully loaded two-and-a-half-ton trucks were heading up the drainage when the driver in the lead truck noticed a flash flood coming at them. A two-foot wall of water followed by a fifteen-foot wall of water reached the trucks seconds after both crews had leapt out and scrambled up boulder-strewn banks. The trucks were slammed together, turned upside down, and flushed into the river, to become part of a new rapid we now call Truck Stop Rapid. Some guides were forced to stand for several hours on a narrow ledge above a Crystal-sized hole.

*   *   *

Another flash flood in 2001 had caught a fully loaded flatbed truck with a thirty-seven foot raft, and a crew van, in the same narrow stretch. The truck tried to back up to safety at Diamond Creek and jack-knifed. The empty van was picked up and carried into the river. It disappeared around the bend, still right side up. It had the guides' tips in an envelope and was uninsured.

*   *   *

The high-water year of 1983 saw many an exciting moment at the take-out. With the current racing by at twelve to fifteen miles per hour and no eddy because of the unusually high water, the first raft in required someone to jump to shore with the bow or stern line to stop the raft before it could float around the corner. If that had happened, the next stop would be Pierce Ferry, fifty-four miles away. Passengers on the next rafts would then throw both their bow and stern lines to people on shore. Sometimes the throws were accurate, other times not. I don't know how many boats wound up at the lake.

*   *   *

On one of my trips, a passenger had asked to row my raft for the last mile. He was engrossed in the story he was telling as we approached Diamond and he failed to heed my suggestions to move to the inside of the current. My suggestions led to urgings, and then to "Get off the oars!" as I jumped on them and pulled as hard as I could to make it to shore. If Michael hadn't run into the river up to his chest and grabbed a poorly thrown stern line, we may have gone down to the lake.

* * *

On my last trip in '03, we arrived at Diamond to find no truck and no vans waiting for us. That could only mean a flash flood had kept them from getting to the river. After an hour of waiting and hoping, a pickup from the reservation arrived and we were told that the vehicles were about a mile and a half up the drainage. That meant we would have to walk our passengers up to them, and if the truck couldn't make it down to the river, we would have to row the rafts another seventy-four miles – the next closest place for a take-out. The elevation of Lake Mead had dropped so much that Pierce Ferry was no longer accessible by river. One more unexpected adventure.

Three of the crew had trips loading out the next day, and they would have to go out with the passengers because if we went down to the lake, we wouldn't make it back to Flagstaff in time for them to go on their trips. My nephew Otis, Eliza's brother, was an eager volunteer to row one of the rafts, but it turned out to be unnecessary. Instead, two heavy-duty pickup trucks drove out from Flagstaff, were able to maneuver down to the river, and we were able to load all our gear and drive them up to the truck. We even got back to Flagstaff in time for the trip dinner.

* * *

Brunch was a free-for-all, like being in a family of twenty-four starving siblings. By the time the crew had loaded all the rafts on the truck, a lot of the food had been devoured. Michael and Star grabbed the last two bottles of iced coffee, and I looked for some root beer, settling for some flavored water instead. I loaded up on shrimp, a small piece of chicken, and some brie, and sat down next to Liz and Doron, who had finished eating. Liz had helped me wash my raft and her hair was still wet. She had on a loose-fitting blouse. She told me how much she and Doron had enjoyed the trip. Doron said she was a little sad that the trip was ending, but happy that she would see her father and brother in Flagstaff. They had been traveling in the States with Elli's husband and son for the past two weeks. I told her they would have a lot to talk about, since her dad and brother had already been on a trip in the Canyon. She said she couldn't wait to tell them about her bow ride in 217. Liz smiled.

The van drivers announced it was time to leave. Sue had offered several options for the trip dinner in Flagstaff, and Mary said she would handle those details and call us at the warehouse with the time and place. They all piled into two vans and headed out. Eliza was riding shotgun. She couldn't ride back with the crew because she wasn't covered by the company's insurance.

The drive out to Peach Springs is an unkind transition from the calm of the river to the dusty, noisy clamor of a loaded truck running over a rocky, pothole-filled road. Some of the crew used to ride on top of the gear in the back of the truck until we reached the residential part of the reservation. We drove past a row of one-size-fits-all government-issue homes. Some had well maintained, grass-free yards, while others were run down and filled with rusting hulks of previously used cars. Still other structures had been abandoned and boarded up.

Once on Old Route 66, we settled back for a short drive through Seligman, a funky western town clearly dependent on tourism. The passenger vans would stop at the most active attraction, Delgaudillo's, a small ice cream shop renowned for its tacky décor, including a 'fifties-era Cadillac convertible, and Juan, an aging owner, who, until his death in 2004, had made tourists laugh for over fifty years by giving them used napkins, a miniscule scoop of ice cream if they ordered a small, a fake stream of mustard that made patrons jump and the rest howl. Plastered on the windows are postcards from the world over, written by happy customers. The food is so-so, but the service is worth the price, and now Juan's son continues the tradition.

The crew wouldn't go there because it would take too much time, and we needed to get back to the warehouse to unload the truck and clean the gear. So we stopped at a convenience store at the end of town and, after ruining our diets with A&W root beer floats and worse, we settled back for the three-hour ride to the warehouse.

Once there, the work really began. We had to unload the truck and wash everything. A pressure washer was used for the heavy stuff, Carla washed all the kitchen stuff we hadn't done in the morning, and the rest of us emptied the sleep kits and separated the sleeping bags, day packs, and sleep-liners to be picked up later by a cleaning service. We emptied all the coolers and tossed the perishable goods. The ammo cans were all emptied and the unopened nonperishable foods were returned to the shelf. Open containers of maple syrup, gorp, and crackers were placed in a shopping cart, along with eggs, butter, sealed cheese, and bread, to be picked over by frugal guides. On about a third of our trips, a guide might be designated for drug testing, and one of the crew would be randomly selected to go pee in a cup at a testing facility. This removed one person from the crew and caused the derig to take longer. Perhaps the most time-consuming job was erecting the tents to check for needed repairs. Sometimes the tents are never used, which makes our job much easier. On wet-weather trips, we have to air out and dry every tent, which means someone has to come back to the warehouse the next day to repack them.

After cleaning up the warehouse, we had a meeting to debrief the trip, receive our checks, load our stuff in our vehicles, and head for the nearest shower. We usually had less than two hours before the trip dinner, and while a few guides would prefer to skip this event, I have always enjoyed the dinner as a final opportunity to interact with our passengers, find out what they looked like after a shower and in fresh clothes, and hear about their reflections of the dawn float and the trip. It's a wonderful way to say goodbye, and remind people to remember the feelings they had during the trip.

I received a real surprise at one dinner. As I was saying goodbye to one of my favorite passengers, she whispered in my ear, "You know, I fell in love with you on this trip." I didn't know what to say. She was with her husband and adult children, and to her credit – and my relief – hadn't acted out her infatuation. I finally stammered something like, "How sweet," and left it at that.

During the derig, Mary called the warehouse and told us they had selected a very popular restaurant in town. After I loaded my car with all my gear, I drove east of town to the place I was staying, took a long shower, did a quick check of my voice-mail, and decided to leave the horrors of my email to the next day. Then I drove back into town. On the way back, I thought about what I would do next. My next trip wasn't for three weeks, and I considered whether I would go back to Boulder, or drive to California to see Sandy and his family. Since I hadn't seen them in over two years, I decided to pay them a visit. I knew that Michael and Sue were scheduled to go out on another Canyon trip in five days, and Floyd was going on a science trip to rip out more knapweed and camelthorn, two of the invasive plants that were taking over some of the beaches. Eliza was scheduled to fly back to Oregon in the morning, and I would be taking her to the airport. To my knowledge, all of the passengers would be leaving in the morning. Liz and Elli, along with their husbands and sons, were scheduled to travel around the west for a couple weeks before heading back to Israel.

By the time I arrived at the restaurant, most of the passengers were already there. I was impressed with how well they had cleaned up, even though I think everybody gets more beautiful the longer they're in the Canyon. They were milling around two long, narrow tables, and some were sitting on stools. Chris gave me a big hug and couldn't wait to tell me how many times she had washed her hair – three – before it felt natural again. Graham was smoking a cigar and drinking scotch on the rocks. He said it would take him some time to bring everything into focus. It was, he said, a spectacular, albeit at times uncomfortable, experience. Mary was beaming and said she had spoken with her husband, who was going to set up an appointment to have her foot x-rayed. She thanked me for all the attention, and reiterated what a wonderful time she had.

The dinner was filled with good cheer and lots of hugs. Tyler was dressed in a soccer shirt, sporting his oversized grin. He told me he wanted to write a poem and send it to me. I told him I would look forward to receiving it. Diane gave me a big hug and said they'd be talking about the trip for a long time to come. Timmy and Ralph looked the same, although both were relaxed, and Timmy thanked me for helping him learn to row. I told him he could do just about anything he wanted, and said I hoped we would stay in touch.

After dinner, one by one, each group departed. Most gave Sue an envelope with a tip in it, and she would divide it all up equally among the crew. In the old days, a good tip was a hundred dollars. Today, that would be considered a bad tip. On a few trips, we've received more than a thousand dollars for each guide.

Finally, I said goodbye to Elli, Roni, and Doron, and then they moved aside, as if to give Liz and me some privacy. I reiterated my interest in coming over to Israel to run a workshop, and to learn firsthand more about the country and its people. I was aware of other eyes on us, and kept a respectful distance. Liz grabbed both my hands, looked me in the eye, and said she would never forget this trip or the times we had spent together. I gave her a hug and she held on to me as if she didn't want to let go. Then, with a final smile, she turned and walked out the door.

I used to believe you couldn't improve on a raft trip in the Grand Canyon, until I took my first String Quartet trip, in 1985. There is something truly magical about the alchemical combination of the energy created by water flowing for eons mixing with the vibrations emanating from the stringed instruments of passionate musicians who love playing in the Canyon.

EPILOGUE

Everybody who travels through the Grand Canyon comes out the other end different. Some are conscious of the impact the Canyon has had on them, and make choices that lead to changes in their lives. Others have had seeds planted that will germinate and blossom at another time. Two weeks after our trip ended, Chris called me from England and informed me that both she and Graham had just submitted their letters of resignation. It took Graham several weeks to put his experience in perspective, and then he wrote me one of the most profound letters I've ever received. One of the things he said was, "If I had known beforehand what was involved, I would not have gone. Now that I have been to the Canyon, I cannot imagine the future without the input of the experience."

I have kept in touch with some on this trip. Mary's foot had a non-displaced fracture. She is now retired in Washington State, and I was able to visit her at her home a few years ago. Tyler is now a trusted assistant on archaeology digs in the West and has definitely lost his baby fat. Graham and Chris are both retired and enjoying life in Cornwall. Graham plays a lot of golf, and Chris has taken up Tai Chi, having become a master's champion and teacher. She's also joined a choral group in town. Frank bought a Native American flute and enjoys it in retirement at his cottage on the Northwest shore of Victoria Island. Ben has fallen in love with the US Virgin Islands and has a wonderful lady in his life. Jeff is married, Ann is a nurse in Chicago, and Tom recently got engaged. Marilyn had a successful initial poetry reading and continues to be an avid hiker. Eliza never became a river guide, but she has been on other rivers with family and friends. She's currently enrolled in a Master's program at Oregon State in Speech Therapy. Antje continues her world travels, and I enjoy reading her posts from all four corners. I was able to visit Ken and Diane at their tree farm in Western North Carolina. I never heard from Liz.

For over a century, writers have attempted to describe the experience of being in the Canyon. It's an impossible task. The words below were written by the world-class cellist on my most recent string quartet trip as her way of saying there are things you can't know about being in the Canyon just from the photographs, standing at the rim, or flying over in a plane:

"I guess that you don't get a sense of how cold the water is, nor how bright and dense are the stars at night, nor how much sand and supremely fine red grit embeds itself into every pore and between each tooth, nor how expert and compassionate and kind and patient and knowledgeable and adventurous and skilled are the 7 river guides who guide us all safely through the womb of the earth, nor how many clothes pegs you need to hold the music on the music stand during rehearsals and concerts, nor how reverberant and musically awe-inspiring are the water-hewn rock bowls and dramatically carved side canyons and caves and natural amphitheatres which are our concert halls, nor how monumental are the giant wave castles in many of the rapids, nor how glorious the beer that has been dragged behind the boats tastes at the end of a long day of hiking, paddling and playing string quartets, nor how peculiar it is to apply sun-melted rosin to heat traumatized bow hair, nor how normal it becomes to squat down to pee into the river whilst carrying on a conversation about geology or fossils or Bach or ants and scorpions with the guy next to you who is also peeing, nor how those mornings of jogging paid off when clambering over boulders and up and along narrow ledges with the cello on my back to play a concert, nor how excellent and voluminous was the cuisine three times a day, lovingly prepared by our guides/chefs, nor how a gallon of water a day was only just enough to keep dehydration at bay, nor how the ever changing and mutating walls of the canyon through which we voyaged could yell their grandeur and eternity so deeply and forcefully into my soul, nor how much we laughed, nor how joyously unceremonious it is to be tossed like airplane baggage off the kayak into a rapid by a laughing wave, nor how much hard work it is to clamber back onto the kayak in a rapid, nor how truly inspiring it was to play Beethoven, Mozart, Bach, Haydn, Sibelius, Elgar, Dvorak, Nielsen, Grieg, Schnittke, Prokofiev, Tchaikovsky, Shostakovich, Brahms, Schumann and Peter Schickele string quartets for our fellow travelers and the insect, amphibian, reptilian, winged and befurred residents of the Canyon, nor how triumphant we are to have successfully negotiated Lava Falls, nor how much wind is generated when a huge volume of water cascades 200 feet into a pool at the base of its cliff, nor how exhilarating it is to paddle the rubber kayak against fierce winds in a torrential thunderstorm where the pounding rain drops bounce up a few inches from the river's surface, nor how we merged into a primordial, mutually supporting tribe within a few days of meeting as strangers, nor how wondrous it is to watch as waterfalls created by the storm breach the crest of the walls above us, nor how the blood red

earth mixes with the rain to fall over the high cliff in a terracotta torrent which changes the Colorado river from green to mud brown, nor how the turquoise Little Colorado river envelopes us with its warmth and magic, nor how humbling it is to see the remnants of ancient lives high in the rock ledges and walls, nor how terrifying it can be to peer over sheer drops to toy boats 100s of feet below, nor what a privilege it is to be a musician in the Grand Canyon and to be alive in this planet.....

How can you?"

Tanya Prochazka
Edmonton, Alberta, Canada

ABOUT THE AUTHOR
CHARLY HEAVENRICH THE CANYON GUY

Charly is at home in Boulder, Colorado, and in the Grand Canyon. He has a BA in US History and an MBA in International Finance from the University of Michigan. An athlete his whole life, he played on Michigan's 1962 NCAA championship baseball team. Charly has been a raft guide in the Canyon since 1978 with over one hundred trips to his credit. His mission is to share the Canyon Experience with the world. His purpose is to support people in exploring and discovering where they want to be and how to be there. Charly is an inspiring Speaker, successful Life Coach, passionate Author, and compelling Photographer with an exclusive focus on the inner world of the Grand Canyon. For information about Charly's presentations and workshop, and how to invite him to Speak to your group, hire him as your Life Coach, or purchase his books, or DVD, go to his website, www.thecanyonguy.com.

Charly's photographs bring the Inner Grand Canyon to the world. He feels honored to know that they are displayed in homes and offices as a reminder of the beauty, richness, diversity, and enduring nature of the Canyon, and by extension, the natural world. You can see and purchase your own Inner Grand Canyon image from his website photo gallery at www.thecanyonguy. com.

Charly can also be reached at his office at 303-545-5414, by email at charly@thecanyonguy. com, or on Facebook and Twitter at thecanyonguy.

RESOURCES
THERE ARE MANY FINE BOOKS ABOUT THE GRAND CANYON. BELOW ARE JUST A FEW.

Stephen W. Carothers and Bryan T. Brown, *The Colorado River Through Grand Canyon* (The University of Arizona Press, 1991)

Edward Dolnick, *Down the Great Unknown* (Harper Collins Publishers, 2001)

Michael P. Ghiglieri and Thomas M. Myers, *Over the Edge: Death in Grand Canyon* (Puma Press, 2001)

David Lavender, *River Runners of the Grand Canyon* (Grand Canyon Natural History Association, 1985)

John McPhee, *Encounters with the Archdruid* (Harper Collins Canada, Ltd, 1971)

John Wesley Powell, *The Exploration of the Colorado River and it's Canyons,* (Penguin Books, 1987)

Marc Reisner, *Cadillac Desert,* (Penguin Books, 1987)

Wallace Stegner, *Beyond the Hundredth Meridian,* (Bison Book, 1982)

Tom Vail, *Grand Canyon, A Different View,* (Master Books, 2003)

Ann Zwinger, *Run, River, Run,* (University of Arizona Press, 1975)

This is a very partial list. For a complete catalogue of modern and less recent publications on the Grand Canyon, contact Five Quail Books at http://www.GrandCanyonBooks.com